THE TRIPLE MIRROR OF THE SELF

THE TRIPLE MIRROR OF THE SELF

Zulfikar Ghose

BLOOMSBURY

First published 1992
This edition published 1994
Copyright © 1992 by Zulfikar Ghose

The moral right of the author has been asserted

Bloomsbury Publishing Ltd, 2 Soho Square, London W1V 5DE

A CIP catalogue record for this book is available from the British Library

ISBN 0 7475 17819

Printed in Great Britain by Cox and Wyman Ltd, Reading, Berkshire

CONTENTS

Part Three: Origins of the Self

PART ONE

The Burial of the Self

1 The Scattered One

I have been resident now for some years in a settlement called Suxavat of fewer than 200 souls in that part of the jungle which subscribes no allegiance to a nation, though from time to time Brazil, Peru and Colombia have professed a claim to the territory, raising obscure legal issues at The Hague concerning colonization and emancipation. I am not a native of this region, no more than the scaly-barked urimbola tree with its broad kidney-shaped leaves which rooted itself to this soil by some accident of the wind. Seeking no further than the immediate objects of nature for additions to nomenclature, the natives named me after the immigrant tree: Urimba, the scattered one.

Something of the characteristics of the Witola tribe, with which the original inhabitants were remotely connected, is still preserved in the native speech with its habit of shortening the words of its acquired Spanish and Portuguese vocabulary; at the same time, the natural human inclination of a secluded group to accommodate spontaneous constructions has led to the evolution of a grammar full of exceptions, creating the impression of a unique language: consequently, a pronunciation that is unrecognizable from either Spanish or Portuguese, or even the Indian tongue, marks the natives' speech. For this reason, my name Urimba is never heard but as *Urim*. A lot that ought to be spoken aloud is taken to be understood, though unheard.

Only three families may still be distinguishable as bearing the features of Witola Indians, though even among these there are some, like the girl Horuxtla who wears pomegranate blossoms in her fine black hair, whose appearance is markedly alien to the indigenous group. Girl, young woman, the daughter of illusions – Horuxtla would pass for a native on the shores of the Mediterranean with her large black eyes and the absence of high cheekbones that are so common to her people; but her beauty alone would make her exceptional in any group, for wherever she is present the air is so scented with her breath that a man, finding his animal senses

3

suddenly awakened, instantly imagines himself lowering his head to touch with his lips, to stroke with his tongue, the moist entrance to her sex, for it is there, in the sharpness of female odour, drawing his own breath in an exhalation of abandonment, that the self seeks the terrible release from desire.

Should all the coincidences of my life, the vagaries of circumstance that exiled me from one continent to another until I arrived at this still centre, under the canopy of the rain forest where light breaks down in a scattering of fragments, lead to my possessing Horuxtla, I would believe that everything that happened had a meaning, that the many bifurcations in the labyrinth constituted a straight line, that chaos itself was a composition of harmonious measures. *You!* I say to myself, what has become of you surrendering to the unwilled choices! Coming to this remote interior as to some ultimate abode of repose from where the next journey must be through that small opening in the earth that takes one to another, perhaps a final, world, I am alive with desire. You escape from one region to another, slipping into areas of denser shadows, and begin to believe the body is at last flattened like a leaf on the muddy bed of a drying river, with a fossil's future of an eternity of death, when the rains or melting snows in remote regions send a wall of water crashing upon you, and you must rise, be born again from water, seek the lovely grassy ground where light falls through the tall trees and catches the sheen of a woman's hair who is just then stooping where a fruit has fallen.

What induces in me a comforting serenity is a conviction, which has no foundation in reality, that it will not be long now before the moment of possession comes, when I shall be able to bury my head in Horuxtla's lap and enter into her sex with no wish to emerge again into the world of light. Perhaps I already have. My mind has an uncanny capacity to transform an imagined future into an accomplished past; and I know, too, that I am quite capable of pretending that what has already happened has not yet happened and is something I wish to occur in the future. In the grammar of self-deception, I change the tenses by the hour. What has become of you! I have lived so long in so many worlds that it is not merely a trick of the imagination to have the sense of not having been born as yet; and conversely, carnal passion, a guise both of self-extinction and of rebirth, might well be a compulsion to remain in the ambiguous realm of being. The mind cannot surmise what former incarnations comprise the layers of one's flesh, there is awareness only of present desire, a longing for the burial of the self.

Most of the inhabitants who were born in Suxavat are the descendants of nineteenth-century *seringueros*, the rubber trappers who were driven into distant regions in search of the precious tree until they had come so far into the interior that their lives no longer had any connection with the commercial and political centres in the east. They are people in whom a memory of blue water has become extinct. More recently, outcasts from the new gold-mining towns have found their way here, their dream of riches abandoned in the mud that released no gold; too exhausted by failure, and too destitute to have the means, to return to the bright cities of the coast, they have settled here because they have nowhere else to go. And had they been the lucky ones to find enough gold and gone to purchase a residence in Salvador or Vitória or Pôrto Alegre their survival there would have been brief, for they were born without rooted attachments, like children left abandoned on a stranger's doorstep. These are people who wish their memory of gold, which was more precious for never having been found, to perish. My companion Tambour, a wiry man in his late 30s, is one of these, though his is a nobler spirit, for he found gold and threw it away to cleanse himself of desire, and sought a habitation where the torment of memory would cease. During the recent rainy season when his spirit was downcast by the sun's month-long absence, he said, 'No, I wouldn't want to return. That world only gave me hunger. I don't want to go anywhere.'

When it was not raining hard, a lighter rain persisted. The river had long burst its banks. Our huts seemed to be standing in the middle of a lake. The children had become bored with the games of water and mud that had first made them shriek with delight as they ran naked into newly formed puddles and kicked up water at one another. The chickens roosted in the trees, the cocks had stopped crowing. The jungle beasts, so terrifyingly loud to anyone not familiar with their nightly howls, had become silent. All living things had a grudge against the world. It was a trial to keep a fire going to cook one's food. Some people fasted, expecting God to notice their protest against His weather. Occasionally, a woman would shout from a window, calling to a neighbour, or a child's crying would rise briefly above the noise of the rain. We slept much of the time, sunk in our muddy world in a slime of dreams.

Tambour came to my hut every three or four days, not caring

how hard it rained or that he had to wade through muddy water. 'These are the times when I think nature didn't intend us to stay in one place,' he said, taking the damp towel I gave him to dry himself. But he observed that I did not complain, and after he had cursed the weather, shouting that we would be better off in the drought-stricken north-east, he concluded by saying, 'No, the north-east can keep its daily sun, its cloudless sky and its dead earth. I don't want to stare at a land that grows nothing. I don't want to go around panting in a land that doesn't give a single sign it cares that I live. You know, Urim, the sky there long ago stopped looking at people. Its stars are turned the other way and there's nothing in nature left to pity a soul.'

I believe he was impressed by the profound inertia that possessed me in the rainy season, my movements in the hammock in which I lay slower than a sloth's. Even when Tambour's words sporadically broke the silence that had fallen on the universe and filled all living souls with an aching sadness, I reposed in the same attitude that I maintained for days, my knees drawn up to my chest, the hands clasped together below my chin, not hearing the sound of the rain, no more than I heard the coursing of my own blood, and discovering an enormous satisfaction in the loss of a sense of my self, trapped there like an oyster in its shell in an unlit world whose essence was water. It was not my deliberate choice to remain thus, sunk in a senseless contentment from which I resented having to rise periodically to serve the body's needs.

I will say nothing of the memories that invaded my mind then. Life in America, in European cities, in India – I will say nothing of the history of passions which may well be the sum of a confusion of dreams with their conversion of dull events into marvellous fictions and their disguising of pain into the grotesquely masked creatures at a Kathakali dance that I may or may not have seen on a wooden platform one autumn evening in a park in Madras. The images forced before my eyes were like a confession prepared by a secret police, threatening extreme torture if I did not sign and claim the ludicrous past as my own. How could I have witnessed those killings on Mohammed Ali Road, an improbable name for a street, I have not left this muddy abode under the rain forest, what could make such information so valuable I must assign it recognition? I do not remember being in the streets where knives sprang up in the air. I do not remember being anywhere.

When Tambour remained silent for a while, the image returned to me of a Canadian poet who had painted his nose, cheeks and mouth a chalky white, and to whom I said, holding my wife's arm, 'I'm going to India.'

Wife? India? I am alone. A dead weight in a hammock. The blood silent, stagnant. The brain depleted of oxygen. So far west, it is uncertain the territory is still Brazil. But that suburban train, is it not in Bombay, going from Sion to Victoria Terminus? Foolish man, go stand under the rain! No, I do not remember dreaming. I never dream. My eyes are always open. I cannot dream. It is impossible.

I must have uttered a groan when Tambour suddenly shouted, 'I want to get out of here!' He was quiet for a few minutes and then said in a calm voice, 'You're right, Urim, it's no use cursing. When I go away, I say to myself I must be like Urim, learn to do nothing. I try it for a while and then I get fidgety. It's like getting an itch, you force yourself not to scratch only for so long and then go at it like a monkey.'

I let him talk uninterruptedly, making only the occasional sound to assure him he was being heard, for that was really all he wished. I knew from the previous year that as soon as the weather improved he would forget his depression with what he called the dripping cave of life, the insult, as he named it, to the spirit of brightness natural to human beings. He was surprised to be informed how he had cursed this portion of the earth, as he was doing now in this rainy season, imploring me to join him on a new emigration – 'To the Andes! Let's climb above the humid line of the rain forest and find a little scoop of land where the sun falls, where it's warm and cool at the same time.' Amazed later that he had made such a desperate proposal, he laughed at himself and admitted that daily blinding sunlight was the last thing he wished for himself, the scattered light under the canopy of the rain forest was an infinitely more desirable habitat, it afforded a natural camouflage.

I got out of my hammock to see him go after a visit. 'It has stopped raining,' he said by the door where the water had ceased its gentle bobbing just below the topmost of the five wooden steps. I looked out. The sky was still overcast but its grey had acquired a silvery shimmer and was no longer menacingly dark. The vast lake-like body of water surrounding the huts was dully grey like a sheet of opaque glass but even as I looked it began to reflect the silver that brightened each moment in the sky. There seemed to be a compact between sky and water as though each constituted a continuous shell around fluid matter which it would take the energy of the naked sun to break before the space in which we resided again became land on which fruitful trees grew.

'Look, such perfect circles!' Tambour pointed to a group of water-lilies floating next to the opposite hut. There were seven of them – six of various sizes around an immense one in the middle. They looked like mossy green discs. There appeared a mass of shivering bubbles on their surface, transforming the green to a reflecting silver before a slight movement in the water made the bubbles disappear. There was a commotion in the sky. A flock of parrots went noisily by, suggesting the illusion that they tore away with their beaks the thick cloud curtain, for just above where they passed a gap appeared where the sun broke through.

'Wait,' I said to Tambour. 'The water will begin to go down soon.'

We stood there for a few minutes watching the sun burn away more of the cloud cover. Suddenly I felt a burning sensation on my cheek and my eyes were caught in a moment's blinding glare. Tambour, as if suddenly stung, snapped back his head and rubbed his cheek. 'Hey, stop that!' he shouted. It took me a moment to see he was shouting at a girl who leaned out of a window in the opposite hut and was playing with a little mirror in the palm of her hand, laughing as she caught with its burning light the faces of the many people who had come to the doors and windows of their huts to look at the sun.

2   The Magic Makers

With the end of the rains, soon after the river had again established its banks, the monkey dancers came – the male warriors of a tribe from upriver with masks of monkey heads wobbling on their shoulders and stiff pieces of rope cunningly attached to their breech clouts to form tails. They accompanied their dance with a ferocious howling, suggesting a raid on an enemy. Their gestures mimicked the shooting of poisoned arrows, the wielding of heavy clubs, the felling of innumerable opponents. It was all an artful rendering of a former reality, for such tribal warfare had long ceased in the region. They could not maintain the pretence for long, and soon buffoonery replaced ferocity and irony the seriousness of the combat, making us laugh boisterously at their antics; and they laughed back, not as humans do, but in the shrieking manner of laughing monkeys in a shrill, rising pitch until it set the distant, unseen jungle beasts howling, so that our own smiling faces took on feigned expressions of terror as if this fearful laughter mocked our situation. But suddenly it ended, and the monkey dancers raised jubilant cries and appeared to be warriors returned from a great victory, young men come back with only superficial wounds, bearing trophies of their success, enriching the tribe beyond its most extravagant dreams.

The jubilant cries signalled the six or seven young girls who had been left sitting silently in the canoes on the river, quietly suffering the anxiety of their fate, to come to the village to be offered as brides. Now it was time to prepare the feast, to light a big fire and to roast the abundant catch of fish, to indulge in uproarious jollity so that the six or seven girls from our own tribe, who would be taken away in exchange in the morning to become wives and mothers in an alien village that they must accept as home, might not feel that they were being robbed from their families but, rather, that they were the honoured and privileged participants in an ancient ceremony.

On this occasion, I feared that Horuxtla would be one of the

9

chosen. As I watched her, the smooth skin of her naked shoulders reflecting the fire as though she blazed with an inner heat, I perceived the essential ambivalence of her situation: her eyes expressed fear that she might have to leave her home for ever but her mouth arranged itself repeatedly in a smile; and I realized that possibly greater than her fear of losing her family would be the insult to her vanity should she not be chosen, that her pleasure of remaining home would be soured by the criticism of her beauty implied by a rejection. I saw that one of the warriors looked frequently at her and that she, conscious of his interest, had shifted her position a little in order to be seen more fully by him, and holding her chest out, took deep breaths that had the effect of making her small conical breasts appear rounded.

My Horuxtla, already my bride! About a fortnight before the rainy season ended she had come to my hut, sent by her mother with a quantity of boiled manioc roots wrapped in a banana leaf: for this miracle of Horuxtla's presence in my hut I had to thank Tambour who after his latest visit had spread the word that I was eating nothing, and so I had received several gifts of food.

When I remarked to Horuxtla, as she stood holding out her mother's offering, that she did not have any pomegranate blossoms in her hair, her eyes lit up and she smiled wonderfully, saying there were none to be had in the rainy season. I rose out of my hammock and touched her hair where the blossoms would have been. She was 15, perhaps 16, a child to my 47 years. I recoiled from my lust. No, no, how can I so simplify the mystery of my emotion? I took the present of food from her hands and placed it on a stool contrived from pieces of bamboo. She turned to go. I touched her shoulder. She looked up at me. I asked her to remember to thank her mother for me. She nodded, smiled. My eyes fell to her breasts, her slender waist, and to the narrow strip of cloth in front of her sex which was her only clothing. When I looked up, her eyes were watching mine, a woman's superior gaze of knowledge and power over the male who is suddenly recognized to be a miserably puny creature. A startled expression came to her face, a quick moment of thrilling pleasure flashed in her eyes, when she instantly intuited the desperateness of male longing. She turned again and as she stepped away I waved the palm of my hand behind her and gave her buttocks a casual pat.

No, not casual at all. It was a lingering caress, the palm holding the rounded flesh while the forefinger slowly traced the cleavage, the whole slow motion disguised as a quick friendly pat, merely the fingertips passing over the curve of her flesh, a casual touch transformed in that brief second of the fleeting contact into a long performance of potent sexuality, and in that second her figure was not receding but pressing to me and I was not standing woodenly but throbbing along the length of her body and we were inseparable, believe me, Urim, it was true, inseparable were we in the mutual transmission of passion. *No*.

No, this was not the last fortnight before the rainy season ended but much earlier, a decade perhaps before I arrived in the rain forest, a memory prior to experience, its images constituted by the force of conceit while I stood in the museum in Baltimore in front of the painting of a girl in Tahiti, a mango in her palm. Or much, much earlier still, when the earth was no larger than a drop of semen that contained in it all possible structures, including the inventions of time, reality and dreams, and including too in that original drop, as one infinitesimally minute fragment of its time-bound programme, that moment of hallucination that possessed me as I lay in a cousin's house in Karachi after the flight from London when I awoke dripping in a darkened room and saw the figure of a girl, her hands held out with an offering, make a phantom appearance and then elude me for nearly thirty years and finally stand before me in the person of Horuxtla.

She was taller than the other girls with whom she watched the monkey dancers and her legs were not as thin as theirs. Her features were so distinctive, her beauty a foreign type unfamiliar to an indigenous tribe, that I began to lose my apprehension that she might be taken away: her singular appearance would be a threat to native superstition. The girls gathered with her pretended to pay no attention to the visiting suitors come in the guise of warriors, who had been joined by our own young men and were together being rowdily ostentatious, and gaily talked to one another while throwing furtive glances at the men.

Tambour's laughter could be heard among the young men as he provoked an exaggerated bawdiness among them with cries of, 'What, is that all?' Eager to amaze him and the rest of our men, the visitors were driven to be crudely inventive in their earthy accounts. There was a woman in a village on the Napa who had trained two parrots to fly down from their perch and sit beside her shoulders every time a man mounted her, and one parrot would cry, 'Do it, do it!' and the other scream, 'Keep on, keep on!' and when the man fell exhausted the two parrots would bend their heads sideways, look askance at the man and say simultaneously, 'Oh-oh, Oh-oh!'

The younger men guffawed loudly but Tambour cried again, 'What, is that all? Don't you know any new stories?' All right, then. Have you heard of the twice-born man? There was a man in a village on the Xingu who climbed up a very tall tree one day to go and look at the sun, hacking the thick foliage out of his way with a machete. When he got to the top there was nothing between him and the sun and so the sun melted him until he became a raindrop and fell down through the branches of the tree. A woman was walking past and hearing a bird whistle from the tree looked up. Her mouth opened as she threw her head back to look up. And plonk, the raindrop fell straight down her throat. Some months later she went into labour that lasted twelve days and thirteen nights, and gave birth to the man just as he had been when he went up the tree, his machete in his hands.

'Ho, ho!' taunted Tambour. 'These are old stories of the forest. Even the ants know them. Come on, monkey heads!'

Well, then. A man sat under the tree of rebirth. He faced the lake in which swam watersnakes around the green disc of the lotus. Upon the lotus reposed the last surviving drop after the evaporation of the oceans.

Oceans? A memory of blue water obscurely disturbed some minds, but they listened to the visiting narrator.

The earth had risen in vertical shafts where the oceans had evaporated. Pointed peaks of the new land rose higher than the clouds. The man had known those heights as his home. Frightened to be so close to the sun, he asked the moon what he should do and the moon said, 'Go where the mountain rises like a wall. Crack a hole in the ice that covers the wall and place in it three drops of your blood and seven lungfuls of your breath. The ice will seal them there and you will never suffer from the heat of the sun.' The man followed the moon's directions early in the morning before the sun's heat could become unbearable. He found that afternoon when he came out of the cool shade of his house that the sun no longer touched him. But seven days later an ache developed in his heart because he was always cold. Now, shivering at noon, he asked the sun what he should do and the sun said, 'Go and look at the place in the mountain wall where you left your soul.' The man was frightened. He had only left three drops of his blood and seven lungfuls of his breath. Why did the sun say he had left his soul there? In his fear he hurried to the wall of ice. To his horror he saw his own face there in outline. The ice was thick and smooth. When he looked one way he could see nothing there but when he looked another way he saw trapped within the ice the very features of his own face. He ran to his house to fetch a pickaxe. He ran back and began to smash the ice, but found that he could scarcely make more than a few chipped pieces fly out of the surface. He stood there the rest of the day and kept on striking blows upon the ice. But he could not reach the face that looked back. Bits of ice flew off into the sky but after each crack the ice reformed as a smooth surface and even before he could strike his next blow he saw his own self looking at him. Night came and the moon rose. 'Look, what you have made of me!' the man cried bitterly at the moon. 'Release me from this prison!' The moon kept going across the sky silently. And when it had reached the west, the moon pulled him up as if he were a wave upon the deep ocean and with the sound of surf breaking upon a beach brought him to our forest and placed him under the tree of rebirth. He sits there, waiting, watching the last surviving drop of water from the oceans that evaporated 10,000 years ago. From that drop of water will rise a cloud and out of that cloud will come in a fluttering of white wings the souls of the next age of the universe. But on a point of light that touches the drop of water he sees the figure of his own arms striking endlessly without sound and without impact the solid ice within which time never passes. Hummingbirds dart up to his frozen eyes and keep stabbing with their long beaks at the frozen moisture in his pupils as though they had discovered the nectar-filled throat of an orchid.

'Oh monkeys, monkeys!' Tambour interrupted. 'Look at your listeners! Their eyes are disturbed. There is no ice in our world, what are you talking about? We have forgotten the blue of the oceans. There is no life-bearing lotus in our rivers. Why are you troubling us with distant dreams?' Before the narrator could answer, Tambour clapped his hands and called, 'Bastianini, Rustomo, come, show these monkeys what you can do. Come on, let's have some real magic. Enough of these stories that trouble the souls of the living. Make room there, stand back, stand back.'

The monkey warriors resigned themselves to becoming an audience. A space was cleared. Bastianini and Rustomo with six of their helpers carrying assorted lengths of roughly cut timber came and stood in a circle. They began to throw the pieces of wood rapidly to each other. Within a few seconds the pieces were flying back and forth among the eight men, but each time a piece landed in the hands of Bastianini or Rustomo, who stood opposite each other in the circle, they took two quick steps forward and performed an action that was too fast to be perceived, and before anyone could tell what was going on the timber had stopped flying, the men stood empty-handed and there, in the centre of the circle, was a perfectly formed table. The audience applauded; some cried aloud in astonishment; some whistled. Rustomo and Bastianini walked in a wide circle round the table, glancing boldly at the visitors with a mocking smile, challenging them to doubt what they saw.

Tambour laughed aloud. Rustomo leaped up into the air and landed on the table where he hopped twice before jumping off, and just as he did so Bastianini leaped up to take his place. They did this several times in quick succession, almost too rapidly to count, and then both stood upon the table together and, accompanied by hand clapping, commenced a rhythmic stamping on it, like flamenco dancing. The visiting warriors were amazed by the solidity of the structure that seemed to have been conjured out of the air. They went and stood round the table, touched it and pounded it. One even took a kick – only to yell out in pain and withdraw humiliated with a bruised foot. The thing was solid as a rock.

Bastianini told them all to stand back. 'Make way, make way there,' Tambour shouted, 'for the master magician!' Rustomo, a tiny finch's feather in his hand, approached the table. He held the feather above the table and looked around at the audience with a bemused smile. He let the feather drop. As soon as the feather touched its surface, the table collapsed, the timber falling to the ground in an untidy heap. The warriors were amazed, puzzled, and finally outraged that a trick had been performed of which they were denied the clue. They looked extremely sullen when they heard Tambour shout at them, 'Such is life, eh?'

But their humour was restored when Bastianini brought out lumps of soft rubber from a sack and began to throw them at Rustomo who had positioned himself with a long spear fashioned out of bamboo in his hands. Again, the action was very fast and the observing eye could not keep up with what it saw, for within a minute the entire length of the spear had lumps of rubber attached to it, each one pierced perfectly at the centre. Rustomo and Bastianini then held the two ends and brought them together, and the next thing, a precisely formed wheel had been set in motion across the cleared earth.

Rustomo stuck two fingers into his mouth and whistled loudly. The audience, watching the wheel rolling away across the ground, now saw a monkey run out of a hut, make straight for the rolling wheel and jump on it. With rapid little movements, the monkey kept the wheel rolling and himself balanced upon it and within a few seconds had disappeared into the jungle. Some of the warriors ran after the monkey. But Bastianini shouted at them to stop. He pointed a finger in the opposite direction. The warriors looked, expecting to see some new trick calculated to drive them out of their wits. But there was nothing, just bushes and trees past some huts. A moment later, however, a great cry and applause broke out from the audience: the monkey, still on the wheel, appeared from that end of the jungle, made straight for Rustomo and, reaching him, jumped off the still rolling wheel and clung to Rustomo's chest. The wheel ran on for a short length, wobbled and fell at the feet of the warriors.

One of them picked it up. The others crowded round him and looked at it curiously. As they tried to see how the two ends of the bamboo had been joined, the thing snapped and they were left holding a straight spear with the irregular lumps of rubber hanging loosely on it. One of the warriors snatched the spear away angrily, furious that nothing could be understood, and throwing his arm back flung it away. It should have fallen on the ground a little distance from him, but instead it flew off like an arrow straight up at the sky. It hit a stout branch of a tree and the force had the effect of making the spear spring round into a circle and to bounce back from the branch. The warriors who had been looking bewildered at where it had shot up were astonished to see a moment later a wheel fall from the tree, bounce high over the ground and roll away into the jungle.

Someone was laughing in a piercingly high-pitched tone, as though he had recently been stricken by a lunatic fit. The warriors looked round to see who could be so afflicted. It was none other than the monkey who had earlier ridden the wheel and who now sat on Rustomo's shoulders, rapidly patting his master's head while he laughed.

This was too much for the visiting warriors. Having themselves come disguised as monkeys, it was too insulting to be laughed at by a creature who had been born one. In the meanwhile, Tambour was mocking them, shouting, 'How's it all done, eh, suckers? You know anything at all?'

They huddled together in a communal sulk, so that the host tribe was now obliged to placate them with some priceless gift. What would they like – turtle eggs? One spat into the ground, another looked angrily at Rustomo. What do you say to turtle eggs? No, no. That rare delicacy, then, the inner flesh of the ant-eater's nose? A couple of bright looks were exchanged, but the common answer was the same. No, no. Syrup from the kyawba tree? No, no. What great rarity, then? A whole inventory of the jungle's riches was offered and rejected, and finally, as though he had just had an inspiration, an elder made a ceremonious speech in which he offered the visitors their choice of the tribe's young girls – and thus ended the ritual of dance, games and tricks, its preordained conclusion arrived at as if by some chance, the anticipated end coming as a happy surprise.

I observed with some anxiety the warriors' choosing of the girls, but I was soon relieved that my judgement about Horuxtla had proved correct, that she was too singular in appearance to be chosen in a ceremony each aspect of which was a communal act and therefore could not include that which was uncommon. She walked away, happy to be excluded from exile but dejected that plainer girls had been preferred to her. No one noticed her go, for the musicians had begun to play on their drums and flutes, food was being passed around, and the festival of life proceeded with new marriages to perform.

It was not difficult to slip away from the crowd absorbed in its high sense of ceremony or amused by the farcical elements contained in the improvised ritual that was made up of memories so remote that their recurrence as fragmentary images seemed comical. The effect was rather like watching Japanese youths performing a rock concert with all the physical gestures of British or American pop stars or coming across on a sidewalk in Los Angeles tall, blue-eyed Americans in orange-coloured robes chanting the praises of Krishna, each group appropriating an alien tribal practice with a sincerity so genuine it is sad to behold.

If I call the inhabitants of our little settlement at Suxavat a tribe, it is only because the word is not inexact in conveying the general appearance of the group; we were not, of course, a tribe as were the Xingu or the Toucanos who for centuries had known no other world than the jungle. We came from different sources, different continents even, from worlds long famous for the rise and fall of civilizations, but we shared no creed or history. Having no established rituals, we tolerated and took a curious interest in whatever got invented. Nebbola's performance of the multiple weddings was one such invention, with its holy fire, saffron robes for the couples, and his incomprehensible chanting, all of which was sufficiently meaningless and mysterious, perhaps having as the general origin of the ceremony some distant experience in Nebbola's memory, possibly even something seen in a television documentary about a remote people, to attract the fascinated attention of the tribe. No one observed the happy and disconsolate Horuxtla going away.

Two steps, and I was behind the trunk of a large tree and already away from the circle of light made by Nebbola's fire, two more and I was screened by a row of bushes, and a quick scurrying down a track and I was on the river's bank where Horuxtla stood leaning against a tree. I watched her as the man in the visiting narrator's story had watched the drop of water upon the lotus, and felt myself connected to her centre as if a blood-filled tube ran from her navel to my mouth and both succoured me with new life and drained from my body my blood. No, she had gone home, it was impenetrably dark by the river, and I remained on the edge of the circle among the spectators watching the solemn and ludicrous spectacle composed of broken memories. No, I was with her, drawn to her even in that absolute darkness. I touched the sadness of her left cheek, enclosing her in the protection of my embrace, I caressed the happiness of her right cheek, and her eyes, dull with misery, closed, and then, aflame with desire, opened. Nebbola chanted. Horuxtla's upper lip was cold, the lower burning. Saffron figures floated around the fire, Nebbola chanted. Horuxtla's right breast was round, full, as with milk. High-pitched now, the words incomprehensible, Nebbola chanted among people who half heard an approximation to an ill-pronounced foreign tongue and yet believed they understood. Horuxtla's left breast was shrivelled, dry. Her heart beat, but her pulse was silent. Drums and flutes, the murmur of the crowd, the floating saffron figures merging one into the other. Smells of food. Horuxtla stood there with her girlfriends, the fire reflecting along her right thigh.

3   The Shadow Man

Nebbola wore a crown of parrot feathers and one earring of a jaguar's tooth; a patched cloak of green, blue and yellow hung from his shoulders. No one in the village had ever felt the necessity of a priest until one year when he arrived and began to invent ceremonies that had the innocent enchanted.

Although he looked to be no older than 40 when he arrived, he introduced himself as the Old Spaniard, calling himself by an aristocratic name of such prodigious length it would have caused a flood had each of its constituents been a raindrop. The Old Spaniard he was for a while, recounting the glories of his native Salamanca – its university where men loved books more than they loved women, its cathedral where men and women found greater ecstasy in God than in each other's flesh, and its women, courted presumably by those who were neither bookish nor pious, the variety of whose beauty exceeded all the species of the earth's flowers catalogued in Duarte Guillermo de Albuquerque's *Natural History of the World*. With his little black beard and glittering black eyes, the Old Spaniard liked to strike a pose, the chin raised and the face turned to a three-quarter profile from the person he condescended to address.

He made grand speeches. The world was poised for conquest, didn't we know, the simultaneous creation of large economic territories and the upsurge of regional nationalism, hadn't we observed, in each of the continents was one symptom, another was the ephemeral hysteria labelled religious fundamentalism, which, didn't we see, was being tolerated by the powerful nations only because the whole world may see its absurdity and irrelevance and therefore welcome its annihilation, the twentieth century, didn't we notice, was dying not like an old patriarch with a future to bestow upon his sons but was being thrown into history like a pauper into an unmarked grave. The Old Spaniard professed to know everything, and turned from one subject to another as if he were at a wine tasting and were the only

18

person there with a certain and intimate knowledge of the contents of each anonymous glass. Wherever he was, words thickened the air, the dust rose in spirals and made the leaves on the trees begin to mutter, and a hot wind blow down our necks.

It did not take him long to realize, however, that no one paid him the slightest attention when, after a fortnight, the novelty of his manner had worn off. His long aristocratic name, flowing with so much majesty from his mouth, had left not an echo behind, and 'the Old Spaniard' was too pretentious for native taste. The exile from Salamanca was left nameless and therefore rendered invisible until one day when a child artlessly said, 'There goes Nebbola.'

Nebbola: the man who talks to his shadow; the man-shadow speaking to divide the man from the shadow; the man whose speech drives away shadows.

Now everyone saw him as for the first time, and several whose brains were set on fire at night by demons until flames sprang from their eyes begged Nebbola to deliver them from their torment. At first, still wearing the learning of Salamanca on his shoulders like a magician's mantle, he recounted his knowledge of alchemy and uttered words vibrant with mystery and splendour – *prima materia*, *hypostatica*, *lumen naturae*, and a whole medieval dictionary that sounded to the natives like the wind blowing over the canopy of the trees. He was quick enough to realize that the people would soon lose patience with his learning and react by abusing and insulting him, that if there were any possibility of releasing the fire in the brain as the *pneuma*, the white dove, then what was required of him was not the hopeful application of esoteric learning but a simple act of charlatanism.

He shaved off his beard and went about throwing penetrating looks with his black eyes; but people stared right back and demanded to know what did he think he was looking at, and he dropped the attitude and began to cultivate a different manner. He shaved his head next and walked about with hooded eyes, always appearing to be meditating with his inner spirit, or, seated in the obscurity of his hut, would be heard chanting in a nasal voice some secret formula that had the air about it of appealing to the gods. It got everyone curious. In public, he kept his eyes lowered, in his privacy he kept his voice raised, a combination that had a powerful effect. The man knew secrets, for sure.

The chanting was a fearful sound that made people want to keep their distance from his hut and at the same time drew them steadily to his window to see what a man looked like who addressed the spirits of the other world with such a passionate rage. Had he been saying *Our Father* or *Hail Mary* at the top of his voice in Latin, we would have understood him even if none of us knew Latin, for even an ignorant observer can intuit genuine religious devotion; had he been saying the mass in Greek, or declaiming the Old Testament in Hebrew, most of us would have caught the drift of his communication with the divine, observed its familiar Christian connections, and paid him no further attention, for the ignorant and the educated alike leave other serious people alone. But it was the mystery of the unfathomable speech that had us captured and held in his power. Of course, some of us strongly suspected it was sixfold garbled gibberish, but the possibility always remained that it was a real language, and what's more, a language uniquely endowed with a capacity for expressing truths our own common speech had been unable to formulate. A man whose face was so intensely contorted in the deliverance of sound that the veins at his neck looked like welts made by an aborted hanging filled us with envy: we lacked the trick, however hard we tried to mimic his chanting, to attain any spiritual vision, ending up instead with a sore throat.

Next thing, Nebbola developed rites that entailed the use of a good inventory of the jungle life – the eggs of a particular fish, the liver of a certain bird, the eyes of a common snake, the sap of the iron tree, all that was available and could be prescribed as a rare potion with the magical power to heal. Using symbols that meant nothing to us, he compiled an encyclopaedia of what grew and lived in the jungle and would consult it with a pointing finger and the oppressed concentration of a scholar trying to find an obfuscating jargon for a banal thought.

Before we knew it, he had become a healer. The sick had to visit him in private, and when they did, screams and yells from both the patient and the doctor were to be heard followed by a portentous period of silence. Sometimes the man emerging would proudly display a bruised head and cuts on his chest as signs of his cure and describe with passion the bitter potion he had had to swallow. Although we did not notice it at first, women had a different appearance when they left his hut: some looked dazed, some serenely contented, and some shocked beyond words, as if their treatment entailed some female mystery that must never be questioned.

Nebbola's early successes emboldened him to look at people – his head raised with the shining pointed chin jutting out menacingly, the hooded eyes gazing knowingly – and declare the odd person to be in desperate need of treatment; and when the poor wretch answered that he was perfectly sound in mind and body, Nebbola opened wide his eyes and so ferociously scolded him for his presumption of self-knowledge that soon the poor man was convinced that wasps nested in his stomach, lizards choked his intestines and that his sperm had turned to rock salt. Women were more readily persuaded, and Tambour remarked to me one day, 'What do you think, Urim? This can only mean one thing, no?'

The speed with which Nebbola acquired sexual tyranny over women and a political despotism over men was all the more astonishing for having been effected spontaneously and without force, but once he understood the power he had suddenly won he began to propound a theory of the healer as a divine presence in a tribe in order to impress upon everyone that his own person was therefore inviolate and must always be held in awe and greeted with adoration. But as yet he was not reckless in his free consumption of the produce and possessions of others, and early devised a method of stifling criticism.

Whenever he sensed a resentment growing among the men, he would go on a fast for several days, eat no food at all, allow no one to enter his hut except for three or four boys who took turns to sit by his hammock where he languished in a silence so terrible that the monkeys in the trees stopped their chattering to listen to it. Each boy, when he had completed his vigil, reported to the group of anxious mothers carrying on a murmurous lamentation outside the hut that Nebbola still refused their offerings of spiced meats and fruit, that he begged them with his dying breath, if they wished to please him, to hold a feast outside his hut, play loud music and tell stories that made men laugh and let the strongest voice in the village stand outside his window and deliver an oration in praise of gluttony so that the fasting man may have a sharper knowledge of the pain of his hunger. Such a request was enough to make the mothers weep and to fill the mouths of men with bitter melancholy. So that when on the fourth or fifth day a boy came out shouting, 'The fast is broken, the fast is broken!' and the man himself came and stood in the doorway, it seemed to the quickly gathering crowd that a wonderful resurrection had transpired before its very eyes. It was enough to make the mothers weep again and for the minds of the men to be filled with confusion.

Perfecting such tricks of the charlatan, he kept a mysterious hold over the society that impassively connived at the gratification of his lust. But then a child with a brain fever suffered real flames in its head and there was nothing that Nebbola could do to save it. His homemade prescriptions, the blood-letting and the mysterious chanting had worked their magic on people who suffered from phantoms or from indigestion; the child was the first with a real malady and Nebbola failed to produce the expected cure.

Anticipating the attack on his power that must follow so visible and pathetic a failure, he declared that the child's death was to be attributed to the tribe's imperfect regard to the principles that governed the cosmos and especially to its omission of a sacred duty. Seeing that everyone looked in awe at the billowing gusts of hot wind coming from his mouth, he went further: until recent civilizations substituted the laws of nature with the laws of hypocrisy, it was true – he announced – of all human tribes that fertility and health were a blessing bestowed by religion and could only be guaranteed by the priest's intercession between a man and a woman whom he joined in marriage, otherwise the offspring ran the risk of being born with congenital malignancies. Everyone looked bewildered. What on earth was he talking about? We beat at the billowing hot wind that was choking us. The air cleared, soon there was only a slight mist of obfuscation before our eyes, and then that too evaporated, leaving Nebbola's vile thought naked.

An outcry arose. He inflated his chest and stopped us with a new gust of hot wind. Intercession, he proclaimed, was the divine principle and without it death and famine overtook a tribe, intercession was the law by which the priest was bound by his sacred duty to take precedence over the newly married husband in the deflowering of his virgin bride. That is when the great cry of revolt went up. Nebbola, accustomed to the success of his charlatan tricks, and hitherto not having devised one with which to possess young girls, had seized the event of the child's death to extract from society a licence for his own vicious ends. A bold stroke no doubt, but as well let loose a pig in the Israeli Knesset.

Before Nebbola knew it, four men had pounced upon him, and the next thing he was being carried to the river with a crowd of men and older boys in pursuit, shouting abuse. The men who carried him flung him on the bank and stripped his clothes. Some other men had begun to light a fire nearby. When flames began to rise from the mass of twigs, four other men held Nebbola by each of his limbs and swung him over the fire, gently lowering him with each swing. He was yelling in Spanish and the crowd was shouting at him in a medley of tongues. The men held him still, suspended over the fire. Flames singed the hairs on his buttocks and he screamed. 'Roast his balls!' someone shouted. 'Turn his prick to ashes,' cried another, and a third, 'And stuff the ashes into his mouth!' The four men turned him about the flames, like an ox being readied for a long, slow roasting, and then began to swing him again, lowering his behind down into the fire and raising him high in the air, again and again. Nebbola roared and screamed. The men swinging him shouted simultaneously, 'One, two and *three*!' and flung him into the river. He fell into it like a huge rock.

Water shot up from where he sank and sent out wide, agitated circles rippling across the width of the river. Nebbola came up, opening his mouth and gulping air, ducked his head into the water, swam two strokes, and raised his head up again for more air. The crowd was jeering from the bank. Nebbola swung around, deciding to swim to the opposite bank. He heard the crowd laughing and swung around again. He saw that the men had taken their revenge and were not murderously inclined, as he had feared. He had only humiliation and ridicule to face; the other bank with its impenetrable jungle offered the dignity of death, a far inferior choice. He climbed up the bank under the glare of pity and derision, and re-entered the tribe as a shadow, truly assuming at last the real worth of the name given him by a child.

The crown of parrot feathers and the jaguar's tooth that hung from his left ear became his new adornments, creating in him an image he had not previously possessed, so that the lascivious opportunist was replaced in the imagination of the tribe by a quiet shaman who, haunted by spiritual visions, devised charming rituals to keep the idle engaged. His tyrannical possessiveness had given way to conspicuous abstinence to such an extent that when, for example, food was laid out for a communal feast, as after the performance of the multiple marriages, he was demonstrative in refusing more than a child's share, insisting that his duty was to bless and not to consume. Stripping himself of vanity and renouncing carnal desire, he had come to accept the behaviour forced upon him by circumstance as a condition he had deliberately cultivated after a prolonged philosophical meditation on the true nature of the self, thus becoming possessed by a nice delusion which, in effect, made him the sole victim of his own charlatanism.

Nebbola's holy fire cast a vivid glow on the saffron robes the marrying couples wore and shone back from the perspiring faces of the brides absorbed in the tension of the mystery of reality that held them suspended outside the selves they had possessed only ten minutes ago when they were summoned to form a circle round the fire. Horuxtla watched with fascination the transformation of her friends into strangers, the expression on her face displaying a succession of emotions: envy and then joy, but again and again a puzzlement that life could so suddenly be overwhelmed by a momentous and entirely unpredictable event, as if she had just been removed from the familiar soft humus of her origin and placed on a rocky land that was prone to earthquakes.

4 A Presentiment

She was safe for the present, her body relaxed with no expectation of imminent violence, her flesh radiant on the edge of the circle of the fire, unmolested by the threat of change as if she were locked within a timeless adolescence; but then she moved in a quick shivering gesture and, standing still again, a shudder went through her limbs: it could have been that a sputtering piece of burning timber had sprung a flying fragment in her direction and she shifted quickly from its path, but the sudden movement seemed to contract her body, the taut flesh loosening for a moment and rivulets of shadows appearing on her breast where earlier there was only radiance, and her eyes were briefly fixed in an expression of deep mourning. Had she glimpsed her future that her mouth opened in a suppressed scream, and then, with Nebbola's chanting giving way to communal singing, let the voice emerge as melody, stifling the cry of pain by converting it to a sound of pleasure, joining the singing voices of the girls around her to reject a troubling thought? The moment passed so rapidly that she could not have retained the knowledge revealed to her had an image indeed been transmitted to her of greater precision than a vague presentiment; and after all it could have been only a cool tongue of the humid air that had touched her bare flesh and she had shivered with its sudden shock. But that brief moment – already long vanished in the community of singing and buzzing voices – stayed with me, enclosing me within its enlarging bubble, so that I witnessed the source of Horuxtla's fears and realized with what awful determinism our separate futures were to collide, seeing too in that prescient flash, which was also an instant of afterknowledge, like a memory of a past become so remote it seems a memory of a former life, that my anticipated happiness and her triumph were the assertion of opposites, that bitterness tinged one and mockery the other, and my reaching for the essential idea was like a snail attempting to climb up a mossy wall who finds the surface too slippery and falls first to its point of departure and then, bouncing from there, discovers itself sunk to the bottom of a pool of crystalline water.

The drumming had slackened, become little more than a throbbing in the air; the shrill flutes were reduced to a heavy and dull whispering. A burst of laughter broke out from a group of men but it had the forced ring of people who refused to abandon an occasion that had already exhausted itself. The ceremonial fire was dying. A few women stood up and began a love-song but after one verse stifled the words for a vague humming and walked away to their huts with a slow, bovine swinging of the hips, and the song, intended to celebrate the recent weddings, dispersed in the air like a weak signal calling their husbands to their beds. The animal sounds of the jungle, which had been present since sunset but had remained unheard over the tribe's festive noise, now rendered futile the last brave attempts to prolong the pleasurable event. Lamps that threw light from the windows of some of the huts were extinguished.

Unaccountably, I remained in the darkness. The land on which I stood, the whole area of the settlement, detached itself from my presence on it, and I saw rise before my eyes a vast black disc that floated up above the rain forest and hung precariously in the sky. It took on the appearance of a hole in the sky, an immense black emptiness. Suddenly, a light sprang up before me. A log that had been smouldering began to throw up flames from a part as yet unconsumed. After the sensation of black emptiness the new flames created an impression of a flashing, blinding light and then made visible fragments of slanting and shivering lines as though long, thin neon lights had appeared across the space, creating a meaningless illumination.

My bride, my demon, Horuxtla, across whose bosom but even now rivulets of shadows had flowed, was at the centre of that brightness, her face turned to me, the smile upon it at once an invitation and a refusal, her all but naked body held in the posture both of submission and withdrawal. Her right arm was raised, beckoning me, while her legs were positioned to spring away and run from me. For a moment, I believed I ran towards her, and when she leaped away lengthened my strides to catch up with her, but the light had me confused and I lost her.

The vision had me gasping for breath. All my former life I had never been tormented by the inexplicable, nor ever suffered my brain to indulge in mystical speculation, and yet my perception now from minute to minute was so invaded by contradictions that I found it impossible to have a secure hold over a sense of present time.

The figure who had appeared in the distorting light and dark was Tambour who hailed me from a distance, shouting, 'All alone, Urim?' Coming closer, he added, 'That makes two of us. Maybe we should join Nebbola. I just looked into his hut. He was chanting away, I guess to take his mind off sex. There's so much of it going on you can smell it in the air.' I made the banal observation that it was only to be expected on this night of many consummations. 'As for me,' Tambour said, 'I thank the Lord I don't have the desire any more. It's true! I have no need at all. Otherwise I'd be back at the old life in Xurupá, a new whore every night and still no end to the body's lust. What a life that was of stupid obsessions!'

5 Xurupá

The bulldozed land was now a sea of mud as far as the eye could reach. The wide western bend of the Xurupá river, which gave the dusty and muddy town on its further bank its name, marked a frontier of sorts, a line beyond which exploration was presumed to be futile; but in every other direction the rain forest had been cut down, its timber long dispersed as black smoke, and the land flattened to a shiny grey evenness. Word had gone out that gold lay deposited beneath the surface as surely as behind the gates of Fort Knox, guarded here only by a layer of soft grey soil, and suddenly thousands of men had come to lay claim to portions of the land.

The earliest took possession of large tracts and the envious later arrivals, coming armed with machine-guns, forced a code of expedient rights for general acceptance that seemed to give each man an equitable share but in reality established the rule of the gun. Half a dozen of the best-armed controlled the land. But thousands of new arrivals still had to be appeased, and many of them, being ignorant and hungry, were simply absorbed by the more powerful by becoming, in effect, their slaves; for the stronger-willed independent minds among the new arrivals a system was evolved of selling smaller and smaller portions of the earth until the very latest to come could buy no more than six square metres, which they greedily purchased at the expense of a lifetime's savings.

Following the general belief that the gold was definitely there and it was inevitably a matter of reaching it if one dug deep enough, thousands of men, dressed only in a pair of tattered shorts, sank their tools deeper and deeper and hauled up pails of mud, and it seemed that the earth had nothing more to give than clawed-up bits of slimy maggot-infested entrails. Parts of the land had been reduced to deep canyons, narrow vertical tunnels of great depth. From dayrise to sunset, as far as the eye could see, there were, emerging from tunnels of their own creation, descending or climbing up a wide excavation that in itself was a vast crater in the land, in chains like termites, thousands of men labouring in the chosen dream of their existence, the grey mud clinging to their bodies like a blackening fungus, working in a slow, weary motion, as must the dead in their eternal punishment, only the whites of their eyes showing an occasional flicker of animation. Among them, Tambour, deep in his own vertical tunnel, shovelled mud into his pail for the ten thousandth time, looked up at the small square of light towards which he must ascend with his load, hoping the rope ladder would hold him for one more time and the earth of the tunnel walls not collapse and bury him alive, and slowly made his way up. To discover that at last he had brought up gold!

When he had converted his gold to cash in the state bank in Xurupá, he left most of the money in the room he rented from cunning old Fatima Parreira and taking a generous amount for his present need went directly to Beleza Teresa's who conspicuously maintained a discreet house on the river with a view across the water of the grey land where men gave their lives searching for gold. Tambour had found small quantities of gold in previous months, enough to pay his rent and to fill his stomach, and most of all to pick up streetwalkers, who infested the labyrinth of squalid alleys in the middle of the town, loitering there in shorts and a bra, their high heels covered with mud, or standing in the bluish light cast out of the doorways of pathetic bars, smoking one cigarette after another. Tambour suffered abominably from lust, but no amount of expenditure in the carnal market brought him satisfaction. He had paid for every fantasy his imagination could conceive and yet could not rid himself of the feeling that the fluid racing feverishly through his veins was not blood but semen, throbbing loudly in his brain with its eternal demand for release.

Striking it rich, he therefore made straight for Beleza Teresa's house. She kept nine girls of varying complexion to suit a variety of tastes and reserved her own black-haired beauty only for exceptional offers. When Tambour appeared before her in his shorts, she uttered a little shriek and sucked in her breath, seeing the man had not had the decency to wash and clothe himself before rushing out to buy pleasure with his newly found wealth. She gazed at the mud that had dried to a flat cake on his head, saw the bundle of notes in his dirty hand, and said in a superior air suggesting she had her standards that no amount of money could lower, 'You don't seem to know where you are, you must have been looking for the shack of some cheap streetwalker.'

Tambour shook his head and smiled, the action dislodging dried mud from his face. Teresa looked down at her light blue carpet where the untidy heap had fallen and then back at him. 'I'll permit no girl of mine to descend so low,' she said imperiously.

'No, no girl, Belezinha, but you,' Tambour said quietly.

'What?' she nearly screamed. 'You come like a dog straight out of the gutter and have the impudence to . . .'

'Please let me explain,' Tambour interrupted. 'I haven't come for the reason other men come here.'

'I wouldn't have you here for *any* reason.'

Not paying attention to her remonstrance, Tambour said, 'I've come for a bath.'

She stared at him incredulously, dumbfounded by what she had heard, and he added, 'Belezinha, I want *you* to give me a bath. That's all. I'll give you all this money for it, see.'

'Let me send for the gardener,' she responded, laughing sarcastically. 'He can hose you down in the vegetable patch, it would save him having to carry compost. Or should I say *manure*.'

'Oh, Belezinha, they tell me you come from a valley in Chile where clear cold streams flow down from the Andes. I think you got your lovely skin from bathing in those streams.'

She was unprepared for such a compliment and stared at him in momentary surprise, and he, seeing her eyes so fixed, went on, 'And nature made your eyes so beautifully black in direct opposition to the sun. You are right to be proud, Belezinha. Your square shoulders and high bosom justify your pride.'

'What nonsense are you talking now?'

'Only describing what I see, Belezinha.'

'You are a silly fool!'

He noticed that her voice had become less aggressive and that he had won her over to an accommodating mood. He thrust out his hand, saying, 'Here's the money. Put it away, and take me to your bathroom.'

The sizable bundle of money had been present in her vision all this time, and now there it was, held up before her, right in front of her bosom. She put up her hand to push his away and to bring the ludicrous interview to an end, but, touching the money, she kept her hand raised for a moment, feeling within her a fine thrill that she

30

always experienced when she touched notes of high denomination, and she ended by snatching the money from him and saying, 'Oh, all right!'

The bathroom had a white marble floor and dark blue curtains. The bath in the centre of the sumptuous room was shaped like a large lotus flower, its petals of sparkling white shot with pink veins and shaped so delicately they seemed to be made of the finest bone china. When Teresa turned on the gold-plated faucets a thin jet of water spouted from the point of each petal and the several jets, each making an arc, met above the middle of the deep bath and fell into it in a vertical stream.

'You'd better get under the shower first,' she said.

He stood there looking helplessly at her. Seeing his filthy shorts, she realized what he expected her to do, and she walked up to him and quickly pulled them down. Then she turned the water on in the shower, thrust him into the stall, and drew the curtains. He flung the curtain open and said, 'Come and soap me. I'm going to need a shampoo, too.'

She saw the stream of mud running down his face and shoulders and was annoyed by what she had let herself in for and yet amused by the funny sight; but she had a sense of commercial honour and would never not give value for money received. So, she went to a corner of the room, removed her clothes, and returned to enter the shower herself.

She was taller than her meek client who, now that some of the mud from his chest had run down to reveal his rib-cage, was also pitiably thin. She held his head under the shower and rubbed it until the dirt was rinsed away. Then, taking a bottle of shampoo from an alcove just above the faucets, she poured a good quantity of it on the man's head, and when she had worked it into a considerable lather and rinsed it out, she repeated the action with a conditioner. Next she soaped his neck and shoulders, his chest and back, and then, having to lower herself nearly to a squatting position, she scrubbed his legs all the way to his ankles, not neglecting his private parts which she rubbed in the palms of her soap-covered hands. The latter action had no more effect on him than if she had been rubbing his toes, and she realized that the man's desire was indeed an innocent one to have himself cleansed and that he had not got her into a situation where he was going to spring a perverse demand upon her.

'Now rinse it all off while I get the bath ready,' she said, leaving him under the shower.

The bath was half full and she poured into it a measure of a perfumed liquid that soon began to spread a layer of bubbles across the water's surface. When Tambour came out of the shower two minutes later, small waves of foam filled the bath. She held his hand, directing him to step into the heart of the open lotus. He sank into it and lay back with his head resting against a petal that arched above him.

Believing that Tambour told me this anecdote to have something amusing with which to fill the tedious hours of the rainy season, I laughed lightly at two or three points in his narrative and then heartily at its conclusion. I congratulated him on his inventive mind. He looked outraged, and said with some force, 'No, that's *exactly* how it happened. It's all *true!*'

He checked the agitation that had come to his voice and went on, 'I discovered I was no longer driven by desire. I can tell you that when I arrived at Beleza Teresa's with the money in my hand I had no thought of what I was going to say to her. I suppose I went running there to get myself laid. Everyone talked of the luxury and style of her establishment, and it's what everyone did when they hit gold, go spend a bundle at Teresa's and come out looking divine. What I said to Beleza Teresa was what came out of my mouth when I stood there before her terrific beauty. In my haste to get to her, I hadn't even looked at myself in the mirror, and it must have crossed my mind when I stood there that I was literally a filthy little animal. Crusted all over with mud as I was, how could have I asked to go to bed with her? I realized I needed a bath more than anything else.'

I agreed it was a logical wish, and Tambour proceeded. 'By the way, she's not called Beleza for nothing. I wasn't blind when she came naked into the shower, and there wasn't room there for her to keep at an arm's length. When she was working her fingers in my hair with the shampoo her breasts were pressed right against my chest. Through the streams of soapy water I saw her lovely face, the long black hair gone wet and fallen over her shoulders, her dark eyes so close to my face, and it was not hard for me to imagine I was elsewhere with her in that delicious moment prior to the release of unbounded passion. Believe me, I was in flowery meadows on the lower Andes where the streams run with icy water, lying beside her on a bank where blood-red poppies grew, or we lolled on a

Pacific beach on the Chilean coast where the sun set upon the world and, sinking crimson into the violet ocean, threw a ruddy glint in the infinitesimal space that divided her lips from mine. Oh, yes, I relished the possibilities when she draped me in a curtain of soapy water. But I realized I was absolutely without desire. I had certain proof of my altered condition when she squatted down and had my cock in her palms and worked up so much lather on it it looked made of foam. Desire had made a complete exit from my body.'

When she had held his hand and led him to the bath he had again remarked to himself how beautiful was her body, each feature perfectly proportioned, even to the slight cushiony protuberance of her belly. 'No wonder men offer her gold as soon as they find it,' Tambour recounted while I lay still in my hammock, the rain pounding the muddy earth outside. 'But I admired her beauty even more because I had no desire to possess it. I lay in the wonderful bath where each pore of my skin opened and what little fragment of desire still lingered beneath the surface was shown the nearest exit.'

6 The Mirrored Man

I had come to Xurupá from the east, travelling to the interior from the coastal city of Natal where I had taken temporary residence at a seaside hotel. Three walls of the hotel lobby, where the attractive young receptionist maintained a tidy desk, were panelled with large mirrors to make the confined area look spacious, bringing into the small room reflections of the swaying fronds of palm trees and a thousand spots of light caught on the leaves of a yellow-flowering acacia, for across the open door opposite the receptionist was the hotel's charming garden.

Each morning, while on my way to the beach, I found occasion to exchange a word with the receptionist for the innocent pleasure of seeing her beautiful smile. On entering the lobby, one saw multiple reflections of her on the walls, caught in a perfect profile in one and in another nearly lost in the dots of light on the acacia, and when I stood there for a minute or two, remarking how perfect had been the papaya at breakfast or how inviting the ocean had looked just now from my bedroom window, I invariably caught my own reflection addressing an image of hers, and the two mirrored figures seemed then to have lives of their own, meeting in a tropical garden with the sound of the ocean in the distance, and for a moment I felt that I should like to listen to their dialogue until the sound of the speaking voice registered on my brain as my own and, hearing the banality of my words, I realized that this was an example of a common phenomenon – our perceiving as enviably sophisticated the lives of others until we come so close to them as to merge with them, when the ordinariness becomes transparent, since it is too familiarly our own, of the most cultivated exchange.

Sometimes, a waitress with a tray of coffee might pass by on her way to serve some guests on the terrace, or another guest might also happen to come to the lobby when I was there, and the room would suddenly appear busy with waitresses going in

34

different directions and several guests claiming the attention of a multitude of receptionists. It was in this latter circumstance that I met Jonathan Pons, seeing his face reflected back from one wall and almost merging with my own profile on another.

He was travelling on some foundation grant from the United States, pursuing, I believe, some anthropological research. In truth, I never comprehended the nature of his research, perhaps because my first impression of him – in swimming trunks with a towel hanging from his shoulder and enquiring of the receptionist if a waiter could bring him a gin and tonic at eleven o'clock on the beach – fixed him in my mind as a hedonist rather than a scholar. I was myself on the way to the beach, a few steps ahead of him, and he, quickly catching up, said as though we had long been acquainted, 'The only thing I miss in this country is my cat whom I named Socrates. Not after the great philosopher but after the Brazilian soccer star.' Assuming him to be a man of culture, I idly responded, 'Ionesco has a splendid joke about Socrates being a cat. In his play about a larger animal,' I added when I saw my reference lost upon my companion and realized that to mention the play's title would only draw attention to his ignorance. Thus, because he did not wish to concede that his culture was inferior and I did not wish to give the impression that I had slighted him, we remained together attempting a vacuous sort of talk which bypassed the delicate question of intellectual vanity but which, keeping us in each other's company, obliged us to pretend there was a growing friendship between us.

My practice had been to take a swim and then to lie on my towel, next to a rock which cast a protective shadow, until just before noon when, taking another swim, I returned to the hotel with a keen curiosity for what the hotel's remarkably inventive chef had prepared for lunch. Pons, however, went for a long and vigorous swim, energetically stroking his way almost to the mouth of the bay where a line of fishing boats was coming in, and on returning flung himself on the sand in full exposure to the sun. A few minutes later, he rose and walked the length of the beach and, seeing that from the end of the wide curve of the beach to where I lay the shortest distance was through the water, swam back and came and sat on the rock.

He mentioned the names of some churches he had read of in a guide to the region and suggested we go and see them after lunch. Then there was the market in town. He had to go to the market.

Markets fascinated him, did they not me? He had rented a car and wanted to see everything. There must be women somewhere too, he added tentatively, and paused to see if I had any knowledge on the subject. I had none, but I did not dissuade him from his many proposals and, finding his excessive energy stimulated me out of the lethargy into which I had sunk, I went along on his excursion to the churches.

A tarnished baroque splendour in dark, gloomy halls and immense vaulted rooms. Seventeenth-century chests of wood scratched and cracked with age and neglect. Sacred vessels heaped in a corner. A moth-eaten vestment hanging from a peg on a wall, its silver threads like thin tumorous tentacles growing in the wall where the plaster had fallen. Outside, a bamboo scaffolding the length of the church, short, bow-legged workers at their dream-like labour, carrying tin bowls of cement from a mixer. One, in a courtyard, a straw hat tilted rakishly upon his head, tapping his mason's hammer on irregularly shaped stones to break them to the required size, as if a geologist were opening a portal into the past. A pot-bellied priest popped his head out of a door, licked his lips, his gleaming eyes glowed a moment as they caught the light falling through a jackfruit tree, and sailed across the front yard to where he saw visitors and, even before he reached them, began to recount a history of processions led by representatives of the Dutch aristocracy. Tap-tap, echoes the stonemason's hammer. There is nothing to lament. It is in this region that the sun rises first over South America, this is where discoveries began, this is where the seed of the mango tree was brought from India.

The whole square is heaped with fruit. Mounds of pineapples, bananas and mangoes. A delicious stink of ripeness in the air. Wide-hipped women carrying pink and green plastic bags bend down to feel the firmness of the mangoes, to pick up a pineapple and to hold it to the nose. A squawking of voices in the air complaining of inflated prices. In the streets around the square, piles of mustard greens, cauliflowers, cucumbers, tomatoes, squash, garlic. Round a corner, another square, fabrics floating from textile shops in an arcade. Handicrafts in a labyrinth of aisles fill the square. Representations in clay of dead figures of doubtful heroism, and of ducks, herons and crocodiles. A folksy poet's verses carved on wood resembling a scroll of parchment. So much re-creation. But the creators are primitive. Were they gods, they would create worlds that looked like pumpkins and were inhabited by amusing little freaks. The remembered past has a funny shape.

Surging humanity in the narrow streets where there's so little air and a potent smell from the stagnant black effluent in the open gutters bring on nausea. Mothers pulling fatigued, reluctant children to clothing shops. Some blocks away from the square of the artisans, where suddenly there's no one in the street, past the corner dominated by the Banco do Brasil, is the Hotel Arcadia. Three stars. American Express. Thomas Cook. Welcome. Welcome. Potted palms in the lobby. Three-week-old foreign newspapers available at the desk, though the only evidence of this is a copy of *Le Monde* which bears the date of another year. A man is leaving the desk, having just paid his bill, a porter is carrying his luggage to the taxi outside. A hotel for businessmen, travellers from abroad, seeking new markets. But take the elevator to the seventh floor, and observe that there are no surprises in this world, only repetitions and mimicry, come out of the elevator and enter representations of American or Dutch or French interiors where women in American and European disguises throw their imperial looks at you and you are emptying your pockets, ready to sell your soul!

That evening, while Pons and I sat together over drinks, he asked, 'Have you heard of Xurupá?' I had not. Then I simply must accompany him! It was the principal object of his study. I'd be fascinated, too, when I heard about it. Bulldozers were eating up the interior, had I not heard, trucks were hauling away the rain forest, and the earth was being prised open for its precious minerals. Another great West was opening up, with wild new towns everywhere, a barbarous frontier drama, with its guns and gaudy whores, with its improvised codes of chivalry on the one hand and utter lawlessness on the other, was taking place on the land of which there wasn't enough for everyone to grab in the thousands of square miles of what from the beginning of history had been no-man's land. Now no-man had been born at last. No-man was everywhere. We just had to go and see the action, maybe even be part of it, for nowhere else on earth right now was there such a naked display of raw lust in all its inhuman forms.

'Why *inhuman*?' he added after a pause. 'Change that to *human*. Only it's so uninhibited, so unmodified by any pretence of hypocrisy, of civilization, unaccepting of any secular or religious law, that it seems a base corruption of what we piously term human.'

It was life on the frontier that attracted Pons, action that drew no distinction between reality and fantasy; the frontier appeared to him to be like an overcrowded ship quarantined just outside a harbour, or like a plague-stricken city that has been sealed off, whose men and women are driven by an unambiguous knowledge that they are alive in a very desperate situation. I thought his similes somewhat anachronistic, if not literary, and pointed out to him that as a native of California he must acknowledge that a more appropriate comparison would be to actors on a movie set who, instructed by the script to slaughter one another, are doomed to act with a foreknowledge of their destiny and yet, in order to be believably realistic, must continue to behave as if they expected to survive all present ordeals.

I agreed to accompany Pons to Xurupá, but not because I was interested in seeing such a society. I did not need to witness a man kill another to understand the nature of his lust for possession any more than I need to drink a bottle of whisky at one sitting to comprehend the mind of an alcoholic. I agreed because Pons's suggestion struck me as an expression of my own unconscious will, to remove myself to a greater distance than I had already come from the source of my original flight.

To reach Xurupá we first had to take a plane to Manaus and from there to arrange for a boat to transport us up the river. After two days of slow navigation against the stream, we disembarked at a village which was inhabited by the listless descendants of the rubber trappers. These were people who did nothing. Their ancestors had worked from three in the morning to long after sunset, wandering the jungle in search of new rubber trees and, finding them, collecting the latex to take back to their smoke-blackened huts where they converted the latex to rubber. In all the decades of the rubber boom, they had not been given time to rest, and now their descendants, inheriting their fatigue, could scarcely bestir themselves for five minutes before they abandoned the task they had reluctantly undertaken and lay down wherever they happened to be. These were people whose blood had slowed down, and they had no memories. Their speech was slow and comprised of very few words.

The village had one enterprising man, named Renzo, who had seized for himself the means of communication since no one else was interested in doing so, and, by using relays of men to perform a very simple brief task each, had found a way of converting the community's lethargy into a slow-motion form of energy, and, commanding that energy, exercised power in the village. It was to him that Pons and I were obliged to apply for transportation to Xurupá. We did not need to seek him out, for he personally met any boat that stopped at the village to see if there was any trade to be had: the boats, even when they were chartered by private clients, carried commodities like coffee and petrol that fetched good prices in the interior, and Renzo bought and hoarded whatever struck him as potentially profitable.

By cannibalizing the parts of a jeep, a pick-up truck and three automobiles, he had constructed a bizarre-looking motorized vehicle: it had a bright red bonnet from a Buick of the forties and huge fins with round tail-lights from a Cadillac ten years younger; the bed of a pick-up formed the main body and on it he had screwed bench seats from another car and boxed the compartment with plywood in which he had cut oval windows, painting one side with the image of St George and the dragon and the other with a representation of Christ in the garb of a shepherd. The top was open and so the car came equipped with two umbrellas neatly attached to a side panel.

It took an entire day to make a tortuous passage through the jungle, travelling no faster than walking pace. It was dark and intensely humid. The vehicle, propelled by the loud engine of an old jeep, laboured in twisting directions over the underbush. Renzo gave the confident impression that he was driving through familiar winding streets at a speed that might cause his passengers a little concern. Occasionally, there was the faint appearance of a track where the ground cover had been beaten down by former journeys, but much of the day it seemed we were crawling in repetitive circles under an oppressively dense vegetation. The fear was uppermost in both our minds that the improbable vehicle could not possibly survive the hazard of such a journey and then when it broke down it would be to trap us in some dark depth of the jungle, but both Pons and I maintained a superstitious silence on the subject and it was only in the relief of deliverance that we whispered a word of it.

That was when we finally gained the highway that had been bulldozed through the jungle. Evening had fallen and very soon it would be pitch dark. Renzo brought out some cold chicken and bread and bottled water. While we ate, he took one of the four large cans of petrol that he carried at the rear and refuelled the vehicle which now enjoyed our affectionate respect. He then produced two hammocks and hung them between trees beside the highway for our night's accommodation, he himself stretching out on a bench in the car. How far was it to Xurupá, Pons asked. Oh, about a hundred and fifty kilometres, just over three hours. Then why didn't we proceed? 'One thing I never figured out,' Renzo answered, 'is how to fix headlights on this car. Mechanics in Xurupá could do it, but at what a price!'

We settled in our hammocks. There was no lingering light at dusk in that part of the world. Somewhere the sun dropped below the horizon and in that moment, as if a switch had been flicked off, all light was extinguished at once and there was total darkness. The unseen beasts began a fearful howling. Images of bats smashing through the darkness and enormous boa constrictors winding up the tree kept one awake in a state of terror. But I must have fallen asleep and the images were perhaps only dreams, for in the middle of the night Renzo was calling out loudly and there was a mysterious sound in the air. I was confused to see some light, and for a moment I did not know where I was and then, remembering, could not think how I had got there.

When I came out of the hammock, I saw the source of the sound – a truck had parked just ahead of Renzo's vehicle, its diesel engine clattering away. Its headlights illuminated the highway and its tail-gate was a fanciful array of red, orange and green lights, all of it creating an eerie glow. The truck seemed empty. I thought I saw the outline of a man's head looking over the tail-gate, but it was impossible to be certain in that darkness. It was just past three in the morning. Apparently, Renzo had heard the truck coming up the highway and, gun in hand, had flagged it down. He had decided to follow the truck and thereby not have to wait until sunrise. He spoke with its driver, and they came to some understanding.

Presently we were on our way, following the truck. Its rear lights, which had appeared so bright when the truck was stationary, were only dimly visible through the clouds of dust rising from its wheels. Renzo's vehicle disclosed reserves of speed on the open road, though the impression on the passengers was that of being flung down a mountainside in a cable car gone out of control. We made perilous progress, hurtling through the darkness in pursuit of the dots of light which threatened to disappear at any moment; and because of the necessity to see something, however dim, we had to keep at precisely that distance from the truck where the whirling dust from its wheels came swooping up to hit our windscreen and to fall upon us from the open top. The road was straight and wide, bordered in the strange light in which we saw it by the black jungle. We had a sense of the undulating land by the speed at which the truck in front of us travelled. Some of the upward inclines were steep enough for the truck to need to labour with a furious roar of its engine in a low gear, and this gave us a little relief from the flying dust, as well as making it easier for us to keep in close pursuit. The downward slopes, however, not only raised a havoc of dust but also put us into considerable anxiety as Renzo struggled with the complications of his machine to keep up with the speeding truck.

We had not travelled in this frantic manner for half an hour when we came to a longer and more precipitous slope than before. The truck gathered speed and began to increase the distance from us. Renzo swore at the wheel and rubbed the dust from his eyes. Pons was in the agony of a choking fit. I held a handkerchief to my mouth, trying not to swallow dust, and had my other arm raised across my forehead to prevent the dust from drilling into my eyes. Of the many lights behind the truck only the two main tail-lights were visible now, and they only as tiny dots and then, too, possibly only because we had been holding them desperately in our vision and would lose should we but blink our eyes.

And then I was certain we had lost the truck. Clouds of dust still attacked us mercilessly but the roar of the truck's engine had become muffled and increasingly distant. Pons came out of his choking fit and, not seeing the rear of the truck when he stared over Renzo's shoulder, cried aloud, 'You've lost him!' A few second later, the dust had stopped flying, there was no sound of the truck, and we seemed to be about to smash into a wall of darkness. Renzo, still believing he saw the tail-lights, though what persisted in his vision was only an after-image, shouted at the invisible truck, 'Mad motherfucker, why don't you slow down!'

Alarmed at Renzo's own madness to be continuing in that pitch black, Pons shouted at him to stop. But as if it had become a question of honour for his machine to continue, Renzo would not stop. The road was apparently straight and wide and for about a quarter of a kilometre, which in the terror of the blind motion in the darkness seemed a very long distance, we drove on. Then we had a stroke of good luck.

Some bushes or low-hanging branches of trees came into contact with the driver's side of the car: instead of crashing into the jungle the car had begun to brush its side against it, and that was lucky because it made Renzo realize that he had completely lost his sense of direction. There was nothing to do but to bring the vehicle to a stop. Relieved that we had at least been saved from a bloody mutilation, we alighted from the car. Pons stepped aside and urinated. Renzo released a loud fart. I felt my knees trembling. Renzo cursed the driver of the truck. Pons said it did not matter as long as we were safe. It would be light in a couple of hours. We fell into a silence.

Five or six minutes later, we heard the sound of the truck, and then saw its two headlights. 'What do you know, the motherfucker's coming back for us!' Renzo exclaimed.

The truck was labouring uphill and its two headlights seemed like two enormous eyes in the immense darkness. Steadily, and as if with a gaze fixed upon us, they came up the road. The truck stopped some twenty metres from us. Leaving the engine running and the lights on, the driver stepped down and ambled across to stand in front of the headlights, his back to the truck. We could see him in silhouette while he had us in the centre of the floodlit area. Suddenly Pons said, 'Oh my God, he's going to murder us!'

The man carried a rifle in his hand. 'You American,' he called to Pons. 'You come here.' He waved the rifle. Pons stepped towards him. 'You, the other one,' he called to me. 'Over here.' I went and stood next to Pons. 'You want to go to Xurupá? Go get your bags and come with me,' he said to both of us.

We went back to the car and picked up our things.

'Hey, you haven't paid me,' Renzo cried in a panic. 'You can't go without paying me.'

A shot rang out. The man had fired in the air, and now shouted, 'Pay him nothing.'

We walked to where he stood, leaving Renzo mumbling curses.

'Did you say something?' the man shouted threateningly at Renzo. 'You two,' he said to us, 'go climb up the back.'

Renzo had gone quiet, grim-faced. As we began to walk to the back of the truck, the man fired two shots at Renzo's car. One shattered the windscreen, the other hit the radiator from which water began to spout.

My earlier impression that I had seen the outline of a man's head looking over the tail-gate had been correct, but it had been only a partial perception. For as we climbed into the truck we saw that it was in fact packed with men. Some had curled up asleep on the bed, too fatigued or too weak from hunger to be curious about the drama outside, others squatted uncomfortably, some stood behind the cab. Pons and I sat down in a corner by the tail-gate. The driver turned the truck around and proceeded with its human cargo. We were too shaken by the experience to say anything, but after a while Pons wondered why the man had come back and not taken us the first time. Renzo had a gun in his hand when he flagged him down, I remarked. It had been cleverer of the man to come back, giving the impression that he had been concerned at losing us and no doubt calculating, rightly as it turned out, that Renzo would have put his gun away.

The truck trundled along in the night, bumping over the uneven surface, jostling the packed men against one another. It was a bedraggled company, we saw as it began to be light. There were twenty-three in all. Thin and emaciated, with many a tooth missing, their skin loosened into wrinkles by the sun under which they had spent their lives labouring for no more profit than an unsatisfactory appeasement of hunger, they looked like criminals who have been incarcerated for so long they have forgotten the crime they committed. We discovered later that they had been employed in the construction of a highway in the interior and that the man who now drove them to Xurupá, who went by the name of Coura, had persuaded them to part with three months' wages in return for the opportunity to dig for gold; indeed, they considered themselves the lucky ones, for there were thousands of others who envied those who could buy their way to Xurupá. Far from lamenting their condition, our weary-eyed and miserably undernourished companions were in fact in a state of hopeful anticipation, dreaming of the gold that must soon be theirs.

The truck halted. We stood up and looked out. There was no city in sight. The jungle still bordered the road. Coura climbed down from his cab, the rifle in his hand. 'You two,' he called to us when he had walked to the rear of the truck, 'throw your bags out and then come down yourselves.'

'My friend here is an American geologist.' I spoke aloud clearly in Portuguese so that all aboard the truck could hear. 'He can tell you where to find gold without your needing to look for it.' The crowd in the truck murmured in astonishment, and I added, 'We'll be worth a fortune to all of you in Xurupá whereas in our bags you'll find little more than dirty underwear.'

43

The crowd saw confusion and indecision come over Coura's face and seized upon that moment of apparent weakness to speak aloud, demanding to be taken at once to Xurupá. Some pounded the side of the truck. Others gesticulated. All shouted, 'Gold, gold, the American will find us gold!' Coura fired a shot in the air. There was a moment's silence. But the crowd burst out again. 'To Xurupá, to Xurupá! Gold, gold, the American will find us gold!' The shouting and the pounding grew louder. To the corporation of men in the truck we were valuable executives on whose enterprise depended the imminent certainty of windfall profits. Coura relented and proceeded to Xurupá with his cargo of frenetic men.

A small plane, with a single-propeller engine, flew over us as we approached Xurupá and landed on a distant field at the end of which was a hangar beside which several similar aircraft were parked. The jungle had suddenly vanished. The land was grey and bald. The road curved into a wide loop, following a river's bank on our right. Opposite was a vast valley, down the far wall of which thousands of men were digging. It was obvious that the land here had been flat, perhaps even hilly, only a few months ago, and that the valley had been formed by men who had hauled away the earth to sieve for gold. We came to a junction with another dirt highway on which an overloaded bus, luggage piled high on its roof, was making for the same turning that would take us over the bridge into the town. Behind it were two trucks. Coura tried to reach the turning first but was narrowly beaten by the bus. It carried a Brasília numberplate. The haggard faces of men whose eyes indicated a terrible fear that a precious dream might be snatched away from them looked out at us, and appeared somewhat relieved to be entering the town ahead of us. Just as Coura made the turn, the two other trucks came up the road. They, too, were packed with men, all standing, like cattle being taken to an auction. The four vehicles entered a square where two buses had recently arrived from the south. Luggage was being thrown down from the buses to scores of clamorous men.

The square was nothing more than a clear space of grey dust. Neither bush nor tree adorned it. Around it were timber houses, each one a shop or a bar. No sooner had we parked behind the buses than several men surrounded the truck and began to shout out all kinds of offers. Whether one wanted lodgings or a title to a piece of land guaranteed to have gold, there was someone to make an incredible offer. Some waved pieces of paper and cried out, 'Official land grants'. Half a dozen boys appeared, selling cigarettes and chewing-gum. The two other trucks arrived a couple of minutes after us to unload their human cargo. Several more sellers of short-cuts to a certain fortune materialized from nowhere to wave pieces of paper at the latest arrivals. It was still early morning but the heat in that shelterless square was intense. There was no air there to breathe; only dust.

Coura came to the back of the truck and unlatched the tail-gate. 'You two stay with me,' he said to us as we disembarked. Some of the men stood around gaping at Pons as if to ask if he could not take them straight to where they could pick up gold. Pons said to them charmingly, 'You'll find me at the hotel when you've got your land grant.'

'You come with me,' Coura said, nudging Pons. He conducted us across the square. There was no escape from the press of frantically pleading humanity. Boys pursued us, offering to carry our bags; a man kept following us repeating, 'Clean American-type hotel, I take you.' Groups of recently arrived men were scattered about the square, looking dazed now that they had reached the centre of their chosen reality. Some kicked at the earth with their bare heels, releasing from that indifferent surface more dust that had nowhere to settle but in human lungs and make them as black as sorrow.

Now a remarkable event occurred. Just as we gained the opposite side of the square, a yellow convertible Volkswagen came out of a side street, its horn blowing continuously and a crowd of people running after it in a noisy rush. A wiry little man stood in the car and was throwing bits of paper out, which fluttered and flew in the air or fell into the dust. The rushing, stumbling crowd was snatching at them and tumbling to the ground, fighting for the fallen bits of paper. The car went past in a cloud of dust and the crazed crowd pursuing it made it impossible for us to cross the street. The man in the car threw out another fistful of the pieces of paper. One of them blew straight at Coura's face. It was a 100 *cruzado* note – the man was throwing away money! Several groups of people in the square saw what was going on and made a dash for the car, which went on to complete the circuit of the square and was again in front of us where scores of people were still picking up the notes. The hundreds who had been alighting from the buses and the trucks were now also engaged in the fight to possess the money being thrown away.

The entire square echoed with shouts and yells. Fist fights had broken out. When the 100 *cruzado* note had come to Coura's face, he had snatched it up and, seeing that some more similar notes were floating to the ground in front of him, made to gather them. Other men went diving and tumbling after them, too; and since to the groups running from where they had been standing in the square it appeared that wherever there was a knot of men on the ground it was because there was money there to be picked up, therefore, by the time the car came round again, the spot where Coura had stooped to gather the notes had become a mound of some fifty or sixty bodies with cries coming from within the pile of people being trampled or crushed. Seeing that Coura was buried in that heap, Pons and I quickly made for the side street and, coming to a number of successive turnings, took them in order to be sufficiently lost should Coura have any breath left to pursue us. Thus we found ourselves before a house from the doorway of which a man greeted us, saying, 'Clean American-type hotel, please come in.'

As we were entering it, the yellow Volkswagen drove up. The man who had been throwing away money shook hands with the driver, and alighted. The car drove away. The man came into the hotel after us. He was looking very pleased with himself.

7 The Act

The visitors who had come disguised as monkeys went back to their village with their new wives, their bearing on that morning after the night of festivities altered as if they had been elevated to a superior rank and must henceforth walk with the chin slightly raised and the eyes superciliously lowered. They left their monkey masks behind, superstitiously disowning the identity that had been abandoned. A few days later, some children were seen playing wearing the masks until Nebbola remarked to their parents that the children courted bad luck by using as toys what had been symbols of ritual, and was allowed to confiscate them.

Suxavat returned to its ordinary routines. A general lassitude prevailed as the last of the puddles left behind by the rainy season dried up and the muddy running stream of the river lost its urgent flow and became a clearer current. An outsider must have seen us then as a lethargic tribe performing its labour in the reluctant motion of people who take no pleasure in their work. But that would have been a mistaken impression. It was not lethargy that had slowed us down, but a wonderful serenity of mind that saw no purpose in the sort of deliberate haste characteristic of societies that measured time as a unit of money.

A short distance up the river, we had cleared an area of land on which we cultivated a little corn and a variety of vegetables. In earlier years, long before I arrived there, the inhabitants of Suxavat still depended on the river merchants from Xurupá for most of their necessities, trading rubber and medicinal plants for them; but the discovery of gold gave the Xurupá merchants a more prosperous market to trade in, obliging the Suxavat residents gradually to evolve a self-sufficient existence. It was this quality of Suxavat, of having largely abolished the need to depend on the world, that attracted me to it when I came there with Tambour. A few of our men occasionally went to Xurupá and bartered some black beans and manioc for coffee, oil and a few tools; more and more of the land around Xurupá grew nothing but the dreams of the daily flow of gold-seeking immigrants, so that we had a ready market for our produce whenever we needed to exchange it for imported items.

After trying the various manly tasks, such as fishing and hunting, and then some, like weaving hammocks and making pottery, at which women were more adept, I found I was most useful in the vegetable garden where I could work in solitude, and it was there that I performed my daily labour, my hands forever encrusted with earth. A hoe on my shoulder and a pair of pruning shears stuck in the belt of my shorts, I walked to the field in the morning and then again after lunch in the late afternoon. A well-trodden path went through the jungle down to the river, proceeded along it for a small distance and then cut across the jungle through an area so dark under the immense trees that it would appear a forbidding passage were not one accustomed to it.

Just up the river, a little way beyond where the path left it, was a small sandy cove where, after lunch, in a corner below the gently swaying branches that hung down from the bank, I sometimes ensconced myself and enjoyed my siesta there in preference to the hammock in my hut. To reach the cove, one had to leave the path and weave one's way through some prickly underbush, but this small discomfort, which obviously kept most other people away, was worth the trouble for the pleasure of lying on the cool sand and then refreshing oneself with a dip in the river before returning to work. I could never really sleep in the afternoon, and my sinking into the sand was a falling into a semi-consciousness with its delicious loss of awareness, as if I were some insentient thing cast there by the river.

Going there after lunch one afternoon, I realized even as I was weaving through the prickly underbush that I had been preceded by someone else. An ancient tree had fallen in the rainy season and its enormous trunk lay above the bank at an angle to it; the tree's branches, still covered with leaves, formed a natural screen, giving additional privacy to the cove and at the same time allowing someone standing behind the trunk, where I found myself now, a concealed position that a voyeur might covet. I saw a youth, a boy of 13 or 14, wearing nothing but a breechclout, hesitantly clambering down the bank; another figure, obscured by the back of the boy, was already there and was stretching a hand towards him in a gesture that indicated that there was nothing to fear and that he should take the short leap. He remained suspended for a moment, shaking his head as though dubious about something, like someone being forcibly inducted into behaviour he has long believed to be illicit. Then he made his leap. Or perhaps he was pulled down by the other person who at that moment became visible.

It was Horuxtla. As usual, the only clothing she wore was a short piece of cloth that hung in front of her sex. She was laughing as she talked, while the boy, when his face could be seen, appeared anxious and worried. She put her tongue out at him teasingly and then, holding his head in both her hands, shook her own head in front of his face, rubbing her nose against his. He withdrew his head and looked amazedly, even disapprovingly, at her. She stamped her foot and spoke something that was perhaps disparaging, or perhaps provocative, for it seemed to touch the boy's sense of male pride. She pushed him playfully at the shoulders, like boys do when beginning to wrestle, and he, perhaps refusing to engage in such a combat with a girl, only stepped back and gave her a surly look. She sprang at him suddenly, clutching his neck with both her arms and trapping his waist in her thighs with her heels locked behind, just above his buttocks. He staggered back and she laughed aloud. Disengaging her legs, she pulled him forward until he was obliged to offer some strategic response to her play, with the result that she fell upon the sand, taking him with her.

It was evident that she had not fallen with the force of the boy's action but had taken the opportunity of his movement to accomplish what she herself wanted, to have him on the ground; but once there, she resumed the pretence of a wrestling match, coming out from under him to climb on his back, to dig her knees into his shoulders and to force his face into the sand. He pressed his hands against the ground and raised himself to throw her off his back. But no sooner had he turned himself over than she sprang on him again, and so for several minutes they pulled and dragged and pushed and tripped each other in the sand. The boy repeatedly attempted to end the game, but each time she said something to provoke him afresh. At last she stood up and ran to the water. She called to him from there and the boy followed her. They swam for three or four minutes, splashing each other, with Horuxtla twice mischievously trying to duck the boy.

I should have left then, for all I had seen so far had been the innocent play of adolescents, both of whom could easily have been boys, and my Horuxtla was still my bride and not yet my demon. Better still, I should have spent that afternoon in my own hut and seen nothing. But I was fixed there behind the uprooted tree, become one of its dying limbs. Even as they were in the water, my mind foretold the painful scene about to be enacted, made me a witness prior to the deed, so that I must stand there to confirm the fulfilling of the prophecy and have my eyes testify that, really, there were no illusions in this world, no fantastic appearances, no reality that was magical, only bits of action, each succeeding one a piece of knowledge so terrible that we could only bear it as reality by imposing upon the visible surface the disguise of metaphor.

Horuxtla emerged from the water, her body shining in the sunlight. Shadows falling on her bosom made her small conical breasts appear superbly abundant. Her thighs glowed with the light drawing the moisture from the smooth, firm skin. She made for the corner where I normally went for my siesta because of the long branches from trees above the bank which swung down in a perpetually swaying motion and made the spot less open than the rest of the cove. She sat down and said something to the boy who had followed her out of the water. He remained standing some distance from her, looking like a child moping in a corner. She spoke to him again. The ring of her voice carried to me, but not the words. It was the taunt of the female, and had the effect of making the boy go and sit next to her. His head hanging low, not looking at her, he listened to more of her talk, and then suddenly he looked up at her, his face showing great astonishment at what he heard. She shook her head enthusiastically in confirmation of what she had said and, as though to prove her point, put her hands to his shoulders and drew him to her and fell back.

His face was against hers and the upper parts of their bodies were joined, but his legs were away from hers, twisted a little awkwardly with his buttocks catching a spot of sunlight that, coming through the overhanging branches, moved on the rounded surface to create a throbbing impression, while her legs remained raised and held apart. They lay thus for a few minutes, when she stretched her right leg across the ground, pushing her heel out and then bending her toes forward and back before raising the leg to its former position, immediately repeating the action with her left leg. As she did so, her hand appeared at her waist, performed a quick action with the string there, and pulled away the cloth and let her fingers press down between her legs, but only for a rapid, agitated moment. He moved from her and turned his knees and she, responding to his action, pulled him to his side and lay along his body, pushing his knees back with hers until their legs were straight against each other.

Even then I should have gone, proceeded to the vegetable garden to put my hands into the earth to gather the carrots that were ready for harvesting. But I remained rooted there behind the fallen tree, an unwilling voyeur, someone whose punishment is to be forced to witness the public desecration of his most private dream. Horuxtla had sat up and turned the boy around so that his head lay in her lap. She stroked his face and said something softly to him. A smile appeared on his face. She placed a hand below her left breast and raised his face up to it. She threw her head back and breathed deeply. He drew up his knees and lay curled beside her, his face attached to her bosom. I looked away and saw a long line of ants scurrying across the tree-trunk. A dragonfly darted up from a leaf, its iridescent green wings momentarily caught by a ray of light, and disappeared into the air. The decaying matter beneath the tree-trunk gave off a pungent odour, sweet and sickening and powerfully attractive, the very smell, so potent that one is driven to attempt to drink it as though it were a fluid necessary to quench the soul's thirst, that comes from the female sex. I knew what I must see when I looked up. The act itself.

8 In the Mirror of the Moon

The last time I saw Pons was, like the first, in the mirror of a hotel lobby. The manner of our arrival in Xurupá had been attended by too much dread and was therefore too inauspicious a beginning to an excursion into the interior for him to feel secure. Indeed, even as we were signing up for our rooms, he said to me, 'A bath, some food, a long sleep, and it's back to civilization for me.' Where would he go? 'To wherever the available transportation is the fastest,' he said. What about his research? I don't believe the blank look he gave me was intended to be an answer.

The other man who had come in said aloud to no one in particular, 'Do you know how many millions I just threw away?' And then, catching my eye, went on, 'Maybe you don't know our money so well, so I'll tell it in dollars. I just threw away about one hundred thousand dollars. And I feel great!'

'What do you mean you threw them away?' the hotel keeper asked.

'Just like this, see?' the man said, picking up a piece of paper from the counter and tossing it in the air. 'All around the square. Four million *cruzados*. It set off a riot!'

'Four million!' the hotel keeper said, amazed. 'Why didn't you throw it right here?'

Pons and I picked up our keys and went to our rooms on the second floor. I heard the man laugh and say to the hotel keeper, 'This place is too clean to throw money at.' And the latter responded with, 'That's no problem. Give me two minutes, and I can make it the dirtiest place in town!'

Our rooms were indeed remarkably clean, though they smelled strongly of disinfectant. I took a shower and changed, but when I went through the connecting door to the larger and more luxurious adjoining room which Pons had taken I found that he had fallen asleep. Leaving him there, I went out and again ran into the local philanthropist, who was celebrating his own generosity by drinking a glass of whisky. Having exercised so much charity early in the morning, he was in a buoyant mood, eager to discuss the affairs of the world; the hotel keeper, at whom he threw the equivalent of $25 for the drink, had become too much in awe of his money to be engaged in serious conversation, and so, seeing me, the man adopted me, before I could have any say in the matter, as the ideal disinterested companion. We left the hotel together when I asked him where I could find a good breakfast and he offered to take me there.

'My mother never told me why she named me Tambour,' he said, 'nor what it meant. I don't know where she picked up a name that no one else has. "Son," she often said, "you never fail to surprise me." It's not that I was always up to some new trick or the other or playing the fool like kids do. It's just that I did unexpected things. Like if she sent me to the market to buy greens I'd come back with an aubergine. The funny thing is, now I don't have her any more, I keep surprising myself. Whatever I aim to do I achieve, but by the time I reach the end I lose interest in the result.'

We were walking through a narrow alley. A young woman in a tight blouse, very brief shorts and high-heeled sandals stood outside a bar, her face excessively painted. She fixed a bright smile at us as we approached, throwing forward her left leg, turning slightly at the waist and thrusting out her breast. 'Hi there, Rita,' Tambour greeted her, stopping in front of her. He pulled out two 500 *cruzado* notes and held them to her. She smiled even more generously and showed fine white teeth behind the shining red lips that almost dripped with paint. Snatching the money, she said, 'Where would you like to go?' Tambour shook his head and said, 'Nowhere at all.' And then, seeing that I was staring at her, he added, 'Unless my friend here would like a little massage before his breakfast.' She glared at me a second, then threw her head back with its mane of curly black hair and smiled. 'Uh, no,' I said. 'Just breakfast will be fine.'

'In that case,' Tambour said to the girl, 'give yourself a treat, dear little Rita, and take the day off.' We went our way, leaving her looking quite puzzled. 'There are so many of them in this town,' he said to me, 'they take shifts and work morning, noon and night.'

During the next ten minutes, as we cut through two more alleys, we came across six or seven more similarly attired young women to each of whom, too, Tambour presented 1000 *cruzados* and left them speechless when they realized the money was a gift, except one who said, 'If only all men were as mad as you!'

'They've all been good to me,' Tambour remarked as we came out into a wider street. 'Rita was the best, even did it free a couple of times when I was hard up. But don't think I fancy myself as some kind of a king walking about in a hospital after a successful surgery, bestowing golden coins on the nurses. I'm not giving these poor whores a reward for excellent past services, no, sir! I'm giving them money because I don't *need* them any more. Yesterday I got a fantastically beautiful woman to give me a bath, it was pure ecstasy. Here we are, the best breakfast in town.'

We entered a spacious restaurant. 'Keep away from fried things,' Tambour advised. 'The pork fat they use will kill you.' They had some river fish which I ordered grilled, together with a couple of boiled eggs and some toast. Tambour asked for a coffee.

'There's a settlement called Suxavat up the river from here,' he said, 'just about where Brazil ends, and God knows whose land it is to claim. A corn dealer who used to trade on the river and knew Suxavat once told me it was a small community of people. They tapped some rubber, hunted, fished. Somehow got by without too much.'

Ah, the simple life, I remarked, eating the fish which had too much salt on it, the old romantic nostalgia for a bucolic sort of paradise. 'No, that's not it,' Tambour responded. 'Believe me, I'm not sentimental and nor am I a simpleton. Until a day ago I was deep in the grey black earth looking for gold. For months there was only one thought in my mind – God, let me find gold, let me find gold! Day after day, I dug deeper and deeper, and would have gone right on digging until I got to the other side of the earth, I was so mad about finding gold. Well, I hit it in a big way. When I went to convert it to cash at the state bank, the manager came out of his office to shake my hand and said he was going to ring up Brasília with the news. That's because the government takes a big cut. I was rich, the country was rich, the world was one great place to live in. The manager was telling me I should invest the money straight away or the inflation would make me a poor man in two weeks. I didn't think of anything then because I was thinking of the most beautiful woman in the whole town and I took my money and left.'

Before he could reach the point in his story he was working towards, a murmurous commotion that had been going on outside suddenly broke into a raucous yelling and some twenty young women burst into the room and made straight for our table. What was this about giving the girls a free day? Fair is fair, give me my share! A thousand, a thousand, give me my share! While these and other cries raised an incredible din in the room, Tambour and I were being crushed by half a dozen of the girls closest to us. The variety of heavy perfumes they wore combined to make the air immediately around us horribly repugnant. Several of the girls had their arms around Tambour's neck or their hands on his shoulders or on his thighs and were attempting to cuddle and paw and stroke him as they shrieked their demand.

'All right, all right!' Tambour tried to shout over their screeching voices. 'All right, all right,' the girls took up his words and began to chant in chorus, 'Fair is fair, give me my share!'

Tambour managed to free his hands and to push the table so that it tipped on its side and sent the dishes and the coffee cups crashing to the ground, an upheaval that silenced the girls for a moment, during which Tambour shouted, 'All right, but get off me! How can I do anything if you're suffocating me?' They retreated a little, and Tambour said, 'Why don't you all get into a line? I'll satisfy each one, but we don't want a riot here.'

The restaurant owner came up and protested against the confusion and damage. 'Let me pay you first, friend,' Tambour said to him, giving him 1000 *cruzado*. The man retreated, appeased. By now the girls had formed themselves into a line, and Tambour began to present two 500 *cruzados* notes to each one. There were twenty-one girls in all. He remembered the names of several and exchanged a joke with a few. But he stared long at one of the girls, and said, 'I don't remember you. I don't think I ever saw you before.' The girl who had just preceded her said, 'She's new, only got in yesterday from Belém.' Tambour looked at the new girl. She was 16, perhaps a year older, with a narrow face and curly black hair. 'Here, take this,' Tambour extended six notes to her, 'for never having tempted me.'

The final girl in the line came up to him when he had only two notes left, and the coincidence made the distribution appear like a precise paying off of his obligations. A crowd had gathered at the door and had been peering in at the strange ceremony. I feared that such an ostentatious giving away of money might attract new claimants to Tambour's charity, making him the centre of a pestering mob which might turn violent if he refused, but people began to go away when they saw him rise after giving the money to the final girl, clap his hands as though knocking off dust from them, and say, 'That's it, everyone's happy and I don't have any more money.'

But he did have another bundle of notes back in his room and it was to his landlady Fatima Parreira's house that we now went. 'As I was saying, before the girls broke into our peace,' he remarked while we made our passage through some crowded streets, 'this place Suxavat is where I want to go.' Oh yes, I responded a little ironically, the retreat from civilization, the serene centre of the maze protected by serpents and a ring of fire. 'I don't know about that,' he countered, 'though I've heard people talk of fantastic travels they dream of as though they longed for some sensational trial for their bored selves. No, I don't know about that. Suxavat just sounds like a nice place to me, that's all.'

Fatima Parreira sat in the darkened front room of her house, a slight figure in a crumpled cotton dress. She had a small, sunken and wrinkled face, with loose grey hair hanging in wiry strands over her ears. 'I want to talk to you,' she said to Tambour when he had fetched his remaining money from his room and had gone to her.

'I just came to pay you,' he said.

'You don't owe me anything,' she answered, 'you've paid me to the end of the month already.' Two teeth hung at the corners of her mouth which otherwise seemed a black hole when she talked.

'I'm leaving,' Tambour said, 'maybe today, maybe tomorrow or the day after. I want to give you an extra month's rent, so you won't have to worry about getting a new lodger straight away.'

'Leaving?' she said with some surprise. 'I wouldn't do that if I were you. The world out there is a treacherous place, with your closest friends ready to stab you in your back. You're happy here. I'm like a mother to you. I plan to make you happier. I plan to make you the master of this house.'

'You got a card you want to put on the table?' Tambour asked.

'Sure,' the old woman said, 'it's the queen of hearts.'

'That's a cute answer, Donna Fatima, but I don't get it.'

'*You* talked of cards. I was speaking plain.'

'All right, keep it plain, then.'

'Were you not born under the sign of Gemini?'

'How do you know, and what's it got to do with anything?'

'I'll tell you what,' she said in her calm and somewhat relentless way. 'When my granddaughter Maria Claudia came to live with me,

56

her father sent me her horoscope an astrologer had cast at her birth. It says in there that she would go on a long journey and marry the fourth man of the house who would be a twin of its mistress. Well, Maria Claudia came all the way from Rio Grande do Sul, you couldn't take a longer journey than that, could you? But I couldn't work out the rest of the saying and I kept thinking and thinking what the fourth man and the twin of the mistress could mean. Then it hit me, just like that, out of the blue. It was when I asked to see your identity card last month to fill out a form and saw your birth date. You're a Gemini. Like me! We are twins, don't you see! The fourth man was easy to figure out after that. I had three lodgers before you.'

'Excuse me, Donna Fatima,' Tambour said in a patient voice, 'but Maria Claudia is a child. She's what, ten, eleven years old?'

'She'll soon grow up, all children do.'

'Just one other question. Why should Maria Claudia's horoscope be binding on *me*? I'm a stranger in her world.'

'Was it a coincidence you came here to be the fourth lodger? And what good is it going to do you remaining a stranger when you can be perfectly at home with people who know and love you? Out there you'll only get yourself murdered.'

'Give me time to think,' Tambour said, seeking to release himself from the old woman's logic.

'Thinking will only drive you crazy,' she remarked as we were leaving.

'Well, that decides it,' Tambour said to me when we were outside. 'I've only got a few old clothes in the room, I don't need them. There's only one thing I want to do in this town, and that's to buy a gun. And then I'm off to Suxavat.'

I remained with him for the rest of the morning. He spent a good hour choosing a weapon at a shop that looked like a military warehouse, it was so large and fully stocked. An infantry brigade could have been armed from its shelves with automatic rifles without the stock looking at all depleted. After a long, technical discussion with a salesman, Tambour bought a Browning rifle. We went next to the river where Tambour talked to several men about hiring a boat.

It was looking at the river that prompted in me the desire to accompany Tambour to Suxavat. I cannot explain the nature of the impulse that possessed me as my eyes followed the river upstream where its grey water emerged from the jungle, but I began to feel an urgent anxiety to enter that remote world. The thought did not become a conscious decision until Tambour came and said, 'It happens tonight is a full moon, and a man can take me to Suxavat during the night. Otherwise, the boats are too busy and I'd have to wait a week.' It was then that I said that I would like to go, too.

We sat in a bar drinking beer and then had a large lunch which included fish, turtle steak and fried eggs. The restaurant had a garden at the back. Tambour asked for hammocks, and the two of us slept for a couple of hours under the cashew trees. It was late afternoon by the time I returned to the hotel. Pons was in the lobby, checking out. 'I'd given up looking for you,' he said. 'Thought I'd never see you again.' He explained that he had had the good fortune of meeting the agent of a tractor manufacturer who had a company plane. He was flying to Brasília in half an hour with some clients and Pons had paid him for a seat on the plane. 'He has only one spare seat, I'm afraid, but here's his card. I told him about you. He's flying back from Brasília tomorrow with two executives and you could go with them when they return, I think he said two days later.'

I decided not to tell Pons about my decision to go to Suxavat, and he, assuming that I would be following him soon to Brasília, picked up his bag and went out, while I, turning to go up to my room, briefly caught his head in profile in the mirror just then separating from my own reflection, which seemed to be beginning in that moment to steal away in the opposite direction.

The moon came up about an hour after we had set sail from Xurupá. At first the general glow cast over the area by the town lights seemed sufficient to make the direction we were to take discernible, but then, when we had negotiated a wide bend in the river, it became pitch dark. For a few minutes, it seemed we had fallen into a solid blackness which was yet without substance, that we were in motion though the movement was not progressively over a real surface but was rather a deluded conception of the mind. But soon one saw that there were layers of blackness within the larger solid appearance, that there was a distinct outline to the blackness of the bank where it met the river and that its shade was not the same black as the water, and there was a darker blackness to the mass of trees rising above the bank that could just be distinguished from the subtly lesser blackness of the sky. No sooner had I formed the conception that discrimination was possible in a world become entirely an abstraction representing nothing, that in an ultimate denial of knowledge one immediately developed a theory of perception and refused to abandon the possibility of deliverance, than it occurred to me that my belief in an undeniable vision in a world without light was only an attribution to surfaces of definitions they did not possess, for what gave form to the flowing invisible matter, to that whole monster body of nothingness into whose throat we had entered, was merely a compulsion of memory. The thought filled me with a peculiar terror which was also a feeling of exhilaration, as if I were being carried like a bubble in one of its labyrinthine arteries into the heart of chaos.

In a seemingly sudden springing into life, the moon came up behind us, the largest full moon I have ever beheld, looking extravagantly proud as it absorbed and reflected the light of the sun that had set in front of us. The river turned to a glittering golden stream. The moon climbed higher up the sky. We had just entered a narrow gorge. Great trees on either bank were festooned with creepers that clung to the hanging branches. The enormous lit-up jungle, liquid the light. Shadows like mysterious ethereal bodies. Light flowed down like milky semen on a silently receptive world where all matter rediscovered its substance and entered again the renewed progression of the wheel of life.

9 Puru Sá

A jaguar had been observed by one of the men, the prematurely bald Raza, who had gone into the jungle to hunt for game. Some thirty kilometres south-west of Suxavat is a region known as the Nazaré Hills which jaguars are known to inhabit, but the one Raza had seen was close to the settlement, less than half a day's walk, in a large diamond-shaped area bounded by four rivers where a huge rock jutted out of the ground. An old Witola Indian recognized the land from the description. It was a village, now abandoned, called Puru Sá where a tribe known as the Puru Sáni had lived until some twenty years ago. They had built their dwellings in a circle round the rock and worshipped it in curious ways. One of their ceremonies was to carry water from the four rivers to the highest point on the rock and to pour it there so that it ran down in rivulets. They attached feathers to the bodies of their dead and left them on the top of the rock from where their souls flew up to heaven. When their women went into labour, they entered a cave in the rock, there to give birth. Out of the rock came their living and to the rock they gave their dead. A secretive people, the Puru Sáni, they married only among themselves. One day a woman gave birth to twins, both male, who were inseparably attached together along their backs: one could not see the other but the two together could see the whole world. The Puru Sáni word for Jaguar was given them for their combined name.

Tiny bubbles of sweat sparkling on his clean-shaven head, Nebbola listened to the story of the Puru Sáni with great interest, lowering his eyelids from time to time over his bright black eyes as if some point in the description possessed a special meaning which only he understood. He now declared that the jaguar our hunter had seen was no ordinary beast but the tormented spirit of the twins, each one of whom had been doomed never to see the other, and the spirit searched in death what was never found in life. So that when the

{"image":"THE BURIAL OF THE SELF"}

party was formed to go and hunt the jaguar to prevent its coming any closer to Suxavat, Nebbola declared that it would be necessary for him to accompany it. 'Our hunters are brave and skilled,' he said, 'but this is no ordinary jaguar, and in case you need to be protected against spiritual unpredictability it's best I'm there to perform that service.'

He was strongly built and his clean-shaven face exhibited a youthful appearance. No one would have objected had he simply volunteered to go as a hunter, but being Nebbola, he always needed to give a special and a mysterious meaning to his actions.

Tambour said to me, 'Why don't you come too? You can use my gun, and I'll go native with a spear.' I picked up his gun, felt its well-balanced weight in my hands, touched the beautiful polished walnut stock, and held the rifle up against my shoulder and looked down its barrel. Standing at the door to Tambour's hut, I moved the gun slowly in a wide arc, panning across the distance in a hypothetical searching of a target in what I took to be the correct stance of the hunter. A red blur appeared in my vision, then came into sharp focus. A pomegranate flower. I lowered the gun and stared. Horuxtla was walking past in the direction of the river. I returned the gun to Tambour, declining his invitation. No, I would only be an encumbrance. The nearest I could come to killing was to pull out a cabbage from the ground.

Tambour, Nebbola and five other men went off to hunt the jaguar. I think that when I stood there with the gun I was about to agree to joining the party. An excursion away from Suxavat that was also a serious mission, and therefore likely to be an interesting adventure, would be a pleasant task. But seeing Horuxtla come into focus altered the resolution that was forming within me. It had been only a few days earlier that I had seen her seduce the young boy. A new anxiety had been born in me.

The boy's name was Mantu. Observed among other youths at their boyish games, he always seemed a weakling. Whenever the play involved the mimicry of some martial act, he invariably slouched off. Nor was he at all good-looking compared to the other boys and he lacked their healthy virile appearance. The way some of them strutted in the presence of girls, it was evident that any one of them would have made a more eager and superior lover to Mantu. Why had Horuxtla chosen him to present the gift of her virginity to? Then the thought occurred to me that I had no evidence that

that was in fact what she had done. Perhaps the gift had been given away to someone else already. I imagined each of the boys being drawn by Horuxtla to the cove or to a hundred other secret areas in the woods, and pictures of a succession of copulations, one act superimposed upon another in an orgy of promiscuity, tormented my mind. I was excluded from the embrace given to the many. They took her being for granted. They possessed her and were possessed by her. The world they inhabited was their communal property. Even the weakest boy, the most beggarly, could claim to belong to her whereas I, the creator in my secret mind of a poetry to her beauty, must remain excluded.

The hunters returned after five days in the jungle. Tambour withdrew to his hut, wishing to have nothing more to do with his companions. Except for Nebbola, the others looked drained of blood as though their combat had been with creatures of the underworld who had inflicted upon them the wounds of monstrous passions. Nebbola, however, had never been keener of appearance, and with the gestures of an orator who knows how to make an impression on a crowd, now folding his arms across his breast, now pointing to the sky, his voice one moment a chant of glory and in the next a mournful sonority, he narrated the chronicle of their strange adventure.

The narrow, constricting passage in your most fretful dream is not so difficult or dangerous as the journey to Puru Sá. It is no simple march on a well-worn path with posted directions to show you your way. The jungle is so thick that to cut through it is to place yourself in a tunnel where no sunshine reaches. Which way must you cut next? No knowledge of reality is of any help. You must be prepared to lose your reason and be guided by instinct. There is no victory either in emerging into the filtered light of the rain forest where creepers hanging from the trees sprout tendrils a metre long before your very eyes and form a net around you when you thought you had gained open space. Each little thing that grows in that world is bursting with progeny even as it comes to life. You do not know where you are but a profound fear which you dare not express in words tells you that the entangled place you have entered must be the brain of the universe where all perceptions are stored and all meanings sealed in the veins of leaves. No revelation is to be had there, however, where the multiplying tendrils might well be shoots sprouting out of an enormous tumour at the centre of the brain. Imagine all this, if you can, and you will understand what it is to find a passage to Puru Sá. The assembled crowd, spell-bound by Nebbola's voice, listened silently.

Ha, but how enchanting it is to arrive in Puru Sá and to stand before the great rock! The jungle ends at a river and, crossing it, you are in a land of undulating meadows of such a gorgeous green all grass elsewhere is but straw. The rock dominates the region, looking like a pyramid from a distance, but, approaching closer, you notice that it is a rounded mass with something of a curved plateau at the top, with a vertical shaft jutting out from its centre. We camped at the base and for two days searched the region for signs of the jaguar.

A bank of one of the rivers had a sandy shore and there Raza saw the jaguar's footprints. In the evening, we positioned ourselves by the trees there, anticipating the jaguar would come to drink from the river, four of us with guns and the other three with bows and arrows and spears. But we waited in vain until night fell, and then suddenly we heard the pounding of the jaguar's feet and the whooshing sound of his body as he tore through the tall grass. We could see nothing, however, in the pitch dark. Lighting a torch, we made our fearful way back to the camp.

The next morning, while roasting the fish we had caught for our breakfast, we passed the time relating the dreams we had had in the night. Now believe me, for every word I utter is true. Each one of us had had exactly the same dream! Each one of us saw the rising sun in his dream illumine the top of the rock, and there, caught in the clear brilliant light of the morning, stood the jaguar, his eyes a fiery green as he stared back at the sun. Tambour was the first to tell his dream and even as he began to speak the others realized he was describing the very images, in precisely the same sequence, of their dream. As yet each of the others thought he was the only one in whose sleep Tambour's dream had coincided. But when he concluded and we all began to say we had had the same dream, we went suddenly silent. A terrible fear gripped us. Such things do not happen for human amusement. What mystery had us in its clutch? Just then Raza gasped and his face went white. His eyes stood out in terror. We looked in the direction of his frozen stare, up at the top of the rock. There the jaguar stood, his green eyes blazing with fire.

The crowd let out a common scream.

As I say, believe me, for every word I utter is true, and what you are going to hear next will fill you with greater dread. We reached for our weapons, but that was only an instinctive reaction. The beast was too distant, far out of range. We would need to stalk it, or build a trap and find some bait to get him where he could be killed. While we kept vigil by the river in the evenings, where twice again we heard him come when it had become too dark to see, during the day we built a pit near a tree in a somewhat forested area. By the third day we had completed our preparations, covering the pit with branches and hanging freshly killed fowl from the tree. We took up guarded positions and waited. It was on the fourth day, which was yesterday, late in the afternoon that we heard his pounding step. We could hear his breath. He had caught the smell of the bloody fowl, and was beginning to grunt and utter a muffled sort of roar.

He burst into the forested area and leaped into the air in a glorious arc and in one breathtaking continuous motion snatched the meat from the tree and landed right in the middle of the branches covering the pit. The branches did not collapse. He could have landed on solid rock! This is when we fired. Four guns emptied their barrels straight into his body. Arrows went flying through the air and three of them stuck deep into his neck. A spear landed in his belly. His mouth opened. The meat fell out. We held our weapons, not shooting again, but watched in terrified amazement as the enormous beast just stood there. He turned his head in an idle sort of curiosity. The branches beneath him began to creak. He looked down at his feet. The branches had begun to give in at last, and then they suddenly collapsed. He fell into the pit like a rock in a pool of water.

We remained frozen for at least a quarter of an hour, remaining rooted to the very spot from where we had shot the jaguar. Finally, we drew courage from the silence in the pit and approached it gingerly. Some of the branches still clung to the sides and we pulled them out. Then leaning over the edge, we looked into the hollow. There was nothing there! Raza picked up a large log and threw it into the pit. We watched it fall in. But it made no sound of hitting an obstruction, and when we peered in we could see nothing. Two of us had stood inside the pit, digging, only the day before, making it no more than two metres deep. As we had all witnessed, the jaguar had fallen into that very space, but when we looked into it we stared not at a man-made hole but at a passage into nothingness. We spent a sleepless night among abominable visions. When we broke camp this morning and hastened to cross the river to this side, we stood trembling, looking from our regained security at the long shadow that fell from the rock and obscured the earthly entrance into the infinite void.

10   Tambour's Rule

It was at this time that Tambour began to train the boys of the community as soldiers. Each morning one of the boys beat upon a pan and made a round of the huts, calling the male youths of Suxavat to duty. They assembled in the centre of the village and then marched down to the river where they lined themselves in rows. Tambour himself setting the example, they performed an elaborate drill which consisted of a series of strenuous exercises. Next, they were handed their weapons – pieces of bamboo deployed as make-believe rifles. Himself armed with his Browning, Tambour marched them off into the jungle. There, they carried on a guerrilla warfare against an invisible enemy, ambushing the shadows of the jungle into surrender. Or they split into opposing factions and, following the rules improvised by their common commander, played at war games in which the greatest dishonour was to be captured by the enemy.

The parents approved of these games. The boys were learning discipline and obedience. At the very least, they were being preoccupied instead of making trouble. Until they were of age to engage in one of the necessary labours of the community, there was nothing for them to do, and when boredom became too unbearable they invariably ended by picking fights among one another. Everyone admired Tambour in his dedication to make men of the boys. I, too, was pleased. At least I could rest easy in my mind that Horuxtla had not gone off to some secret place with a boy.

In fact, the girls, becoming resentful of the new mystique that the boys seemed to have acquired, disporting themselves as a superior race, formed a disciplined group of their own. In the mornings, we saw the boys marching off in one direction and the girls in another. The community enjoyed a wonderful quiet with the children no longer shrieking like monkeys from the trees.

No one noticed that Tambour had assembled the boys earlier than usual one morning. We were awoken by a hammering, and before we could stir ourselves from our hammocks and see what was going on, we had become prisoners in our own huts. For days, Tambour had got his army to cut timber in the jungle and now had carried out his plan of barring all our doors. At each door, a boy recited a formula he had been taught: 'If you wish to be set free, repeat after me, "Tambour is the governor of Suxavat and I am his loyal subject." If you do not accept Tambour's authority, you will remain confined without food and water.'

I was quite shocked. When Tambour had begun to train the boys, the thought had occurred to me that he who had lost his desire for women had perhaps discovered one for his own sex, but I realized now that he had gone mad.

'You gone crazy, Tambour?' Nebbola shouted at him from his window.

Tambour stood not far from there with his rifle, surveying the alarm and commotion that was arising in several of the huts. 'Remember Puru Sá?' Tambour shouted back at Nebbola. 'Who was crazy then?'

'That was for the peace of everyone,' Nebbola answered. 'That was truth of the mind.'

'Truth, ha!' Tambour mocked. 'We never even got to Puru Sá. We lost our way. There never was a jaguar. Raza told a lie because he was too ashamed to come back without catching any game. He made us lose our way because he didn't want us to get to Puru Sá and find there wasn't a jaguar there. Everyone knows there are no jaguars this side of the Nazaré Hills. And that's the truth.'

'What I said was true nonetheless,' Nebbola insisted. 'The jaguar's descent into the earth is a truth as old as history.'

'Don't give me your humbug!' Tambour shouted, raising his gun and firing a shot over the roof of Nebbola's hut.

'But what has that to do with this situation?' Nebbola demanded. 'What's this about being governor?'

'There'll be no more lying in Suxavat,' Tambour shouted back, and turning to face the huts in the opposite direction and firing a shot over them, said, 'You hear that, there'll be no more lying in Suxavat.'

Now Rustomo spoke from that direction. 'Nebbola's story bothered no one. No one believed it to be true and therefore it could not be said to be a lie.'

'You and your monkey tricks!' Tambour cried at him. 'There'll be no more of your deceptions either.'

'What good is life without magic?' Rustomo asked. 'If you explain everything, the only mystery left will be death.'

The old Witola Indian spoke from his hut. 'You've barred our doors but left the windows open. What confidence can we have in a ruler who forgets an important detail?'

'Windows are to let air in and not to let people out,' Tambour answered.

By now, several people, perhaps already missing their breakfast, had taken the oath and been released from their huts. They came and stood near Tambour, stooping slightly and smiling ingratiatingly. Seeing that he offered them no menace, many others followed the example of the first to surrender, and soon the majority of the community had assembled in the centre of the village. Tambour ordered them to sit on the ground and, standing before them, made a speech. 'There is too much deception in Suxavat,' he began. 'We live in a maze of lies and believe in disguises. That is the way of treachery against the soul.'

I was amazed at the evangelical manner he had acquired. The crowd, finding there was no threat in his generalized abstractions, listened quietly and then, becoming bored, in a mood of absentminded resignation. Nebbola, hearing the speech from his window, took the oath to have himself released from his hut, and came to Tambour and knelt before him. The latter paused in his speech, looked down rather contemptuously at Nebbola, and ordered him to go and sit at the back of the crowd. Nebbola's glittering clean-shaven head remained obsequiously bowed for a moment and then he rose, waving his hand up and down with the palm up just below his face in a respectful gesture as though before the statue of a deity, and walked to the rear of the assembly in an affected show of dignified ceremony. I understood the meaning of his little act: he had concluded that Tambour had gone mad and decided that the best way to deal with him was to humour him, as in the court of an insane emperor where the courtiers' conniving impersonation maintains the appearance of their monarch's sanity.

Tambour now proceeded to proclaim several decrees. There was to be a redistribution of jobs and huts as a first step towards a rational reorganization of the society. Hours were prescribed for work and recreation. Meal times were established. He delineated the areas where children could play. He took up one aspect after another of our communal life and defined the conduct that was to be observed.

As he spoke, it soon became clear that the life he was demanding we live was precisely the one we already lived. By the time he finished his long proclamation, all he had done had been to describe, catalogue and codify as rules the details of our conditions of existence as they had prevailed for as long as anyone could remember. Nothing at all was to be changed! We had always bathed in the river, and now Tambour, waving his gun in the air, decreed that we should bathe in the river. His long speech seemed a remarkable exercise in saying nothing at all.

And yet in the months that followed there was a subtle change in our condition. The same actions that we had performed naturally, freely and willingly were now an obligation imposed upon us by a tyranny, and though no one was expected to behave differently from the past the fact that a madman drew a peculiar gratification from seeing the tribe's ordinary and normal behaviour as a strict observance of *his* will made people resentful and begin to loathe as an affliction the very actions that had formerly been a source of satisfaction and even pleasure.

Tambour's little soldiers, armed with pieces of bamboo, marched all day long, making their irritating appearances where people happened to be working peacefully, and demanded in the name of the governor that everyone do his duty. Tambour himself sat in his hut from where he sent the boys out on tours of inspection and received hourly reports from them. Sometimes he himself would make an appearance where he was least expected. Now it would be by the river where the fishermen would be hauling their nets and, seeing that the basket in which they put their catch was already nearly full, he would say, 'It is your duty to bring in a basket full of fish.' Or now he might appear where a woman would be preparing a fire outside her hut and, seeing that she had beside her a bowl of beans soaking in water, he would say, 'Make sure you do your duty and cook some beans for your family's dinner.' When a person saw him approach, he at once became uncomfortably aware of what he was doing, knowing that Tambour was just about to tell him that that was what he should do. It was the utter redundancy of his commands, mildly amusing at first, that became so increasingly annoying it began to seem one lived under a hateful dictatorship.

I once saw him come upon a small girl of 3 or 4 who had picked up a fallen mango and was eating it; Tambour stooped over her, wagged his finger in front of her face, and said, 'It's a good thing you're eating that mango, for that is why it fell from the tree, so that you could pick it up and eat it.' The mango at its mouth, the child stared uncomprehendingly at Tambour and then, dropping the fruit, burst out crying and ran in the direction of a hut.

Two or three of his armed boys always accompanied him and kept guard over his hut when he slept, thus preventing any attempt to surprise Tambour in order to snatch away his gun. But no one desired to use force, of which the tribe possessed more than its lunatic ruler, to disarm Tambour. For a time, Nebbola discarded his robe and, wearing a breech clout and carrying a piece of bamboo, tried to make himself one of the boys. He looked remarkably youthful and did not appear absurdly out of place in the company of the boys in spite of his clean-shaven head that made him strikingly distinct in any group. His original plan was to find an occasion to disarm Tambour and win for himself the admiration of the community. But he discovered that youthful male companions provided him with a new pleasure, finding an especial enjoyment in such games as wrestling, so that instead of relieving the tribe of its suffering he became committed to prolonging it. When he went for his siesta in the afternoon, he took a boy with him, having persuaded Tambour that the tribal priest should be guarded, and on some occasions, when he emerged from his hut later in the afternoon, he appeared to be vitally refreshed by his rest.

The old Witola Indian and two men went and sat outside Tambour's hut one morning and began to talk loudly so that he could hear them through the window and open door. 'I'm the leader of this conspiracy,' the Indian said. 'There has never been a ruler who has not been detested by some of the ruled who then become obsessed with wanting to overthrow him.'

Tambour came and stood at the door, his gun in his hands. The two other men now spoke. 'As a conspirator,' said one, 'I am bound by the oath I have taken.' 'And I,' added the other, 'am solemnly committed to the conspiracy.'

'We are agreed, then,' the Indian said, 'that it has been our destiny to come to the house of the governor and carry out our conspiracy.'

'As surely as it is the destiny of the fisherman to catch fish,' responded one of his companions, while the other said, 'As is the destiny of husbands to be married men and of fathers to have children.'

'Now, if there is a conspiracy against the governor,' the Indian said, 'then it becomes his destiny to surrender.'

Tambour had been looking with an eager sort of interest at the three men (who ignored him completely), fascinated by the dialogue which seemed to him to possess a logical force that appealed to him. Observing that Tambour always believed any action being performed in his presence to be an expression of his own will, as though he were the author of the drama he witnessed, the old Indian had hit upon the idea of enacting a scene before him of which the necessary ending would be the surrender of his gun.

Tambour left the door and came to where the men sat, who, giving the appearance of being surprised, quickly stood up. 'It's a good thing,' Tambour said to them, 'that you are conspiring, otherwise I could not believe that you were conspirators. Clearly, truth would not be served if you were faking a conspiracy, and therefore, since only a successful outcome can guarantee that you're not liars and scoundrels, but honourable conspirators who should be known as such to all history, I am left with no choice but to hand you my gun.'

Later, the Indian gave me the gun for safe keeping, together with a box of ammunition he had taken from Tambour's hut, saying that I was the only person in Suxavat who was not given to violence or showed signs of madness. Tambour's surrender brought an exhilarating sense of freedom to everyone, with the possible exception of Nebbola, who was depressed to see that the boys were actually relieved to lose their leader, freeing them to pursue new games among themselves. Tambour, who had avoided me during the period of his lunatic government, resumed his old position as my companion, and talked with no memory at all of the months of his derangement.

11　The Offer

Two men dressed in orange-coloured overalls arrived from Xurupá one day and asked to speak to whoever represented authority in Suxavat. Except for the aberration of Tambour's brief government, no one had ever assumed such a role for himself, nor been designated to it, and therefore, after some discussion, it was decided that the triumvirate of Rustomo, Nebbola and the old Witola Indian should speak for the community.

The visitors informed them that they came on instructions from the Interior Ministry to announce the government's plan to relocate the people of Suxavat. Where were their documents, what proof did they have? Nebbola demanded. The law was the law, they responded, they didn't need documents. The law of which country? asked Nebbola. Did they know where Brazil ended and where Peru began? They ignored Nebbola's questions, and made their announcement.

The government was opening up a new era in the region and was offering free land grants. People in the villages in our area were the first to receive the offer, in fact the community of Suxavat was the very first to know of it. We really were the lucky ones, winning a lottery to which everyone in the nation had a ticket. Soon peasants from the north-east and the south would come pouring in to claim bits of scrappy land. We would have taken the choicest parts. What was more, a nice little bursary came with the land. What greater luck could we ask for?

'What you have not said,' the old Indian remarked thoughtfully, 'is what value you place on Suxavat that you want its people to leave.'

No value at all. Look at the village. Open your eyes and just look around. What future could children have in this small place? There was no potential for development at all.

'But you must have a plan for Suxavat,' Nebbola said, knowing something about schemes intended for the betterment of others.

'Something you need it for, otherwise you wouldn't be wanting to entice us out of it.'

It was well known that the present government was the most far-sighted the country had ever had. It had a plan for every part of the nation. What did it concern us if a rubber factory or a timber mill were planned for Suxavat provided we were well looked after? A happy people trust their government.

'What makes the government think we're not happy here?' Rustomo asked.

The government knew where we would be happier.

The three went aside to deliberate. The visitors sat smoking and drinking from a flask. The voices and the laughter of girls came from the river.

The old Indian returned with the answer. 'We thank you,' he said to the visitors, 'for your courtesy in calling on us and making us your offer. However, we must decline. We know the world in which we are and have no desire to leave it for the unknown.'

The men exclaimed that we were out of our minds to refuse the generous terms of a new life. When misery struck us, as it surely would in this isolation, we would bitterly regret the refusal. Consider again, and be earnestly advised to accept.

'There's nothing to reconsider,' the old Indian answered. 'Come what may, we are content here.'

Free land, money, and we turned it down! It was unbelievable, the visitors said aloud in their amazement. We must be mad to cling to this dark little village when we could have the sun shine on us from a wide open sky.

12   Within the Sealed World

Whether it was the loss of his youthful male companions or some hidden process of nature that brought on a profound change in his appearance was impossible to divine, but almost from one day to the next Nebbola had shoulder-length hair and a long silvery beard. His eyes seemed to have become sunken, with rings around them. His shoulders stooped as he walked with lowered head, his hands clasped at the stomach, a grey robe of coarse cotton falling heavily about him. He walked among the shadows of Suxavat, avoiding the spots of sunlight that fell through the canopy of the rain forest. He might have wished to look preoccupied with some great question of conscience, but the person we saw wandering uncertainly had more the appearance of being mentally distracted. Women pitied him and sent him dishes of fish and game that they prepared with aromatic herbs in the belief that the body, roused by fragrance and sated by quantity, entered a deeper oblivion in its sleep and, thus becoming stronger in its combat with internal demons, could therefore vanquish the mind's troubles. Soon, Nebbola's belly grew enormous and his face became bloated, but his eyes regained their former eagerness.

The rainy season set in, arriving in a marvel of illumination and explosive thunder and a roaring wind that sent the trees spinning. The perplexed monkeys ran across the sky among the tree-tops, squealing like pigs as they scrambled down the branches and, eyes wide open in amazement at the chaos pouring out of the cracked brain of the planet, swung into the darkness of the undergrowth. Then a steady downpour settled over the rain forest, coming down in crashing streams and cataracts without a moment's lessening of intensity for three continuous days. Children went screaming into the wet wilderness and tumbled laughing in the liquid mud. The downpour ceased, and now a drizzle fell like a misty curtain across our doorways and windows, sealing us in our inner world.

THE BURIAL OF THE SELF

As in previous years, I was at first content to let a loss of will overcome me and to surrender myself to a torpor so extreme it seemed the machinery within my body had come very nearly to a halt. The body's desuetude, a state as closely resembling the annihilation of the self as was possible without collapsing into a lifeless coma, was, I believe, the one condition I desired for myself. A minimal residue of consciousness, which I had expected would give me proof that the body was nothing but a complex of hungers and itself incapable of any abstract cognition, became blazingly alive, however, and my very senses, which ought to have been useless while my body mimicked death, were so keenly active that I seemed physically to enter other states of being which were not my own immediate being and yet which belonged to no one other than myself. I realized that this was the force of memory. There was a part of my mind which was always engaged in the preservation of identity by relaying to my consciousness fragments of brilliant images that were stored in my memory. But I recognized that some of the images were not unique to my experience. My memory was also the repository of fabulous fictions of the self.

These thoughts produced a nervous tension within me and I found it difficult to remain suspended in my hammock in the condition of inertia which I had at first welcomed. Now it seemed that the more lifeless became my body the more riotously sensational became the imagery in my mind. I was a traveller in the desert to the north-east, or one of a mountain tribe in another northern province, or a resident in a populous city where no one else had the same pigmentation of skin that I had, and at another time an enormous eagle had picked me up with its beak snatching my collar and held me suspended over a great plain, the sharp point of its beak piercing my neck. This is not the force of memory, I almost said aloud, this is a collection of disturbing dreams submitted to some celebrated seer with the hope of receiving from him an interpretation that would solve the complex riddle of the buried self.

I left my hammock and paced about the narrow area of my hut. Outside, the air was like misty spray, the atmosphere heavy and saturated. A row of five huts across the clearing from mine, which were close enough for me to see whether it was potatoes or onions that the woman sitting outside the middle hut was peeling, had become remote – partial and vaporous impressions as of an imagined reality. It was only my knowing that the hut furthest to the right was Nebbola's that made me convert into the figure of his person the large grey blob that came out of it and went back a few minutes later, otherwise I would have seen only a discolouring or the falling of a darker shadow on my field of perception that was already generally grey under the massive cloud cover.

I went out in my restlessness, deciding to surprise Tambour with a visit. There was very little firm ground, and everywhere one walked with one's feet in mud. Going past Nebbola's hut, I came across a short, heavy woman leading two boys who carried a large basket between them. I heard Nebbola greet the woman from his door and looked back to see him standing there with his hands held together upon his tremendous stomach. The woman, who had a screechy voice, spoke rapidly back. She was bringing him fish and chicken. Nebbola roared out his approval, welcoming the woman's offering. I proceeded to Tambour's hut but found him not there. A neighbour of his said he had gone to the river.

Tambour's temperament demanded he do the unexpected and the unconventional. Everyone loathed water when the rainy season reached the stage of seeming to be interminable, but it was precisely at that time that Tambour discovered anew its delights and would submerge himself in the river up to his neck and watch the rain fall on the water's surface. I went in search of him but saw no sign of him on or near the river. My venturing out had been futile and, frustration now added to my restlessness, I made to return to my hut. A short distance away from the river, just where I had to go through a small grove of trees, I looked back to see if there was any clue that I had missed. In that action of glancing back I saw a movement at the base of the trunk of a tree which I would not have noticed otherwise. A boa constrictor was just coming out of the underbrush below the tree. I left the scene quickly, thinking to myself that if I was going to leave my hut at this unpredictable time of the year when the whole world was water and the creatures in it become crazed by novel longings then I should at least carry the gun that had been given me at the termination of Tambour's dictatorship.

The woman and the two boys were leaving Nebbola's hut and, passing them, I warned them about the boa. Amazement, fear, and a desire for adventure came to the boys' eyes, and the woman, sensing their response, screeched at them, 'Keep close to me, you hear?'

Nebbola sat just inside his doorway, having laid out the contents of the basket before him, and, holding a whole quarter of a chicken by the drumstick, had his teeth sunk into its flesh while he tore the bone away from his mouth. His other hand had already plucked up a second quarter of the chicken by its leg, and poised thus to work on it the moment he finished with the first quarter, he was rapidly and loudly smacking his lips, his eyes darting at the chunks of fish in a wooden bowl, which sight was producing another anticipation and making him consume the chicken all the faster. I stood there a moment, watching him. He remained unaware of my presence. When he began to eat the second chicken quarter, he transferred it to his left hand and, unable any longer to postpone eating the fish, picked up a piece and bit it greedily. Swallowing, he took a bite of the chicken, and then quickly another of the fish. He seemed to choke on a bone and paused very briefly to cough. Bits of food flew out of his mouth. With a claw-like hand he tore the chicken's breast clean off the bone and stuffed it whole into his mouth.

I returned to my hut, having gained nothing on my expedition and without having lost the restlessness with which I had set out. I took out the gun and sat cleaning it, wondering how I would deploy it should I find myself in combat with a boa constrictor or some other animal, I who had never used a gun in my life. I stood at my door, the gun held to my shoulder, my stance imitating a hunter about to fire, panning the murky, watery gloom. The grey blob of Nebbola's body left his hut and transformed itself in my perception to a large black circle. I held the gun pointed at its centre. My finger was at the trigger. All I had to do was to activate my finger and the bull's-eye of Nebbola's body would explode. Would it be as easy as that to kill a person? I withdrew from the door, having come out in a sweat.

Word soon spread that there was a boa in the village and by late in the afternoon bands of boys, keen for glory, braved the torrential rain that had begun to fall and searched among the trees and the underbrush. But the great snake had disappeared. Darkness fell early under the heavy rain. Our sleep was a submersion in black water, and many dreamed they floated in the boa's vast belly. In the grey morning, with no light breaking through the canopy of the rain forest in spite of the wind having torn holes into it, we discovered our huts were surrounded by water. Although the rain had stopped, the level of the water was rising visibly, as if the earth that had been saturated by it were being squeezed. Muddy, slimy tentacles of the rising mass were reaching out towards the doorways of our huts, looking like eels and slippery snakes slithering on the edge of the encroaching water.

As if not surrounded by water but immersed in some great depth of interior thought where menacing images persisted to startle self-awareness into the discovery that all progression had been completed and there remained only the acquiescence of the self to accept the termination nearly at hand, I had awoken to the dream of my future. A turbaned boatman rowed by silently. From the opposite hut, a female voice reached me with the words, 'Soon the ground will be covered with hyacinths.'

13   The Theory and Practice
of Illusions

Sunlight had broken through and the drying earth sprouted new shoots while the vegetation that already grew accumulated upon its branches a fresh brightness. Rustomo and Bastianini, their pet monkey now on the shoulders of one and now clinging to the waist of the other, were rehearsing new tricks early one morning by the river. Rustomo was the theoretician of the non-existent, Bastianini the engineer of illusions: one demonstrated that the solid surface of an object had no mass while the other created impenetrable solidity where there was nothing, and both of them, simultaneously showing two antithetical perceptions as one impression in the minds of their spectators, made the commonest reality an example of the unreal or the object of perplexed speculation.

I had long realized the futility of questioning either of them concerning their theory and practice. They scorned analytical talk, and once, when I tried to engage them in it, I was met with evasion from Rustomo and elicited from Bastianini the remark, 'Did you ever see a hologram? There you have perfect proof that the artist is the inventor of reality and that reality is only an illusion.' Observing them closely at their rehearsals was equally inconclusive, for it was like attempting to divine a great painter's genius by observing him execute, one at a time, a succession of brushmarks upon a canvas.

Their present preoccupation was at that stage of chaotic trial when the scattered tools and props made the scene appear to be a lunatic's habitation. Rustomo had conceived the idea of placing a camouflaged length of water-filled tube vertically along the trunk of an urimbola tree and connecting to it a device which could be activated from a distance, setting off jets of water in a series of arcs as if the tree had spontaneously become a fountain. Bastianini, who was never content until an idea could be so elaborated that it seemed impossible at the very moment that it was suddenly made to appear before the eyes of a dazzled and startled audience, first wanted each jet of water to be in a different colour, and then, finding that development not sufficiently impossible, wanted several trees to be prepared so that a splashing ring of rainbows would fill an empty space where there had been nothing else a moment before but a beam of sunlight.

It was not vanity that made Bastianini desire to execute the seemingly impossible. He was indifferent to the applause of people who he knew could not distinguish between his obsession with complexity and the tricks of an ordinary magician. When I once asked him why he spent so much labour perfecting an event that was over in an instant, and which was scarcely appreciated by his audience, he answered, 'I am now thirty-five years old. I may well live to be seventy. What am I to do with all that time?'

The two friends pondered the problems they had created for themselves and invented new ones no sooner than they hit upon the solutions. I left them when Rustomo suggested that the fountains along the trunks of the several trees should be started not by a remote device but by the monkey successively scampering up and down the trees.

Some of the muddy ground under the trees had not yet dried out. Seven adolescent boys lay in a long snaking line in the wet mud. The second held the boy in front of him by the thighs, with his head between the first boy's shins; the third was similarly attached to the second, and so on to the seventh. Led by the first boy, they dragged themselves as one body through the mud. There had to be girls somewhere though I could not see them until I had walked past the human snake, when I discovered them crouching beside a tree, waiting with both dread and excited anticipation to be surprised by the advancing body coming to devour them. I did not wait to see the outcome of this game among the adolescents, knowing from past observation that the initial pretence of having been stung would be succeeded in the minds of some of the girls by the belief that they had actually been bitten, a mental condition that would make their bodies collapse, allowing the boys to carry them off into little clearings in the forest already marked out for the purpose. Something else had caught my eye: a red spot floating in the darkness under the trees which I perceived a moment later as a pomegranate flower fixed above the right ear in the black-haired head of a young girl.

Horuxtla had detached herself from the group of girls and was walking away towards the huts. The game her companions were playing was perhaps too rudimentary for her: she did not need a make-believe situation in which boys and girls fell on each other, pretending they were wrestling, or resorting to some other metaphor, such as coming to the rescue of a snake bite by sucking at the wounded flesh. She had experienced the reality itself of what her companions' pretend game signified. It was only the force of habit, or a bodily instinct, that kept her attached to the adolescent group, but she would soon become bored by what to her mind was childish and wander away, as she was doing now, leaving in apparent disgust the very group she had expected to engage her mind with excitement.

I followed her at a distance. We were both going the same way, but I did not wish to catch up with her and start a conversation, believing her to be in a resentful mood. That, however, was my first impression. I thought her to have become frustrated that the level of her companions remained naïvely youthful when she believed herself to have become an adult and that she therefore resented her friends. I was pleased with the conclusions I was reaching, for they somehow made her more accessible to me: was not a rejection of her youthful friends a form of making herself older and thus closer to me? Her body, quickly slipping through the forest, was momentarily touched by beams of slanting light, so that the vision before me of the female form of my most ardent desire alternated between a glowing illumination and a shadowy spectre. She was there and not there; when she was present, it was as a sudden brightness that took me a moment or two to recompose the yellow-golden radiance as the naked back of Horuxtla; and then, when she re-entered the shade, she disappeared altogether and briefly it seemed that the universal light had been eclipsed before my mind could distinguish a lighter shadow in the general darkness and recover its belief that the object of my desire had not been altogether illusory.

I was content to pursue her in this manner of seeing her and not seeing her while knowing that she was always present and no one but I had any connection with her. But why was she remaining under the trees and not coming out to the path that led to the huts? She was too far away from her friends to be concerned that they would have noticed that she had slipped away and would want to call her back; in any case, by now they must be sufficiently accustomed to her singular behaviour to leave her alone when she was being so different from them. And yet the way Horuxtla dodged beneath the trees and kept herself hidden struck me as an act of deliberate stealth.

I was walking along the path and saw her only because I had noticed her when she had just left the group and had since kept my eye on her; otherwise, as with the jet soundlessly crossing the sky which one would never have seen had one not looked up when the sun just happened to throw back a gleam, I would not have known of her presence.

As the path came to a succession of clearings where our huts were, the edge of the jungle where Horuxtla walked meandered away to form a sort of coastline at the back of the huts. Some people walking in front of the huts distracted me for a few seconds and when I looked back to the jungle I could no longer see Horuxtla. I instinctively made for the direction in which I had last seen her go, but quickly retreated, realizing the foolishness of my action. But I was puzzled by her behaviour, and began to think of her appearance of being stealthy indicative not of wishing to remain undetected by her friends that she had left, but suggesting rather than she did not want anyone to see *where she was going*. I realized with considerable anguish that I had been observing not a young girl who had slipped away from her friends out of boredom but a woman who had an assignation to keep with a man.

I paced the area outside my hut for a few minutes, finding again the restlessness that had come over me during the rainy season was filling me with an inexplicable discontent. There was nothing I wanted to do, or be. We had come out of many weeks of wet gloom which had isolated us, each in his own torpor; renewal was at hand with light pouring through the torn roof of the rain forest. I had risen early that morning with an anxiety to be beside the river and then had walked along the old familiar paths which had been uncovered by the subsiding flood, just as people in northern cities are driven to go to the park when the daffodils are first out, as if the blood within us were a kind of sap that could flow freely only when our feet were planted on a resurgent soil and there had arisen within us a complex primeval desire to be among the newly growing things or a passion for things changing to regain a former brilliance, to both of which, the desire and the passion, we gave the simple word *instinct*. I had wandered about the wooded fringes of the jungle and felt that peculiar happiness we experience when we have a simultaneous sense of our own being as a living phenomenon which is one with all nature, to which we contribute a singular individual role, like a drop of moisture on a leaf; and yet we sense no supremacy of identity, as if the drop of moisture, falling off the leaf and no longer existing, did not diminish nature's fullness. My wandering had taken me to the cove in the river where some months previously I had seen Horuxtla seduce the boy, and my mood changed suddenly; transparency and lightness were replaced by a gloomy heaviness. It was only coming to Rustomo and Bastianini at their rehearsal that restored some of my earlier lyrical spirit.

But then I had seen Horuxtla disappear into the darkness where I could not follow her. And I wanted myself to disappear into that darkness. I thought I should go away for some days, as devotees of certain cults do who go away on a retreat or deliberately seek that condition where the body must be punished by hunger and solitude, and see if I could not regain my contentment with life in Suxavat. I stopped pacing and stood in front of the entrance to my hut. I resolved to go away at once. Perhaps what had stirred within my breast early that morning was not merely a desire to be among growing things but the surfacing of a different instinct, to embark on a pilgrimage, only in my case the shrine to which I wished to go was in a place I would not know until by some miracle, or coincidence, I arrived there. I entered my hut to see what I should take with me. I spent some fifteen minutes choosing the few things to put in a canvas bag: a shirt, a pair of shorts, a pan in which to cook and another in which to collect water, a couple of knives, and a few other items, such as a small ball of twine that I happened to have. Then it occurred to me that I should take the gun. God knows where I was going to go, but less than a hour's distance away from Suxavat the jungle was full of dangers. I put the canvas bag down, took the gun and sat down just inside the entrance of the hut to practise loading it and accustom my hands to the weapon's general manipulation.

It was then that I saw the sight that was such a great shock to my heart that my breast was filled with a frenzy of palpitation. I could not believe what I saw and yet, obliged to believe the evidence of my eyes, was filled with unspeakable pain. I saw Nebbola come to the door of his hut, look out, turning his head left and right, quite obviously looking to see if anyone was about, and then withdraw; a moment later, Horuxtla walked out hurriedly, quickly went round the hut and disappeared into the dark wooded area at the back. Nebbola came out to the door when she had exited, and stood there smiling at the empty world; his long white beard rested on his huge stomach bulging out of the doorway, his eyes darted this way and that as if seeking the direction from which his next gratification was to come.

The gun in my hands was loaded. I raised it to my shoulder and, resting my head against the stock, looked down the barrel. I had Nebbola's enormous stomach in my sight. I was surprised how absolutely steady my hands were. The air and the ground had become perfectly still. There was not a fraction's tremor. And Nebbola himself would not have been standing so like a statue had he been facing a firing squad. The index finger of my right hand was at the trigger. There was only one thought in my mind: the world had been taken away from me by this greedy Spaniard.

A succession of shots rang out. Blood burst from Nebbola's stomach and he fell to the ground. Now my hands were trembling. The gun slipped out of my hands. Another shot went off. I looked to see in which direction the gun had fired when it hit the ground. During the next minute, while not being able to discover what I might have hit accidentally, I became aware of a very peculiar silence; normally, the daytime silence in Suxavat was composed of the cries of children, women occasionally calling across a clearing, the pounding of manioc roots and corn, the continuous singing and twittering of birds with the sudden loud screeching of a flock of parrots; but this silence, as I looked for the harm my accidental firing might have done, was devoid of all sound. And then I heard more shots firing. I looked at the gun which lay upon the floor.

I picked it up and checked it. I saw that it had not been fired at all. When I had held it and had Nebbola's great stomach as my target some other gun had gone off and it was only the coincidence of my being poised to fire, the agitation of the moment and the fact that the consequence which followed – Nebbola's being shot and falling dead – was precisely the effect I had wished for that naturally did not lead me to doubt that I had murdered Nebbola. But now I saw that my gun was fully loaded, that more and more shots were going off, and that the silence which had been broken had been replaced by cries and screams and a confused shouting suggestive of a crowd gone out of control.

Three men in orange-coloured overalls, armed with automatic rifles, went running across to Nebbola's hut. One looked in and fired two or three random shots. Another paused beside Nebbola and shot him twice more. The third ran into the next hut from where loud screams came a moment before several shots rang out. In the meanwhile, the first man had run to the hut beyond that one, and the second, a small bald man, who had made certain that Nebbola would not rise again, was already on his way to a fourth hut. There were shots being fired in the surrounding clearings where there were more clusters of huts. I realized that Suxavat had been invaded by the people who had some months earlier come to offer to rehabilitate us elsewhere in exchange for the land we occupied; having been met then with our refusal they had now come to possess the land by the method used by earlier invaders in the Americas, by exterminating the inhabitants rooted there.

It was not the time, however, for me to lie in my hammock and speculate upon the repetitions of barbarism perpetrated in the name of spiritual or material progress that made of humanity such a hopeless cause and not at all worthy of the great minds that had brought to it that supreme refinement, the imagination's possession of aesthetic bliss, for my own life was imperilled. I realized that it was only the chance of the direction from which the three men had come that they had gone running towards the huts opposite mine; the only other alternative entrance into this particular clearing with its cluster of huts would have brought them first to me. It was obvious that they would finish their bloody business across the clearing in a few minutes and then come to my side. These thoughts ran through my mind in an instant, for already I was clutching the canvas bag and the gun and looking out to see if I could not make a dash to the wooded area behind Nebbola's hut.

But the three men had quickly ended their murdering frenzy and were marching in my direction even as I came to the resolution to make a run for it. I could withdraw to the back of my hut, but there was nowhere there to hide and the best I could hope for was to delay being discovered by two or three minutes. In any case, I momentarily lost all power to decide or move, for my mind went dead and my body froze. All I could see were the three men marching with their rifles aimed at me. Suddenly one of the men stopped and laughed aloud, pointing in the direction to the right of my hut. The other two stopped, too, and also began to laugh. I looked to my right. There was Rustomo and Bastianini's monkey wearing a green satin waistcoat and a little fez cap, his mouth open so that his teeth seemed fixed in a grin, riding a single wheel as easily as if he jogged upon a treadmill. He made straight for the men. Seeing that their attention was entirely absorbed in the monkey I readied myself to take my chance and make a dash, waiting only for the moment when the monkey would go past the men and they would look in a direction away from me.

As the monkey neared them, however, the small bald man took a shot at him but missed. The monkey made straight for him, who readied himself to fire again but stopped, seeing the monkey swerve away and begin to ride rapidly in figures of eight. It was at this moment that I held my breath and ran, not pausing to look though I could hear shots being fired and imagined that the men had seen me. I got past Nebbola's hut, seeing his corpse in the corner of my eye as I ran and observing the flies collected at his mouth, and looked back from a concealed position behind the hut. The men were still firing at the monkey, which had now begun to ride at a remarkably fast speed in a wide circle around them. He seemed to be making them furious with their inability to hit him and they were dodging about, seeking new positions from which to fire, and in the confusion the bald man shot one of his companions. The man fell dead. The other two stared at each other; the man who had witnessed this shooting made an angry face and said something that appeared to be harsh for it made the bald man react by raising his gun, but just then the monkey, which was passing behind the first man in that moment, jumped off the wheel and landed on his shoulders, surprising him and making him drop his gun. The small bald man who appeared angered by the other's remark ran forward just when the monkey had landed on the other's shoulders, making him turn his head and raise a hand to push the monkey away; catching his companion thus defenceless, the bald man shot into his chest, killing him instantly. The monkey fell to the ground, rolled over and, springing up, did a somersault. The man felt himself being mocked. Having murdered a human being for a harshly spoken word, a monkey's mockery was more than he could bear. But the monkey seemed to have a charmed life and hopped around the man and then took long leaps across the clearing, and the man, firing at the monkey several times, ran towards him each time he missed. The monkey's leaps brought him to where Nebbola lay, and he looked curiously at the mound of the dead Spaniard's stomach. It was in this moment that the monkey's pursuer caught him when he was not moving, and shot him.

I stood frozen some ten paces away. I knew then that I should raise my gun and shoot him for having killed the monkey. I told myself that I had not the skill. The truth is I feared giving away my presence and kept still mainly out of cowardice. Soon he was running in the direction of my hut and I entered the darkness of the jungle, unsure whether it was the dense vegetation that stifled the light or whether it was a psychic blindness I had brought on like a film across my pupils so that I did not see where I went.

For a long time my progress in that darkness must have been a circular one, for I continued to hear screams and the firing of automatic weapons at a constant volume. Perhaps I was unconsciously reluctant to leave Suxavat until I was certain that there was no more a Suxavat in which I could live. I knew that I had again resumed my flight but that I moved as on a treadmill, covering theoretical distance while remaining trapped in a narrowly confined space. I stopped several times and listened with a more intense attention to the sounds of my environment. On one such occasion, there was a continuous firing of a succession of guns, producing in my mind the image of a crowd of people forced into a small clearing and massacred. I could still see nothing, but a picture seemed to be lit up before my eyes of a crazed English general commanding his soldiers to shoot at a crowd trapped in a square, and I was about to pity myself for having begun to hallucinate when I remembered a name, General Dyer, and saw in that moment a golden temple, and was filled with another sensation, as if a terrible past had begun to heave out of that jungle's darkness, giving me the impression that I stood upon layers of centuries which were projecting fragmented mirror images of one another through cracks in the humus. Chance excluded me from the massacre, but made me its eternal witness so that the victims appeared before my eyes in an obsessively repetitive re-enactment of their fatal agony. On another occasion when I stood holding my breath a heavy silence seemed to have fallen over Suxavat but the air about me was not without sounds, being composed of spiralling currents that seemed to echo some absorbing harmony, and then, as I tried to interpret the sound that charged the silence, I realized there was no silence at all but a murmurous lamentation, the continuous soft cry, which is almost soothing to hear, of pain.

A more real and a more immediate sound made me assume a posture of greater immobility than the one in which I already stood. I reassured myself that it was too dark for anyone to see me, just as I was unable to see who had entered the murky interior where I was hiding. But I remained frozen for some considerable time, anxiously scanning the grey-black shapes that could not be other than the trunks of trees. Nothing moved. I held on to my position a little longer and became aware of voices coming from the river. The shooting had stopped. The invaders were leaving. Another party would arrive the next day to dispose of the massacred tribe, and in a week or a month the land would have become someone's official property and the gold that lay buried in it would begin to be mined.

Dispossessed and alone, I detached myself from the tree against which I had long remained pressed. Slowly I walked through that gloom not knowing which direction I had taken. But I had not gone a dozen paces when I heard a crackling sound, that of a foot stepping on a twig. I slipped behind the nearest tree and held my breath. It must be my imagination, I thought, when I heard nothing. I began to walk again, pausing after each step to listen to the sounds around me, and then, becoming confident on hearing nothing out of the ordinary, proceeded without interruption. I came out on a path and after following it for a few minutes realized that it was the path I had daily taken to the area where we cultivated our food. I stopped, thought for a second, and turned round and began to walk in the direction of the settlement. But I stopped again, thinking that the invaders might have left two or three men behind and, suddenly finding myself experiencing for the first time the real horror of what had happened and imagining in excruciating detail not the massacre of a tribe but the murdering of individuals whom I knew and some of whom I loved, I could not make myself go and see them hideously transformed into figures of carnage. Once again it seemed that another time, another bloody past with its history of murders, reflected its images from the shattered mirror of the present. *Whose heaped bodies are these?* a voice within me echoed. Suppressing the abominably demonic power of hallucination, I turned again to the direction I had involuntarily found myself taking and began to walk hurriedly, wanting to be as far away as possible before night fell from the land I was having to leave.

Past the vegetable garden, where, not wanting to be held back by a sentimental attachment, I kept my eyes averted from the patch I had been tending since the end of the rainy season, and from the new shoots of the okra seeds I had planted, past the cornfield where the path followed the slope of the land towards the river, disappearing, before it reached the sandy bank, into a small thicket of nut trees. An hour's walk beyond the thicket, an ancient bend in the river had been cut off from the main stream and formed a wide, curving lake in the shape of a horseshoe. Here we had stocked fish for those times when the river failed to provide for us. Twice a year, some wild fowl descended upon the lake. Frequently a beast from the jungle would come there to drink. The lake had been an inexhaustible resource for the people of Suxavat and every male of the tribe had had there his first lesson in hunting and fishing. I walked along the shore of the lake until I had reached nearly the apex of the wide bend. The jungle vegetation was thick there and spilled down to the water. A couple of camouflaged shelters had been built among the trees where a hunter could spend the night or from there have the advantage over an animal come to drink at the lake's edge. Using the footholds cut into the trunk of the tree, I climbed to one of the shelters, deciding to ensconce myself there until that time when the direction of my passage to a different world could be determined.

I remained there three days, and might have stayed longer, perhaps indefinitely – for the lake provided me with water and food, a few emergency supplies left in the shelter giving me the rudimentary tools for survival – had I not become suspicious that I had been followed. On the third morning, having been awoken by sounds that suggested animals trampling through the undergrowth, I was looking out of the shelter in the direction of the shore and saw two beasts the size of full-grown deer drinking from the water's edge. In the dull light among the shadows it was difficult to discern their identity; in any case, I was not thinking of killing largish game for my food and therefore, not having a pressingly personal interest in the animals, was not bothered that I could not see them clearly enough: it was sufficient that I had them under observation to make sure they presented my own being with no threat.

They raised their heads from the water, looked around, and lowered their heads again. But then suddenly they sprang back, darted along the shore line and, swerving in unison, shot into the jungle. The noise of their violent departure died away but I still heard a pounding sound. I realized I was listening to my own heart, for the fear had seized me that another person was present nearby and that I had not been mistaken when I had made my escape from Suxavat and had had the sensation that someone was following me. Whoever he could be, what surprised me was that remaining so close yet he kept his distance. If he was near enough to frighten away two animals with his presence, then he surely knew where I lay and had possibly known it for three days. He had had the advantage over me during this time; why, then, did he not, whatever the intention that made him so grim a pursuer, accost me?

I had two alternatives before me. To accost him myself or to give him the slip and continue my flight alone. I was uncertain as to what I should do; disinclined though I was to challenge an unknown adversary who might well have a mortal design upon my life, to succeed in running from him without ever discovering why he had pursued me would leave me puzzling the mystery to the rest of my days. As it happened, I did not have the opportunity to choose.

Later in the morning it became necessary for me to leave the shelter. I climbed down the tree very stealthily and stood behind it on reaching the ground. I looked carefully in each direction. I did not see my adversary but noticed something else. Where the undergrowth had been trampled upon by the animals who had recently come to drink from the lake there was in fact a passage that the same, or other, animals had previously taken. It was possible, by stooping, to penetrate the thick jungle, and it seemed to me that chance was showing me the direction of my escape. I took it, without thinking, but vaguely imagining I would come out to some hospitable region.

The tunnel-like passage through the undergrowth required not only that I stoop but in sections that I should crawl. After about half an hour I came out of it to an area where large vertical rocks with rounded sides jutted out of the ground. Among them was a jagged mass, an enormous granite boulder. Standing on the top of it, brightly lit by the sun and looking down upon me where I stood seized by amazement and fear in the rock's shadow, was the figure of my adversary in a saffron robe and a large monkey mask for a head.

The first thought that passed through my mind was that my pursuer was not one of the invading men who, seeing me escape from Suxavat, had followed me and waited only an opportunity to exterminate possibly the sole living witness of the massacre. In my relief I wondered if the person behind the mask were not Tambour, for I imagined the disguise could be intended as a joke, and I shouted, 'Is that you, Tambour?'

There was no response, and I shouted out two more names. 'Rustomo? . . . Bastianini? Is this some magic trick?'

The figure on the top of the rock remained motionless. I was suddenly reminded of an image which I first thought had come to me in a dream and then realized I had heard it from Nebbola when he had invented the story of the dreadful journey to Puru Sá and described the jaguar with blazing green eyes standing on the top of a great rock, and I was filled with dread, wondering why one man's fiction should have been a mysterious form of prophecy for another. 'Is this some kind of a joke?' I cried aloud at the still figure.

A hand emerged from inside the robe and then the other. The two hands were raised to the head; the mask lifted. Horuxtla looked at me, but at that distance I could not judge with what passion.

I had so often longed to possess her and to be warmly embraced by her that the realization that we were the sole survivors of a world now lost struck me as a connivance by fate to make my wish come true. The whole progression of my days, the transit of my body across continents, believing I contrived my own destiny when each departure was a form of involuntary exploration, an anxiety of the self to confirm an image half remembered from a dream, the enormous accumulation of fragments, like images in a shattered mirror, which constituted my life had, I had reflected, only this ultimate end, to effect a conjunction of my body with Horuxtla's. Oh, it was not merely an older man's lust for a lovely girl's small breasts and her tight vagina, for it was not base pleasure that I craved. I felt no lust, only a desire to be, as it were, taken into her and sealed there beyond the penetration of light.

What tormented me now that she had become my companion, silently going ahead of me and sometimes walking by my side, was that the desire still potently throbbed within me although by now I had become an embittered man, having seen her give her body so thoughtlessly to others. It was not jealousy that made me resent her behaviour. If I had seen her courted by a youth whose looks, and especially whose actions, made her accept him for a lover, I would have congratulated the young man on his good fortune. Instead, I had seen her seduce an unattractive boy and then observed her go and serve herself to the monstrously gluttonous Nebbola. She had been completely insensible of her own value and, in my eyes, she had degraded herself. And what made my torment so painful was that were I now to fulfil my desire it would be worse than to receive no gratification at all, for her blood had become polluted by what to me was the hideous corruption that had flowed into her from her intercourse with worthless men.

But though she was still the young female arousing a sexual desire that, while strong, could no longer bring to my wandering male spirit the contentment of a final home that it sought, a desire not for possession but for an ultimate surrender, she had become transformed to a second and a third self within her beautiful body. The young – to my perception, the eternally young – Horuxtla walked at my side or before me. But there was within her the demonic guide who, disguised with a monkey head, had pursued me silently and, conquering my spirit, remained speechless, offering no explanations of her connivance, if she knew of it, with destiny, but quietly led me into an unknown region.

For weeks now, she had been my silent companion, and that moment when I first saw her remove the monkey mask from her head and then come down from the top of the rock and touch my arm and point to a direction we must take had already become so distant it seemed to me almost the beginning of time, for my memories of a life before then were blurred, confused and of the nature of illusory perceptions. Whether it was she who directed me or whether there was no choice but only one direction to pursue, I do not know, but usually she walked ahead with an air of assurance, glancing back from time to time with a look that seemed to confirm that we were on the right track. She knew what roots or berries were edible; she sensed the presence of animals and reptiles and knew in advance which were dangerous and to be avoided and which to be killed and eaten; in the thickest part of the jungle she knew which way to take to arrive at a river and, following the river, she knew when to cross it. That whole interior world seemed to be a memory come alive in her mind of which she recognized every detail.

At night she made her own secure nook in the jungle and showed me where I could rest out of danger. Our speech was limited to an expression of needs and not the exchange of memories of our life in Suxavat. She never explained why she had followed me, nor why she had first disguised herself with the monkey head. Plucking some reeds from the edge of a stream, she would tell me how to make a little trap in which to catch a bird; or, stopping and holding my arm, would whisper into my ear that an animal lurked in the vicinity and then instruct me how it could be killed. There were no ideas to talk about. As the days, and then the weeks, passed, it became with me a habit to keep on going in her steps. Perhaps it was my resentment of her past behaviour that made me suppress my thoughts, and that conscious willing of the self to disengage itself from thinking led to a numbing of my mind so that it functioned like a brain drugged to have no thoughts, but I became merely an automaton following wherever Horuxtla led me, like a soul become aweary of the sun.

She had long thrown away the saffron robe and monkey head. Watching her bare legs and round little buttocks, I wondered at my incapacity to feel a sharper particular lust than the general longing I had to merge with the abstract female. In this strangely hallucinatory journey, my senses seemed alive but my emotions dead. But one afternoon, when we had come out of the jungle into open land, under a sky closed in by heavy clouds, and had arrived at a wide river with a sandy beach upon the inner curve of its wide bend, and I saw her run into the water with a spontaneous abandon and almost a childlike delight, I felt within me the reawakening of desire. She came out of the water cleansed of the dirt that had clung to her from sleeping the previous night on uncovered ground, and sat on the beach, her elbows on her raised knees and her chin clasped by her palms, and looked pensively at the water. I needed to bathe too, and an absurd immodesty made me walk some distance away from where Horuxtla sat and enter naked into the river. The water was cold, almost icy, but exhilaratingly so since the air outside it was hot and extremely humid. I saw Horuxtla look in my direction and then turn her face away. I swam a few rapid strokes and came out of the water. My muscles seemed to have become cramped by the cold water and I fell on the sand, shivering. A few minutes in the hot, steamy air revived me, though my skin had taken on a shrivelled appearance.

Except for the excessive humidity, the landscape before me looked surprisingly European. The sky was overcast and the murky light, made gloomier by a mist that must have risen thickly from the river in the morning and still hung about late in the afternoon, transformed the ghostly presence of the great tropical trees on the further bank to the outlines of magnificent oaks and sycamores. All the landscape needed was a small group of well-fed cows lying on a grassy patch above the bank and the illusion would have been complete of a perspective in Suffolk or Utrecht. Visibility penetrated less than a mile of the darkened, greyish environment.

When I joined her, Horuxtla told me to go and collect as much firewood as I could gather from the floor of the jungle. She got me to pile the wood in four heaps about ten feet from each other, so that we had four fires burning that night as if on the four points of the compass. First I thought the fires were to protect us from all four directions, but as night fell I realized the protection was not against animals but against a chill wind. We slept adjacent to each other in that ring of fire, the closest we had yet lain to each other. There seemed to be a fullish moon in the sky, for sometimes the drifting clouds would be illuminated from behind, occasionally filling the night with a milky glow. I slept more soundly than I had in the nights in the jungle. Once or twice I awoke when touched on my shoulder by a sharply cold tongue of air and thought, before I fell asleep again, I had arrived in a northern climate from the tropics and, my body a reservoir full of heat, found the play upon my skin of cold air a welcome variation. And once I was awakened by a sound that took me a moment to realize was Horuxtla carefully placing more wood upon the fires.

Horuxtla showed no inclination to move from there the next day, which she spent bathing and lying about on the sandy beach. Nor on the days that followed. Each morning she directed me to a particular part of the jungle where I would find a certain fruit-bearing tree or an animal, instructing me what to bring back for our food. My afternoons were devoted to the labour of gathering firewood. Breaking off a long vine, I used it as a rope with which to tie the bundles of broken branches which I carried upon my shoulders. Horuxtla would not have moved from where I had left her after my previous delivery, and somehow it gave me pleasure to be thus serving her. She had surprised me with her knowledge of the jungle, but for which I would long ago have perished.

On the second night I shook myself awake from a terrifying dream of being alone in a European city where men in uniforms spoke accusingly to me in a language I did not understand, part of my terror being that I had begun to dream again after having gone without dreaming for so long that I had begun to believe I never dreamed, and, awaking, saw just then the milky glow in the sky become suddenly intense. In the next moment, the cloud cover broke to reveal a bright full moon. I sat up, startled by the revelatory radiance. A long passage of light shone from the river. Near me, Horuxtla turned just then and the skin on her shoulder became luminous. Flying clouds were lit up by golden light. But as suddenly as the sky had opened, it closed again, and the darkness that fell upon the earth after the momentary light that had been revealed was all the blacker.

94

THE BURIAL OF THE SELF

The mist was heavy on the river the following morning. The distant bank was invisible. I wanted to ask Horuxtla for how many days longer we were to remain by the river. It was not that I had a better, or indeed any, alternative to suggest, but simply that I had an urge to engage her in a dialogue a little more complex than the few words she spoke to do with our needs, and thought that if she could be made to express an idea to do with a plan or a hope, then, by enlarging the scope of her abstract ideas, I could enter that aspect of her world which was a mystery to me. But each time I looked at her with the intention of beginning such a dialogue, my own mind went blank and I could think of nothing to say. And so I wondered why I should not be content simply to be with her.

I could not. Nebbola's gross body and his vile breath invariably came to my mind when I saw Horuxtla's glistening breasts and almost hairless sex as she emerged from bathing in the river, so that the very image which was the most beautiful and evoked the sharpest desire was also loathsome and made me believe that the extinction of my self would be preferable to wanting to belong to a body so abused. It was not pride or excessive self-love that made me think this. I was not, like some Othello, enraged by a Moorish frenzy for purity. Only, I had fallen into some darkness and was like someone who knows he is wronged but has no one to whom to address his complaint.

But on that third night, before I had fallen asleep, the wind rose and whipped across the river in great icy sweeps and then, with a continuous roar that lasted an hour, it ripped across the sky with a howling fury. Our circle of fire was useless. The cold hurt. Horuxtla wailed and came and huddled close to me. Then suddenly, just when it seemed we had entered an infinity of windy cold, the wind died. One of the fires had a breath of life in it and I heaped what branches had not been scattered too far by the wind. Horuxtla stood behind me as I waited to see the fire catch. When flames began to appear, she sighed and sat down near the fire.

The wind had carried the clouds away. The sky was brilliantly lit up by the moon, which seemed no less full than the night before, and also by such a bright profusion of stars and planets it seemed that all the galaxies yet discovered, and then some more, were here revealed. I went and lay on the opposite side of the fire from Horuxtla, above me a wider universe than I had known. I had become so enthralled by the immense dazzle that I had missed noticing a strange dark mass on one horizon, as if even as the universe had exploded into light there was already a blackness that had begun to encroach upon it. I looked again at the moon and the wild dance of the stars around it. Just then a shadow fell across my body. It took me a moment to realize that the blackness on the horizon was solid, unmoving, and not the cause of the partial eclipse that hid the moon from me. The shadow was formed by Horuxtla standing between me and the moon.

She lowered herself. The moon reappeared behind her shoulder. She sat beside me and touched my cheek with her fingertips. She lay down and pressed her body to my side. I remained on my back. Her hand was moving over my chest in a caressing motion, her knee was pressing against my thigh. She raised her head and pressed her lips upon my chest and then held her face close to mine. I believe I put my hand to the back of her neck and held her head so that her lips would be placed against mine; I am certain that a little later she rose and sat across my thighs; and I have no doubt that I saw her rise and fall in an accelerating rhythm and then, a sharp cry escaping her lips, she flung herself forward and collapsed upon my chest and lay there for a few minutes. I witnessed all that, as if I were a voyeur of the actions of some other.

A few minutes later, Horuxtla stood up and walked to the river. I heard her jump into the water. I must have fallen asleep soon after that, for I did not hear her return. When I awoke the next morning, I saw first that Horuxtla was not beside me and then that the dark mass I had seen in the night was the outline of snow-covered mountains, the nearest of that vast and impressive range perhaps no more than ten miles away. For some fifteen or twenty minutes, I assumed that Horuxtla had gone off to the jungle as she had done each morning, and occupied my imagination with the perfect triangular shape of the nearest mountain peak. But then I began to wonder what kept Horuxtla away so long.

When about half an hour had passed and she had not returned, I walked to the edge of the jungle, which I knew well from having spent so much time collecting firewood there. I called her name out several times and heard some bird high upon a tree answer back. There was no sign of her. Walking back towards the river, the beauty of the mountains struck me afresh, especially the nearest peak which, a dazzling white against the deep blue sky, a trick of perspective made seem much closer than it was. It must be one of the great peaks of the continent, I imagined, wondering whether the magnificent range of mountains from which it stood out had a name. If I had to name it, I thought I should call it Suxavat, after the settlement that was no more. No, I decided. I would call it Horuxtla.

It was in that moment, even before I looked away from the highest peak and the jagged line of the range against the intense blue and was repeating the name *Horuxtla* in a whisper, that I realized that, like Suxavat, she was no longer there. I glanced at the area where we had slept within the circle of the fire. On successive nights, we had built the new fires a few feet away from the previous night's, so that after three nights the ashen remains of twelve fires formed nearly a precise ash-grey circle. The ground was charred and little heaps of ashes lay upon it. There, Horuxtla had come to me, lain upon my body, covered it completely. There, I had felt no sensation. No heat from her, nor the fire of her eternal youth. I could not feel what she took from me. She rose, and was gone. Looking at the circle of dead fire, I thought I saw the ashes left behind of a recent cremation.

The angle of the light had changed in those few minutes while I stood staring at the charred ground. The glaring whiteness of the mountains seemed tinged with a suggestion of pink. I could not call the region *Horuxtla*, I suddenly realized. This great range of mountains already had a name, which I remembered. It was of Indian origin though somewhat altered by the European conquerors of the region. When, looking at the jagged peaks against the blue, I uttered aloud the name *Horuxtla*, an echo sounded in my brain a little while after the word had died on my lips and repeated the name differently. There was no Horuxtla. The name echoing in my brain was not *Horuxtla*. Staring at the high peaks, in a land of origins, the sound I heard was *The Hindu Kush*.

I spoke it aloud. *The Hindu Kush*. And now very quickly, even, it seemed, as I looked amazed at the dazzling spectacle of the snowy mountains against the blue sky and was repeating the name, dark clouds blew in and long grey-white tongues of mist began to rise from the river. In an instant the mountains vanished and the grey-black mass of clouds hung low over the land. The long tongues of mist looked like smoke rising from a huge land-fill where a multitude of small fires have been lit to burn the accumulated dead matter.

And then the mist spread fog-like over both river and land and it seemed I stood in the middle of a swelling ocean beneath a dark grey sky. But as when you are in a plane cutting through a cloud mass and the interminable grey is broken by quick-passing shafts of light and in a vast darkness suddenly there is a strange ethereal shape that a trick of the piercing light makes appear glitteringly solid, so there, at a distance from where I stood in the floating banks of fog, appeared what looked like an enormous egg, its dull, greyish-white shell ringed by a golden line of light of which the source was invisible. It remained supported as on the spume of an agitated ocean and filled the spatial infinity above the churning water. It seemed to move, as if the life within it had begun its mindless clamour for existence. No, I said to my soul, do not dream of rebirth.

PART TWO

Voyager and Pilgrim

1 The Realist on Machu Picchu

I had received a grant from a philanthropic foundation in New York and taken a year's leave of absence from the university in southern California where I worked in order to pursue my research project on Robert Browning's *The Ring and the Book* as a source for dramatic themes in popular Italian films of the fifties; before leaving for Italy, I had, in order to refresh my mind after a gruelling academic year during which I had consented to take on the associate deanship in charge of minority recruitment which had left me no time to teach, gone down to South America for two months with the idea of acquainting myself with the ruins of the Inca empire in Ecuador and Peru. It was on the heights of Machu Picchu on a breathtakingly beautiful day somewhat spoiled by an excessive number of French tourists who stood around in groups of three or four in every direction that one looked, arguing loudly and hotly disputing the accepted history of the place while making a thousand gestures which looked like directions to invisible workers to relocate all the rocks up into the sky or down into the valley, that, while changing lenses on my Nikon, I ran into the renowned master of Latin American realism, Valentin Sadaba. Rather, it was he who ran into me, for I was standing still while a wave of Frenchmen burst past me; I had just succeeded in placing the 50 mm. lens into my camera bag and was taking from it the 85 mm. lens to attach to the camera to take a shot of a yellow flower growing from a weed in a crack on the wall, when a person, who I assumed was a Frenchman too absorbed in some lunatic theory to look where he was going, banged into me, making me almost drop the lens. 'Ah, *merde!*' I cried, but immediately, on hearing an apology in Spanish, realized that not only had I made an error but also conveyed the impression that I myself was French, thus wronging myself for having given the appearance of being what I was not and wronging the French race by representing it as barbarously vulgar. I am very precise in all things

101

and cannot tolerate leaving a false impression, and therefore I felt obliged to take the Spanish-speaking person aside and to inform him that I was not a Frenchman and, what is more, was not in the habit of shouting obscenities in public, which I had done involuntarily and only because of the oppressive presence of the French.

Now Valentin Sadaba, as anyone knows who has read Liliana Andagoya's biography of him, which I had once browsed through in a bookshop in Santa Fe, is a very private man, and normally would not have revealed his identity. But like me, he was caught in an unusual circumstance, and it seemed afterwards that we had been brought from our different spheres to that arena by the *deus ex machina* of jumbo jets in order to complete a drama that some minor god – this is Sadaba's image, by the way; I myself am never possessed by extravagant figures – had left abandoned. Sadaba never wished to go where he was likely to encounter large crowds, but this visit to Machu Picchu had been in the nature of a pilgrimage; after nearly twenty years during which he had exiled himself from a South America which, from Colombia to the north and Argentina to the south, Brazil to the east and Chile to the west, was run by regimes of terror that tortured their own people or engaged them in civil wars for no discernible cause, Sadaba had returned, as he said, to breathe again the divine air of the Andes which had been the source of all his inspiration. One of the promises he had made to himself was to go to Machu Picchu and stand on a certain spot which his friend Pablo Neruda had confided to him was where he had stood and found himself overcome by a premonition of his great poem. That Sadaba had to suffer such a large contingent of French tourists in addition to the usual crowd of visitors to Machu Picchu did not bother him; it was like having that many more steps to climb to the shrine of Our Lady of Guadeloupe which to the penitent going up them on his knees must appear not as an additional punishment but rather as an indication of a certainty of a reward that must await him when he had uncomplainingly performed the penance.

When I apologized to him for my rudeness in French, which I assured him was neither my style nor my native language, and beseeched him not to conceive of me as a French tourist for in reality I was a scholar from America abroad on research, his response was to smile graciously and to say that he was an American, too, though the country of his birth had the Andes for a frontier, and why was it, he demanded, that people in the United States thought they had the exclusive right to be called Americans?

By now I had fixed the 85 mm. lens to my camera, and thought I could mollify his hurt pride by offering to take his portrait – something, incidentally, that I'm very good at, and have a project for a book of portraits of people of the Nile valley which, if the grant from the National Endowment for the Arts comes through, I shall have to give precedence to over my proposed research in Italy. No sooner had I raised my Nikon to my eye than Sadaba immediately struck a pose, presenting a three-quarter profile to the camera. Even before I focused and clicked – I'm very fast at doing this, by the way, and have no need for those new auto-focus cameras which give fumbling amateurs the illusion of being slick professionals – the name came to my lips: *Valentin Sadaba*. I had looked at the photographs in Liliana Andagoya's biography in the Santa Fe bookshop, and seeing him through the viewfinder of my Nikon, I was looking at the same pose as in the frontispiece. With the help of my camera's power winder, I fired ten shots in very quick succession, and then held out my hand to him, saying what an exceptional pleasure it was to meet the greatest living Latin American realist. I believe he was flattered to be recognized by an American scholar. When I had introduced myself – succumbing to a rare compulsion to give also my middle name, so that Sadaba seemed impressed when he heard, 'Jonathan Archibald Pons, professor of literature from California', and shook my hand most warmly – he held my arm and said, 'Look here, Archie, let's get out of the crowd where we can talk.'

We journeyed back together to Cuzco but we were mistaken if we thought we had left the French tourists behind. An army of them had taken over the town since I had left my hotel early that morning. A group of them, young men and women in blue jeans and red and white sweaters, marched around the Plaza de Armas chanting the *Marseillaise*. There was not a seat to be had in any of the restaurants. From the doorway of every bar could be heard a Charles Aznavour or Edith Piaf sound-alike accompanied by a lively accordionist. I congratulated myself on having a suite reserved in the best hotel where I had enjoyed a perfectly undisturbed sleep the night before, and invited Sadaba to join me there; but reaching the hotel found that I had to struggle through a lobby packed with Frenchmen watching a soccer game on a television set that showed a snowy black and white image, shouting partisan advice at the players. It was a fifteen-minute labour just to obtain my key from the desk. The staircase to the second floor was crowded with women who, apparently separated from the men watching the soccer, were making speeches calling for feminist vengeance.

There was a new obstacle to negotiate when we came out to the corridor on the second floor. Campbeds had all but closed the passage. Large men slept in them and in one, exactly outside the door to my suite, a young couple lay asleep in an embrace, the two heads in profile facing each other, their shoulders naked above the sheet that loosely and partially covered their bodies, exposing, at the lower end, their bare legs from the knees down. At last, I got to the door. My suite was made up of two rooms, the first a sitting room with a small desk and chair, a long sofa with deep cushions, and a round table in front of the sofa with a vase full of cut flowers; although I had arrived in Cuzco the day before and expected to leave it after one more night, I liked the idea of having more than a cramped bedroom in a hotel, finding it especially necessary to have an area that theoretically offered me the space and the facility where I might do some work. Before retiring to the bedroom the night before, I had sat in the sofa for an hour or so with a couple of drinks enjoying the satisfaction derived from looking at a fine arrangement of yellow and mauve chrysanthemums and thinking to myself that all I had to do was to place upon the desk the laptop computer I carried on my travels and, if not draft the notes of some ideas, at least play a game of chess. Well, now when I welcomed Valentin Sadaba to my suite, I discovered that my luggage had been brought from the bedroom and placed next to the desk and that some sheets, a blanket and two pillows were heaped in a corner of the sofa. I did not need to check the door to the bedroom to find that it had been locked, for already we could hear the loud voices of a couple arguing in French. 'This is too much,' I cried to Sadaba, and picked up the phone and called the front desk.

It was repeatedly engaged and, the furious argument raging in the adjacent bedroom making me angrier by the minute, I dialled again and again until finally I got through. The receptionist answered the phone in French. I exploded with the two Spanish oaths I had learned from a Chicano mechanic in Los Angeles who was the only person I could trust to work on my 944 Turbo, and getting the man's attention asked him what was the meaning of locking me out of my bedroom. When he had understood the meaning of my tirade, he put me on to the manager who charmingly declared that he had been looking for me: I had come into a piece of luck. 'What the hell are you talking about?' I asked, my language still tinged by anger and far from my own usual standard of refined and civilized speech.

'We refund you two hundred dollars for the bedroom,' the manager said.

'But I paid only a hundred and twenty for the suite!'

'The French couple, they pay four hundred dollars for the bedroom. We share fifty-fifty, okay?'

Just then I heard crashing sounds from the adjoining room. They appeared to be throwing shoes at each other. 'Why didn't you give them the whole suite?' I asked sarcastically. 'Their sexual foreplay calls for duelling space.'

'You want to leave? A couple offered five hundred dollars for the sofa. Okay, what do you say, we split fifty-fifty?'

I had a word with Sadaba. 'Take the money,' he said. 'It's a deal,' I shouted to the manager, and then, putting down the phone, enquired of Sadaba, 'What's to be done now?'

'Always take money that's offered you,' he said, and began to look through the pages of the phone book. 'That way you're always in a position to buy what you're looking for.'

'What, buy the very thing I've accepted a bribe to surrender because it's so unobtainable?'

'That is the fate only of the ignorant who neither understand nor can cope with reality. Always take the money, I say. It makes it easier to think.'

He found the number he had been searching for and dialled it. He spoke for five minutes in a very rapid Spanish, finishing which, he said, 'Okay, let's go.'

It was no easy matter to proceed, however. First I had to seek out the manager to get my money from him; he, in turn, had to find the French couple who had offered $500 for the use of the sofa; and then no porter was available to carry out my luggage. It was at least an hour before we were able to leave, and when I finally walked out of my room with my portable computer under my arm and my camera bag hanging from my shoulder I saw that the young couple outside my door had changed position: the man now lay upon the woman, their lips were joined, and their bodies, barely covered at the waist by the sheet, were heaving up and down, and they were oblivious of the fact that the metal legs of their campbed had collapsed.

2   The Infant Inca

A truck deposited us outside a small wooden door in a high stone wall halfway up a steep street. Having no luggage himself, Sadaba carried my computer while I staggered past the door with my suitcase and followed him down a long, poorly lit passage. We stopped – for I desperately needed to rest my arm – when we reached the top of a winding stone staircase, and I asked my companion where he had brought me. 'Where you'll be safe from the European invasion,' he answered and began to descend down the steps.

I followed, holding the suitcase in front of me with both my hands, which obliged me to lean my shoulders back to prevent the weight of the luggage from dragging me down. Sadaba's feet echoed on the stone steps. Several times, needing to rest my arms, I had to call to him to stop, for in that darkness I could barely see his outline even when he was only two steps below me. I lost count of the number of times we stopped and could not tell how far down we had descended when finally we reached a passage at the foot of the stairs that was more brightly lit than the one at the top. A man in a bright yellow shirt sat there on a stool, leaning against the wall. Sadaba spoke to him in a language foreign to me and presently the man led us round a corner to a hall and pointed to the second of three doors on the right. Sadaba nodded his head at the man and proceeded towards the door, saying to me, 'Here you are.'

It was a bare room; walls and floor of stone; two slits on one wall for windows. Sadaba placed the computer upon the ground near my feet, walked to a corner and lay down upon the naked rock surface. Did he expect me to do the same in the opposite corner? By now I was extremely tired and longed to be in bed. To stretch out on bare, cold granite was not my idea of rest. Sadaba's murmured response suggested indifference to my plight. But when I went to the corner and sat down, the ground felt quite pleasantly warm. I had not expected to lie down there but found myself doing so. It was a most peculiarly satisfying sensation I experienced then, with my head upon the convex surface of a rock and my body stretched out on a hammock-like curve carved into the granite that formed a remarkably comfortable position. It seemed as if I had fallen not upon hard and foreign ground but upon a familiar mattress which was already grooved with years of accommodating my weight so that I fit there snugly and felt perfectly at home. A drug could not have put me to sleep faster.

Slanting yellow beams of light fell through the window slits. I saw across the room that Sadaba had also just woken up. 'We can wash up at the airport,' he said. 'The amenities here are primitive. What's puzzling you, Archie?'

I was staring at the windows and wondering how they could be catching the sunlight when, after entering the building, we had descended down a winding staircase that had taken us deep underground. Sadaba was amused by my question and, pointing to a window, said, 'Why don't you take a look?'

The window was too high but a groove had been cut in the wall a few feet from the ground and by inserting a foot into it one could spring up and, grasping the windowsill, be able to look out. What I saw, though it filled me with wonder and surprise, only intensified the mystery. There was nowhere to look *out*, but only *in*. Sadaba had lifted himself to the second window and said, 'Quite incredible, eh? The room of ten thousand candles in the temple of infinite brightness. Could the human imagination ever conceive this?'

Thousands of tall white candles had recently been lit. Indeed, a man, whose naked chest blazed yellow in that light as if his skin had been covered with gold leaf, was still in the act of lighting the candles in a distant corner. It took me a few minutes to glimpse shapes in that brightness; after observing the man lighting the candles, seeing him first because he was moving, I noticed a column with a sphere upon it in the centre of the room. The sphere, a globe with a diameter of about five feet, seemed to attract the light of the 10,000 candles and to flash it back to illuminate the huge room with a brilliant dazzle. 'All gold, solid gold, Archie, can you believe it, eh?' I heard Sadaba's words as if they came to me from some great distance. 'The walls, the floor, that huge door. Gold, all gold. You think the world is made of air and water and the flames of periodical fires? What a foolish illusion! Just look, Archie, the womb of the world is pure gold.'

The man lighting the candles departed through the door, leaving it open. The enormous blazing sphere seemed to throw out 10,000 rays of light. Presently, four men, bare-legged and bare-chested, entered carrying a golden chair on their shoulders which they lowered and placed in front of the sphere. A human child of 2 or 3 years of age and of indeterminate sex, with its hair all shaven, reposed upon gold-coloured cushions in the chair. 'The infant Inca,' Sadaba whispered. 'Matrika Hualpa, who rules the earth from below. The eternal child of the golden womb. This is its daily resurrection, as banal and as necessary and as miraculous as baking the daily bread. The ceremony of sunrise, look!'

The oldest of the men lifted the infant Inca from the chair and carried him with his arms stretched, one hand supporting the child at the neck and the other at the bottom, and held him in front of the golden globe. The light beaming from the globe absorbed a shimmering and distorted reflection of the infant as the man holding the child slowly encircled the globe. 'Matrika Hualpa is the sun that rises,' Sadaba whispered as if repeating a prayer. 'Matrika Hualpa is the shadow thrown by the sun, Matrika Hualpa is itself and its opposite.'

When the man had thrice walked round the globe, he stopped and held the infant Inca's right shoulder against the sphere. Another man, a golden dagger in his hand, approached. God, I thought, they are going to kill the child! The theological mind seems everywhere a bloodthirsty one. The dagger raised in the air, the arm gesticulating, and the eyes of the man taking on the appearance of having fallen into a trance, the outcome seemed grimly fixed. But the gestures were symbolic, for when the man brought the dagger down to touch the flesh of the infant Inca it was only to prick the shoulder. Matrika Hualpa ritualistically gave his blood to the earth. Now the other two men began a nasal chant in a compelling rhythm and, carrying mirrors, approached the infant Inca from opposite ends until he had become trapped between the mirrors. From where I stood I could see into one of the mirrors: an infinite series of images of the infant Inca drew my eyes into an unending tunnel of golden light broken by shadows, and when I attempted to come out of that brilliance and focus again upon the living child I could not find him: every point of light that pulsed out of the globe was now a reflection of the eternally multiplying god.

By a coincidence, Sadaba and I had both been booked on that

VOYAGER AND PILGRIM

morning's flight to Lima. Ever since we had met in the crowd of
Frenchmen at Machu Picchu and he had drawn me aside so that
we could talk, one thing or another had interfered and we were
yet to have a conversation. But having constantly been together
in our various attempts to escape the tormenting presence of the
French we had formed a sort of attachment that seemed based on a
longer history of friendship than was in fact the case, the illusion of
being old acquaintances suggested by the decisions we made for each
other in our common attempt to escape a succession of difficulties
because of the European invasion.

Sadaba explained what it was that had come to his mind when he
had wanted to talk to me on Machu Picchu. When I had introduced
myself as a professor of literature from California it had occurred to
him that I could relieve him of a certain duty and at the same time
possibly advance my career. However, he remained vague about
what it was that burdened him which would not be so to me but
would instead be accepted as an enviable gift. 'Archie, you were
destined for fame,' he said, I believe jokingly, and wrote down his
address in Lima where I must visit him in three days' time. Why
the wait? I asked. Because of the weekend. The banks were closed.
What could he want to get from a bank? Gold? He laughed. 'Perhaps,
Archie, perhaps. Your eyes have been bathed by the light from the
temple of infinite brightness. You've seen more gold in one minute
than the Spaniards took out of South America in four centuries.'

Several questions occurred to me, all of which Sadaba eluded
though he talked charmingly at length. When I asked him to whom
he had talked on the phone and arranged for us to spend the night
where we did his response was to engage my mind with an absorbing
talk about the history of the region, and, coming to his conclusion,
he invited me to observe how well we had slept, that what had
seemed forbidding rock was in fact a perfectly comfortable bed. I
refused to believe, however, that the scene I had witnessed in the
room of the 10,000 candles was what he had represented it to be,
for surely, I remarked, word would have got out by now that there
was a room made of gold to which the pretender to the throne of
the defunct Inca empire was brought each morning. 'Word would
have got out, by whom?' Sadaba asked.

'Well, you seem to have known about it.'

'But I know so many things, many of them unbelievable to
anyone else!'

'You are the great realist. The *maestro* of realism. The whole world knows that.'

'And that is precisely why I keep nine-tenths of my experience to myself.'

'All right,' I said. 'Now *I* know about the temple of brightness and the infant Inca. I could write a piece for the *National Geographic*.'

Sadaba laughed. 'Too bad you didn't take any photographs,' he said. 'No one will believe your word.'

I remembered that laugh several weeks later when I had returned to California and had just had the eighteen rolls of film I'd used on the trip developed. One of the rolls came out completely blank. At first I could not understand why. When I had examined all the photographs I realized that I did not have a single picture of Sadaba although I had taken ten when I first saw him on Machu Picchu. That was the roll that had been in my camera while we were flying together from Cuzco. I had taken a shot of a peak of the Andes from the window and then, leaving the camera on my seat, had gone to the toilet. Sadaba must have opened the camera while I was away, and spoiled the film so that I would have no more evidence of having met him than of having seen the infant Inca: indeed that I would have nothing from him but the remarkable gift he was to give me in three days, not even proof that it was he who had given it to me.

3   In Dangerous Territory

Leaving the Gran Hotel Bolívar, where I had spent the three days in my suite reading the previous Sunday's *New York Times*, the latest available *Time*, *Newsweek* and *Sports Illustrated* – a perfect recipe, incidentally, for the strained and overworked research scholar abroad to recover his sense of balance – leaving the hotel from the city centre I expected the taxi to transport me to one of Lima's elegant residential districts for my scheduled rendezvous with South America's great realist. To my considerable surprise and increasing apprehension, however, the taxi followed a route on which one street lined with dilapidated buildings was succeeded by another in a worse state of disrepair, so that after half an hour of such progression, regression rather, the worsening environment had reached a stage of extraordinary devastation with several buildings reduced quite to rubble. The driver, who had greeted me cheerfully enough when I hailed him outside the hotel, had become quiet when I gave him the piece of paper on which Sadaba had written his address. As we proceeded, the driver added a sullen manner to his taciturnity. I thought him a most contrary type, for I had never come across so uncommunicative a taxi driver in all of Latin America. When I asked him if he was familiar with the address, he merely glanced mournfully at me in the rearview mirror, and when I tried to win his Latin sympathy by denouncing the World Bank, all that my libellous abuse evinced from him was a slight twitch of the shoulder which might have been intended to be a shrug of indifference.

A mountainous heap of broken masonry, rotted timber and shattered glass and little hills of piled-up trash blocked the road. The taxi came to a halt. The driver glanced wearily at the meter and then slowly turned his head, looked sadly at me and said, 'You'll have to walk from here.'

'What place is this?' I asked.

He pointed to the meter and said, 'I got work to do.'

111

I should have thrown his money at him and banged the door behind me on leaving, but instead I gave him a large tip, thanked him, wished him a good day, and closed the door so gently that he was obliged to reclose it, for, as I walked away, I saw him lean back, push the door out and pull it back with a loud thud. Half a dozen urchins appeared, offering me a variety of services to do with the lust of the body and the craving of the addicted mind, one of them uttering repeatedly the quaint formula, 'You fuckinca, you fuckinca?' which took me a moment to comprehend, while another kept shoving an open tin cigar box with a heap of white powder in it up to my nose, saying, 'You wanna coca?'

A man whistled from a doorway. The boys around me froze, looked at him and then ran away. Short and muscular, with a sloping forehead and straight black hair, the man looked Indian. He came up to me and I understood him to ask if I were a Spaniard.

'No, Americano,' I responded.

He stared at me a moment, said, 'Motherfucker gringo', spat on the ground, and began to walk away.

'Hey, hold on,' I called after him. 'You speak English? Can you tell me where this street is?' I put my hand into a pocket of the denim jacket I was wearing and realized that the piece of paper with Sadaba's address was not there. I had given it to the taxi driver and not taken it back. 'Shit!' I muttered.

The man had stopped and was looking at me. 'Shit yourself,' he said, spat again, and walked back to his doorway.

I cast a more searching glance at where I was and saw that I stood on the edge of a shanty town. The dilapidated buildings ended opposite the heaped garbage, which seemed a permanent sort of blockade erected on the road from the city. Past it, the road was no longer asphalted, becoming a narrower strip of dirt lined on either side by makeshift huts. Men and women milled about the street. Throngs of little boys were absorbed in brutal games. Dogs were slumped on the edge of the gutters, their eyes watching the movement around them. Some walls on which there was space for graffiti had the sign of the hammer and sickle painted on them and also words of which the only one I knew the English for was *Muerte!*

I realized why the poor taxi driver had gone silent when I gave him the address. This was obviously dangerous territory. But why had Sadaba got me to come here? It must have been a mistake, of course. A letter missing in a word that changed the street's name from one in a superior district to one in a shanty town. Or, the taxi driver had perhaps not been sufficiently educated to read perfectly correctly and had seen 'Avenida Arequipa' as 'Avenida Aguirre'. But supposing there had been no mistake? I could only surmise that the great South American realist was playing a cruel joke upon me, and I must say that I felt vastly embittered standing there, aware that in the windows of the broken-down houses there lurked people who awaited only a slightly more favourable moment before they could leap out and indulge upon my person their love of violence.

I tried to remember the particular name taken by Peruvian terrorists that television programmes and news reports in the *Times* had made familiar to American intellectuals, something *luminoso*, but it escaped me just then. In fact, I suffered from a total loss of memory as regards South America, and wondered what the hell I was doing there. I mean, I was spending $5000 of my grant, which is to say, I was *investing* $5000, in Peru, and what the hell was I getting in return? The privilege of being ambushed, if you please, by a bunch of thugs!

'Hey, Archie!' a voice suddenly called, and there, emerging from the very doorway to which the Indian had returned, was Valentin Sadaba! He carried under his right arm a bundle wrapped in brown paper. I saw that above the doorway, where the plaster had partially fallen off, part of a sign painted there still read 'Banco Real'.

'I expected you'd be on time, but not that you'd be *early*!'

'I was sure I'd got the wrong address,' I said. 'Surely, you don't *live* in this part of the city?'

'I'm a man of the people, Archie. I *belong* to the people. Come on, let me take you to my house.'

We skirted past the heaps of trash and entered the shanty town. Short, overweight women watched us from doorways. One or two dogs raised a head and then let it collapse on the edge of the gutter. Groups of boys continued to tumble about the dirt as they wrestled one another in the street. Men leaning out of windows greeted Sadaba, addressing him as *patrón*. The street stank to high heaven, a giddyingly potent mixture of decomposing matter and human excrement. Loud music blared out of the huts: Andean flutes and drums from one, powerful rock from another, the high-pitched yelling on a radio commercial from a third, a combination that rang through the street as an ear-pounding noise. From several of the huts the electronically amplified noise came intermingled with the shouts and screams of men and women or the wailing of children. At one corner, half a dozen men sat on folding metal chairs drinking beer outside a hut which had a tin Coca-Cola sign on it; more of them could be seen inside, standing by a counter.

A flowering hibiscus bush, the only bit of vegetation in the street, grew beside the entrance of a hut, and when we reached it, Sadaba said, 'The only extravagance I permit myself, hibiscus flowers that I can see from my window.'

It was unbelievable. The greatest living South American realist, who was avidly read in such distant worlds as Iceland, New Zealand and Japan, to say nothing of the millions in North America and Europe who devoured his words, lived in a hut made of mud that had not even been painted and had no door to protect its famous inhabitant.

The interior space was divided into two rooms. One contained a small school desk, designed probably for primary-school children, with a tiny hole in its top right corner for an inkwell. A dogeared notebook and a ballpoint pen were placed upon the desk top. Tucked underneath the desk was a wooden folding chair. Three cushions were placed on the ground against the wall, otherwise the room was bare. The other room contained a narrow bed and next to it a wooden chest. And that was it! God knows what he used as a bathroom, where he prepared his food, and where he kept his books and papers.

'I take it this is where you conduct your business,' I remarked when he invited me to sit down on a cushion. 'Surely, you live elsewhere?'

His response was clearly a refusal to enter into a personal dialogue. 'Archie,' he said, 'the Americas were called the New World some centuries ago. There was nothing new about it, I can assure you. It was simply an extension of the Old. A larger territory for the same greedy governments to exploit. The new is yet to be born. You are sitting in the very womb where the embryo is taking shape.'

The question passed through my mind why he was called a realist when he was given to fanciful expressions and seemed to have a special fondness for the womb as a metaphor. He placed the bundle he had brought from the bank on the notebook on the desk and, taking a cushion, flung it on the ground in front of me, sat down and went on speaking. 'The revolution is about to erupt from the great hungry belly of South America.'

He proceeded to lecture vehemently against the power of American corporations, the greed of British and Swiss bankers, the duplicity of French arms dealers and the cunning of Japanese businessmen. It was quite a foamy torrent of abuse and I felt as though I were riding the white water of the Columbia river in a rubber dinghy, now crashing down a series of rapids, now being sucked into a whirlpool and then hurled out of it to go spinning down the rushing gorge. But I remembered suddenly a recent scandal among the intellectuals in New York when the State Department refused Sadaba a visa to attend one of those conferences American intellectuals are so fond of, to which they invite celebrities from South America and Eastern Europe and then, with sublime masochism, submit themselves to ferocious abuse from the visitors for America's 'cultural imperialism'. Sadaba was hurling the abuse at me which he had no doubt prepared to deliver in New York, seeing me as a representative of the American intellectual establishment, which, of course, I was not, being only a scholar abroad in pursuit of research. Well, when he began on the kids in his street not having shoes while kids in California had closets full of Nikes and Reeboks, and tore about their neighbourhoods on Hondas and Yamahas while the kids in his street did not even have a soccer ball to play with, well, I threw up my hands then, and interrupted him with, 'So how is your *new* world going to be free of the old European strings, tell me that! The revolution you're talking about is socialism, and don't tell me *that* was invented in Lima!'

'No, Archie, you're wrong there. I'm talking of values that were already prevalent in these parts long before any Spaniard set foot on this land. But clearly, you Americans have made up your minds and never hear what we have to tell you. Your tragedy is that you see the world only as your investment.'

I saw that he was resorting to the old trick of a person who has no argument to offer and therefore takes on a martyred appearance, adopts a wounded voice and pretends to be resigned that he is misunderstood. I was about to reiterate my point when he stood up and picked up the brown-paper parcel he had placed on the desk, saying, 'This is why I wanted to see you.'

I stood up as well. Untying the string, he said, 'When I ran into you on Machu Picchu the other day and you said you were a professor in California, I thought you were just the man for this.'

'What is it?' I asked. I had assumed the parcel contained bank notes that, given the country's inflation, were worth some $20. But I was mistaken.

He pulled away the string while continuing to talk. 'And then when we were thrown together on Machu Picchu, I said to myself it had to be fate. There had to be a reason for it. Coincidences don't happen but to advance some plot. I should be the first one to know that! Well, here you are!'

He let fall the brown-paper wrapping and handed me a bundle of school exercise books tied together with string. On the top book was the single word *Urim*. Again I asked what it was.

'You're a scholar,' Sadaba said while I held the bundle and looked at that mysterious word. 'You're familiar with techniques of research and should be able to establish for yourself what it is. I think it is an account of life in the interior, somewhere up the Amazon perhaps. But it's written in English, and could well be one more sad attempt by an Englishman to emulate the Latin storytellers. I didn't read it all. I don't have patience with imitators. I've done my duty and saved it, now it's up to you. As I say, you're a scholar, you should be able to . . . well, *do* something with it.'

'How did you acquire it? Where did it come from?'

Just then a boy with a basket of fruit on his head was passing by the window and Sadaba shouted at him, 'Pablito!'

The boy came to the window. Sadaba gave him a coin and took a fruit from the basket, a guava, I noticed. Sadaba turned to me, held out his hand and said, 'And here's another small present for you. You saw how I acquired it, but who can tell where it came from?'

4   The Incomplete Text

Having been enlightened by Sadaba that the bundle of exercise books contained nothing more intriguing than notes of an existence in the interior, I lost my curiosity to know the meaning of the word *Urim* inscribed on the top book and indeed had no pressing inclination to untie the bundle. On returning to California, I placed this gift from the great South American realist in a small closet where lie heaped piles of books bought from remainder catalogues that will one day, when I can afford the glass-fronted book-cases imported from Denmark, enhance the air of scholarly distinction of my study, and, I have to confess, I soon forgot about the little bundle entirely.

I had my Italian research to prepare for, and spent a fortnight of the three weeks that remained before I was scheduled to fly out to Rome reviewing my collection of videotapes of Italian movies in order to become more familiar with the subject of my study. I replayed some of the scenes and made mental notes of their dominant themes of love, greed and the acquisition of power, reminding myself that I must obtain a copy of Browning's *The Ring and the Book* before I left the country. To give an idea of how busy I was – there were phone calls to make to the agency in Rome from which I was renting a villa, and to colleagues already on sabbaticals in London and Paris to give them dates of my arrival, for I had promised a few days' visit to each on my journey out – I had no time to check with the bookshops and the library for a copy of the Browning until, remembering a few hours before my departure, I sat down with one final drink and called Dalton's – only to be told that nothing of Robert Browning was available, though, the man added helpfully, a deluxe edition of *Sonnets from the Portuguese* by Elizabeth Barrett Browning happened just then to be on sale.

Well, it turned out that it did not matter being denied a glance at Browning, for during my sojourn in Rome – seven months of intensive preoccupation with the object of my research, from which I took time off only twice, once to escape a cold spell by seeking a week's refuge in Egypt, and on the second occasion going to see the early spring flowers on the banks of Lake Como, stopping in Milan on the way to take in an evening at La Scala (a rather indifferent production of *Turandot*, I'm afraid) – I concluded that a book on the subject of the Italian cinema of the fifties and Browning's poem, though it would be welcomed by scholars in the field of literature and popular culture, was not the work with which I preferred to make my début as a critical scholar. It was just as well, I thought when I returned to California at the end of the summer after taking my holiday in Switzerland, which I needed in order to brace myself for the rigours of the upcoming teaching semester, that I had not transferred my mental notes to the laptop computer that I took everywhere, and therefore I had nothing in writing with which to fall into the temptation of easily putting together a publishable book.

There was a week left before classes began. I poured myself a drink, sat down in the back patio, and reflected on the past year I had spent abroad. I congratulated myself on the intellectual growth I had acquired during those twelve months, for, in retrospect, it seemed to have been a most fruitful time. There was one thing I had proved to myself absolutely: I knew what need *not* be done. This knowledge provided me with a fine sense of freedom, liberating me from the tyranny that afflicts ignorant people, of making them waste their time on fruitless labour. I was a superior scholar for knowing what scholarship not to attempt. I was soothed by this reflection, but then, rising to replenish my glass, I was struck by the panic that classes were to begin in another week. I realized that I needed to start thinking of a new project. But *what*?

It would depend, of course, on which grants were available. I had during the previous seven years received funds from five different foundations which support humanistic study and so had exhausted the most likely donors. I went the next day to the university and spent the morning in the office of the vice-president for academic affairs, checking with the computer there for the latest information on available grant money. This is a very dispiriting exercise for a humanist. There is column after column of governmental and corporate grants available to scientists; what the poor professor of literature gets is a packet of salt-free peanuts. There really was nothing that I could apply for – it made me think I lived in the third world.

But one tiny entry caught my attention. A foundation in Nebraska offered research grants to persons who undertook the completion of a work left incomplete by the untimely death of its author – and to elucidate the sort of proposal the foundation supported, it added: 'For example, the completion of C. K. Scott-Moncrieff's work by Stephen Hudson, or Franco Alfano's contribtion to the *oeuvre* of Giacomo Puccini.'

I took away with me the foundation's name and address but little hope that I could come up with a winning proposal. Perhaps it was the thought during an embittered moment when I looked at the enormous sums available to scientists to work on Strategic Defence Initiative research that had made me think of myself as a person in the third world that triggered off the association that reminded me of my last visit to South America and that, in turn, of my meeting Valentin Sadaba and of the bundle of exercise books he had given me. I must have had at the back of my mind the Nebraska foundation's curiously riddle-like description of the kind of research it supported for when I returned home, I went straight to the closet where I had left that bundle of exercise books. I untied the bundle in a state of intense trepidation, as if I were about to glimpse an important clue to my future, glanced quickly at the opening, and then turned anxiously to the end to see if it showed any potential for appearing incomplete. To my considerable happiness, to my immense relief, the last two exercise books were completely blank – clear evidence, to my mind, of an incomplete text.

5 Prologue to the Life of Zinalco Shimomura

The text is in my hands. I think I will call it *The Burial of the Self*. I have spent a considerable time reading and rereading it. From the outset I have wanted to keep myself out of the picture, which is why the first four chapters of my commentary have been kept deliberately brief and sketchy and contain no more of myself than has been absolutely essential: I was aware of the necessity to show how I came into possession of the manuscript before I performed my scholarly duty of editing it. One consideration, however, obliges me not to ignore myself as peremptorily as I had wished. While I read the manuscript, with my interest in it heating to no greater degree than mildly warm, I suddenly sat up with a start. I was reading my own name! What's more, I was present in the text, making an appearance in a city called Natal and a somewhat convenient exit from a frontier town called Xurupá. I can testify that I have never been to either of those two places. As a matter of long-established principle, I simply do not travel to destinations to which I cannot fly first class, and the manner in which Urim and his 'Jonathan Pons' go from Manaus to Xurupá is simply not my style. I place my own name between quotation marks because I do not accept that I am the person represented. And yet, the use of my name is not a coincidence; and though the ludicrous person seen to bear my name performs actions that I never did, yet *I* know that Urim was thinking of *me* when he invented that person. What is more, he was thinking of me *maliciously*. It will be asked: Why?

To reveal the secret of his true self, that is why! To make sure that at least one person – *I* – would know, and reveal to the world, *his* identity. Vain man, thinking only of himself!

My first reaction was that of any ordinary mortal: to avenge myself for his distorted portrait of me by publicly revealing the name I had, as a joke among friends, coined for him in private when I knew him:

'Zinalco Shimomura' – an amalgam signifying a Spanish gypsy, for such were his features, black hair and sunburned copperish skin, and birth in the Orient, though not in Japan as the second name, with deliberate intent, misleadingly suggests. The oriental part was my mocking rendering of the nickname he had acquired when he lived in England: Shimmers. As it turned out, the foundation in Nebraska approved my proposal and when, after a year's labour, my work showed sufficient progress, the foundation was sympathetic to my appeal that not to be afforded the opportunity to do the additional research necessary to produce a publishable text would be defeating the purpose for which the original grant was given. It therefore granted me funds for two more years of research. I thus had the opportunity to travel extensively in the Orient as well as renew my acquaintance with those areas of South America where Zinalco Shimomura had travelled or briefly resided. In the process, I made discoveries that changed my opinion of the man, his life and his times. I realized that I could not behave like any ordinary mortal and take revenge for a pettiness committed against me, for I had been given a glimpse of something larger and more important than myself.

I had seen that the only perception possible of truth was through art, and that all the rest, including science, merely played with illusions. You see, I had become possessed by my subject. And the name I had given him in mockery I now spoke with affection, as though it embodied my own creation. I ended by wanting to protect him, for his secret being, which I had wished to revile, was now in my soul.

Yes, I had known him. I must have passed him several times in the corridor on my way to the faculty mail room in the liberal arts building before I actually saw him. It is not that there was nothing distinctive about him; at a time when most men wore their hair long, cultivated a beard or at least a moustache, and adorned their necks with some beads if not a gold chain, his black hair was cut short and neatly brushed, his face was clean-shaven each morning, and, most surprising of all, when everyone else came in blue jeans, he always appeared in a lightweight suit with a discreet tie hanging from the starched collar of either an off-white or a light blue cotton shirt. The truth is that when one walked to the faculty mail room one assumed a preoccupied manner, as if the inner mind contemplated some exquisite metrical device of Milton's, in order to conceal one's excited hope that the mail might contain an answer from Berkeley or Stanford with a spectacular job offer or the successful outcome of a grant application or at least a free copy of an anthology published by W. W. Norton & Company.

This was in a small state university in Arizona, so close to the border that, standing on the clock tower on moonlit nights, one could see the Mexicans breaking through the fence erected by the US government, and on some mornings the campus police would discover an illegal alien hiding among the rocks in a dry creek at the back of the university's air-conditioning plant. Zinalco Shimomura had joined the faculty during a year when I was away on research – if I'm not mistaken, it must have been the year I spent doing a comparative study of theatre productions of Shakespeare in London, Corneille in Paris and Sophocles in Athens – and so I hardly noticed him during the routine walks in the corridor. Then one day Arthur Williams, who always stopped me for a chat, pointed to the receding figure of a man in a tan-coloured suit, and casually said, 'Didya know he published a sonnet in the *Atlantic Monthly* last year?'

I was quite shocked that a colleague of mine should have published anything, but said in a dismissive manner, 'A bit late in the day to be writing sonnets, isn't it?'

Arthur's eyes beamed at me through the thick round lenses of his glasses. 'Zactly whatta think,' he remarked, and gave a short laugh with a little giggle to punctuate its end, looking much cheered by my response. I don't know how he ever found out about the rejection notes collected by his colleagues, but Arthur's favourite subject for a corridor conversation was which one of our colleagues was the latest whose article had been rejected by which journal, and he had been considerably shocked by Shimomura's success. 'We all talked 'bout it while you was on search leave,' he now said. 'Jim hit we all's saintiment when he said, "Hell, anyone can publish a poem, it's articles that count."'

'A *sonnet*!' I sneered, leaving Arthur greatly encouraged, assuring him that I had put the upstart in his place.

Of course, after discovering that we had on the faculty a sneaky scribbler eager for fame, I paid him no attention whatsoever. If hitherto I had looked at him without actually seeing him, from now on I scrupulously refrained even from looking at him. I must be one of the few people in my profession who does not need to pretend to be preoccupied. I *always* have some idea deeply engaging my mind. In any case, my own career took an exciting leap at that time. I received a job offer from a college in San Diego and was thrilled to have the opportunity at last to get out of provincial Arizona and secure a foothold in southern California. In other words, I never met the man I had derisively named Zinalco Shimomura when Arthur and I and some others on the faculty used to talk about him among ourselves during the seven or eight months before I departed from Arizona. But the remarkable thing is that when, on reading the exercise books Sadaba had given me, the reference to myself immediately brought the image of Shimomura to my mind, I saw him clearly, though, when he had been passing me in the corridor, I did not look at him at all; and then, remembering Arthur and the others, I found that not a single one of them had any shape or distinctive quality that I could force my mind to remember, and it has been out of desperation to simulate reality that I have given Arthur a pair of thick-lensed glasses, a short laugh and a little giggle, none of which characteristics he possessed in real life. I am quite pleased that the facility to create a credible picture of a man has come so naturally to me; what is remarkable still is that when I began to investigate the past and again met the living Arthur, I imposed upon his unspectacled blue eyes and gentle, restrained voice the features of my invention and gave him a preposterous speech which was not his way of talking at all, and thus never saw or heard the real man again.

And so, initially merely to satisfy my own curiosity, I began to reconstruct the life of Zinalco Shimomura, and soon found myself obsessed by a passion for certainty, becoming very fastidious about eliminating the slightest doubt. I ended by believing – I am convinced with complete justification – that the character developing in my composition of his several facets could have had no other existence than the one emerging from the images I was hunting down, just as some figures in a dream have a being only in the mind of the dreamer who, for some necessity, sometimes a demonic one, has unconsciously willed his mind to summon that particular dream.

6 From the English Notebooks

The P & O liner *SS Stratheden* has entered the Suez Canal. I had been standing on the deck above the propeller and staring at the widening wake, imagining the churned-up water of the Red Sea flow back through the Gulf of Aden into the Arabian Sea and a tongue of it be carried on a current to a beach in Bombay and touch the boy playing there on the wet sand. A charming sentimentality had me bemused for a moment as I pondered the phenomenon of the divided self. My body was voyaging towards England. My mind throbbed with pulsations as it received impressions of the world's novelty. But I had the startling intimation that while my mind and body were inevitably interdependent there was a third aspect to the self, being, which could assume a detached existence, as though it resided on a shore now become foreign. And this being, bound within time and space of fixed and unchanging dimensions, was one of many successive beings that the mind was constantly called upon to judge as a legitimate representative of the self. But the cry went up, *The Suez, the Suez!* I remained a minute longer where I stood, like one prolonging a sad farewell.

A sandy bank on either side of the narrow channel, a desert beyond each bank. Occasionally, an Arab and his camel are to be seen as if placed on the horizon to fulfil a preconceived idea we all have of this world. It's a long, dull canal which must be navigated slowly. The English, going home, went through here. There are many on this ship. They have finally given up their tea-plantation bungalows in Assam, their villas in the suburbs of the cities where under the tall palms and wide-spreading flamboyant trees they tirelessly grew their roses and azaleas. They are crowded on the deck and stare at the desert, their eyes seem puzzled by some enigma of the land. The young woman whose name I've overheard as Catherine is in the crowd. Between breakfast and beef tea at eleven, she sits on a deckchair with her face to the sun. Her white skin has acquired a warm, dark tan, which gives a startling intensity to the green of her eyes. A tall blond-haired man who always seems to be seeking her out has come to stand next to her and is pointing at the distance and saying something. He is smiling as he talks. But she has a slight frown on her forehead and her eyes look as if they cannot see what he is trying to show her. If he's being funny, she doesn't get the joke.

This is our fifth day out of Bombay. After beef tea on the deck, Catherine goes and sits in the lounge where small groups of the English passengers are always assembled around drinks. They seem to drink all day long. It's amazing. A few Indian passengers go into the lounge in a self-flaunting sort of manner, eager to show their familiarity with English customs or to assert their new independence which no longer need segregate them from their former rulers. Two young Englishmen are usually already there when Catherine goes to the lounge. She sits with them, smoking cigarettes. She has her first drink at noon, a shandy. The blond man seeks her out then. Every time he pretends that he is surprised to see her there. The two other men make room for him. The three men buy one another rounds of beer and seem to become competitive in showing off to Catherine how manly each one is. She meanwhile sips from her half-pint of shandy and laughs at their stories. I walk past their table to buy cigarettes at the bar and hear some of their talk. I cannot believe how pathetically trivial their talk is and think if only I could be alone with Catherine I would astonish her by comparing her to a summer's day and announcing to her, my dark lady, *Not from the stars do I my judgement pluck.*

I have never seen the English from so close or heard their speech so clearly. The men do not sound like Robert Donat or Charles Laughton. It takes me a couple of days to remember the word *Cockney.* Sometimes when I come across Catherine alone on the deck sunning herself in a bathing suit I wish the wind would take the magazine that she drops by her side and blow it to my feet so that I could return it to her and have her eyes look at me as I say, 'I believe this must be yours.' The thought that I could come so close to an English woman as to touch her breath with mine is so unbelievable it fills me with terror and excitement. Why terror? The breath of women, the light of their eyes, the vibrant ring of their voices come from magical sources and make a young man's nights dreadful.

We are in the Mediterranean, we are in Europe! We stopped in the harbour of Port Said after coming out of the Suez Canal. Egyptian merchants rowed out in boats to where the ship had cast anchor. There were scores of them shouting at the passengers crowded on the decks, holding up souvenirs – the Pyramids, a Sphinx made of brass. It sounded like a bazaar. They threw up a rope for people to haul up a souvenir in a little basket in which they sent back money after haggling over the price. But we soon sailed away, the East behind us. Knowing we are in the Mediterranean has made everyone feel different. I had a funny sensation when I saw myself in the mirror. I'm in Europe, I said to myself, and could not believe I was looking at myself. Catherine seems affected by being closer to home. She has become serious about her relationship with her admirer. I believe she has decided to give herself to him, and may already have done so as I write this. There was a swell in the sea this evening, making the ship rock, and most people retired to their cabins directly after dinner. I walked on the decks and on the topmost one came across Catherine and the blond Englishman. He had his arm around her shoulder as they walked some distance ahead of me. They came to the door into the passage from where one descends to the lower decks and were about to go in when they stopped and spontaneously embraced each other. They remained leaning against the wall, their heads moving in eager kisses and their hands agitated about each other's shoulders. I decided that I could not stay on the deck any longer and was obliged to go past them to the door near which they stood. On hearing me approach, they looked up and seemed to come to an unspoken decision. They quickly entered the passage and began to go down the steps. I could not help but follow since I was making for my cabin. They hastened away like a couple eagerly seeking privacy. When I reached my floor I saw them at the end of the long corridor where they entered the man's cabin. This is going to be a dreadful night.

Past Crete, past Sicily through the Strait of Messina with fire glowing on Mount Etna lighting up the evening sky for hours, past Sardinia, we proceed on a heavily swelling Mediterranean that makes the ocean liner sink low now to the left and now low to the right and from time to time raises its bow high above the water and then smashes it down with a crack. Hardly a soul comes out to the decks. The bars and the restaurants remain deserted. Occasionally, a steward is seen struggling bravely down a corridor with a tray of sandwiches or whisky and soda for some passenger bound to his cabin. I hold on to a handle near a port-hole in a bar and stare at what land appears through the misty commotion created by the rocking ship. One moment, the whole side of the ship seems to be going down, down and it seems that in a moment we will crash against the water; but just then the ship holds itself and begins to rock in the opposite direction; and the water leans back, revealing the land on the horizon and then making the land dominant and appear so close one could swim to it; but the ship continues to roll backwards and the land sinks away and the brilliant blue sky appears. It is as if the land were trying to emerge from the ocean and kept falling into it, as if I witnessed the birth of Europe and simultaneously the drowning of its land mass, as if by being both there and not there the land offered a homecoming to some and suggested to the others, the new immigrants, that it was actually not there and that it would be hazardous to attempt to disembark on what was essentially an illusion just as the disturbed sea threw up so much spray that from one angle, as the ship heaved up, there appeared a rainbow erecting its great arc over the entire width of the ocean which, though one knew it to be a trick of the light, seemed as substantial as an iron bridge. This is a two-sided world. When we were closest to Mount Etna I thought the sky reflected the fiery volcano though it was the dark blue of evening just before sunset. I realized that we were at the southern gate of Europe and Europe had placed as its sentinel there a burning mountain ready to pour out its fire to block the intruder's passage. Here was the shore of the deadly whirlpool and of the six-headed demon. I was in the sea full of sinister islands which suddenly stood out against the deceptively tranquil horizons as pastoral kingdoms where the lotus profusely bloomed and the air was perfumed more sweetly than a lecher's promises and whispered to the self on its voyage to come ashore and surrender itself to that seduction which would extinguish in it the torment of being. I feel no nausea that travellers in such conditions normally suffer. Something in the atmosphere has overpowered me. I alone step out on the decks. Every one else is in their cabins. But for the brave stewards, I would think I was the only voyager on the ship which had lost its crew and sailed on a ghostly course that pitched me from one end of the Mediterranean to the other.

The Pillars of Hercules now, and the great rock of Gibraltar, another sentinel at Europe's other southern gate, the Union Jack flying. But how can I record what happened in Marseille? I don't know what is boiling more in my blood, shame or disgust or the sadness of a missed opportunity. Just when it seemed the ship was bound on some circular demonic route, it came away from the treacherous islands and sought a safe harbour on the continental land mass. I had not expected this gift, the arrival in Europe on French soil. It was spring. My next birthday fell in two days when we would be in the Bay of Biscay – which seasoned travellers said would be rougher than any ocean we had so far survived – and my father had given me some money to spend ashore. The day before we arrived in Marseille the ship was still going through heavy seas but one or two passengers had begun to emerge from their cabins and to find their legs once again. One of them was a young Englishman named Ted Minton, who was one of the men Catherine used to join in the bar for her midday shandy. Seeing that I was the only other person on deck, he came up to me, introduced himself and asked if I'd like a game of quoits with him. He was the first Englishman ever to talk to me, so naturally I responded with enthusiasm. Though he was eight years my senior, we got on so well together that after our game – which was farcical because the rolling ship had a way of making us stumble or fall on our knees frequently at the wrong moment and in the opposite direction to where we wished to be – we stood smoking and talking for half an hour. I discreetly mentioned Catherine's name. 'Bleedin' bitch on 'eat's wha' she is,' he declared calmly. I found it difficult to understand his accent at first but soon grasped at least a gist of what he said. He abused the blond man, whom he referred to as Jack, saying, 'Wha' 'e needs is a plumba to put a washa on 'is cock, it bleedin' drips all the time.' But the next morning when Jack and Catherine appeared at breakfast, I saw Ted go and sit with them and have a good laugh over whatever it was they talked about.

Everyone went ashore in Marseille, where we were docked for a whole day. I think that when I stepped on the land my mind was so taken by the idea that it was I, this being, this body, who was in France that it could not cope with the immediate reality, since much of it had already been overwhelmed by images from Victor Hugo even as the ship was approaching the coast of France. I toured the city in the morning with my parents and a group of Indians but witnessed nothing of what they saw. My imagination was visiting the nineteenth century. Victor Hugo's characters populated the streets. Our little Indian group returned to the ship for lunch, but I slipped back into the town with no sense of my present being but become a roving eye among exotic streets from another time. Had I not accidentally run into Ted Minton I might well have lost myself completely. He was alone in a bar when he saw me walking past outside and ran out to stop me. Did I have any money? he wanted to know. His friends had gone away – 'Off to pick up some tarts,' he said – and he found he didn't have enough money to pay for the drinks. I happened to have some money and so paid his bill. We walked away together towards the docks. Whether he guided me there or we arrived there by accident, I do not know, and nor do I know how Ted with his Cockney English came to a perfect understanding with a stout old French woman who sat at a counter in the dark hall just inside the entrance to a narrow building and spoke French rapidly in a screechy voice, but next thing we were climbing up a creaking wooden staircase with two girls in front of us.

In a tiny, poorly lit room, I am alone with a woman. She is older than I had thought when she walked ahead of me up the stairs. I cannot tell what age she is. Her gesture is weary as she holds her dress by its skirt and raises it up her body and over her head and wearily drops it upon a chair. There are tufts of black hair at her armpits. Encased in a cotton slip, she is wide-hipped and has heavy breasts which are unsupported and wobble with considerable agitation as she walks wearily and sits on the edge of the bed. Her exposed thighs are thick and heavy. She raises a weary hand to her head and expels her breath loudly, impatiently. There is a mirror above the bed which catches some light from a high slit window and reflects it upon the woman's cheek and lips. There is a sickly aspect to her skin, as if there were areas where the blood beneath the skin had died. But her lips look full of life, as if they had lately sucked fresh blood. Her eyes are on me, dull, tired eyes. I take a step towards her to see if the light will not throw a gleam from her eyes. I cast a glance at the mirror. Instead of seeing light there I catch a shadowy image and realize it is a reflection of my own self. I step back quickly, suddenly frightened. Again I see her blood-saturated lips and know my desire is too terrible to express even if I could speak her language. She is sick and ugly. Her blood is diseased. She says something and makes a gesture with her hand, beckoning me to her side. I stand rooted to the ground, terrified by my inexpressible desire. It is only a brief moment of time, three seconds perhaps, but my conception of standing there is of much longer duration, an age perhaps. It crosses my mind simultaneously that really she is beautiful and only appears sick in the sinister camouflage cast upon her by the room's dim, shadowy and mirrored light, that here is the moment I have dreamed of in my male preoccupation with a longing to enter the female, and that no, no, no, the flesh upon her is almost lifeless and her dull, weary eyes do not see, that the sickly pallor of her skin cannot be disguised by the dark red rouge which in the room's darkness appears like a black splotch on her face or the disfiguration left by a severe burning. Beautiful, ugly, pitiable woman! I want her to drive her teeth into my breast and to suck my blood. '*No!*' my voice bursts aloud suddenly from my throat, and I turn and run down the stairs. Outside the building, I stand open-mouthed, nearly panting. When Ted emerges, he grins and asks, 'Get a good fuck for yer money, then?'

We have come out of the Mediterranean. The Bay of Biscay has proved calm so far. Everyone is in a mood to celebrate. A fancy-dress party in the dining room, an Old Vienna Evening in the ballroom. Jack and Catherine who seemed to have become inseparable by the time we had reached Marseille and remained attached to each other when we sailed past Gibraltar now do not even look at each other. She seems determined to enjoy herself and is seen laughing in groups of men or dancing with one of them. There's a desperation in the air to extract from what time is left of the voyage the greatest possible pleasure. Ted has not been interested in talking to me since we left Marseille. The last time I greeted him he was with a couple of his English friends and he looked surprised that I should think I knew him.

England has been sighted! It is a cold, grey morning with nearly a gale blowing, but everyone comes running out of the bars and the cabins and crowds upon the port decks. We peer at the horizon.

Masses of grey cloud go racing past. There is a hum in the watching crowd as if people scanned the sky for a comet's expected appearance and pointed to speculative sightings. Suddenly, but only for half a minute, the wind pulls away the clouds. A thin green line appears on the horizon. A cry goes up from the crowd. England! One man claims it's the coast of Devon, another Dorset. A third, looking through a pair of binoculars, announces with a definitive air, 'That's Brixham.' The first man is triumphant and exclaims, 'I said it was Devon!' But the clouds fall down upon the green. The grey thickens. A fog descends. The land is lost to our sight for hours until we enter the Channel and have navigated to the mouth of the Thames.

7 The Flight West

The American Airlines 727 took off in the grey afternoon from Kennedy airport and within a few minutes had flown down the eastern edge of Manhattan when, still ascending and weaving in wide banking movements, there appeared in the still bay waters far below its starboard wing, clearly visible to the passengers who sat by the windows on that side of the plane, perfectly caught in a spotlight of sunshine breaking through the clouds, the Statue of Liberty. Looking out from where he sat in the non-smoking section, Zinalco Shimomura recognized the statue, but the vision was momentary, for just then the plane entered a mass of low cloud. There was nothing but grey darkness outside for some ten to fifteen minutes, and that quick glimpse of the statue, suddenly appearing and disappearing, was like a moment's unexpected illumination to someone lost in the dark, and therefore possessed a sharper and a more lasting brightness, keeping revealed in the mind's eye the images surrounding the bright centre, so that Shimomura continued to see the raised arm with the torch and the little boats plying the river on the margin of the spotlight even as he listened to the noises coming from the galley and wondered how long it would take the flight attendants to reach him with the drinks. He was desperate for a Scotch. The plane, instead of getting over the business of climbing out of the cloud mass and settling on its cruising altitude, was still weaving about. Shimomura imagined dozens of other planes going to and from the several airports in the area engaged in the same weaving dance in the dark sky. He looked down the aisle to see how much longer it would take for the drinks to reach him, leaned back, closed his eyes, and tried to concentrate his mind upon the picture it still vividly retained of the statue. He thought of the many thousands of immigrants who had sailed past it on their arrival in America, coming as it were to be in the presence of a shrine after a fearful pilgrimage, and remembered sentimental images from movies that showed faces aglow with rapture and adoration when they first caught a view of the statue.

He had not expected to see the Statue of Liberty when he left London that morning and was uncertain whether he should perceive any significance in what had been a passing apparition from a sky otherwise determined to show him nothing of the land below. He could appreciate symbols in monuments if he wanted to, but knew the ambiguity inherent in all such symbols, and the appearance could be interpreted as a welcome to the new immigrant as convincingly as it could be read as a mockery of his dream for freedom, just as a beautiful young woman who bestows a gorgeous smile upon a man leaves him unsure if he has received an invitation or merely had flung in his direction that provocative kind of cynicism which flaunts before his eyes the very pleasure from which he is excluded. A little bump made him open his eyes and look out. The plane had just risen above the mass of cloud cover and was climbing higher into the undiluted blue of the sky with the sun blazing from the west. The drinks arrived. 'A Scotch, please,' Shimomura said to the stewardess. 'Make that a double. No ice.'

As he cracked open the first miniature bottle, the captain's voice came over on the public address system, filling the cabin with a crackly sort of incoherence from which Shimomura caught a few key words. Virginia, Tennessee, Arkansas. Thirty-five thousand feet. The captain was giving their route to Dallas. To the newcomer, the ordinary, everyday names of the states were touched with mystery and splendour, and he repeated them to himself as if they were a refrain in some initiation ritual. He looked out and saw that the cloud mass below was breaking up. The grey became patchy, then scattered, and then vanished altogether to be replaced by a weak cumulus system and then, after he had turned away from the window to open his second miniature bottle and taken a sip of its contents, when he looked out again he saw that the sky now was absolutely cloudless. The smell of food was coming from the galley; the fumes of whisky rose pleasantly to his brain; outside, he could see all the way down to the ground, the wrinkled land of America, forested with pines and lined with rivers, with clusters of towns in the valleys or enclosed in the wide bends of rivers, little plumes of smoke puffing out of a power station or a factory.

He drank a glass of red wine with his meal. A deep contentment came over him. Not a tremor disturbed the smoothness of the flight.

He marvelled at the crystal clarity outside. The light possessed an uncommon purity. The undulating greenery of the land suggested a primordial forest. *Virginia, Tennessee, Arkansas*, he chanted to himself, the land of myth and legend, the country of 10,000 movies, of perpetual dramas that exacted human blood. The folds in the deep green suggested hills, some whose considerable height was set off by the rivers that cut through the valleys.

– It reminded me, he wrote to his wife Isabel in London, of a flight over another land. A decade ago that was. No, longer, longer! God, when was I there? Taking off from the Malabar coast, climbing over the mountain range and then flying over the great plateau. The green parched to brown to ochre. Oh the endless land! There was no real comparison, of course. Only this feeling of being in the same space, of being hung in the sky while the planet slowly rotated. And lands merge one into another, like two circles, one within the other, rotating in opposite directions at such speed that there is no longer any distance between land masses separated by thousands of miles but the east becomes superimposed upon the west and the movement of opposites ceases, there is stillness, at last.

The green flattened out. The sun, falling closer to the horizon, lit up a body of water, a long, broad stream of golden light sparkling from the land. He leaned his head to the window, his forehead touching the perspex.

– The Mississippi! There was a moment's wild fluttering within my breast. As if my soul had become agitated, restless, tormented. Then we were flying directly over the river. And a great calmness came over me. All was serene. The river seemed to be proving the country's identity and defining the frontiers of the states even as its banks were shifting and collapsing infinitesimally, and I thought I saw in the golden glow of its muddy water the whole continent drifting in a myriad particles of sand, each grain a golden America, indissoluble and inviolate, a soil untouched by the immigrant's foot. It was a trick of the distance perhaps, of the great height from where I gazed down in envy of the earth, or a distortion perhaps of the intervening air with its illusion of pristine clarity, or a memory perhaps of a dream in which the land appeared untenanted and undivided and a voice spoke its name, America, and the soul, filled with an anxiety for wholeness, became agitated, restless, tormented and then, recklessly believing the great golden river caught and dispersed the light of the whole continent, became calm and knew serenity, at last.

He turned his head and kept gazing at the river until it could be seen no more. He leaned back in his seat and fell into a deep sleep from which he was awoken about an hour later by the plane's change of motion as it began to make its descent towards Dallas. In that dreamless sleep, in that hour's absence of images, there was within him only an awareness, as if the mind could enter a dimension unconnected with space and time where black darkness glowed with illumination and be able to intuit the interminable presence of the self as a passive receptor of unuttered knowledge.

After half an hour's wait at the Dallas-Fort Worth airport, he boarded his connecting flight to his destination in Arizona. The plane took off at dusk, the western sky a brightly glowing fiery red ribbon on the horizon dissolving into shades of pink, mauve and blue. Soon night fell. Shimomura declined the offer of another meal but took a glass of red wine. The plane was flying in clear air over the desert. The black night seemed covered with a sparkling golden canopy. The stars were pulsing with light, the planets were so bright they appeared to be brimming over with golden liquid. The half-consumed glass of wine in his hand, he fell asleep, overcome by a melting feeling within himself, as if the ordinary organs and the common blood within his body had become redundant in this ascension into the realm of pure light and that emptiness must occur of base matter to which the self was abominably tied so that the subsequent release, coming as a moment of transfiguration, would be in the form of a blinding explosion of light, a flash that in an instant burned out a lifetime's accumulated energy.

In his sleep, his head slid across the backrest and rested against the convex edge of the window. He shifted his legs, stretching the right one out by sliding the foot under the seat in front of him. His hand turned over and the wine remaining in the glass spilled over his right thigh, staining the grey material of his trousers and gradually seeping to his skin and waking him with the uncomfortable sensation of a numbing cold advancing up his thigh.

135

8 In the Desert

In that part of the United States, Shimomura's features so resembled a Latin American's that even his neatly groomed appearance and sartorial elegance inspired no more complex a fantasy in the general faculty than that he was a visiting professor from Mexico City or perhaps Caracas come to do some research on Hopi Indians and from whom one might expect to hear a lecture on the seventeenth-century migratory impulse into the northern interior of South America, resulting from the European conquest, of the Carib Indians.

Being Latin American, or mistaken for one, in the Southwest of the USA, with its majority of non-white population of Mexican origin, guaranteed a person's anonymity, and so no one paid much attention to the new wanderer of the corridors of the liberal arts building, and only the Dean of Humanities and a couple of his associates knew that he had done more than to have published a poem in the *Atlantic*. The Latin identification was reinforced when his wife joined him at the end of the semester, by when Shimomura had established his immigrant status, for she was a Peruvian named Maria Isabel Valdivieso. Black hair that she wore in a thick plait which reached the small of her back, slightly protuberant cheekbones and very dark brown eyes, together with her Spanish name, and of course the native fluency with which she spoke Spanish and the accent that coloured her use of English, made her so emphatically a Latin that people simply took it for granted that her husband was of the same racial type, and both no different from the local Chicanos.

Shimomura's anonymity was helped by another factor, that of Isabel's carving out for herself a career at the same university. She succeeded in joining the Sociology department and became prominent in the university's politics. Because of the domineering image she projected of her own character, the majority of her colleagues assumed that she was one of the new feminist recruits from an ethnic minority whose ideas were to be liberally applauded

136

without investigation if one were not to be damned by their collective vindictiveness. Her spouse seemed to fit neatly into the category of the husbands of the new species of highly motivated and politically aggressive female professors. He appeared meek, obscure and submissive. Though false, the appearance suited Shimomura who did not have the interest in society that Isabel had. He preferred to go unnoticed than to have to endure the boorish talk of a colleague. Isabel, however, was always desperate for company and action.

Her father had served as Minister of the Interior in a government considered by the intellectuals of the time to be repressive, and he had decided that Maria Isabel's university education would be best undertaken outside Peru, fearing that among the liberal agitators who infested the university in Lima she was bound to hear of his own role in the repression. Communist lies, of course, as far as he was concerned, the rumour about institutionalized torture and a secret police, but he wanted to protect his daughter from such representations of his work. He offered to send her to Paris, thinking that the very name of the city would dazzle and increase her affection for him; being at the age when the slightest hint that someone else made decisions for her was to the young girl an outrageous affront, Maria Isabel thought about her father's proposal and made up her mind that if she was to leave Lima it would be only for London. It made little difference to her father, however, who was astute enough to guess that had he proposed London to her she would have insisted upon Paris.

Going to London, she had dropped the Maria from her name, feeling that she needed to shed her alien identity. She struck a deliberately independent pose and avoided becoming attached to groups of South Americans who met in one another's flats in Earls Court and Clapham and listened to records of Violeta Parra or Nara Leão and talked obsessively about 'the political situation' prevailing back home. After a somewhat lonely first year, she found herself in a crowd of artists and writers – most of them English but several from France, Italy and Spain – among whom the only allegiance was to the latest trends in the cinema, rock music, fashion, and anything that had the potential to become, however briefly, a passionate obsession. By the time she had taken her degree in sociology, the international set she moved in had split up, regrouped, altered, so that in her fourth year in London the circle Isabel most frequented was made up of young writers and artists who met in Highgate and among whom she was regarded with considerable esteem for having published in a national left-wing weekly a series of articles on the living conditions of immigrants in east London.

Although during these years she twice returned to Lima, once for a Christmas holiday and the second time with the idea that, having got her degree, she ought to settle upon a career, she found that her adoption in London of friends who were almost exclusively European had so altered her thinking that she had become impatient of native customs that were somehow unbearably suffocating. Also, the very reason her father had got her out of Lima now made it difficult to return to it: a change of government had exposed past brutality, and that old rumour about torture had not been a communist lie at all. She could not go to a university and expect to be employed by people who had suffered vicious surveillance, and in some cases personal affliction, at her father's direction. She went back to London, but now with an ambiguous feeling that she was both rejecting her country and had been rejected by it, so that in her new life the more she wanted to think of herself as a European the more she thought of herself as a South American in exile, and where she had earlier attempted to expunge the alien accent from her English speech she began to preserve it so deliberately that she sometimes sounded like a Hollywood caricature of a Spanish señorita.

Zinalco Shimomura was one of the group of people she mixed with in Highgate. There is no documentation that I can draw upon to describe the relationship between them that led to their marriage. I know the two of them best when they were not together because then they wrote to each other. I have been able to trace only three of the other people who were part of the Highgate crowd, and their recollections have been vague, speculative and sometimes contradictory – though one of them was to give me a small group of important letters, from which I shall quote in the course of this narrative. One thing the Highgate group did agree upon, however, was the idea that Isabel was attracted to the young man from India because his features were indistinguishable from that of a Peruvian while his speech, education and the poems with which his literary career had begun in the same left-wing weekly in which she had published her articles made him, in her eyes, perfectly English. I thought this an absurd conjecture and a piece of idle gossip, but was reminded that while she adopted English habits of thought Isabel never gave up wearing her long black hair in a thick plait which had once made Shimomura say that she looked just like the village girls in Gujarat.

One of the Highgate crowd, who was born Richard Dunlop and was nicknamed Monsieur Michelin by the smart set as he grew pneumatically enlarged about the waist in his late 20s, was my source for the story that what decided Shimomura to propose to Isabel was reading a biography of James Joyce from which he learned that Joyce had married at the registrar's office in the very borough where Shimomura resided, and he thought it an auspicious thing to do on the next anniversary of Joyce's wedding the same thing at the same spot as Joyce had done. The charm of literary history produced a fantasy in the young man's mind and an irrational craving for its gratification hastened his conviction, which perhaps came from an oriental cast of mind, that he was fated to marry Isabel. A second person from that Highgate group, Judy Morris, who thought it extraordinarily witty to call Dunlop a tiresome bore, dismissed his story as the nonsense of a thoughtless male too sexually conceited to admit that women had the greater say in questions of matrimony. Isabel was too strong-willed (Ms Morris responded to a letter full of questions I had sent her), and would never have consented to some idle notion that amused the poet's fancy. She always was too serious, my correspondent emphatically declared, and added, 'You have to be, to be a social scientist, don't you think?' It was Isabel – Ms Morris had no doubt about it – who decided the date of the wedding, and elected to honour the memory of President John F. Kennedy, whom she had greatly admired, by choosing the American Independence Day as the day of her wedding.

That incidental, almost an arbitrary, commitment to American independence changed Isabel's political views in the course of time. Just when, a few years later during the Vietnam war, it became fashionable for European liberals to denounce the United States, Isabel took the opposite position, abandoned her allegiance to the left-wing weekly and submitted several articles to the popular conservative press. Her pieces were rejected politely: the right-wing newspapers had no need to parade lapsed socialists in their columns, just a straight reporting of the policies of the Labour government then in power was enough to demonstrate the errors of socialism. It was at this time, too, that military dictatorships became the rule practically all over South America and, unconsciously needing an association with her origins of which the unqualified 'American' was the significant factor while the qualifying 'South' implied shame, disgust and guilt, Isabel therefore advanced the principle of the Americas being only America and so could call herself, without suffering from the guilt of having repudiated her own segment of the hemisphere, simply an American. And when Shimomura received an invitation to a semester's visiting professorship in a small state university in Arizona, an appointment funded by a bequest from a rich widow who had stipulated that the job go to a minority poet in Great Britain (who she believed would be Welsh or Irish or Scots, never dreaming that Indians, Pakistanis and West Indians would constitute a new minority there), no sooner had he accepted than Isabel began to discuss with him the strategy by which the position could be made permanent so that they could both emigrate to the USA, and she could enjoy the satisfaction of having her ideology, her origin, and her residence all denominated by the common designation, American. With socialism seemingly entrenched in Westminster, fascism continuing to fester in the Iberian peninsula, and what little there was of Europe that was still tolerably free become abominably decadent, she longed for her old New World.

This portrait of Isabel prior to her immigration to the United States is drawn from the facts given me by Richard Dunlop and amended with many a qualification from Judy Morris, who tediously insisted on calling herself 'Dunlop's tireless critic'. Isabel was attracted to the American Southwest as soon as she joined her husband there and found the desert reminded her of the barren seaboard of her native land.

– I'm so enchanted by the desert, Isabel wrote from Arizona to Caroline Hadfield, the third of the Highgate contemporaries, her dear friend Caro to whom she appears to have been the closest and who gave me photocopies of the letters she had received from Isabel, some, as you will see, with shocking revelations.

In their black Mustang, a Bach cantata in the cassette player, they drove fast on the straight, unpoliced road off the interregional highway, the narrow black strip bisecting the flat, dusty land where only the occasional cactus grew. The sky's presence was overwhelming. They camped in the middle of the desert, pitching a small tent in which to sleep. But one night when the air was of such absolute clarity that the stars seemed to have come nearer, they could not remain within the tent and spread the sleeping bag upon the ground outside and lay upon it with their faces to the sky. The stars seemed to be no more distant than an arm's length. Light gleamed golden from the stars and its throbbing created a wild movement in the sky as if the millions of stars were jostling and nudging one another or going on little races across space. It was quite cold, but they spontaneously removed their clothes and made love.

– Believe me, Caro, there was something quite special about this experience. Oh, people make love all the time in all kinds of funny places, but I'm not talking about prurient curiosity. I mean sex not as an act between a man and a woman but a moment of contact between the thing called *me* and the universe. I don't know how to put this so you can understand. Not *mis*understand, rather. Have you ever had the feeling that what was pouring into your body was pure *light*? Sounds awfully mystical, I agree, but even the memory of it makes me shudder, it was so *physical*, believe me. As if the light were entering layers of my flesh. A ridiculous comparison comes to mind: it's as when you make lasagne – you know, pouring the sauce between layers of pasta, that's how the light slips in. Oh dear, I can see you smiling and saying, 'Poor Isabel, she thinks sex is nothing but spaghetti and meat balls!' But there was something else. Something hideous and terribly frightening. The wildly moving heavens suddenly went still and I thought the light grew brighter in that instant. But that lasted only a moment. A dark outline cut into the brightness and the whole sky took on the features of a wolf. I was so terrified I ran to the car, a sudden oppression inside me, as that of unbearable heat, choking me, and I wanted to gulp air and could only think of the car's air-conditioning. The key was in the ignition and I quickly flicked it to turn on the air. The first thing that came on was the stereo. The Bach. The chorus, you know. Very loud and unbelievably magnificent.

While driving back after a deeper excursion into the desert than they had attempted before, they found themselves arrived at an Indian village. As was their practice, they avoided the main highways, choosing from the state map those roads which were least favoured by the cartographer, being assigned a weak black line as though the road represented some fissure in the earth. Even the narrow paved road disappeared, giving way to a dusty track bordered by prickly-pear cactus, and a sign constructed of weathered timber gave Kailost as the name of the village which could be seen fifty yards down. The suffix in the village's name seemed to mock curious intruders when they arrived there but the complete name was in fact a literal description of a scattered remnant of the Kai tribe that centuries before had shared the land with the Navajo and the Zuni. Half a dozen adobe houses built around a circular open ground constituted most of the village, with some shacks in a cultivated field on the western side.

It was late afternoon when Shimomura and Isabel arrived in Kailost. One of the adobe houses had a Coca-Cola sign above its open door and a pick-up with rusted dented fenders was parked outside it. Shimomura stopped the Mustang behind the pick-up and leaned towards Isabel who had a map open before her with a finger pointing to a dot. 'What does it look like to you?' she asked. 'I'm sure we're *here*. This was our last turning, and now we should be *here*. It doesn't mention this place at all.'

Shimomura stared at the map. She was right. The map didn't show any settlements. Only the black line of the road until it reached the lower bank of the Colorado and then ran along it. 'Maybe there's someone in there,' he said. 'I'll go ask.'

'Shim, do be careful,' Isabel said, seeing a man had come to the doorway and was looking in their direction, and then, putting the map on the seat and opening her door, added, 'I'll come too.'

As soon as he emerged from the car, Shimomura became aware of a strong and strangely familiar smell, and said to Isabel, 'This must be an Indian village,' just before he saw the man in the doorway who had straight black hair, and, wearing only a pair of shorts, displayed a vast expanse of flabby flesh and an enormous stomach. Coming up to him, Isabel said, 'Would you know how we can get to . . .' while simultaneously Shimomura had begun to say, 'There's no mention of this village . . .' when both stopped, looked at each other, turned to the man and again spoke simultaneously, though by chance they uttered the same words: 'Where are we?'

Beady black eyes sunk above fat cheeks moved slowly from Isabel to Shimomura and back to Isabel. He raised his neck a little, setting off a ripple effect on successive layers of fat that joined his head to his shoulders. 'Izzano problem,' he answered in a falsetto voice. 'Hotnuff for you? Howbout ice-cold beer? Doctor Pepp-or Mountain do.'

'The store's closed, Harfo,' a female voice scolded from the dark interior. 'Quit acting Mister Salesman of the Month, it don't go with your personality.'

'Store's closed,' Harfo said, laughing as though it were an excellent joke and setting off a commotion of ripples all over his torso.

'That's okay,' Shimomura told him, 'we didn't really need anything, only wanted to know . . .'

Before he could complete his statement, Harfo answered back, 'Izzano problem,' and slapped the sides of his thighs, so that the loose flesh of his triceps seemed to flap out like a bat's wings.

'Harfo, you waiting for the tortoises to walk back to the creek?' the woman asked from the darkness.

'No, ma'am.'

'Then go fix yourself for the dance!'

A moment later Harfo's figure in the doorway was replaced by that of the woman, whose person was equally large, though a few inches shorter. She saw the two visitors outside the door and immediately said to them, 'You come to see the tortoise dance? The old days must be coming back when tourists get to hear of the tortoise dance.'

'Actually, we only stopped to ask some directions,' Isabel said.

'What is the tortoise dance?' Shimomura asked.

'Wait till sunset and you can see it. Ten, twenty minutes and you'll see it like in the old days. Well, maybe.' She seemed to reject her own prediction. 'The name's Mokhwa Jaghès.' She offered her hand to the strangers and invited them in. 'Though everyone calls me Mizmemm Ree,' she went on and, anxious to show that nothing escaped her and that she herself was exempt from the errors of her race, added, 'Funny and stupid, ain't it, the way folks talk? But that's the truth. I'm the last person left on earth with any memory. The whole world's forgotten everything. No one has dreams any more. The planet's gone dead into coma. You want to know why? You want a beer? No? No. I'll tell you why. It's like you're spinning round and the momentum just keeps you going. You have no reason to stop, no expectation of stopping. Children join you and you keep spinning away, the whole population keeps on spinning. And then you're suddenly staggering, like the earth was quaking under your feet and kept on shifting and changing levels and dropping you down holes, and you know any moment you're going to fall endlessly, that's when your mind flies out of your brain, and how can anyone have dreams after that?'

'Maybe I will have a beer,' Shimomura said.

'Why don't we split one?' Isabel suggested.

Mokhwa Jaghès pulled two cans of Pearl out of the refrigerator, closed its door by giving it a push with her right elbow, and stretched out her hands to the two visitors. When Isabel raised a hand to receive the can she saw that the Indian woman, though enormously fat, had a young face and thought her to be not yet 30. 'I guess I could drink it all,' Isabel said, taking the beer. 'Slowly.'

Shimomura took a long swallow from his can and realized how unexpectedly thirsty he was. 'Mizmemm Ree, ha!' Mokhwa Jaghès seemed to have drawn a wondrous supply of oxygen for herself from the refrigerator. 'They come to me, the old men of the tribe, and Mizmemm Ree, they say, tell us what happened to us. You wore a crown of eagle feathers, you painted your body with the colours of the earth, you brought back the turtles from the other shore and we were able to speak to the dead and the dead lived in our houses again and then were taken in a dancing procession back to the other shore. Oh Mizmemm Ree, the old men say, tell us more. You wore shell beads round your neck, you rode the winged ponies across the plains, and you brought back antelope meat, you brought back fish, you brought back trophies, and there were girls by the willows on the river-bank waiting for you, singing of secret desires, filling the air with longing, calling you to the dream flowing from their laps. But it is as if I told stories to kids, no one remembers anything at all. The connection's lost.'

There was a thudding sound. Harfo came from an adjoining room, stamping his feet exaggeratedly on the floor. A crumpled length of grey material hung from his neck down across his chest and, over the great bulge of his stomach, to his knees. He had stuck two bluejay feathers in his hair. 'Ah'mreddy, ah'mreddy,' he cried eagerly, making mock leaps across the room and going out.

Mokhwa Jaghès gestured to the visitors to follow. Shimomura drank the rest of his beer, put the can on a counter, discreetly placed a dollar bill below the can, and walked behind the Indian woman who had begun to guide Isabel out. Isabel held on to her beer can, and said to her new companion, 'I'm from Peru, you know. We have Indians there, too.' Mokhwa Jaghès acknowledged the information with an appreciative smile, but had to give her attention to two boys who had run up to her and were repeatedly saying 'Mizmemm Ree? Mizmemm Ree?' and somehow expecting the interrogative tone of their clamouring voices to state the question of which they did not utter the words.

'Yes, yes, I know.' Mokhwa Jaghès waved them away as she would have flies. 'Go fetch the tub.'

The sun was still quite high, Shimomura saw. In fact, when Mokhwa Jaghès had said that they should wait till sunset and then added, 'ten, twenty minutes,' he had briefly been puzzled, believing that it was only late afternoon and there were at least another three hours of sunlight, but had thought that perhaps he had been mistaken. Four other men, much in appearance like Harfo in that they were wrapped more in layers of fat than clothes, were lethargically walking from the several houses towards the centre of the open ground. Groups of three or five people were also emerging from the houses and from the scattered shacks in the fields, staggering lazily to the centre.

Mokhwa Jaghès pointed to a log lying abandoned in the open space and said to Isabel and Shimomura, 'You sit here and be comfortable while I run the show.'

The two boys who had earlier beseeched Mokhwa Jaghès for instructions now staggered past carrying a tub no more than three feet in diameter. Shimomura, who was still standing, saw that it was half filled with murky water and that it contained a couple of shadowy objects. The boys walked some twenty paces from where Shimomura now took his seat next to Isabel and placed the tub on the ground. Harfo and the other four men slowly walked towards it. The groups of people assembled in a loose circle, two of the men taking up the little space on the log on either side of Shimomura and Isabel, obliging them to inch closer to each other. No one in the scattered audience spoke a word but looked in the direction of the tub and the five men as though they were about to see an unimagined spectacle and turned their eyes again and again to gaze at Mokhwa Jaghès.

'Remember, this is the tortoise dance,' she said aloud, and held Harfo's hand and gave it a push, making his arm swing out like a pendulum. He looked amazedly at his arm as it swung back and came to rest against his thigh with a slap. The four other men stared curiously at Harfo who slowly turned his torso to gaze helplessly at Mokhwa Jaghès. '*Dance*, remember?' she cried at him. 'And you, Mani,' she said loudly to another who suddenly looked terrified. '*Song*, remember?' Harfo stumbled forward and then jerked himself back. Mani stood petrified, staring open-mouthed at Mokhwa Jaghès who yelled at him, 'Song, song!' Harfo took half a step to his right, seemed about to lose his balance, and strained his body to his left. Meanwhile Mani had discovered the independent existence of vowels and had begun vocal experiments with brief, stifled sounds. The other three now imitated Harfo and tentatively practised the art of stumbling forward and back or shuffling to the left and to the right, but all very slowly, and from time to time they also felt compelled to mimic Mani's vocal example, and thus a chorus of unconnected grunts and bellows broke the astonished silence in which the small crowd watched the ritual. Having the tub on the ground, though not knowing what it had to do with them, their stumbling gradually placed them in a loose, wide and irregular circle around it, and now Mokhwa Jaghès began to clap her hands, walking in front of the watching members of the tribe, gesturing to it to clap, too, but only two or three understood her meaning and softly let the fingers of one hand fall upon the palm of the other without making any sound.

Suddenly Mokhwa Jaghès cried out, 'How the dead come back to talk to us!' and she pushed the two boys who stumbled forward and then looked back at her as if to ask what she expected from them. 'The tortoises,' she hissed at them, giving them another push. The boys ran to the tub and each brought out an object from it and placed it upon the ground. Harfo gave a little jump as if he had suddenly stepped upon live coals. One of the objects was a dried tortoise shell, the other a flat piece of wood; a short length of string was attached to each and, after some more prompting from Mokhwa Jaghès, the two boys began to drag the objects away. Harfo, who seemed to have warmed up to the extent of taking two side steps at a time, looked round at the boys and, trying simultaneously to shuffle forward, failed to defeat the law concerning the centre of gravity and collapsed upon the ground. Mani's vocal experiments had emboldened him to attempt a continuous wail, for which excessive effort he felt obliged to close his eyes, so that he collided against the fallen Harfo and collapsed upon him. The three other men were led to believe that the two fallen heroes were not on the ground by accident and so allowed themselves to assume a similar position, and one of them, convinced that he had come to a wrestling match, flung out his arms and gripped the man nearest him and he, revolted by the embrace which he thought a disgusting piece of opportunism by the man, about whom he had had his suspicions, punched him in the face. Harfo had received a sharp blow from Mani's elbow when the latter had fallen on him and was still crying out in pain; the frustrated wrestler was yelling that his nose was broken; and with Mani continuing the display of his vocal virtuosity, the two men still silent realized they were in error and so began to wail.

The assembled crowd, watching in a dull sort of amazement the mysteries of their tribal memory, believed the five gallants were wailing for the dead just then being dragged away by the boys, and began to cry. Mokhwa Jaghès walked round a wide circle, staring silently at the pitiful sight of the members of her tribe scattered around that open ground, and came and stood in front of Isabel and Shimomura. To them she said, 'Nothing comes back of the past, ceremony is dead in us, and though we inhale the smoke of the forbidden leaf and call to our brains to summon ancestral apparitions, no stimulant works, no dream awakens, nothing comes back of the past.'

– But, oh Caro, memory, don't you see, is both what we are, a preserver of the self's chaotic chronology which it sometimes recalls with coherent vividness and sometimes in a confusion of confounded time, as well as our eternal torment, for we're locked in a succession of acts. You surely remember the line Shimmers used to quote so often. Things ill done or done to others' harm. You know that my father died last May. A part of me has been numb since then. No, it's nothing to do with grief, nor with the ambivalent feelings I experienced towards him when he was alive. It's to do with knowing I have no feelings at all! I must have loved him terribly when I was a child. There are buried memories that show mysterious glimpses from time to time. And when he served as a minister in the dictatorship I think I unconsciously blinded myself to what was going on. I did not want to know that my father was involved in brutality. I was defensive about him. I mouthed the slogans handed down by his office. You know, the usual clichés about communism, American imperialism, one or the other coupled with patriotism. Then I ran away. When my father asked if I wanted to go and study in Europe and I chose to go to London, I knew the real reason was that he didn't want me to become a witness of the repression. But I pretended he was doing the dutiful thing for his daughter, giving her the best available education. We talked of one thing and knew we were talking of something else. In my heart, I knew all along what we were both doing. Yes, silently I agreed not to be a witness, I ran away. Don't you see, Caro, I was conniving with my father in continuing the tortures? Some people who were my companions when we were teenagers and thought Lima was our golden city were never seen again. I murdered them by saying to my father yes I will go to Europe for my education. So you see why there's a part of me that's numb. *I don't want to feel.* For I know it's the only way I can protect myself, and not fall into the terrible reservoir of guilt I've created for myself. Shimmers has divined all this, I know, although I haven't told him anything and he hasn't said that he understands. I've caught him not looking at me when my head falls with the memory of unutterable sadness, and his not looking is an acknowledgement that he sees everything. Things ill done! And done to others' harm. Is that all we can say of our past? No, I say to my soul, I'll wash away the blackness yet and continuously attempt its purification. Shall I tell you how it is to be? This one life is flawed and I may not have another. But I have it within me to create new life and express my repentance through it. Aha, I hear you say, Isabel has made an extraordinary confession, full of pain and sadness, only to say she's pregnant! No, Caro, I am not, yet. But I have understood that reproduction is a form of salvation. Shimmers won't agree – I know, without asking him. For him it is only a form of vanity, a projection of the self's love of itself, or a sort of instinct he considers base. Of course, I don't agree and will have my way. I don't have to tell him anything, do I? You at least, I know, will agree that this is one subject on which the exercise of power is solely the prerogative of the woman.

Isabel well understood her husband's unspoken thoughts. Her perception of character was exceptionally developed – which would explain her rapid professional success as a social scientist when she had established herself in Arizona. She knew Shimomura the poet and storyteller and consequently had acquired an instinctive insight into his thoughts. I was able to confirm this idea I had formed of husband and wife when on reading the correspondence with the three Highgate friends I asked Richard Dunlop how anyone could be certain about Shimomura's real thoughts and he said, 'Just look at his little novel, the unfinished one. Driven by the contradictory motives of wanting to be known but preferring to go unnoticed, he published it in an obscure magazine. He worried over the prose fragment and said he would never be able to finish it because he was incapable of drawing upon autobiographical facts. He deliberately left it as a fragment. You can't write about yourself and then say *The End.* Alas, the soul's history is endless. The longest version cannot escape being a fragment. Very curious little fragment it is, too, in which the *I* becomes a *You*, as if the man who composed it sat, like a painter working on a self-portrait, in front of a mirror.'

I had already been indebted to Richard Dunlop for letting me see Shimomura's English notebooks which he had left behind with Dunlop, presumably for temporary safekeeping, when he first went to Arizona. Now he offered me a short text of extraordinary revelatory significance. But before I recall that fragment I need to show you the future from which Shimomura scrupulously excluded himself, when Isabel, having rejected her native land, was yet compelled to embark on a pilgrimage to the northern oases of Peru and beyond to the great silence of the Andes and of their melting snows, to be at the sources of the rivers flowing east, and, in a mysterious way, to become absorbed by the same landscape which would draw her husband to its icy heights.

9 Novella Isabella

i Becoming American

'It's strictly family,' Isabel said, using the kitchen phone. 'Shimmers will look after the barbecue. Harry's already been assigned to take care of the beer. No, Celia, dessert is *my* department.' She doodled on the margin of a calendar in front of her at the kitchen table where she sat while listening to Celia remonstrate, and then glanced out of the window at her front yard. The leaves on the banana tree hung limply. Another hot day. 'Okay, a gallon of ice-cream for the kids. Sure, vanilla will be fine. Make it simple for the kids is my motto.' She knocked her pencil against the cereal bowl her daughter had left on the table while Celia got sidetracked on some remark about her children. 'I know,' Isabel said into the phone, 'Nickie's like that, too. She had to run out for the school bus this morning without even finishing her granola. I guess I must be stricter with her.' She rolled her eyes up and held the phone away from her ear, wishing she had not called from the kitchen but had picked up the cordless phone from the den instead, for with that she could at least stroll about the garden while listening to her friend's ceaseless chatter. Celia was irrepressible. Mention one thing and two others came to her mind. Now she was going on about the school buses not having seatbelts. The prospective horror of mutilating injuries to young children led to an association in Celia's mind with unborn babies and she next began to restate her strong views on the right to life movement, and the phone call that had begun with an invitation to a poolside party ended with observations on abortion clinics.

Fortunately for Isabel, Celia's chatter was interrupted by her observing through the window that the brown UPS van had halted outside her house and its young driver was coming out to deliver a parcel to her, and she was obliged to conclude the conversation. Isabel was herself expecting a man from the company which had recently installed a sprinkler system in her front yard, where she was determined to have as perfectly green a lawn as any she had seen in England – unlike the other people in the neighbourhood who had replaced their front lawns with water-conserving xeriscape, filling their yards with cacti, gravel and sand where there had been expensively watered grass and flowering beds.

Shimomura had not wanted the lawn, for he approved of the logic of his neighbours who derived their landscaping inspiration from what was natural to the desert Southwest. In fact, he would have preferred a small house in an unpretentious district, but had submitted to Isabel's insistence on living in the best American style. The house had to have a double garage, a den with a forty-inch TV and an entertainment centre, a play room for their daughter Nichola, a master bedroom large enough to accommodate a king-sized bed and a dresser imported from Denmark, and of course the kitchen had to be equipped with technologically advanced gadgets and the two bathrooms had to have marble fixtures; there were to be no compromises, and so the cacti and some oleander bushes at the front were torn up to be replaced by a lawn, and the rather pleasingly barren area at the back, ochre-coloured with its hard-baked sandy soil where some thorny bushes grew, now had at its centre a sparklingly blue kidney-shaped swimming pool surrounded by a bricked area on which were placed tubs overflowing with zinnias, marigolds and periwinkles. A gazebo on which trumpet vine had been trained to grow provided a shaded area to the right of the pool and housed a picnic table, with a barbecue grill conveniently near at hand.

Shimomura did not care for barbecue either, finding the gluttonous consumption of rudely roasted meat an offensive piece of barbarism, but Isabel's fixed purpose to adopt the native custom countermanded his objection; but if he must peform the American male's weekend summer ritual, then he did so by discreetly altering the recipe, replacing the coarse American idea of a sauce with a marinade rich with spices from India.

That sort of detail with its private intention of making an indi-vidualistic gesture was lost on Isabel. Herself impressed by the glossy veneer of bourgeois pretensions, she saw little beyond the generality of form. She loved America, she eagerly declared, not realizing that what she meant was that she loved her bright red Thunderbird which had replaced the black Mustang and in which she drove on weekend shopping expeditions to the malls that ringed the city. Her excuse for any acquisition was that she wanted her daughter to grow up in a normal household. Early after immigrating to the country, Isabel had, professing an interest in enlarging her mind, audited courses in sociology at the university. At the start, it was something to do. She would drive to the campus with Shimomura and while he taught his courses spend her day at the newly constructed high-rise social sciences complex from the upper floors of which one could look across to Mexico.

In between attending an undergraduate lecture class and sitting in on a graduate seminar, she had an hour to pass, and she did so by visiting the professors who taught those courses. At first it was to request to be enlightened upon questions apparently left obscure in the classroom, but these visits soon became a mid-morning social event over a cup of coffee, especially with Professor Ed Mossman who ran the graduate seminar and who, finding Isabel quite expert in his field, unwittingly slipped into the habit of letting her talk in the seminar as if she were a co-teacher, thus diminishing the pressure upon himself during the ninety-minute session. Isabel, naturally disputatious and gifted with a memory for references, so that when arguing a point she could support her position with allusions to seemingly authoritative texts, perceived the impression she made on the students. It almost became routine at the end of a seminar that some of the students should stay behind to ask her for fuller bibliographical references. But she always paid Professor Mossman the compliment of being the real authority in the field and quickly followed him to his office to leave with him a hastily scribbled list of the texts she had referred to so that when she directed the students to him he could give the superior impression that, of course, he knew all about those texts. Without planning to, Isabel placed Professor Mossman in her debt, and when the next semester she decided to pursue a higher degree she won his support in obtaining both a fellowship as well as a position as an instructor. It was more than any graduate student in the department had ever been awarded.

During the first semester, while teaching an elementary course, she looked among the papers she had brought with her from London and found the articles on the living conditions of immigrants in east London which she had published in the left-wing weekly. She realized she needed to search no further for her master's thesis, and then had another idea. By changing the ordinary language with its journalistic simplifications to the more complex prose, with its exquisitely obscure jargon, of her professional discipline she could, by adding also some diagrams and footnotes, publish the series of articles as one impressive contribution to the international study of sociology.

It took her only a week to perform the necessary cosmetic surgery to her simple English prose. The resulting lengthy learned article was submitted to an eminent learned journal in the discipline. A committee of learned experts in the field pondered the article for four months and recommended its publication. Its future publication was announced in the next two numbers of the journal. Isabel distributed photocopies of the announcement not only to the professors in her department but also to the dean of the college and the president of the university.

The article would not be published for another year, but she was already a person of distinction in her department. Academic merit, however, would not have advanced her career as rapidly as her charming habit of visiting the department's politically active professors and finding some common interest with each. The older male professors delighted in her company and were pleased to have their prejudices complimented as a sign of principled independence while their younger female colleagues found Isabel a champion of feminist rights.

Isabel never consciously thought she was building a career for herself. It was simply her instinct to create for herself a position of some prominence and then to protect it. In her own mind, she was merely being a good American, using the opportunity available to her. At the same time, she was convinced that she brought to her profession a superior mind and therefore was justified in receiving a superior reward, and it did not occur to her that her rapid advance was a consequence of ruthlessly pursuing a cunning political strategy, even though she did so in a manner that seemed wholly innocent. She quickly realized how the system operated and adopted its procedures. When her article on the immigrants in east London had been published, she cast the same piece in terms of mathematical models – a type of discourse that had recently become trendy and that, she was quick to see, gave to the banalities of the social scientists the aura of heavy-duty physics; by asking Professor Mossman two or three simple questions she created in him the illusion that he had provided crucial advice and therefore must be considered a co-author of the article which she then submitted to another scholarly journal.

Soon discovering that there were dozens of journals in her field, she recast her article four more ways, giving each a new title and different footnotes, in the last one of which she cited the previously published versions. The university was impressed by her publishing record. While Shimomura cultivated anonymity, Isabel served on several committees and courted publicity by conspicuously participating in popular causes, such as demonstrating outside an abortion clinic, that were reported in the city paper and twice received statewide media coverage.

The one academic subject on which husband and wife co-operated was the scheduling of their classes. By the time Isabel had become a full-time member of the faculty, their daughter Nichola had been born and so they planned their combined timetable to leave one of them at home to be with her when she was not at the day-care centre or in school. Shimomura had wanted Isabel to resign her position and to spend all her time with Nichola, but did not suggest the idea, knowing that he would be accused of being a male supremacist. In any case, having become a two-salary family, they could not afford to lose half their income and continue to live in the bourgeois splendour that Isabel demanded.

– It's a far cry from those Highgate days, she wrote to Caroline Hadfield when her English friend chided her for having communicated no news for a long time. It's such a remote time now, like a dream of someone else's past, those years spent in that absolutely ghastly little flat in Shepherd's Bush which we then thought so charming. Remember how everyone used to come for high tea on Sundays, and there was so much passionate talk, all about Harold Wilson and Rhodesia – God, what a miserable waste of energy! And then those long seminar-like talks in your place in Highgate, bundled up in all those woollies, from this distance it looks like a ghostly Bloomsbury group in a room thick with cigarette smoke suffering guilty agonies over Empire. Do you know what was wrong with all that? It was all awfully sterile. I know your eyebrows will hit the ceiling when I say that no woman can have a real sense of life who has not had a child. You do not, dear Caro, make a political statement by remaining childless. That's only a stubborn rebelliousness, resentful and vindictive. Ever since I've had Nichola, I've felt stronger as a woman. Shimmers didn't want a child. *He* is the old-fashioned feminist in this house! But I feel politically freer, being a mother. Shimmers is sweet and gentle, of course, and devoted in his way, but I'm not sure if he really thinks of himself as a father, I don't know if he has any paternal instinct in him. When I knew I was pregnant, I didn't tell him at first. He never wanted to start a family. Whenever we talked about it, whenever *I* began to talk about it, he just glowered, you know how he has that dark, gloomy look, you'll remember he'd sit in a corner and brood while everyone else talked at those high teas, well then he was only dreaming up some offence to his soul so that he could write a poem about it, often, you'll smile to know, it was nothing more than a longing for everyone to leave so that he could take me to bed, but he never wanted to have a child and when I conceived one I broke the news to him speculatively. What if there were, etc., you know, the proverbial beating about the bush. He went into one of his huge silences when the idea finally broke through to his mind. I thought his horror of children was only a literary pose. In our earlier talks he'd shown me passages from people, Flaubert I think was one, who rejected the idea of having children. That's all men, I complained, what do *they* know? And then he pulled out Virginia Woolf's diaries and thrust before me a page he'd marked. I was quite horrified to see what dear old Virginia had written. It's stuck in my brain ever since. Yes, even to have children would be useless, she'd written. Even. God, how horrible that *even* is! But I got over the shock and continued to think it was only a literary pose with Shimmers, he was only making himself think the way he thought his favourite writers had done and that when the child came he would naturally be filled with a love for it and be accepting of life. But to tell you the truth I don't know what he really thinks. We live as before, I believe. Well, perhaps some things have changed. We make love less frequently and that too in a detached sort of way as if the act were a tentatively experimental indulgence of a disenchanted celibacy, but that could be just the passing years. Well, oh dear, what I meant to say, dear Caro, is that you really ought to have a child, in fact I urge you to, I implore you to, because otherwise you will remain incomplete. Incomplete that is not as a woman but as a *feminist*. I know this is going to make you mad, I'm sorry, and yes, I remember your rejection of sex with men because it is always a re-enactment of the woman being raped, but dear dear Caro, there must be a way of remaining sexually pure and becoming a mother, and how else are you ever going to know what it really means to be a woman?

When Caroline Hadfield made her letters from Isabel available to

155

me, she cautioned, 'You must remember, Mr Pons, that dear Isabel was a very temperamental person. Her Latin blood, I suppose. She would blow in like a hurricane and devastate me with the sheer quantity of her news and then not be heard even to breathe for months. Twice it was years – until the final catastrophe, which I still can't bear to think of, the sheer horror of it is too awful to contemplate.'

I reminded her that she had visited Isabel in Arizona, and she said, looking up from the file of letters in her lap and appearing quite bemused, 'Oh yes, my spring in the desert! After the sheer dreariness of one more February in London it is quite exhilarating to fly into sunlight. But of course I don't need to tell you about the light and the air of the desert. You come from there! It does penetrate one's being though, all that brilliance.'

She closed her eyes for a moment and breathed in deeply, filling her lungs with a memory of the desert air – which, of course, was a false memory, being a perception only of a stranger for whom the novelty of the environment lent it a pristine condition it did not possess, for the reality was that the air she had breathed in Arizona was considerably polluted. 'You spent a fortnight with Isabel?' I prompted her, wanting facts about the Shimomura family and not some revelation of Miss Hadfield's mystical attachment to the desert.

'It's such a tense experience, seeing a friend after so many years,' she said almost sadly. 'It can be sheer murder!'

'What happened?' I asked, anticipating her digression into another generalization.

'Oh, it was very charming, of course, being with dear Isabel. But one couldn't *talk* with her about anything. It was all the child with her, Nichola this and Nichola that. The little girl must have been two years old and was still too precious to be vulgarized to *Nickie*. So it was *Nichola, Nichola* all day long. A dear little thing, I admit, but I thought I'd die of sheer boredom, admiring her eternally. Luckily, Isabel had to go and teach some of the afternoons. I went to the campus with her a few times or stayed back to talk to Shimmers. He'd gone quieter since leaving London. Tended to brood. But when he talked at least it wasn't about the child. In fact, he said nothing about the child. He just left her in her room to sleep and if she began to cry he let her cry. Once I thought the crying unbearable and got up to go and see but

156

he said I shouldn't, he didn't want, he said, to spoil her with attention.'

'What did he talk about, then?'

'Oh, he was very polite. Asked about my work. He wasn't interested in gossip about his London acquaintances. And he certainly wasn't interested in talking about himself. Or in reminiscing. He had an absolute hatred for nostalgia. It occurred to me afterwards that he had already given up.'

Her final phrase startled me, and I asked, 'What do you mean, *given up*?'

'Well, I didn't think he was interested in life.'

Was that not an enormous presumption, I wondered.

'Well, what I mean is life as it is ordinarily lived.'

I could not help smiling and asking how else could one live it but ordinarily, there was only one way of breathing what little air the planet still afforded us.

'He knew he had to,' Miss Hadfield said, 'live that is, in the ordinary way, but he did not strike me as being interested in paying attention to doing so. He let it happen in a resentful sort of way. I mean on Saturdays, for example, they had poolside parties. Two or three families would come over. There was one friend of Isabel's whom I remember quite sharply. Celia, who had an opinion about everything and an eagerness to express it. One could tell Shimmers quite despised her, for while he remained aloof from the controversial talk of others he'd occasionally take a cynical jab at Celia. Half a dozen children screamed and splashed in the pool. Shimmers kept himself busy at a distance. Attending to the drinks, making the barbecue a much more elaborate ritual than it is. One could tell he simply wasn't interested in being there although it was his own house. That's what I mean, he'd given up.'

I asked if she knew who the guests were. 'Social scientists, all of them,' she answered. 'Friends of Isabel's mainly. A terribly old-fashioned group, really. Male professors with wives devoted to advancing their careers. A rather provincial lot, if I may say so, with the worst bourgeois pretensions. Quite a sad spectacle, really, those eager females jealously guarding their husbands' careers and completely ignorant of any feminist principle.'

I assured her that she did not offend me by thus characterizing my colleagues and their families, and exclaimed, 'You're right on the money!'

'Everyone admired Isabel, and that was the main thing. I rather suspect that she had gathered around her as her favoured friends those of her colleagues who would flatter her and among whom she would appear brilliant. None of them had any idea who Shimmers was, except that he was Isabel's husband. Perhaps I'm mistaken when I say he'd given up, for he could have been merely protecting his anonymity and letting Isabel enjoy the attention she craved. But no, I don't think I'm mistaken. I do believe his world was elsewhere.'

Caroline Hadfield sat with the file of Isabel's letters in her lap. While she talked, she idly turned the pages without looking at them. 'You know,' she said, 'I suddenly said to Isabel one day that I had a craving to travel by Greyhound bus, and so I went away to Los Angeles for five days. Of course, I had no such craving at all. I needed to escape from her, can you believe it! It's terribly sad to think one goes out of one's way to see an old friend only to experience a pressing need to avoid her! Shimmers drove me to the bus station. Talked about the smog, about Beverly Hills, in other words he did not talk at all. And when he picked me up five days later, it was I who talked about the smog and about Beverly Hills. I had three more days to spend before flying back to London. The tension was worse now. I think each of us knew I'd gone to LA so that we wouldn't get on one another's nerves but insisted on pretending that I'd gone out of natural curiosity and, to sustain this fiction, felt obliged whenever we were together to talk incessantly about my visit to California, a dialogue that was inevitably hollow and confirmed the existence of the very idea it was meant to suppress. It was sheer agony, I can tell you! Do you know what I did to survive those three days? I became utterly absorbed in little Nichola. I discovered a deep passion for children! I wanted to do everything for the sweet little girl. Walk in the garden with her in my arms. Sit by her bath where she splashed water while playing with her plastic ducks. Change her clothes. Do everything for her. Isabel was entranced, of course. She really thought she'd converted me to desiring motherhood. I don't think Shimmers was taken in. But I held on to Nichola to the moment I had to board the plane, clasping her against my bosom as Shimmers and Isabel drove me to the airport, and not letting go of her until the flight was called, talking all the time about her pretty little dimples, her little black eyes, her little long fingers, her sweet little chin, and provoking from Isabel the sort of maternal commentary that is a great bore to hear. I don't know how Shimmers put up with it all. At the final moment, it was he and not Isabel who took Nichola from me. Of course, if I'd known then what was going to happen, then perhaps I'd not have felt the relief I did when I entered the plane.'

She stood up, pulling out from the file the photocopied pages she had made for me. 'It's awfully sad, isn't it,' she said, 'that afterwards we always want our experience not to have been so pathetically miserable as it was? We would revise reality if we could, but alas, in the living present we always fail ourselves.'

It would be difficult to detect from Isabel's letters the tension that Miss Hadfield had described. For several months Isabel wrote long gossip-filled letters as if her friend's visit had been a socially brilliant event and she must be sent the latest developments of a drama in which she had recently starred. She was given long soap-opera details of the lives of people she had met during a barbecue, possibly talked to for five minutes, and whom she could no longer remember. Isabel was obsessively engrossed in the small social world of which she saw herself the centre. That, the politics of the university, and Nichola constituted all her life. The striking thing about these letters is that there is scarcely any mention in them of Shimomura.

– I have decided to become a US citizen! she announced to her English friend some time later when their correspondence had again become irregular. She had recently spent a holiday in her native country, having taken Nichola with her to show her off to her family. Do you know, she had written, people live in little fortresses, with armed guards? Life in Lima has become quite intolerable. Everyone is a prisoner in his own house. There is of course a large political debate going on; where is there not one? But to reduce a people to killing? She was revolted by what she saw. And returning to the opulent contrast of her Arizona home, she felt the necessity for an attachment more committed than that of a resident alien. America was, after all, her daughter's native land and by now Nichola's future had become more important than her own. But in this letter, too, there was no mention of Shimomura.

There was one striking, and remarkably romantic, outburst after she had become a US citizen. Oh South America, she suddenly seemed to cry aloud, why do I still dream of the Andes! Oh, Caro, you cannot know this most invisible of all pains that comes from having had to reject the origins of your self. Returning there, I found it had become a degraded land. It no longer seemed to be the same country my childhood had discovered to be its own, whose very trees and birds were objects in a nursery of perpetual delight.

Isabel discovered in her emotions a necessity to return to those scenes she had deliberately wanted to exorcize from her memory: the passion with which she became an American also created within her an urgent anxiety to return to her native land in order to appease her conscience by offering it evidence that her rejection of it had been correct. It is almost as if she wished to experience the harsh misery of common Peruvians so as to be confirmed in her conviction that the cancelling of her past identity had been a necessary sacrifice. She returned to Lima twice within a year, taking Nichola with her. The barricaded homes of her aunts alone were sufficient symbols, but she witnessed more: a male cousin, who had driven to a hospital one afternoon to visit a friend recovering from wounds suffered during a car bomb outside a bank, disappeared for three days and then was found staggering about naked in the Campo de Marte, his chest covered with cigarette burns. All he could recount was that three men had attacked him in the hospital car park and then driven him away in his own car. Beyond that, he had no memory of what had happened to him and how he had arrived in the Campo de Marte.

Each time Isabel returned to the States it was as if she had escaped from some brutally authoritarian territory, and for a short time at least it was thrilling to be again in Arizona. But the anxiety that had taken her to Peru would return. She decided she needed a stronger bond with the USA in order to expel from her mind her sentimental attachment to the scenes of her childhood. Perhaps this was only a rationalization of a stronger instinct with her: she concluded that she needed to have more children so that a growing American family about her would inhibit the tormenting dreams of her native land. At least a new anxiety distracted her for a time: how to persuade her husband of her pressing need. She knew she would have to take a reckless risk with her marriage and pretend that there had been an accident and not some secret plan to trick Shimomura into accepting another child. When the time came to tell him that she had again conceived, she hoped that he would, as he had been with Nichola, be accepting of what could no longer be reversed; but there was no guarantee that he would not believe that he had been deceived and that her scheme which was calculated to resolve a conflict within her soul would end instead by creating a fatal conflict within her marriage.

When she was certain of her pregnancy, she kept the information to herself for longer than was necessary to prevent the question of a possible abortion even to be suggested by Shimomura. She simply could not bring herself to make the revelation. The long summer vacation was at hand and again she was taken by the idea of going once more to Peru. She wanted again to be in the middle of the scenes of her childhood and to confirm to herself once and for all that the scenes were now irrelevant and possessed no sentimental value, that her emotions could no longer be touched by her past, and that it was only the future now of her children in their country that held any meaning. The thought that one more visit to Peru would finally rid her of any emotional necessity again to return to her native land ironically made her desperate to fly to Lima, and she could not wait another ten days so that Shimomura could go with her, as he wanted to: though the semester had ended, there was some business concerning the dissertation of a post-graduate student who worked under Shimomura's supervision that delayed the start of his holiday. It was decided that he would follow Isabel and Nichola to Lima a fortnight later.

As it turned out, Shimomura never saw his wife and daughter again.

On the flight to Los Angeles, Isabel wrote a short letter to Shimomura in which she told him of her pregnancy. She posted the letter from the international airport before boarding the flight to Lima.

ii Peruvian election

'I've a memory,' Isabel said to Tía Lourdes, 'of going to the mountains with Father. But funnily, the mountain peaks are somehow mixed up with a dense tropical jungle.'

Her aunt Lourdes, a stout woman in her early 60s, looked up from her cup of coffee at the grey mist that was thickening to a fog over the Pacific, and then smiled at Isabel, her pointed chin raised in her direction. 'That's two trips Mario used to love,' she said. 'Don't you remember a river, too?'

'Why, yes,' Isabel replied. 'With very large ships sailing on it.'

Tía Lourdes laughed. 'Well, they were quite large, but you were so small then everything must have looked gigantic.' She glanced

161

at the ocean and remarked, 'I'm afraid we're not going to be lucky with the weather. It's not clearing up. Quite the reverse.'

They were sitting in a café in Chorrillos late in the morning, having driven down from the aunt's house in Barranco, encouraged by the optimistic weather forecast to go for a walk on Playa Agua Dulce. But the mist, swirling sluggishly on the ocean as though ghostly white figures swayed drunkenly on the water's surface and then fell in slow motion to be drawn into the cold depth, became denser and the grey light turned gloomier.

'What were they, the two trips that Father so loved?'

'There is a town in the north,' Tía Lourdes said, a memory of her own childhood released by Isabel's. 'Huaraz, trapped between the Cordillera Blanca and the Cordillera Negra. We went there as children. Your grandfather was a great one for putting his whole family in the American car he was so proud of and taking off on long trips. Poor Mother was always terrified. The roads were bad in those days. Mostly dirt and potholes. But wherever there was a track to be seen in the jungle or on the side of a mountain, Father made for it. The children have to learn geography and economics, he would say. The best education in the world. He said that to placate Mother. The fact is, he loved his country. He could not take his eyes off her or leave any part of her untouched.'

Isabel had never seen her grandfather, who had died in a small plane, crashing in the jungle, before she was born. But Tía Lourdes's memory filled her suddenly with an unbearable passion for the recovering of her own childhood memory of the interior of Peru. It filled her, too, with nostalgia and with regret. She had spent so much of her life in exile! And now, having become an American, she found herself unexpectedly tormented by the thought that she had rejected the true, the vital America, that Andean and Amazonian America which was peculiarly her own, created physically within her by memory, which, she realized, was the strongest mentor of the self. The present, she knew she could come to terms with; but the past, with its huge gap of absence, would become, she feared, if it was not already, a source of infinite sadness.

'In Huaraz, Mario must have taken you where our father took us. On a long uphill walk from the town. Past the cemetery and up through the pine forest to the mirador. Halfway through the forest I'd begin to whine. I was a tremendous whiner as a kid, I'm afraid. So that Father would pick me up and hoist me on his shoulders. And

I would reach the mirador high on Father's shoulders. And I would scream out, *There, there!* Father would pull me up and, holding me at the armpits, swing me around so that the little index finger at the end of my arm that I had flung out to point to the peak of the Huascarán would make one circle in the air and I would be saying *There, there!* at the entire horizon. Now my finger would be pointing at Huascarán, now at Huandoy, and now at San Cristóbal as the great Andean peaks swung about my head.'

As Tía Lourdes described her childhood memory, Isabel believed she was experiencing her own past. That was exactly how her father had swung her in the air! The memory had remained forgotten all these years and had begun to surface, distant and dreamlike, since her arrival from Arizona. Returning to Peru for what she had thought was going to be one last time – though she did not preclude coming again as a tourist or to visit the family – returning the last time still with attachments to sever that she had considered redundant on becoming American, she had discovered that each cut resulted in new growth of unexpected vitality.

During the first fortnight, she had enjoyed the visitor's delight in meeting former acquaintances and listening to the family gossip. In spite of the violence that had increased, it gave her pleasure to take Nichola with her and walk in the squares in the centre of Lima, and especially in those streets in their vicinity that held some special association – a theatre where as a schoolgirl she had come under the spell of Calderón de la Barca, a café she had frequented at the age of 15, convinced she was very grown up, in the company of a journalist with whom she believed herself fallen in love but who turned out to be using her to pry out secrets concerning her father who was by then a minister in the government. Nichola was only 7, and Isabel's several little pilgrimages to the city were really only a private indulgence: but the mother was resolved to hold her daughter's hand when she silently re-experienced her own past, so that the living child, as well as the one coming to life in her womb, would receive the transmission of her own memory as an unseen gift.

On arriving in Lima, she had not telephoned Shimomura. She did not want to call him until she first heard from him, either on the phone or by letter, his response to the news she had posted him from Los Angeles, that she was pregnant. He had remained silent. His plan had been to fly to Lima a fortnight after she had left Arizona, but he did not come. Isabel let a few more days pass, and then Shimomura's silence and absence began to bother her. Finally, she called the number of their house in Arizona. There was no answer. She tried for two days, calling at different hours, but received no answer. She phoned the offices of several of her colleagues at the university. No one picked up the phone. The semester had ended, finals and commencement were done with, the university was closed until summer school, which she remembered began in another week.

When that week, too, had passed and Shimomura still had not been in touch, she tried calling the university again and finally contacted Ed Mossman. Explaining her perplexity to him, she persuaded him to go to her house and to see if he could find any information about her husband, giving him a day to discover what he could. When she called him the next day, he reported that he had seen no one at the house. There was no sign either of anyone being there. The front lawn was burnt, the dead grass already the colour of the desert sand. But there was an automatic sprinkler system, she cried aloud, as if the loss of the lawn were somehow more momentous than the mysterious absence of the husband. Ed Mossman guessed it had been switched off. He'd contacted some friends in the English department. No one could tell him where Shimomura was, though someone speculated he could have gone to London.

Isabel could not think why he would wish to go to England. But her apprehension grew that his disappearance was a reaction to the news she had sent him. If so, then it seemed to her a monstrously unjust reaction. Why did he not tell her that he hated her for having conceived again, if indeed that was what he felt? Why was he not indignant, why could he not express his outrage? And get this damned bad temper over with! For all she knew, the child she carried might be his son. Was there a man who did not want a son? What was the matter with him that he went into a huge sulk and pretended he no longer existed? Isabel thought that she was getting quite mad with her husband. She would have a monumental row with him when he came out of his stupid sulk.

Shimomura's silence and absence irritated and perplexed her, but affected her quite differently at the unconscious level. Not finding her husband, the search she began was for herself. And when she heard Tía Lourdes describe how her father had swung her on the mirador just outside Huaraz and she had seen the great peaks of the Andes, Isabel's own buried memory of her own father doing the same to her

164

suddenly came vividly to the forefront of her mind. Her immediate decision, still unexpressed because as yet unconscious, was that she must take Nichola to Huaraz and show her the wonderful peaks of Huascarán, Huandoy and San Cristóbal – only, alas, little Nichola was not little enough to be carried on her shoulders and then swung in the air.

But Tía Lourdes had begun to describe the second of her father's favourite journeys into the interior, and Isabel realized that a second revelation was at hand, a restructuring of her memory of the jungle. 'Up through the heart of the country, with stops at the oases in the northern desert. This land has everything, your grandfather was fond of repeating. He taught us to know colours by looking at the country, from the virgin white snow on the Andes to the inky blue-black shadows in the jungle. The ochre desert was eerie. It made Mario and me go dumb, too scared to talk. All that empty barren space, if you half closed your eyes you could see ghosts where the wind was shifting the sand. Sometimes we went another way, not through the desert, but east over the cordillera.'

As Tía Lourdes talked of her childhood, Isabel remembered her own and arrived again at the river towns, one year in Pucallpa on the Ucayali, another time in Yurimaguas, from where her memory of the ships came.

Tía Lourdes was most vivid when she talked about arriving in Yurimaguas, but Isabel hardly heard her, discovering within herself an overwhelming recollection that came from a time when she was so small she could not say it was her own history she remembered and not some images from a magazine or a film, and she eagerly asked her aunt, 'Tell me, could my father have gone there later, could he have taken me there?'

It took Tía Lourdes a moment to leave the train of her own thoughts to attend to Isabel's question. 'Why, yes!' she answered. 'There was a famous incident on the river Huallaga. You must have been three or four. Mario had taken his family to Yurimaguas and had the bright idea of renting a boat and sailing downriver to Iquitos. Just past one of the small river towns' – but before Tía Lourdes could say precisely where and describe the event, Isabel was alive again on that day which was, she knew without needing to calculate, thirty-three years ago, and they had sailed out of the little town of Santa Cruz where they had taken on supplies of which she could remember only a huge bunch of green bananas.

Chug-chug-chug laboured the little boat, its small engine straining even though they sailed with the stream. After one bend in the river, they seemed remote from any human habitation. Huge trees with massive trunks grew on the river-banks, long loops of creepers hanging from their thick branches, and behind them the jungle, dark and motionless, was periodically pierced by the sharp cry of a single bird. Little Isabel stood on the deck, holding her father's leg just below the knee, and stared at the land that seemed to bob up and down and looked for the bird which struck her as being in pain. Past two or three more bends, the current forced the boat close to a bank where a fallen tree lay rotting a few feet below the surface of the water. Before they could navigate away from the bank, the boat had got stuck and the engine gone dead.

'Oh, Mario made a great drama of it,' Tía Lourdes was saying, and it seemed to the child Isabel that a voice hovering above the boat was describing what she experienced, the worry not that they were stuck but that the bird with its piercing cry had gone silent. A waiter pouring more coffee in Tía Lourdes's cup drew Isabel's attention to her immediate circumstance and awoke her to her aunt's voice. 'You were caught in the decaying vegetation in a corner of a bend in the river, some distance from the flowing stream, and though three or four larger boats sailed past your cries for help went unheard. A young man who called himself Captain Boquerón and was in charge of the boat turned out to be pathetically incompetent. Your mother said afterwards that he ought to have been thrown overboard and fed to the crocodiles.'

Isabel looked across at the grey, foggy ocean, but saw where they had been caught in the river. Actually, only one boat went past, and that a small one with a noisy engine. So, her father must have made the incident into a terrifying dream! Isabel was amused to think that her father's story, as now recounted by Tía Lourdes, was more interesting than her recovered memory of the event as largely boring. But she realized that in her live experience of it she had yet to come to the moment of terror. Night fell. Captain Boquerón had but one lamp on board. The darker it got the louder were the screams and the shrieks from the animals in the jungle. But even that was not the terror that awaited them.

It was in the morning, Tía Lourdes was saying, and now Isabel recognized the literal truth of her words, that a boat came up with three men in it who had seen them.

Captain Boquerón was suspiciously quiet and submissive, letting himself be taken first into the larger boat where he appeared to be locked into a cabin. It was realized later that he had not been incompetent at all, that the previous day's misadventure had in fact been planned with him as a key accomplice. Isabel and her parents were next taken on board and believed themselves to have been rescued from their marooned boat. But the three men were not very communicative and proceeded to sail silently downriver. It was when instead of continuing towards Tres Unidos they made to go up a tributary that flowed into the Huallaga that Isabel's father became alarmed. Now the men did not even give laconic answers to his questions but merely stared grimly. 'I don't like this,' he whispered to his wife and she, looking over his shoulder, gave a sudden start. One of the men who had gone into a cabin was just coming out carrying a gun.

Soon all three men were armed. The boat sailed slowly upriver. Isabel slept in her father's arms. They docked at a wooden jetty by a clearing above the bank where a few primitive huts had been constructed. A group of seven or eight men and half a dozen women, several of them armed with rifles, stood about the clearing. Isabel was taken by one of the women. Her father remonstrated, shouted abuse, but was pulled away by one of the armed men and taken into a hut. The mother was placed in another hut. Isabel cried in the arms of the woman who held her strongly, preventing her attempts to jump to the ground and to run after her father.

As Isabel heard the story from Tía Lourdes of the time she and her parents were captured and remained prisoners in the jungle for five days she realized why the memory had remained suppressed all these years. 'The mercy was they were not so brutal in those days,' Tía Lourdes was saying. 'There was some sense of honour and decency among would-be revolutionaries – though no one knew who your captors were, whether revolutionaries or merely thugs out to make money. Today, either group would end an episode like that with a blood bath. This country has gone rotten.' But Isabel was thinking, Why yes it was I in the jungle a little child witnessing the humiliation of my father and did not want to remember all these years but the jungle was there all these years in my blood the slow winding rivers of the interior beyond the Andes all these years the dark men in the canoes who drift along the banks waiting to ambush some adventurous soul, and repossessing her past by the suddenly illuminated memory she wanted to take her living daughter and her unborn child to the same interior, as if there existed some shrine to the father that had become buried under the jungle's fast-breeding layers of vegetation and the father's memory demanded an obligatory pilgrimage of discovery and restoration.

There had still been no news from Shimomura when she set out for the interior with Nichola. At first she decided to rent a car but, considering the violence prevalent in the country, thought that to be driving alone with her young daughter would be dangerous and so was persuaded to seek the security of numbers and to travel by bus. She chose the most distant destination that could be fitted in her schedule, Pucallpa on the river Ucayali, determining that once she had seen the real images that constituted a recurring dream of rivers, she could then fly to the northern interior and return by bus via Huaraz, where she would complete her pilgrimage and, she hoped, be released for ever from what gripped her to this strange land of her birth, by displaying her daughter and her unborn child to the Andean peaks of Huascarán, Huandoy and San Cristóbal as she herself had once been by her father.

The full bus headed for the mountains and the central highway. She was delighted by her daughter's endless curiosity in the passing scene. Nichola remarked upon the rosy-cheeked Indian children in their pathetic dwellings in the foothills. Or, where streams flowed down the side of a mountain, she was amazed to see banks of red, orange and purple flowers growing in a wild profusion. Even the scattered fog that floated above valleys as the bus climbed towards the Anticona Pass filled the young girl with wondrous delight.

Isabel had not expected the bus to leave the highway for short excursions to small towns and villages where it dropped off and picked up passengers. But she was relieved to notice that Nichola was not, as she had feared, bored by what appeared to herself as unnecessary interruptions of their natural progress. In fact, Nichola gave a little cheer each time the bus slowed down to make a turning on to a narrow road. Perhaps it was because two of the stops had been at cafés where she had been treated to a Coke. Though she herself found the diversions from the highway to be tiresome, Isabel was not prepared to admit to being bored, for she persuaded herself that she thus saw more of her country than she had bargained for and that it was in these unexpected variations to a routine that one sometimes experienced the rare, the unimagined event.

After crossing the Anticona Pass, the bus stopped at a larger town which was served by the highway. Everyone, including the driver, got off for a twenty-minute break, the stop being at a popular restaurant. Two other buses were already parked there. The long counters where people ate snacks and sipped coffee or soft drinks were crowded. Long queues had formed in the lavatories. Babies were crying and older children were running wildly among the adults standing patiently to be served. When alighting from the bus, Isabel felt impatient for the first time with the frequent stops they had been making, especially as she observed the crowd and realized that they were going to have a frustrating delay. But stepping down to the ground, she happened to look across the wide car park.

They had come to one side of a large treeless square with a diminutive football pitch at one end. A small crowd stood in the centre of the square gaping at a curious object. A few military policemen, armed with rifles, kicked their heels in the dust. There were shops and smaller cafés on the opposite side. Finding from the driver how much time they had, Isabel decided to go to a less crowded café across the square. But while she had the driver's attention, she remarked to him, 'We've been stopping in every little village, how will we ever get to Pucallpa by tomorrow?'

'Pucallpa?' the driver asked, astonished. They were standing by the door of the bus, and the driver beckoned Isabel to take a couple of steps to the front and look above the windscreen. The sign, she saw, read 'La Oroya'.

What should she do now, she asked, realizing her error. Nothing but go on to La Oroya, the driver said. Catch the next day's express to Pucallpa from there. The thought that they had made the several excursions to the villages and were making the present stop only because they had caught the wrong bus somehow vexed her. The knowledge that her experience would have been different had she not committed an error led her to resent the stops as if they had been forced upon her by some malevolent influence: that which she had been prepared to find charming when the side trips seemed part of the natural progress she now felt to be a form of punishment, for where she had wanted to see the grander vistas of the mountains she was being dragged away on petty excursions and shown trivial little villages in which she had no interest.

Luckily, Nichola was still cheerful. Isabel took her hand and crossed the road in order to walk across the square. The crowd in the centre of the square was staring in wonder at a black saloon car that was festooned with garlands of paper flowers and red ribbon. With strips of ribbon stretching from the front bumper, over the bonnet and down to the rear bumper, the car looked like a gift-wrapped present waiting to be opened. Through the window, a man in a bowler hat could be seen in the driver's seat, his lips parted in a self-contented smile. He nodded at the crowd and raised a white-gloved hand as if acknowledging cheers. The crowd, however, merely gaped silently. Isabel was too preoccupied with her own vexation to become curious, and proceeded to the café on the opposite road. Inside, when she and Nichola were seated at a table, she heard a man two tables away say, 'Why do we bother with elections in this country? They're only an excuse for more killings!'

The remark and the crowd in the square suddenly brought to the front of her mind an idea Isabel had suppressed since it did not concern her in any material sense, for she was no longer a citizen: municipal elections were being held in the country and were both a test of the strength of the democratic movement and a prelude to the presidential election six months hence. An acquaintance in Lima had talked about trouble in the country, with the Sendero Luminoso group determined to sabotage the elections, and had said, 'This is not a good time to be travelling.' But she was obsessed by her own interior compulsion which she saw as possessing such spiritual purity that any question of physical danger seemed irrelevant. She had simply refused to become concerned by the country's political situation. But now, vaguely anxious, she asked the waiter, 'When are the elections?' He looked at her with surprise at her ignorance. 'Tomorrow,' he answered, 'that is, if the communists will let anyone vote.' No, there wouldn't be any trouble, a man at the next table said. They were expecting the most popular of the presidential candidates in another hour. He was making a campaign swing to calm people's fears and to show his support to his party's candidates in the municipal elections. He was going to fly right into the square in a helicopter. Did she see that car in the square? The future president was going to be driven in it round some of the villages. No, there wasn't going to be any trouble. Another man disputed this conclusion. The lively argument that followed somehow added to Isabel's vexation. The nation's politics depressed her, the causes that roused people's passions seemed so terribly hopeless when she thought of how drug money had begun to corrupt the country.

170

When fifteen minutes later, holding Nichola's hand, she hurried back across the square, the crowd around the presidential car had grown. More military police arrived and were looking up at the sky. The helicopter was not due for another hour, however.

Isabel hurried past the crowd and wondered why she had been feeling unaccountably ill at ease the last quarter of an hour. Something that ought to have been there was missing. The cold mountain air ought to have been refreshing but it was heavy with dust and carried a smell of decay. The town seemed to be on a plateau and afforded no views of the mountains. It was difficult to see far through the dusty yellow haze.

As she had feared, the twenty-minute stop proved frustratingly long. It was an hour before they again climbed up the highway. As they drove away, she saw the military police in the square holding the crowd back from a marked-out area where the helicopter was due to land. When the bus was a short distance out of the town, the highway stretched before them in a series of wide loops as it descended into a valley. There was no traffic. The driver took the bus sailing down the first loop at a safely controlled speed, but then he inexplicably slowed down and proceeded more with his foot on the brake than on the accelerator. He kept looking at the rear-view mirror. Twice he slowed down to a crawl, and then, making a show of changing gears and pumping the accelerator pedal, he spurted noisily up an incline and glided smoothly down another loop. But again he slowed to a crawl and held his head sideways, leaning forward with his left ear directed to the front as if he heard suspicious sounds from the engine. He changed down to second gear and pumped the accelerator pedal furiously as though charging a dying engine to remain alive. Then suddenly he began to drive fast. Some of the passengers clapped and shouted their approval, being relieved that the bus was not about to break down. But a moment later the same passengers screamed aloud when the driver took a bend in the road at a dangerous speed.

On a straight stretch they were overtaken by a pick-up truck. As it sped past, Isabel saw that three armed men in khaki jackets stood behind the driver's cab. The pick-up cut in at the front of the bus and slowed down. One of the men was making some gesture to the bus driver. The pick-up left the highway and halted on the narrow grassy margin. The bus stopped behind it. 'What's happening?' Nichola cried, grasping her mother's arm.

'Shh.' Isabel craned her neck to see through the windscreen. 'Remain quiet and still,' she whispered to her daughter.

'Why? What are they going to do?'

'Nickie!' Isabel scarcely moved her lips when she spoke.

'I want to go home,' Nichola protested.

Some of the other passengers were murmuring to one another. The majority stared out in deadly silence. A few hung their heads low, their eyes tightly closed and their lips silently moving in prayer.

Two men jumped off the pick-up and jogged to the door of the bus. One of them fired off his semi-automatic rifle in the air before stepping into the bus.

'All the men out, come on, quickly, up and out, at once, one two three, come on!' He waved his rifle above his shoulder and then held it against his side and aimed it at the seats as he shouted. His companion stood by the door and as the male passengers alighted he ordered them to form a line up the road, on the edge of the grassy margin. The third man on the pick-up bed stood there pointing a mounted machine-gun at the assembling line. Isabel counted the men as they left the bus. There were seventeen of them.

From lower down the mountainside, a truck laden with timber could be seen slowly climbing up the highway and approaching a wide bend in the road. Three cars drove behind it, waiting for an opportunity to overtake the truck. Because of the tilt of the land, the small convoy could be seen from the bus, but the position of the vehicles on the road, though it afforded them a partial view of the bus, blinded them to any possible oncoming traffic and so the drivers proceeded cautiously.

When the men from the bus, except for its driver, had been assembled on the edge of the grassy margin, a man who had been sitting next to the driver in the pick-up came out and, brandishing a revolver, began to shout out some phrases. Only the odd word reached Isabel. Women and children inside the bus had begun a lamentation. Some were crying loudly, some talking crazily. Nichola had begun to sob.

The timber-laden truck came up the highway. The drivers of the cars behind it, seeing the empty straight stretch, overtook the truck but, having the slope against them and being in a low gear, could only do so slowly. Each driver watched the roadside scene as he drove past. The driver of the truck, who could only crawl up the highway with his load, leaned his head out of his window and looked at the line of men held up on the roadside as he drove on.

The man with the revolver was still shouting at the lined men when the truck reached the top of the incline and went out of view round a curve. The women inside the bus were crying hysterically. Nichola sobbed. Isabel was mad with herself for not having flown to get her wretched pilgrimage over with, or at least to have rented a car. How could she have been so sentimenal about some mountain peaks, she asked herself bitterly. It was no longer her country, she was rid of it, and its natives, the barbarians!

She could see clearly only a few of the seventeen men who were being shouted at. They looked to her to be all illiterate peasants. Their faces showed confusion, incomprehension and fear. They had done nothing to be chosen as victims. 'Shh.' She patted Nichola's cheek and stroked her hair. 'I want to go home,' Nichola cried. Isabel gently passed her hand down Nichola's neck and leaned up to look through the windscreen. The man with the revolver was walking in a military style in front of the line of peasants and shouting out some command. Three of the peasants stepped forward. They were ordered to climb up the bed of the pick-up. Their wives and children in the bus began to cry aloud and scream. 'Mommy, I want to go home,' Nichola wailed. 'Shh.'

The pick-up drove away. The remaining fourteen men broke their line and ran to the bus. Women and children were still screaming. The men were crowded in the door of the bus, shouting at one another. Two at the front staggered forward and several behind them burst in. The driver shouted at them, 'Hey, you don't have to smash up the bus!' Isabel held Nichola's head and pressed it against her shoulder. The bus began to move, the driver announcing he was going back to the town they had recently stopped at. It was the safest thing to do since La Oroya was in the hands of the Sendero Luminoso.

Isabel wondered how the driver knew this as she watched him make the dangerous manoeuvre of turning round the bus on the narrow highway. But she listened also to the men who had returned to the bus. The three who had been chosen at random were being taken away to La Oroya. The guerrillas were staging a big demonstration there. They were going to make sure no one voted in the elections. They were going to cut people's index fingers off if they tried to vote. The talk of the men only intensified the hysterical wailing of the wives whose husbands had been taken away. No reason was given for their abduction, and that only increased the terror experienced by those still free. But then, just as they were entering the car park by the restaurant where they had stopped less than two hours ago, one of the men stood up and shouted at the driver, 'You're one of them, aren't you? You were expecting them, you kept slowing down.' The driver stopped the bus, pulled the handbrake quickly, and rose to leave the bus. By now several other men had stood up, too, and were shouting at the driver that he was a collaborator. The wives of the missing men had begun to scream at him. The driver dashed for the door but a crowd of men and several women were up with him and a mass of them seemed to tumble out of the bus. In a moment the bus was empty except for Isabel and Nichola. Isabel sat stroking her daughter's head, finding tears come to her own eyes when she heard Nichola repeatedly say, 'I want to go home.' As she comforted her daughter, Isabel noticed that the square was now empty. The presidential candidate must have arrived and commenced his tour.

When Nichola had quietened, Isabel led her out of the bus. She did not want to see what the crowd was doing to the driver and hurried to the restaurant. The cries and the shouts could be heard all through the restaurant. The driver was being beaten to death by the mob. The crowd in the restaurant pretended that nothing was happening. Isabel described her luggage to a boy who minded people's cars while they were in the restaurant and offered him a good tip if he could collect it for her. In the meanwhile she began to ask among the waiters if there was any possibility of renting a car in that town. At first there seemed to be none, but a man who was not a waiter overheard her enquiry and said, 'García Moreno has a car all dressed up and nowhere to go.'

What did he mean? García Moreno ran a spare parts dealership in town and had offered his Lada to drive the presidential candidate on a tour of the villages. He'd dressed up the car with ribbons, as for a wedding. But the candidate had cancelled his visit at the last minute. Word had reached Lima of the stepped-up Sendero Luminoso attacks in the region. García Moreno was all dressed up, too. Did the lady say she would pay in US dollars? García Moreno might just be willing to accept her offer.

With the boy carrying her luggage and Nichola holding her hand, Isabel was led by the man to García Moreno's store in a street off the northern side of the square. She saw the car from a distance. Parked in front of the store, the black saloon gift-wrapped with paper flowers and red ribbon looked even more incongruous than it had in the square. García Moreno, a small fat man in a swallow-tailed coat and bowler hat, stood outside his store, smoking a cigarette and admiring his car.

When he had been apprised of Isabel's offer, he lifted his hat, revealing thin black strands of hair combed across a nearly bald head, raised his face up as he opened his lips in a wide smile that showed nicotine-stained teeth, and then bowed deeply. Well, asked Isabel. No, he could not rent his car. He could not trust anyone to drive it. She would pay him to drive it, she suggested. A hundred dollars if he could drive her to Lima. No, no, not to Lima. Impossible. Not even for $500. García Moreno did not want to admit that his car would never make it back over the Anticona Pass and so pretended he was a busy man and could not afford the time to drive to Lima. But he had no intention of losing an opportunity to get some dollars. He let Isabel fret for some minutes. When he saw her begin to despair he offered to drive her to La Oroya for $200. But that was where the trouble was, she exclaimed. What trouble? García Moreno dismissed the rumours she'd heard. The government was determined to hold the elections. There were extra troops in the cities. The country was safe because everyone was worried that it was dangerous. Then why had the candidate cancelled his visit? Ha! That was for two reasons. The government wanted the Sendero Luminoso to be filled with an exaggerated sense of its own power and so become reckless and fall into the trap prepared for it. And secondly, the candidate was not Julius Caesar – his wife had a funny dream and said he must cancel his tour and so he cancelled. Men listened to women nowadays, García Moreno added, bowing respectfully to the woman before him.

Isabel was persuaded by García Moreno's statements because they were what she wanted to hear. There could be some trouble in La Oroya but she saw no reason why it should affect her. And nor, in agreeing to be driven to La Oroya, did she pause to wonder what she would do there. It had simply become in her mind a necessary destination, as if it would afford her first safety and then the means of easy transportation to Lima. She vaguely thought of being in an aeroplane without knowing whether or not La Oroya was served by an airline.

García Moreno pulled out a pair of white gloves from a pocket of his swallow-tailed coat and ceremoniously put them on. He untied the red ribbon from the rear bumper, unlocked the boot and got the boy to put Isabel's luggage in there, and retied the ribbon. Isabel gave the boy a generous tip and he stood there on the pavement gaping at the foreign-looking lady who had so much money. García Moreno bowed and opened the door to the rear seat, gesturing with a hand for his passengers to enter. Isabel hesitated a moment and wondered whether she should not ask him to remove all the ridiculous decoration. 'Why don't you get rid of all that . . .' She waved a hand in the air. García Moreno stared at her in disgust. 'Get rid of it?' he cried. 'Excuse me, but can one ask a lady to get rid of her Sunday dress?'

'Oh, don't be absurd,' Isabel said impatiently. 'You know it will look quite silly for me to be riding as if to a wedding.' García Moreno now looked at her with contempt. 'These decorations,' he declared with some vehemence, 'were approved by the committee to welcome the future president of Peru. If they are not good enough for you . . .' He shrugged his shoulders, indicating that she could go elsewhere for her transportation. He was stubbornly reluctant to remove the decorations because in his mind he had anticipated the image of driving the presidential candidate across town and into the neighbouring villages with so much pleasure that he was loath to abandon the fantasy now that the candidate had not turned up, and in order to complete his fantasy he wanted to chauffeur his dollar-paying client as though she were the candidate's surrogate. 'Oh, come on, then,' Isabel said, having become desperate to get away and deciding not to waste any more time.

There was a strong sickly smell of a perfume with which the interior of the car had been sprayed. The back of the front seats had been decorated with paper flowers in the colours of the presidential candidate's party. Isabel and Nichola sat back. García Moreno walked around the front of the car and climbed into the driver's seat.

Some minutes later, they were out of the town, proceeding slowly down the wide loops of the highway. Isabel gave Nichola a bar of chocolate she had hastily picked up at the restaurant. The moment's association with the restaurant made her reflect on the fate of the bus driver. She shuddered, and looked out at a pine forest across the valley. García Moreno drove on sedately as if he led some grand procession. There was hardly any traffic. Twice they were overtaken by cars and the amusement with which their occupants looked at García Moreno's car and its occupants reminded Isabel how absurd she must appear. Little could they tell how she hated her present situation, but saw instead a person who appeared to be proceeding according to some eccentric or burlesque notion of a festive pilgrimage. They must consider her a country simpleton or some rich woman fulfilling a lunatic fancy.

Nichola's head had fallen against her shoulder. Her eyes were closed. Isabel chided herself for putting her little girl to such unnecessary hardship. She leaned her own head back and closed her eyes, thinking of the child in her womb. The memory of the mountain peaks was forgotten, as was the quest for a river remembered from childhood, and she wondered at the senselessness of the longing that had brought her to Peru. How abominably one was a victim of contradictory persuasions!

García Moreno saw her in the rear-view mirror and observed that she had fallen asleep. He was approaching a turn-off to a road that wound down to a village in a valley which had been the first planned stop on the future president's tour. This was the region where the peasants got their livelihood from growing coca. The presidential candidate had wanted to see for himself the evidence of the coca trade. García Moreno had a payment to collect in the village. His spare parts store was only a front and his reputation in the town as 'a character' was only a disguise: García Moreno made his money as a middleman with connections in Colombia. His getting up the car to look like a country man's idea of presidential grandeur and dressing himself as a peasant's notion of a European chauffeur was part of a larger world of appearances that the town had prepared with which to deceive the future president.

Seeing the turn-off approaching, García Moreno looked again in the rear-view mirror. The lady was asleep. He decided to go down to the village to get his payment. He could always say he was taking a short cut to La Oroya. A series of hair-pin bends obliged García Moreno to step on the brakes and change gear frequently. Nichola woke up with a start and began to cry. Isabel, still asleep, mechanically stroked her head, and then suddenly shook herself awake. 'Where are we?' she cried at García Moreno. He put on his idiot grin and said to her image in the mirror, 'We'll be in La Oroya within the hour. I know the quickest way to get there.' She looked out at a plantation of young trees which she did not recognize and said, 'But this isn't the highway.' García Moreno nodded his head and answered, 'Like I said, I know the quickest way.'

The road straightened as it approached the bottom of the valley and then began to follow the bank of a winding river. Going round one of the bends, García Moreno was obliged suddenly to brake to a halt for just round the blind corner an old truck blocked the narrow road. A man who was engaged in changing the rear right tyre stood up with a start, letting go the spare that he had been in the process of fixing to the wheel. He made a gesture that indicated to García Moreno that he ought to have been driving more carefully, he had almost smashed into the crippled truck. On his part, García Moreno was furious that the man had not exercised the common rule of the road and placed a warning sign on the other side of the bend. The man's thoughtlessness had almost caused an accident.

The man leaped back and flung up his arms into the air, throwing his head back and seeing, as he did so, the small hut high on the mountainside in its camouflage of pine branches. He gave the impression of having gone out of his wits at the sudden fright of almost having been killed in a crash, for in that instant he was dashing to the river-bank from where he took a flying leap and dived into the river. But the manner in which he had flung up his arms, waving his hands like one possessed in some ceremony of black magic, was read in the hut as a signal by one who sat watching from there, his hand on a detonating device, waiting to carry out his commission to blow up the truck and with it the presidential candidate and whoever else accompanied him in the car which would be decorated as for a country wedding.

10 You

You are tucked inside a blue eiderdown sleeping bag, upon which are heaped three grey blankets, in the attic room of the flat in Drayton Gardens. Flannel pyjamas finally feel warm. A prickly, coarse woollen vest close to the skin, two pairs of grey socks pulled up to the knees, you are woolly warm inside the sleeping bag, but the stuck-out nose is ticklish in the cold air and the black locks of hair feel the wind of the high mountains blowing through them, in the slate-roofed attic flat. The milkman's dray-horse is already in the street going clippety-clop when the milkman whistles walking to the doorstep of the next house in a tinkling rattle of bottles three pints please two gold tops and one silver clippety-clop whoa there tock-tock stop and a rattling shifting of milk crates with a tinkle-tinkle of empty bottles. You are asleep in London in the dead middle of the twentieth century. The pink-faced schoolboys running in the playground among the soccer games with tennis balls, black blazers flying behind them, stopped and shouted in glee and instantly made up a song *Here comes the sav Here comes the sav Here comes the savage Who lives in the coconut tree* and went wild with malicious joviality. But one, a tall fifth-form Latin prodigy, Brian Humphreys, constant quoter of Catullus who when walking away from people sadly intoned *Omnia qui magni dispexit lumina mundi*, sighed at the foreign sound and then laughed when informed the name could be translated as a brightness, a light, as something that shimmers. *Shimmers! Why, that's splendid!* declared Humphreys and befriended the stranger because he could say to a third person in some future conversation *My luminous friend here*. And even your mother now shouts up the narrow uncarpeted wooden staircase to the attic room, *Shimmers!* and you throw the blankets away and stand up in the sleeping bag and hop around the room like in a sack race looking for the school uniform and then let the sleeping bag fall and step out of it quickly grabbing the white shirt with the soiled collar from the chair and the grey trousers from the ground, quickly put them on over the pyjamas, double-quickly grab the school tie hanging from the chair already knotted and slip it over your head and pull it tight, then a green sleeveless sweater and a grey full-sleeved sweater over that and then the black blazer, now treble-quick put on black boots, sprinkle face with cold water, brush hair, munch toast, swallow tea, grab coat and cap and briefcase fat with homework and go running down Drayton Gardens past the Society of Authors, stopping for breath at the corner with Fulham Road where you stand a moment outside the cinema and wake up in a dream looking at the stills of Elizabeth Taylor. The smoggy-smelling cold air sets you marching briskly up the road but your whole life is ruined as you enter the school building because you remember that you have a gym lesson in the morning and you are still wearing your pyjamas. Benson, the school captain and cricket captain and number one scholar bound for Balliol, is with the prefects at the school gate but you have your foot in just before the bell rings, not like last time when you were two minutes late and placed Benson in a moment's moral dilemma: should he wink and let you pass because you were his best batsman in the summer and super useful come Easter at Rugby fives or should he appear to do no favours and book you for detention with the usual lazy sods, and you are certain he'll take you aside for a private word to give the appearance of conveying a severe warning and then let you go with a wink but are shocked that he clenches his jaw, suppresses any consideration of partiality, and takes down your name. Your name! An hour's detention after school. What a way to treat your best batsman, like any other lazy sod! At four o'clock you go resentfully to detention. You sit there first angry with Benson and then thinking of the English films in which the British officers rose above favouritism and prejudice, the judges were never corrupt, and there was honour even among thieves. It is a long hour. Justice is blind. You sit there and realize come the cricket season you are going to do your damned best for Benson. He's a jolly good fellow. You are never late again. But you are a proper fool keeping your pyjamas on when you have a gym lesson first thing after the milk break. Entering the school, you start limping. You limp past the door where the PT master Mr Clay is standing getting his form, noisy 3B, into order and you say *Good morning, Mr Clay*, so that he sees you limping past. Every term there is a boy who is convinced he is the first to think up the remark that Mr Clay's wife makes a mug of him. *Watch it*, you shout at a boy who has bumped into you, *I got a sprained ankle*, and limp extra hard, glancing back to see if Mr Clay heard that. After registration you limp up to your form master and ask permission to be excused from assembly because it would be hard on your sprained ankle to stand up for the hymn. When the whole school is in assembly and is shouting blood-rousing commands at Christian soldiers marching as to war you slip to the school secretary Mrs Tyndall's office and ask if she has anything you can put on a sprained ankle. She produces a bottle of Sloane's liniment and a bit of cotton wool. You rub some on, thank the kind lady like a good boy, and limp out, having established a useful alibi. But she calls you back. She saw something when you pulled the trouser leg up and the socks down to rub the liniment on your ankle. *Do you have pyjamas on under your clothes?* she asks in a shrilly rising voice. You stare at her, gone totally dumb. *Uh it's uh special winter underwear, miss*, you say at last, and appealing to the Orient's reputation for mystery add hopefully *from Kashmir*. You almost forget to limp, making a second exit. Mr Clay does not even look at you when you ask to be excused from PT but quickly agrees. The boys are changing in the steamy room where many smells from bodies unwashed for weeks are trapped and a strong sweaty odour is rising from the naked chests and thickening the already sickening air. Mr Clay blows his whistle and says it's turning out fine, they'll go and have five-a-side football outside in the playground. You realize Mr Clay has some trouble on his mind, he's not thinking or seeing anything, and doesn't want to work. It's turning out fine, he says. It's miserable cold outside. But the boys give a cheer and go running out with nothing on but shorts, though a few put their shirts back on as they dash out, and are already dividing up into teams. You slip away to the empty form room, take a seat by the hot radiator near the window and get a thrill reading 'Porphyria's Lover' aloud, *her cheek once more Blushed bright beneath my burning kiss* and instead of the pink boys giggling at your funny accent there is a respectful silence in the class followed by thunderous applause. Class standing, applauding. Headmaster moved to tears. First prize for declamation. From the window you can see the boys down in the playground, several almost naked in the freezing cold, others with shirt-tails flying, running up and down in two games of five-a-side, what a funny lot the English to think it's turning fine when the clouds are like muddy buffalo hide. When you came on a white ship ten months ago, sailing across the gorgeous blue of the

Arabian Sea and the marvellous Mediterranean, under sunlit and moonlit skies, suddenly the world's brilliance was dimmed. Grey the passage into the Channel, grey the mouth of the Thames, grey the docks at Tilbury and dark dark dark the landscape from where the doomed were led manacled to the hulks moored in a perpetual melancholy mist. But O then came April then came May with the buds on the chestnut trees and the hawthorn bursting in white and pink glory and you knew this was an ambiguous land, its days successively so foul and fair you had not seen such contradictions in the air that alternately so soothed and tormented it seemed the breath now of angels and now of witches. Off you walked one foul and fair day, coming out of the tube at Elephant & Castle, choosing a magical name on the map for your setting forth south of the river, walking past the pub at the crossroads where unshaven and dull-eyed men in dirty, ragged coats loitered uncertainly. Black soot on the unrelieved rows of brick houses. You hurried to the Oval seeking the relief of green grass but the ground was locked and the glimpse through the bars of a gate showed only a yellowish patch of the boundary. You proceeded then along Clapham Road walking faster to get past the dreary façades of buildings and to escape the nauseating fumes from the buses and the box-shaped black taxis, recovered your breath in the Common, stopped for a cup of tea and a cigarette, Senior Service, and went determinedly along, past Putney on the Upper Richmond Road, past Barnes, pausing again when you saw green grass, in Barnes Common. The magical names had all been enchanted into the habitation of the doomed and the wretched. This was the city you had heard sung about. You were going to walk the length and breadth of it, your eyes were mad to possess its details, even to the fact that the trunks of the silver birches in Putney were not silver but an ashen grey that looked ghostly white. You remembered Hardy as you walked on and on, you remembered, *He was a man who used to notice such things*. But the black soot that hung in the air was catching at your throat as you walked for hours, for cold grey hours. And then you came to Richmond Hill and saw from an eminence the river shining as in a fanciful picture of arcadian beauty and you entered the wide spaces of Richmond Park where deer roamed and saw from a hilltop the distant city now suddenly gleaming, the sky a large golden disc behind the buildings which had shed their gloom in the late afternoon's momentary burst of sunshine, and all of London was there before you in that surprising golden light. You would walk the length and breadth of it yet, you would see the city from other heights, from the sky even, coming down again and again from visits abroad, from new exiles yet to be endured, but that sudden burst at the end of the grey day presented to you upon Richmond Park a complete vision of the city and it seemed that nature connived to reward you at the end of your weary pilgrimage. You took the tube back to Gloucester Road after a cup of tea on Richmond station and a Senior Service cigarette. Still charred black spaces among the buildings in Kensington, now five years after the war. Still the smell of death and in the eyes of men and women the unhappiness that death brings. So many eyes looking at absence and loss. You have become a wanderer in this city. Again and again on gloomy winter afternoons, you come to the river and walk in a fretful haste from Chelsea to Blackfriars as if all transport had broken down and you had urgent business in the City and then back via the Strand and the lit-up shops of the West End. Some days you loiter in the fashionable streets as if you had purchases to make in Bond Street or Jermyn Street where you avoid the eyes of the supercilious chauffeurs standing by their parked Rolls Royces. You become acquainted with the trees in the streets and squares. When you are on the last part of your walk home, your back beginning to stoop under the heavy overcoat and your legs beginning to hate each additional step, you still must go out of your way when you come to Brompton Square, and walk to its very end, only because there is a tree there behind the railing in the square and you can never go hurrying down Brompton Road but must walk up the eastern side of the square, stand a moment to look at the tree and then walk back. It is one of your favourite trees in all London. You will never tell anyone about it or whether it is a chestnut or a plane or a beech or a birch. But you will never walk past the square without going to look at your tree. When it is too cold to walk you sit in the Circle Line for two hours. There are always lonely men in the tube, smoking Woodbine cigarettes. They come in at Notting Hill and leave at Victoria. They come in at South Ken and leave at Temple. Thin men in cloth caps, smoking Woodbine cigarettes. They seem possessed by some bitter compulsion. Their eyes won't stay still. In one station and out another in the constant agitation of men cursed to inexplicable restlessness. Then there is no reason why you, getting out at Gloucester Road to go home, descend instead to the Piccadilly Line and go hurtling through the lowest darkness of London. You are frightened to think where you are. In the primeval clay. Fossils of complete creatures, monsters of the past that you sink among. At Piccadilly Circus you become one of the great crowd come there for shelter against the falling bombs as if all the living had thought they had died and had voluntarily come down to the floor of a vast tomb to lie one next to the other. You are placed among the living dead at the mouth of the black tunnel. In February there are crocuses in St James's Park, in March under the broken grey and blue windy sky there are daffodils. You keep coming up from the darkness of the underground to the surprise of blood red tulips. From the window you look at your classmates running and yelling at their five-a-side games. The sun comes out a moment and goes in for a quarter of an hour. Murky, miserable. Mad, the English, to think it's turning fine. This is a world full of contradictions. When you come to be among the poets they will have abandoned poetry. Once more you give Porphyria's cheek a burning kiss, reciting the verses almost by heart. A lovely hot day in August coming to a close, the sunlight lingering late in the evening, when you enter Parliament Hill Fields, cricket bag with the bat's handle sticking out in your left hand while your right hand clasps the double-folded fat on the fleshy waist on Eliza Masefield's Devonshire double-cream yellow-white body. The light is dissolving among the great oaks and the copper beeches and the wonderful chestnuts and little Eliza with her wide hips and bulging behind, her ample bosom and round face looking shorter than her five foot four and younger than her 27 years trips along beside you as you hasten to a secluded spot on a slope under some elms you had discovered the week before. You were playing cricket in Surbiton but thought of Eliza all afternoon and hurried to London and took the tube to Archway to run to her flat where she lives with an aunt. You'd met her at an away match a month earlier, in the second game with the club you played for after the school term, at 17 the youngest in a team of solicitors and stockbrokers from Surrey, being taken up by the club because one of the solicitors was the father of one of your school team-mates and had seen you bat when the First XI played Parents and Masters. Eliza had been in charge of the tea at the away game. She had come there with an older man and his tea-making wife and a rain shower that interrupted the match somehow brought you and Eliza together for twenty minutes. You were alone and quiet, not sharing the small talk of the older men, and Eliza seeing that you couldn't be one of them came to talk to you. That's how it began. You liked the name Masefield. The same as the Poet Laureate. And you have been meeting her three or four times a week in the parks and the commons and mostly here in Parliament Hill Fields, the nearest to her flat. You have been standing in the shadows against the great chestnuts and it has been so comfortingly cuddly to clasp the many creamy roundnesses of Eliza but most of all it has been her long buttery lip-nibbling and tongue-stabbing kisses, that has kept you attached, her thin rosy lips throbbing with a sexual mystery you have never felt before. Last week, when you discovered the grove on the slope, the secluded spot under the elms, you spread your mac upon the damp ground and Eliza collapsed upon it, laughing softly, and pulled you upon her, little mounds of her body everywhere, spongy beneath her clothes, and you remained upon her, kissing, and now as you hasten towards the grove you are remembering how last week she let you pass your hand up her inner thigh, how she let your mouth fall on the bulging flesh that showed below her neck. She is talking now and you are murmuring assent, agreement, willingness, every word in the thesaurus that signifies yes yes yes, there are ghostly men walking about, pulled this way and that by their dogs, there are lovers lying embracing in the shadows and some in the softly falling last lingering sunlight, and Eliza's voice is hotly female, it is melting hot sex itself and your mouth is already dripping with it. You throw down your cricket bag against the elm, take off the mac that you have been wearing on this hot rainless day for the purpose of now spreading it upon the ground, and Eliza is already clinging to you, standing up, on her toes the little round woman ten years older than you but you are only thinking of woman woman woman, and she takes off the long coat she had thoughtfully brought, and in a moment the two of you are as inside a tent. There among the boys screaming at their five-a-side football is Peters, with his broken front tooth, with whom you happened one day after school in the summer term to be walking down Fulham Road and coming to a barber's he walked in, and shamelessly and without embarrassment, in his school uniform mind you, and loudly so that the customers having their hair cut could hear, said, 'A packet of Durex please' just like that, like he was buying razor blades, and that gave you the idea to arm yourself for the future and so there and then, outside the barber's, you offered Peters a profit of sixpence to sell the packet to you, whereupon he re-entered the barber's and as if it had been sweets he had purchased a minute before and consumed with greedy haste bought a second packet. You're a funny fucker, though. What thrills you is that this is Keatsian country and the munificent lady bouncing on her buttocks is Miss Masefield and though you have at last risen above a dependence upon bananas that in Bombay you used to chop off at one end, scoop out half the fruit and make there a nest for the onanist bird that went chirping in and out in and out like a busy wren and then cawed like a wet crow, it suddenly occurs to you even while Eliza has you deeply tightly grasped than any banana you could fashion in your most outrageous fantasy and you are amazed to know you are right in the middle of hot melting sex even then, you're such a funny fucker, it suddenly occurs to you that Michael Masefield would make an excellent pseudonym. There you are, coming to a climax deep inside the vast globe you have attached yourself to, and the image that crosses your mind is some editor receiving a sheaf of poems by the new poet Michael Masefield and being wonderfully impressed by the alliterative felicity that outshines the Poet Laureate's name. Mere John Masefield is eclipsed for ever and the mellifluous Michael Masefield reigns in his stead. The little round lady is sighing in her pneumatic deflation and you choose that moment to talk about your poetic dreams. She sighs away like a punctured rubber tube immersed in water, and when you are in the bus to Archway she says Poetry pooh you should become someone in the City. With the tube to catch and home to get to before your mother wonders what sort of game your cricket is, there is no time for the registration on either brain of intellectual incompatibility. But before the summer holiday ends you have an opportunity of no longer waiting for darkness under the elms and making love hurriedly with all your clothes on. Eliza's aunt has gone off to Cornwall for her holiday and nothing stops you sitting naked in the flat all day long the whole Sunday. Suddenly the little lady is coy. You'd thought when you rang the bell that the door would open and she would be hiding behind it to surprise you with her nudity but she is dressed from top to toe, even her neck has a scarf around it. She wants to talk of serious things. She makes a pot of tea and brings out a fruit cake from a tin. What are you going to do when you get your A-levels? she asks. You stretch your hand and pinch her thigh and say you're going to get your A-levels right here. She insists on remaining serious and you are obliged to answer again. You have a choice of two universities, you say, and then quickly jab your index finger and say, poking now her left tit, This one, and poking now her right tit, Or this one. She has begun to giggle and you know you can carry on this game to a successful conclusion as presently you do when she is obliged to ask what you propose to study and you say in all seriousness that the subject is a hard one. By now she is shrieking with laughter and has thrown off the absurd scarf from her neck and is eagerly leading you to her little bedroom with the pink walls. Well, you proceed to prove to yourself that what has been taking place in the darkness of Parliament Hill Fields has not been some fantasy while you were still manipulating the old Bombay banana trick, you are on and inside real flesh. And what flesh! Eliza's body is a marvel of rotundity. Whatever of human flesh could be circular is upon her body fully rounded. She is a miracle of globes and spheres, moons and suns. Cantaloups and watermelons grow upon her. She is the whole circle of the known world, Britannia herself of the kindly beaming face and the devouring all-consuming body, full of amplitudes, and you are like a little lozenge melting in one tiny moist corner of her flesh. This cannot be reality, otherwise you would not, bouncing upon the spongy flesh, be thinking of Hedy Lamarr. Your pleasure therefore comes not as a climax but as a dispersal, you are scattered far and wide in a world of slender women, tall Joan Crawfords, thin Margaret Leightons. You sit on an edge of the bed and look longingly at your clothes heaped on the floor. Eliza has begun to talk behind you. She is bent on having a serious talk. You glance back. There is a pink mound on the bed which it takes a moment to distinguish as the many globular lumps of her body and you wonder what on earth have you been looking at all these weeks. She has begun to talk about marriage. A laughable subject. But you appear to ponder seriously her Alma Cogan concept of love and marriage and her Doris Day version of a secret love while you are thinking how best to make a super-fast exit from the woman your romantic imagination first conceived as a fluffy cloud when what was floating past your eyes was very like a whale. Your longing for women is done for and years will pass before you overcome the havoc of hesitations and uncertainties that make of your desires a complete catastrophe. You cannot believe the thin arm you touch is not fat or the slender girl not many round lumps stuck together of clay. Miss Eliza Masefield has put all your aesthetics into doubt and you find yourself seizing opportunities to go up the hills and mountains of the British Isles to escape the illusions of London. But it will be in an old part of London where you will recover your confidence. You come out of Whitechapel Gallery where you had gone to see an exhibition of Pop art and instead of proceeding to the tube station you unthinkingly walk in the direction of the West India Docks, not realizing your mistake until you are in a confusion of streets. There is a pub at the opposite corner from where, remarkably in this ancient part of London, Indian film music can be heard. It is what has arrested you in your thoughtless progress. The exhibition at the Whitechapel disturbed you. Western culture has lately begun to take a gleeful pleasure in applauding the mediocre and to proclaim its delighted approval of the trivial as though it were the astonishing invention of some genius. You spent longer at the gallery than you had planned, slowed down by sadness, and when at last you left a mourning sort of mood overcame you. The world is suddenly full of wrong directions. But the female Indian singer's voice stops you. You look at the sign on the pub. Charrington's. Toby Ale. But there is a picture on the sign of a blue elephant with a dark brown turbaned youth above its head sitting in front of a scarlet and green howdah. Below the picture is the name of the pub. The Howdah. You cross the street and go into the pub. It is one large, curiously shaped room, being a pentagon of unequal proportions: the two walls that meet at the furthest apex are the longest and the two on either side the shortest. The room is poorly lit, but the murmur of voices that can be heard as an undertone to the Indian singer, whose voice is quite shrilly loud, as well as the dense cigarette smoke that fills the room, immediately creates the impression, which you confirm as soon as you become accustomed to the dim light, that groups of people are sitting at the several tables. A long mahogany counter joins the two further walls like the horizontal stroke in the capital letter A. The other walls have large mirrors on them but the surface of each mirror is dulled and tarnished, so that the reflections that appear in them are indistinct and shadowy, especially when seen through the smoke-filled atmosphere which seems to make things remote and insubstantial. You have no desire for a drink and you are about to leave when the song ends. In the brief relative silence from the tape recorder the voices from the tables are suddenly loud and the language that you hear is Hindustani. By now you can see clearly. Mostly men sit at the tables, all of them brown-skinned, some so dark as to be very nearly black. The whites of the men's eyes are conspicuous when they are turned to look at you. Then you see the young woman who looks surprisingly familiar. She too notices you in the same moment. And because your eyes meet neither can pretend not to have seen the other. You take a step towards her remembering where you have seen her. She keeps her eyes on you and begins to smile. You have seen each other at a party at a common friend's flat, in Highgate, but not met, and where you wondered who this girl was with the thick black hair with a long plait, she looked she came from Gujarat. Yes, you say to each other, exchanging names, it was at that party at Highgate. You glance at the two men with whom she has been sitting. They are middle-aged Indians of a somewhat impoverished background. One of them, seeing himself being stared at, quickly picks up his half-pint in which there is less than an inch of beer left and drinks from it as if it were full. A new song commences on the rather loud speakers, a painfully agitated voice lamenting a lost love. You look at the young woman, whose name you have heard as Sybil, and see that she is folding shut her reporter's notebook and saying something to the men. She rises from her chair. You step back to make room for her to come out of the narrow space between the tables and the two of you begin to walk out as if you were close companions and you had come there at a previously fixed time in order to escort her away. Outside, she stares at you with a smile and says, 'Well?' You say you have been convinced she is from Gujarat, or possibly from Bengal, from Calcutta which is so full of sophisticated girls with a refined sense of culture, but *Sybil*, could she be from Goa? She laughs. 'It's *Isabel*! and I'm from *Peru*.' Then what was she doing among all those Indians? Research, she says, for her thesis. And you begin to walk towards Whitechapel, exchanging history and expectations. You stop at a Lyon's corner house for a cup of tea. A thin middle-aged Cockney waitress who seems permanently overwhelmed by sadness serves you. Emaciated men in cloth caps and with large watery eyes sit smoking cigarettes, the cup of tea before them gone cold. When you leave, you ignore the tube station where crowds are descending. She puts her hand through your arm and you enter a labyrinth of streets and for two hours you are cutting across the layered memory of the City, past old churches, past ancient walls, adding to that memory the echo of your footsteps, past warehouses and offices from where the clerks and the secretaries are flowing out towards Cannon Street, towards London Bridge. Absorbed in each other's words, you turn into this street and that, blindly. Lombard Street and Threadneedle Street, Monument and St Paul's, Mansion House and the Bank of England, this way and that round and round you go, proceeding only because you are arm in arm and are hearing each other's history and want the moment to be prolonged. You are enclosed in the City from which people are leaving, you could be its only living souls adding the echo of your footsteps and of your voices to the old old streets where nightly the fog flows in from the mouth of the great river and enfolds in its long swaying arms additions to the City's memory to deposit them on the architraves and cornices and steeples and domes and paving stones, wherever the day's soot settles, adding on this evening the fine film of your first attachment to each other. It is also the first of your pilgrimages together which will take you to the planet's shrines, to the high-spired cathedrals from where Christ ascends and vast temples where the Buddha sleeps, the heights of Machu Picchu and the pyramids of the Sun and the Moon, to cities with triumphal arches where eternal flames burn. But you are in England now, alone in your five-year exhaustion after the one summer of circular acrobatics with the Britannic globe, for although you go off to university and have dull associations with new excitements your senses have somehow been crushed by Miss Masefield. That time has marked you. And even when the years pass and you are with Isabel and you think you have recovered she will catch you staring out of the window like one looking at another time. The five-a-side football has been over a long time. Winter settled deeply over England. Spring came, then summer. But it is winter again and you are sitting at the window next to the hot radiator and trying to imagine a light warm breeze blowing through the poplars at the end of a cricket ground in some slightly hilly part of Surrey but there is too much dark grey in your mind as if between this winter and the last there has been no intervening sunlight. You force your mind to summon that image of summer but you cannot remember what green looks like. Winter has settled over England. The air is grey, like galvanized iron. *Thump*, it falls on your head when you walk the streets. Full of black soot, the atmosphere. You've fallen into a labyrinth in a coal mine. Where is that England of the Blackie readers with their Rossetti and Constable reproductions whose blues and greens had your eyes throbbing with desire? War-black is Buckingham Palace when you walk past it to cross into the grey park, St James's, grey the ice on its pond, you make for Parliament Square, war-black the

Houses, war-black the Abbey, and you look at the ghostly men in grey coats and you want to ask them do you remember green do you remember blue but their grey eyes are smarting with the flying black soot and they seem to see nothing before them walking like the bereaved in a funeral procession. You look for Clive, you look for Warren Hastings and Macaulay. Thomas Babington. Education of India Act. Where is that England of Fox and Bentham and Mill? War-black is Whitehall. Great gaps where monuments stood. Anxiety shakes your heart. You join the queue outside Parliament, seeking admission to the source of the laws. You go to the visitors' gallery. Tensing Sherpa is walking down a hall, a visitor come from climbing the world's highest mountain, wide beaming Cheshire-cat face, smiling inside the mother of parliaments, being shown imperial icons by two hush-hush whispering hosts. You climb to the gallery and look down. A lot of roast-beef pink faces rolling in the benches. There stands Churchill by the dispatch box, a large bald head, not that searching-eyed grimly determined Karsh-of-Ottawa Churchill, his speech slurred, his body almost swaying reminding you of men who collapse on the pavement outside a pub. The little man on the opposite bench with quick-darting beady eyes is Attlee. You will, some years hence, sit next to him at a dinner preceding a university debate, and you will talk about India, but only as if it were some forgettable film you both had seen and were discussing the implausibilities of the story or remembering the funny characters in it. But it is a sleepy time in the House. The back-benchers are slowly nodding their heads, their eyes nearly closed on a dream of brandy and cigars. *Hyah-hyah*, a voice suddenly coughs like a crow from an unseen branch of a tree, and a coughing echo disturbs the gloomy air a moment. You hear no speech on foreign policy. There is no debate on the human condition. No law seeks passage. The Prime Minister's slurred words vaguely answer a question about some petty economy in the national health service. The members sink lower in the benches. The gloom is permeated by a numbed drowsiness. Your heart aches as though of hemlock you, too, had drunk. You are always at the window. Another winter passes. The Queen is crowned on a grey wet day one summer. Then one school day she goes in a procession down Fulham Road and all the boys get to stand on the pavement and wave. You stay inside, linger in a corner of the cloakroom while the masters march out their forms to go and assemble on the pavement. You don't know why you feel ill. You don't want to stand in the grey air and wave at the Queen. Her Britannic Majesty. Who was Princess Elizabeth the Emperor of India's daughter. You stay in the corner where it is dark. Everyone has gone out. No one can see that you are crying.

11 From the Desk of Jonathan Pons

An editorial note at this stage of the narrative will probably be viewed as an irritant, but I do have important information to convey to the reader who, hearing it, will readily assent to the necessity of this brief stoppage just as, in the late steam age of glorious memory, passengers in trains crossing great continents accepted the necessity of the locomotive stopping in the middle of nowhere in order to take on water.

But permit me first to use this occasion for a little, but necessary, incidental business. Since the world knows me to be an American, a mere academic in the late twentieth century who is putting together the curious life of one who has gravely provoked him, why, it will be asked, is the spelling employed in my text British? This question has given me considerable pause. I have fretted over it, and also over the choice of a deliberate archaism in certain expressions, a great deal.

Having undertaken an investigation into biographical truth – for such is my solemn pledge to the foundation in Nebraska which is underwriting the considerable expense of my research – I am obliged to be uncompromisingly precise even though all biography is, in the end, a fiction: I may be American but my subject is British and therefore it is in his language that I must write. When the alien philology has vexed my native instinct I have restored my mental calm by reading a few pages of Henry James. So, let no editor, critic or student, on this subject, cavil.

Though the pursuit of truth may be no more than a succession of conjectures in which the mind weighs speculative fictions, I have, most excitingly, this to relate, that in pursuing my researches on three continents, picking up a lump of clay here or a bit of granite there somehow to bring together the various discovered fragments to sculpt the figure of the man whom I sometimes believe to be my adversary, sometimes my nemesis, and occasionally my friend, that as the shape has become both monstrous and perfectly beguiling, I have finally found myself confronting the man who might have been real. The image came to me not in Isabel's papers, nor in the misleading pages of the Suxavat manuscript which, but for the reference to me, I would believe was a joke on the part of Valentin Sadaba, who wished to confound admirers of his famous realism by broadcasting a virtuoso example of the real method buried in his prose, that of – the label is his own – the Poetical Hermeneut, and nor did the image come to me in the various scattered revelations from former acquaintances of Shimomura in America and in England. It came to me in an old Moghul palace, high above the bank of a sacred river in the heart of India, where I found myself in a hall of mirrors and suddenly perceived the true identity of my man, knew at last what the story was that I had to tell, the fiction that there was to invent yet of the century that was all but dead and become a memory.

It was then that I realized that I must concern myself only with that language which would rediscover, oh, not some miserable truth which is but a paltry thing, but the precise detail embedded in the florid, passionate, miraculous and infinitely elusive figures that haunt memory, to reinvent the idea itself of reality after discovering that reality, poor thing, has no existence at all.

PART THREE

Origins of the Self

1   The British Subject

The English soldiers were at drill. Left-right, left-right. The boy watched them in the parade ground a hundred yards away from the balcony of the second-floor flat and although his mother called to him, 'Roshan, come and drink your milk,' he remained watching the soldiers with fascination. Pink-red faces they had. Left-right, left-right. He mouthed the words, then spoke them aloud. Amazed, he looked round to see if anyone had heard him. 'Stand at ease!' he shouted, repeating the words that reached him. He was speaking English! He dropped back from the balcony and slapped his bare feet on the grey tile floor, shouting, 'Attention!' Then he commanded, 'By the left, quick march!' And began to march up and down the confined area, looking askance at the soldiers and mimicking their actions.

Left-right, left-right. Suiting the action to the words, thrilled by the perfect match of one with the other. His new school had been A-for-Apple, B-for-Bell. Large pictures, huge letters and bold words. D-for-Donkey. And Miss Nogueira making her red-painted lips go in a circle and then straight into two lines. O-for-Onion. Then at last the Cat sat on the Mat. A classroom of an incongruously mixed group of Indian boys, 6 to 15 years old, yelled *The cat sat on the mat*. But the words meant nothing. They merely identified pictures in a reader or were an exercise in pronunciation. It was not what the English soldiers spoke to each other when they came out of the next building in which they were billeted and went in groups to the parade ground just across the wall below the balcony from where he watched them. A rush of words from the pink-red faces in the sun. What were they saying? The cat sat on the mat. No. They were talking about important things. Voices full of confidence, certainty. Hosh posh billydo coopityclam howdudo ohyessno sir! He looked behind him. There was no one around to hear the funny words. Finaytlee see you hosh posh boobydo come now byby ohyessno sir! He looked at the soldiers. Red shining faces in the sun. Beyond the parade ground, all the way to the railway lines, was a depot packed with jeeps and lorries and anti-aircraft guns. Sometimes the soldiers drove away the jeeps and the lorries, trailing guns behind them. Then more vehicles and equipment arrived. The English were a mystery to him. Left-right, left-right, they went, up and down the parade ground. Then suddenly on the double trot-trot-trot in their black boots some jumped into jeeps some into lorries and crunch-crunch the big wheels on the pebbly sandy ground and they were gone. A whistle blew, more came out of the building trot-trot on the double. Complete mystery. But he had begun to speak their language! Left-right, left-right, stand at ease! Complete hosh posh ohyessno sir!

He climbed up the balcony again. His ears had caught the sound of the train before he saw it. Not the clattering suburban trains that went past every five minutes. But the gliding, sweeping motion of the electric locomotive that produced a smoother sound as it pulled the red carriages of the Punjab Mail, still some ten miles from Victoria Terminus, slowing down for its penultimate stop, Dadar. He stared at the train and was filled with a feeling of magic. Lahore one minute and shoo-shoo clickety-click tucka-tucka-tucka pishoooo you're gliding into Bombay. And there he was in the women's compartment with his mother and his sister Zakia looking out of the window at the long Lahore platform at last disappearing. The huge steam engine down the curving track heaving, throwing out a great cloud of black smoke. Choocho-sho choocho-sho and over the river ctunk-ctunk clack-clack clack-clack through the iron bridge. Fast then across the vast green plain. Delhi. Agra. Names from memory, from history lessons, stories told by his father with a huge illustrated book in his lap. Domes in the distance, minarets, sandstone, marble, ghosts of armies charging across the plains, the horses of Moghul kings kicking their heels. English soldiers at the railway stations, marching down the platform on steel-tipped boots. Clack-clack tock, clack-clack tock, the metallic sound drilled to be precise, efficient and powerful. Crowds of people. Turbaned men. Veiled women trailing children. Now across the middle of India. So much dust. The earth ochre, almost orange in patches, swirling up in clouds of dust. Cough cough. But then the steam locomotive is disconnected, along comes the square-faced electric engine and we're gliding down the mountains whoopie with the air now moist and the breeze coming from the ocean, the magical Sindbad-the-sailor ocean, the Arabian Sea. Full of pearls it must be, emeralds and rubies. One minute Lahore and then pishoooo you're gliding through forests of coconut trees and the little bits of blue glass shining in the distance are bits of the Arabian Sea like little presents wrapped in blue paper hanging from the trees.

The Punjab Mail glided past smoothly beyond the soldiers marching up and down. Every day he saw it come and stared at the mystery of remembered landscapes that the red coaches must have gone through. There were the other trains that came from parts unknown. The Howrah Express with its green coaches going clickety-click cutta-cutta-cutta all the way from Calcutta. The Deccan Queen swooping down in a rush from Poona. The Madras Mail. And on the other line, just visible from the roof, on the line of the Bombay, Baroda and Central India Railway, the silver coaches of the most magnificent of trains, the Frontier Mail that came from Peshawar, bearing in its closed air-conditioned first-class carriages the mystery of originating from a remote region which pulsed with barbaric passions and yet, coming through the familiar landscapes of the Punjab, evoking in the young boy memories of adobe houses and emerald-green rice fields. From every direction came the great trains. Each time he saw one of them it was like seeing all of the India the train had come through, bringing the people of every province to Bombay. Bengalis, Punjabis, Madrasis, Pathans even and Gurkhas, and Hindus, Muslims, Sikhs, Christians, all of India was tumbling into Bombay coming to the wonderful city in the wonderful trains while the English soldiers were going left-right left-right hosh posh jimblijoo boobydo carrodim dibbetyloo look here left-right left-right stand at ease well done!

Z-for-Zebra. The school was up on a hill above a railway station. Stripes of light fell through the jackfruit and mango trees that covered the hill, almost concealing the church built by the Portuguese. The schoolroom was a small clearing with a thatched roof supported on bamboos. The boys stared at the red lips of Miss Nogueira, their ears listening for the special sound of the Deccan Queen as it entered and left the station below in one sudden rush with a force that seemed unstoppable. The hill was a vast jungle when the bell rang and the boys went running into the striped light. It was an interior of complex adventures. The dense shade looked like dark tunnels and caves under the huge trees. Cobras guarded hidden treasures, and you were dared to go running through a tunnel. You took a deep breath and made a dash for the little mirror of light. A thousand snakes sprang at your ankles. The jungle hissed. But the mirror suddenly flashed blindingly and you came out into an explosion of light, your ankles scratched by thorns. The whiteness turned blue. There, far to the west, was the Arabian Sea. It hissed. Like someone behind you saying, 'Listen, come here, let me show you something, see this?'

Roshan saw an ocean liner on the horizon one day and his older friend Mangal immediately made up a game. 'Lie down quick! The invader's coming.'

Seeing Mangal fall upon his stomach, Roshan bent his knees a little but Rusi, who had recently turned 13 and considered himself above boyish games, remained standing erect in the light and said, 'What rot, Mangal, it's only the British.'

'Your *friends*, I suppose.' Mangal spoke sarcastically, annoyed to be denied his game.

Holding his hands like a pair of binoculars in front of his eyes, Rusi said, 'Soldiers from the UK. For the Burmese front.'

Mangal stood up and brushed the dirt from his shorts. 'The enemies of India,' he said, adopting a disgusted look on his face.

Roshan straightened his knees and kept quiet. He did not know what his friends were talking about. Mangal was smart. He knew things. Rusi was taller and fairer and looked down on the dark-skinned Mangal, a few months his junior. They were always disagreeing and were therefore inseparable. Mangal once explained to Roshan in an aside, 'He's a Parsee, what do you expect?' Roshan looked baffled, and Mangal added, 'They're so white, they think they are British substitutes.' Mangal was repeating phrases he heard his father speak to his friends, expressing racial distinctions and prejudices. Roshan remained unenlightened. Mangal was very clever, he thought.

The hill was their fort, Mangal declared. Rusi suggested a name. The Red Fort. Mangal looked at him with scorn. 'That's in Delhi, stupid!' Roshan, who had been impressed by a magazine photograph of Windsor Castle, said, 'I know. Windsor Fort.' Mangal stared at him in disbelief. 'Ba-ritish?' There was so much contempt in his voice that Roshan instinctively stepped back from where he stood. Rusi gave a little laugh and said mockingly, 'And I suppose Golconda would be Muslim.' Mangal took a deep breath and threw out his chest in a defiant posture. 'India,' he announced, 'is *ours*. And this is Fort Free India.' He had apparently rehearsed this speech, for he brought out a small orange, white and green flag from a pocket and began to march up a path that led to the top of the hill. Roshan and Rusi followed him at a short distance.

'Fanatic Hindu,' Rusi mumbled but receiving no response from Roshan went silent. Roshan did not know what to say. He did not understand why Windsor was so wrong a name. He had thought it a neat idea. India is ours. Of course. Everyone could see that. Why make an issue of it? But he did not want to confess his incomprehension and, pretending that he was wise to the subtleties of their argument, kept quiet. He did not want to be told he was too young to play with them. Other boys his age were like children. And he was as tall as Mangal and as fair as Rusi. His father had told him stories from history about kings and queens and great battles. He was older than boys his age. They had never heard of Nelson or where Alexander had died. Alexander the Great. Akbar was great too. Akbar the Great. Best to keep quiet about what Mangal and Rusi were arguing over. India is ours. Best to agree. Suddenly, Mangal stopped and turned round holding one hand up like a traffic policeman and the other to his face with a finger on his lips. Roshan and Rusi halted. Mangal retreated towards them and then, from a few yards away, waved them to follow him into the undergrowth.

The three crept gingerly past some thickly growing bushes. Roshan imagined Mangal had spotted some new enemy. Mangal led them through the undergrowth in a semi-circle until they were opposite from where he had retreated. They came to a granite boulder. Past it, the land fell into a hollow with a rocky bed, forming a little area that was without the entangled vegetation that covered the rest of the hill. Branches of nearby trees formed a canopy over the area, making it appear a perfectly concealed hiding place. Only, there was an opening on the right edge of the boulder, between the rock and the trunk of a jackfruit tree two feet away, from where the boys could look down.

The first thing they saw was the naked torso of a woman lying on a pink sari folded and placed upon the ground. Her large breasts were held by two hands while her own hands clasped the back of a black-haired head that was sunk between her spread thighs. Her eyes were closed and she was trying to suppress some sound that was escaping from her throat.

Mangal held his finger on his lips. Rusi stifled a giggle. Roshan stared, unbelieving, the blood throbbing at his temples.

The man raised his head and lifted himself. Placing his knees on either side of the woman's chest, his buttocks suspended over her stomach, he placed his penis between her breasts and began to knead them with his hands.

'Damn good!' Rusi whispered.

'Shh.'

The man held his penis and rubbed its tip in circles around each breast. They shone wet. He fell upon them with his mouth, his tongue licking now one and now the other. The woman could check her throat no longer, and let out little cries, throwing her head to the left and to the right.

'God!' Rusi cried in a whisper, his hand inside his shorts.

'Shoosh,' came from Mangal though his eyes were filled with amusement.

Roshan felt funny and scared. Then he saw the unbelievable. The man placed himself between the woman's legs. Roshan's blood was going wild now. Rusi was beginning to pant. A louder cry than before escaped the woman's lips. The two bodies were joined now and beating against each other. Rusi leaped back and went round the boulder. Mangal grinned silently, watching him go.

In the afternoon Roshan watched Miss Nogueira walk up and down the aisles in the classroom as the boys copied the letters of the alphabet on ruled paper. Her wide green skirt swung as she walked. It brushed his knee when she went past him. He smelled talcum powder. But there was a smell behind that smell. When she walked across the front of the classroom he saw where the orange blouse was stretched over the swelling roundness of her breasts. It was funny what that man had done to that woman. Naked in the shade of the jackfruit tree. He must have heard that cry that came from Rusi. Ooooh. He looked up then, his eyes wild, and then dropped his head to the woman's shoulder. A moment later the couple stood up and dressed hurriedly. Roshan saw the man's swollen penis was uncircumcized. The woman's face was pitted with smallpox. Rusi came from the other side of the boulder. The couple began to walk away. 'That was damn good,' Rusi said, 'what do you say, hey Roshan?' Mangal laughed and, pointing a finger at Rusi's shorts, said, 'You better walk in the sun, Rusi, if you want those spots to dry.' Roshan asked, 'Did he hurt the woman?' Rusi laughed aloud and exclaimed '*Hurt!*' Mangal admonished Rusi, saying, 'He doesn't know, he's only a kid.' Rusi held up his left hand and shaped it into a loose fist and repeatedly stuck the index finger of his right hand into the hole between the thumb and the first finger, and said, 'That's how you were made, little fucker.' Mangal said, 'Oh, leave him alone. That was great,' he added. 'Never seen it done like that, in broad daylight with the man's arse in the air where a crow could land on it.' Rusi hooded his eyes a moment and said, 'That was damn good. You Hindus can't stop breeding,' he taunted Mangal, 'you're at it day and night, night and day.' Mangal declared he was proud to be a Hindu. He was going to do it day and night too when he got married. His sons were going to be proud of being Hindu and proud of being Indian. Roshan did not understand what Rusi meant when he mocked Mangal's exclusively Hindu nationalism. He thought it must be something that the naked couple had been doing. Roshan held his breath when Miss Nogueira's skirt went swinging past him again. But the smell reached him. The smell behind the smell of talcum powder. He was sitting in an air-tight chamber surrounded by that smell. Returning in the aisle, Miss Nogueira stopped and put her hand on Roshan's head. 'You're dreaming,' she said.

He entered the dream of his future. The crooked letters of the alphabet began to flow into words. There was a new language in his throat. Jack and Jill went up the hill.

There was the picture of Princess Elizabeth and Princess Margaret in the magazine. One serious, one smiling. They were beautiful, his sister Zakia said. She said their father was handsome. King George. Akbar the Great. Alfred the Great. Father said he burnt the cakes. Funny king, what was he doing in the kitchen? Counting all his money. The king was in his counting house. King George the Sixth. Not Great. The Sixth. The Emperor of India. Ohyessir! Queen Mary was his mother. Queen Mary was a ship. The boy stood on the burning deck. The Deccan Queen came rushing down to Bombay. He came from the Punjab. In the women's compartment with his mother and sister in the Punjab Mail. Whole night and whole day, clickety-click, tucka-tucka-tucka, such a large country, and the whole day he had stared out at the endless dusty plain, the ochre, orangish landscape blowing its wild dust before his eyes, with the word *India* stuck like a fishbone in his throat, choking him.

Suddenly there was nothing but the rising dust. Orange turning ochre as it rose, dimming the sun to a dulled iron-grey. Not the ghost of a tree in that world of dust. Not a sparrow. Not a pebble. The sound of the train stopped. The women vanished. He could not see himself. His throat hurt.

2   On Forbidden Territory

Baldev Singh from one of the neighbouring buildings was known as Mona because he cut his hair. In the flat below lived Chandrasekhar whom everyone called Chandru. When Roshan had mastered the English alphabet and begun to make his sister mad by reciting nursery rhymes at the top of his shrill voice he was considered qualified to be moved from Miss Nogueira's hillside school for boys of all ages, with its promise 'English coached', to a high school run by Catholic missionaries from Italy. Even before he changed schools he had become closer friends with Mona and Chandru, who had the double advantage over Mangal and Rusi of being his own age and also his neighbours. Soon a crowd of them assembled after school every day and walked through the rust-coloured iron bridge over the suburban railway line to play cricket on a dusty field at the foot of a forested hill which the boys had named Pavilion Hill.

Bamboos growing wild at the foot of the hill made a wide arch below which fell a permanent area of shade that became known as the changing room in the pavilion. There was nothing to change into, however, since most of the boys wore the same pair of shorts for months at a time. Nor was there any equipment to store in the pavilion. The team possessed only one bat and that had been cut from a piece of flat wood by Chandru's father; another boy, Raman, usually brought a worn tennis ball, making everyone believe he received it from the English soldiers with whom he was on intimate terms when it was common knowledge that he got the balls from a club run by Hindu businessmen where his father worked as a peon. No one questioned Raman's claim to friendship with the English soldiers as long as he provided the team with tennis balls.

From the pavilion they went out into the dusty field with its clump of coarse grass, thin brown legs sticking out of the dirty shorts. Some of them wore no shirt, exposing a narrow, bony rib-cage that made them look more like scrawny chickens than cricketers, especially when they ran after the ball with a competitive fervour. When he walked out of the pavilion, Roshan always held up his head as he had seen Walter Hammond do in British Movietone News when his father had taken him to see *Pinocchio*. What a big man he was, Walter Hammond. Beautiful white flannel trousers, striding across green grass, which you could see was green in the grey black-and-white picture. Ohyessir, he was Walter Hammond, tall, heavy man who was weightless when he stroked the ball and ran an easy single. No, what am I talking about, I am Bradman! Small man with the eyes of a falcon and the strength of a savage in his arms. Here is Larwood pounding up to the wicket. Here is Maurice Tate. What a nice name, Maurice Tate. Roshan Tate. Hammond is nicer. Roshan Hammond. Ohyessir, here comes Roshan Hammond! Mister number one batsman of all India on the green grass at Lord's. Mister perfect all-rounder, medium pace from the Nursery End, and what a fielder, he runs one hundred yards on the leg boundary, dives through the air for ten feet and, whew, what a catch just inside the boundary one inch from the ground. Beautiful white flannels, shirt of cream-coloured viyella, silk cravat, white buckskin boots on the lovely green grass. Mister perfect number one of all India.

The boys around him, from different parts of India, chased the ball in a dusty confusion, fell upon one another, cursed in Hindustani and made up in English. Shake hands on it, old boy. When they chatted while crossing over the iron bridge, their origin would sometimes make one utter a chauvinistic remark that asserted the pre-eminence of his native province. Niran from Dacca was the most assertive about his beloved Bengal, provoking the south Indian Raman to mock him with a mouthful of Telugu. At such moments, Mona, the hair-cutting Sikh from Amritsar, would hold Roshan's hand, and utter some nonsense in Punjabi. And Chandru from Madras would taunt the Goanese Freddie for taking on European airs when he was as dark-skinned as any Maharashtran. But such provincial rivalries were brief, for soon they were on the cricket field and the game had to be played by English rules.

Although their common language Punjabi should have made Roshan and Mona the closest of friends, Roshan and Chandru became more attached to each other. Mona's parents were ambitious for their son and made him study on some evenings with a private tutor, so that he was often obliged to remain away. Sometimes Roshan and Chandru would abandon the game on the cricket field and climb up Pavilion Hill to look at the view from the eastern slope. Far on the horizon were the foothills of the Western Ghats beyond which was the Deccan Plateau. Looking at the Western Ghats reminded Roshan that he was on an island, as if on a separate colony with its own peculiar composition of an exiled but unified humanity, gazing at some real country, that India over there with its continuously bloody history. From the top of Pavilion Hill they could also see out to the harbour of Bombay and get a glimpse of the ships docked there, among them sometimes a beautifully white sparkling P & O ocean liner at which Roshan and Chandru stared in awe and wonder.

The ship to England! Women with milky-white skin in floral dresses and wide-brimmed straw hats, with a little Pekinese dog on a leash, would be embarking. With them, pink-faced men in double-breasted suits or white linen jackets and loose drill trousers, and officers with a polished leather belt coming from the shoulder diagonally across the stomach, a small stick under the arm. Going home. Home leave. Some maharajah among them, some rich nawab, going to London for Ascot, for Wimbledon. But now the war was on. The War. Mostly soldiers came and went. And rulers who had to rule when people were dying. But to the young Indian boys who had only recently slipped into English as their common language the white ocean liners possessed mystery and power. At first it was an envy of the unknown, and they suppressed that envy by imagining themselves as the English going home to a familiar world of beautiful gardens and King George VI riding in his carriage across London town, as they had seen in magazine pictures. Then, as they grew older and began to understand the language heard among their parents' friends, the ocean liners became an object of nationalistic resentment, so that seeing them made Roshan and Chandru feel more Indian, their sense of the ocean liners as a symbol of the ship of enchantment, with its latent promise of taking one to a land of pulsing beauty, being replaced by a sense of the ocean liners as malevolent carriers, as if each were a ship of death come to ferry them to some overwhelming darkness. And in this ambiguity of intuitive knowledge, which rendered the fascinatingly attractive as a pestilence to be avoided and equated desire with the forbidden, they watched the ships with longing and with loathing, looking away at last towards the continental mass and beginning to talk about the great trains running the length and breadth of India.

During the afternoon, both of Chandru's parents would be away, making it possible for Roshan to visit his friend every Wednesday, when school ended early, without feeling guilty that his Muslim presence was polluting a Hindu household – as he had felt the first time he innocently called there: Chandru's father had opened the door and for a second had looked aghast at the Muslim boy before recovering his composure and deciding to let him come in. Roshan had noticed the look and realized his blunder but having been invited in he was obliged to enter. The host and the guest were each other's victim and suffered from the necessity to pursue the normal motions of hospitality. Invited to sit, Roshan went to a bentwood chair with a plywood seat and placed himself gingerly on it, not presuming to take a place on the flower-patterned cushion on a wicker sofa for fear that he might oblige the Hindu family to go to the expense of calling a priest to purify it again. Chandru arrived and looked hopelessly embarrassed. His father noticed and attempting to improve the situation made it worse.

'What are you staring at?' he said to Chandru. 'Why don't you offer your friend a glass of water?'

The statement was spoken in a casual, familiar tone that was intended to cover Chandru's embarrassment, but Roshan could see the father at once realized he had made a mistake. 'No, please,' Roshan said. 'I'm not thirsty.'

The father now felt the necessity of forcing upon the young guest the very hospitality that would create a crisis in the family, and perhaps he felt compelled to do so in order to impress upon Chandru that he needed to be more careful in his choice of friends. 'Water? What am I talking about,' the father remarked loudly, theatrically slapping his forehead with his right hand, 'bring him a lemonade, come on now, double quick!'

Chandru ran off. Roshan felt hot and uncomfortable. 'Make it quick now, don't keep your guest waiting!' the father called after Chandru.

Chandru came back with some lemonade served in a brass cup. Roshan was horrified. Should he touch the brim with his lips? He thought he saw a shadow move in the next room. Chandru's mother was watching. Moisture had formed on the brass surface. Should he, like a Hindu who does not want to touch his lips to a vessel that has been soiled by another's drinking from it, throw back his head, open his mouth wide and pour the liquid in a stream from a foot away from his face? He did not have the confidence to do so and feared the lemonade would fall on his upturned nose or below his chin, down on his neck. As he wondered what he should do, he was uncomfortably aware of the father staring at him and knew that the thought in the father's mind was that he would have to throw away the cup after it had been touched by a Muslim's lips. 'Drink up, drink up,' he said encouragingly – and perhaps he was encouraging himself to endure the situation which was nothing short of a calamity.

Roshan held the cup in front of his lips, trying not to touch the rim, and tilted it to his mouth. Some of the liquid was dribbling down his chin but once it began to flow down his throat he was grimly determined to drain all the contents in one go. Sweat burst out of his forehead, his cheeks had darkened. From the chin, some of the liquid fell on his neck and trickled down his chest. Mercifully, the ordeal was over, though as he handed the cup back to Chandru he saw that the front of his shirt was wet and he realized that he did not have a handkerchief with which to wipe his mouth and must twist his neck to reach the sleeve of his right arm – a lapse of etiquette expressly forbidden by his mother.

It was many weeks later that Roshan's courage was restored and he was able to enter a Hindu household. It was easy to be brave when the parents were not there. It was natural since Chandru had become such a constant companion and they had begun to read books together and, growing older, were sharing a wider range of ideas than cricket fantasies that had first made them friends, that they should get together in the flat when the parents were away. It was easier than carting books to Pavilion Hill.

Roshan appreciated the silence and tidiness that prevailed in Chandru's flat. There was very little furniture in it. The two bedrooms with their cleanly swept tile floors had no beds in them, only some rolled-up bedding in a corner. One thing that took getting used to was the smell from the kitchen. From that smell you could tell you were in a Hindu household. Asafoetida it must be; and fennel. When Roshan looked into the kitchen he saw that it was the most immaculately cleaned room in the whole flat. Brass utensils shone brightly from the far wall. The stove was on a little raised area to the right of the room. Chandru did not mind his Muslim friend entering the kitchen but Roshan knew that Chandru's mother would go out of her mind if she were to find out that Muslim feet, with shoes on too, had polluted her kitchen.

Roshan imagined that she would need to get a priest to come to the flat, or even have to make a pilgrimage to Benaras. Hindus were single-minded about being Hindu. But Chandru was not like that. And he himself as a Muslim was not like the Muslims who lived on Mohammed Ali Road who had to be Muslim and nothing else. Invoking the name of Allah all day long. Like other boys who had entered adolescence and were close friends, Roshan and Chandru had taken to holding each other's hand when they walked together in the evening to where they could see girls. They gave each other a signal with a quick double squeeze of the hand when spotting a pretty girl and multiple squeezes, like a May Day signal, when a stunningly beautiful girl was to be seen.

Mona, who lived in the flat above Chandru's, ran into Roshan one day when he was leaving his Hindu friend's flat. While constantly sharing ideas with Chandru made him a special friend, Roshan found that hearing two words of Punjabi from Mona made him special in a different, much more intimate way. Mona's parents had left Amritsar three years before Roshan had been brought to Bombay from the Punjab, but each time the two boys met they greeted each other loudly with some choice Punjabi obscenity, which better expressed deep mutual regard than did the sophisticated kind of greeting Urdu-speaking people employed or the non-committal, defensive and uncontaminating joining of one's own hands that was the universal custom of Hindus, fell upon each other in a spontaneous embrace and then proceeded to talk rapidly in English.

Mona's parents happened to be away and he invited Roshan to come to the flat. Being on a higher floor, the ocean breeze blew through the open windows. There was a quality of luxury in the flat that Roshan had not seen before. A sofa upholstered in light blue velvet, its frame of solid teak, and not like the flimsy rattan and wicker in his own flat; a spongy carpet on the floor; a glass-fronted cabinet full of ceramic birds and animals. What attracted Roshan the most was a small sculpture of a nude woman in white marble. Mona caught him staring at her, and said, 'Go ahead, fondle her tits, I do it all the time!' Roshan was shocked to have his mind read so easily. But he was pleased, too. For it opened the subject that had recently begun to obsess him and which he had not known how to start talking about with Chandru. It was some years now since he had seen the couple on the hill when he was with Mangal and Rusi. He had thought then that what he saw was an act of brutality by a man upon a woman, though at one buried level in his mind his intuition gave him a different knowledge altogether, but it was a knowledge that remained suppressed because he was too young to see his mother in the role he had witnessed the woman perform. Only, he had been confused by the smell that had emanated from Miss Nogueira, which was strangely exciting and terrifying. But by now he well understood what it was that had made Rusi go behind the boulder, so that he felt not at all embarrassed to pick up the marble statuette and to pass his fingertips over her tiny breasts the size of cherries and say to Mona, 'You should keep her in the bathroom.'

'Son of a pig!' Mona exclaimed in Punjabi, using a phrase that being the most offensive to a young Muslim was therefore the highest expression of endearment between friends, and burst into a short laugh before saying, 'Let me show you what I do when I conduct this lady to the bathroom.' He took the statuette from Roshan, held her breast against his lips, closed his eyes, made a moaning sound, and beat the empty air in front of his shorts with his fist, so that Roshan exclaimed out in admiration in Punjabi, 'Sister fucker!'

'You want to try it?' Mona offered the statuette back to Roshan.

'What, *here*? No, sir!' Roshan protested, though he felt aroused and took the statuette from Mona and began to stroke the curve of the tiny breast.

Mona saw the small tent that had risen on Roshan's shorts and laughed. Pointing a finger in that direction, he said, 'Yours has been cut, no?'

'Every Muslim's is,' Roshan said, closing his eyes and imagining the cold marble to be living flesh.

But suddenly embarrassed, he quickly opened his eyes, placed the statuette on the small table beside him and crossed his legs.

'Already done it today, eh?' Mona teased, glancing at him brightly.

'What about you?'

'Twice,' Mona answered proudly.

'I heard you Sikhs have big ones.'

'Not like you Muslims, yours are so big they've all got to be cut!'

When they stopped laughing a minute later, Mona asked, 'Did you ever do it on the picture of Princess Elizabeth?'

'Sure, and on Princess Margaret.'

'Put it there, sister fucker!' Mona said, stretching out his hand, so that Roshan smacked it with his hand, completing the familiar gesture of total camaraderie and implicit understanding of each other's habits.

They proceeded to discuss the film stars who had received the same favour. They both had felt that the desire aroused by looking at the pictures of actresses always seemed illicit, as if they had fallen on evil ways and were about to be the ruin of their family, and was therefore a sharper and dangerously exciting passion, while their imagined affair with British royalty was somehow noble and, being doomed to a tragic conclusion, worthy to be the focus of national admiration and consolation. Realizing that their thoughts on this subject were identical, they again smacked hands, while at the same time each threw at the other an outlandishly obscene phrase in Punjabi.

Roshan heard the sound first; a second later Mona. They rose spontaneously and went running to the balcony. Although trains had been going past all the time that they had been talking, each had identified the particular sound of the Punjab Mail. They saw it go in the distance, gliding smoothly towards Victoria Terminus, and watched it in silence without realizing that they were holding hands. There was a throbbing within their bodies, as if their arteries were tracks on which the train from their native land ran in a ceaseless flow.

Although they had teased each other about their solitary sexual practice and made remarks that could have been interpreted as hints that what was done in solitude could more interestingly be performed together, Roshan and Mona remained modest in this respect, and it was surprisingly with Chandru, with whom there had been no prior dialogue on the subject with the same openness as with Mona, which could have been an appropriate prelude to the action, that Roshan found himself engaging in mutual exhibitionism. Perhaps it was because the two were more often together in Chandru's flat and the regularity of their companionship facilitated the transition to a sexual attachment as almost a natural development of their friendship.

They had, as often when they got together in the empty flat, been reading. It was a poem of Shakespeare's. Chandru's voice, with his Madrasi sing-song accent, was rendering the verses most musically. 'She red and hot as coals of glowing fire,' made both boys hopeful, and soon another line, 'Panting he lies and breatheth in her face,' sent another signal that they should keep alert, for the imagery here referred to the subject foremost in their thoughts. 'I'll be a park, and thou shalt be my deer:' Chandru read, paused, looked knowingly at Roshan who nodded his head eagerly, and continued, 'Feed where thou wilt, on mountain or in dale;' and stopped again because Roshan cried aloud, 'O God! *Feed where thou wilt!* That's too much!'

'On mountain or in dale,' Chandru repeated, and Roshan snatched the book from him. He saw where the line was and read aloud the couplet that followed:

> Graze on my lips; and if those hills be dry,
> Stray lower, where the pleasant fountains lie.

'Shit, that's too much!' Chandru said, snatching the book back to see the lines for himself. 'Pleasant fountains! That's damn good. Graze on my lips and if those hills be dry stray lower where the pleasant fountains lie, bloody hell, that's damn good!'

'I wasn't going to do it today,' Roshan said, 'but that's too much.'

Chandru understood what he meant and said, 'It'll be my third time today.'

'Damn good!' Roshan said in a congratulatory tone.

What the two did next seemed a long-established routine although it was the first time. Without either making a suggestion, they walked together to the bathroom, and, standing side by side in front of the shower stall, unbuttoned their flies. 'Stray lower, brother, stray lower,' Chandru said, seeing Roshan begin while the latter remarked, 'Here come the pleasant fountains.'

'That wasn't a fountain, that was bloody Niagara,' Chandru said, running water from the shower and then working a thick brush over the tiles, directing the spillage into the drain. 'Funny thing, being cut like that,' he added.

'It's better than having all that loose skin hanging for nothing,' Roshan answered.

From that afternoon it became part of their private vocabulary to ask each other, 'Been to the pleasant fountains today?' When Mona had heard them say that a number of times, he wanted to know what they were talking about. 'You know,' Roshan told him, 'like doing it on Princess Elizabeth's photograph.' Mona was always delighted with any reference to the subject, and laughed aloud, but he wanted to know what pleasant fountains had to do with it. Chandru recited the verse from Shakespeare which both he and Roshan knew by heart. 'That's *printed* in the book?' Mona asked, incredulous. He had to see it. He loved to see dirty words in books. *Vagina* in the Concise Oxford Dictionary had been his most thrilling find. Chandru told him to come along to his flat on Wednesday afternoon.

That first visit implicitly made Mona an active partner of their enterprise, though he was not always free to join them. Roshan and Chandru remained the principal protagonists in the ritual, almost liturgical recitation of Shakespeare's verses to be followed inevitably by self-arousal and a visit to the pleasant fountains. What added to their excitement was that the event was attended by a double sense of criminality: it was wrong for a Hindu to let a Muslim do it in his house in the first place, but to encourage and assist him and to have him reciprocate was positively, shamelessly and deliciously evil. They read all of Shakespeare's poems and then several of the plays, looking for erotic images. Often two hours of frantic reading would lead to no new discovery and, desperate not to lose the opportunity before Chandru's mother returned, they went back to the well-thumbed page that had first provided them with the revelation that while poetry moved the mind with its fine thoughts it also moved the hand with a craving for urgent agitation. Whenever Mona came, he brought a film magazine with him, and they looked pantingly at Veronica Lake or Virginia Mayo. The photographs showed the actresses in sweaters and in evening gowns; the exposure of female flesh was minimal – a *décolleté* gown revealed the most: but they had only to see slightly parted lips, the hint of a nipple behind the sweater, or a knee negligently bared, and their imaginations invented a throbbing gorgeousness which they began eagerly to ravish.

Much as they appreciated, and took good advantage of, Mona's magazines, it did not occur to Roshan and Chandru to deviate from reading Shakespeare when they were without Mona's delightfully corrupting company. The great poet's words were ransacked in a rushed, uncomprehending reading which stopped only to take note of the amazing suggestiveness of certain words, as of the final one in 'My wife is slippery', that conjured up an image of a lascivious woman, naked, available and covered with soap that made embracing her an erotically novel experience, or when they were rewarded by some explicit phrase, like 'Kissing with inside lip', that sent them in an ecstasy of wonder at the unending surprises that sexual pleasure held in store. Although the climax in the bathroom was always the same, they were more like an amateur play-reading society trying out their voices with new parts than two 13-year-olds hunting for sexual stimulation. But whenever Mona came, the scholarly atmosphere changed to a boisterously earthy one. Roshan observed to himself that while he considered Chandru to be a closer friend the sight of his penis always repelled him whereas Mona's did not, although it looked exactly like Chandru's, being, like the Hindu boy's, uncircumcized. When it came to mutual touching there was some pleasure in doing it to Mona but with Chandru he found himself using only the thumb and fingertips, and not the full fist as with the Sikh boy. He thought that this must be because Mona was such a naturally warm-hearted person or because their common Punjabi background created instinctive sympathies between them from which the Madrasi Chandru was excluded. But many years later, when in spite of his professed agnosticism he could not lose the born Muslim's repugnance for pork, Roshan understood the real reason why he had found it repulsive to touch Chandru's penis. Chandru was a Hindu. The realization shocked him. He loved his friend. They held hands when they walked together. And yet at a deeper level an ancient prejudice was stronger than love.

One day, Chandru had to go away after letting his friends into the flat. He jokingly told them to learn *The Rape of Lucrece* by heart during his absence. Left alone, Roshan and Mona instinctively scouted the flat for forbidden territory. They came to the kitchen. 'Damn clean, these Hindus,' Mona said. 'Real spick and span.' The two looked at each other. It was both terrifying and thrilling to be standing in the spotless kitchen with its gleaming pots and pans. As they stared at each other in a self-admiration of their bravery in entering the forbidden place, each realized that he was silently daring the other to commit some act of particularly vile sacrilege.

Mona grinned. Roshan smiled back. Mona held Roshan's face and suddenly kissed him lightly on the mouth. 'Hey, stop it, that's disgusting!' Roshan said. Mona put his hand in front of Roshan's shorts, squeezed his penis, and said, 'What about this, then?' Roshan did the same to him, saying, 'That's better.' Mona pressed his face closer again and forced a longer, firmer kiss on Roshan, and then said, 'Not bad, eh?' Roshan screwed his lips in a sulky gesture, and said, 'Well, not that bad. But this is better,' he added, having got his penis out. Mona's eyes brightened, and he said, 'Hold on, I've got an idea. Let's make a Hindu–Muslim curry.' He went to the end of the room and picked a gleaming brass pan from the wall, returned to where Roshan was, and said, 'All right, let's get some good Muslim chopped-up meat cooking in this Hindu you-tencil.'

Holding the pan in his left hand, he began to stroke Roshan's penis into it. 'Dhamma-dhamma,' he said with each stroke, and then, accelerating, 'Dhamma-dhamma, dhamyatta, dhamma-dhamma, dhamyatta.' His eyes closed, Roshan began to chant, 'Ram-Ram, Ram-Ram, Ram-Ram!' Mona beat out a furious rhythm, 'Dhamma-dhamma, dhamyatta,' and then, 'Dhamyatta, dhamyatta, dhamyatta,' until Roshan, panting 'Ram-Ram,' cried aloud, 'Ram-Ram, Ram-Ram, Ram-RAAAAAM!'

The boys stared in astonishment at what looked like the white of two or three eggs floating at the bottom of the pan. Mona went to the sink and tipped the pan over, saying, 'There go the Muslim leftovers.' He glanced inside the pan and hung it back on the wall.

'Shouldn't we wash it?' Roshan asked.

'Nah, forget it.'

'But Chandru's mother will see it shining wet.'

'She'll think some ghee dropped into it.'

3   The Gathering

'Welcome, welcome!' his father's voice was booming from the stairwell. The guests were arriving for Sunday dinner. Roshan and Zakia had been standing on the balcony from eleven in the morning watching people get off the bus that came every fifteen minutes. It was not till twelve-thirty that Tilak Singh, whose long white beard made him visible in the middle of the night, was seen getting off the bus to become the first visitor, his young wife Manika trailing behind him in a gold-bordered purple silk sari. 'My, my, look at Miss Fashion Parade!' commented Zakia. 'Some people have to be noticed from ten miles away.'

'Zakia, why do you have to be so catty?'

'Purple silk, my dear! And on a green satin blouse, too! My oh my! Where are we going, to the Palm Court Hotel for the King's birthday?'

Roshan found his 12-year-old sister's non-stop satire amusingly ridiculous. 'You're just jealous,' he taunted her.

'Jealous? Oh, yes, like a dove is jealous of a crow. One thing I can tell you, Mister Number One Know Nothing, I won't ever marry an old man. With such a long beard, too!'

'He can't help having a beard, he's a Sikh!'

'But a *white* beard? And why doesn't he tie it up instead of carrying a swallow's nest hanging from his chin? I can just imagine it, he goes to kiss Manika and twenty swallows go flying out of his beard.'

'Look, there come the Samudras in their chariot.' Roshan pointed.

A twenty-year-old black convertible Morris on wheels that appeared to be wobbly came and stopped in front of the building. Mr Samudra, wearing a white linen suit and a Panama hat, with a cheroot in his mouth, continued to sit stiffly at the wheel after he had turned off the engine, waiting for the shuddering bonnet to go still. His small wife, who had tiny slits for eyes so that the red dot on her forehead gave her a cyclopean look, sat staring at the vibrating

217

bonnet as if she expected some magical trick to pop out of it, her head shaking helplessly with the motion that shivered through the frame of the car. Behind them sat Mr Menon in his usual sailor suit.

'There's Menon in his perpetual fancy dress,' Zakia commented.

'He's an officer in the British Navy,' Roshan said, defending the man whose uniform he coveted.

'Officer, my foot! Why should the British make an Indian an officer?'

'He says so himself.'

'He says! And I say King George is my uncle. Roshan, you are so dumb! If he's in the navy, what's he doing on *land*? There's a war on, didn't you hear?'

The old Morris finally went still. Mr Samudra pulled out the cheroot from his mouth, threw it on the pavement, opened the door and heaved himself out of the car. His wife alighted, too, drawing the end of her white cotton sari as a veil over her head, and while Mr Samudra puffed out his chest and walked purposefully she shuffled behind him with her head bent. Mr Menon stepped out of the car as if some lackey had opened the door for him and saluted him while he strode towards the high officials assembled to greet him fresh from his heroic exploits on the sea.

'What a pity Mr Samudra was born with such a dark skin,' Zakia said. 'He would so love to be thought an Englishman. Thinks he's Winston Churchill himself. Can you imagine, Bulldog Samudra!'

'Welcome, welcome!' their father was shouting down the stair-well.

Roshan and Zakia saw a large American car come speeding down the road and make straight for the rear of the parked Morris. Its brakes were applied hard and it came to a noisy halt an inch behind the Morris. The doors of the 1938 dark blue Chevrolet flung open at once. A balding middle-aged man jumped out of the driver's side.

'Anwar-bhai's here!' Zakia clapped her hands.

No sooner had Anwar-bhai come out of the car than his wife and seven children came tumbling out. The children, four girls and three boys aged between 12 and 4, immediately ran towards the entrance to the building.

'Get ready for the hurricane!' Zakia said, leaving the balcony and running to meet her special friend, the eldest girl, Salima.

Roshan followed her although the Anwar boys were all too young for him to play with. But the entire Anwar family was fun to be with, especially the father who was so universally liked that everyone added the fraternal suffix to his name, so that even his wife fell into the habit of calling him Anwar-bhai, making him joke to her, 'You're the mother of all my nephews and nieces.'

'They're here, they're here,' Zakia shouted into the kitchen as she ran past it. Roshan repeated the words, stopping a moment at the kitchen door and seeing his mother bent over the stove and blowing at the coals that were sending up wisps of black smoke. Two of the servants, the old Maharashtran woman known to the children as the Chutney Lady because of her knack for transforming any vegetable or fruit into a chutney, and the young Pathan, Nabibullah Khan, who was never seen to smile and spent his free time fashioning pieces of wood into guns and daggers, were also standing beside the stove and trying to stimulate the fire. Near them, placed on a long wooden platform, were several pots and pans containing food that had already been cooked – some the night before and some early that morning – which was now to be reheated. 'They're here,' Roshan said again into the kitchen and ran on down the corridor to the door where the Anwar children had already arrived.

Just as Zakia had predicted, a hurricane hit the flat. The children went stampeding through the four rooms, which had been tidied in anticipation of precisely such an invasion, while the elders gathered under the ceiling fan in the sitting room and talked loudly. Film music from the Cossor radiogram added to the noise. Zakia took her friend Salima to the rear balcony overlooking the parade ground to see the English soldiers walking about there at their Sunday ease, telling her as they looked down at three young Englishmen standing talking, 'This is my Sunday roast-beef picnic. Scrummmp-chuss!'

Roshan left the two girls ogling the Englishmen and went to the sitting room. More people had arrived. Mr Richardson, who claimed to be an Anglo-Indian although he was as dark as a Madrasi untouchable, stood near the Cossor radiogram with his rotund little wife in a pale blue frock, talking to Tilak Singh whose wife Manika, shaking her head to the music, seemed absorbed in the sentiments of the love song blaring out of the radiogram. Mr Samudra had lit a new cheroot and, tilting his head, was blowing smoke at the ceiling fan beneath which he stood while near him Anwar-bhai was poking at Mr Menon's ribs with an index finger and saying, 'What good is your navy-shavy when the Japanni armies are going to come tumbling through Burma?'

Roshan went past the crowd to the balcony that looked over the road. Some street urchins had gathered around the parked Morris and Chevrolet. At the bus stop, among the people alighting from a bus that had just arrived, he saw his friend Chandru. He must have gone to the Hindu gymkhana to which he went some Sunday mornings. Chandru disappeared to the side of his building, making for the rear entrance to the flats. Roshan stood in the balcony for a while, watching the traffic go by. Two jeeps with English officers in them left from the next building. Probably off to Delhi. Busy lives they led. Off to Burma. Off to the Khyber Pass. Borders to protect. Harbours, shipping lanes. The advancing enemy to repel. But. British go home. Quit India. The whites of Gandhi's eyes over the rim of his glasses are watching you accusingly. We've got to weave our own cotton. Home-spun.

Inside, the film music on the radiogram now turned low, the men were talking about the British. Every dinner party warmed up to the independence movement. 'War, war, what war?' Mr Samudra was asking Mr Richardson. 'Why should India lose her sons because the German hyena is at UK's door?' Roshan remembered that in his French class his clownish companion Bhatia had written, 'I kay, you kay, he kays, we kay, you kay, they kay,' and added beneath that a variation that turned the last two words to an Urdu one, go and see, 'I say you kay dhékay.' Mr Richardson answered hotly, wagging a finger, 'But a promise was made by His Majesty's Government!' Mr Samudra laughed cynically. 'Yes,' he said, 'just like in 1914. Come die for us and we will give you independence. They gave us General Dyer instead. The butcher of Amritsar.' Mr Richardson glared at Mr Samudra and said, 'The fault was not the Crown's! There's always a black sheep in the family.' Mr Samudra quickly interrupted him with, 'And India is a luscious pasture for all your black sheep. Ba-baa!' Mr Richardson held out the palms of his hands and shrugged his shoulders. 'Believe me, if we can win the war, India will be yours.' Anwar-bhai, who had heard the last statement, looked amusedly at Mr Richardson's dark skin and remarked, 'And will you be going *home*, Mr Richardson?'

Tilak Singh's beard had begun to shake. He was talking agitatedly in Punjabi to Roshan's father until Mr Menon asked him in Hindustani why he spoke the tongue of a secessionist and Tilak Singh switched in mid-sentence to English: '. . . Sikhs are going to be left in the lurch, that is the plan of the Congress Party in collusion with the

Muslim League.' Mr Richardson turned aside from Anwar-bhai's ironical question and said to Tilak Singh, '*Exactly* what I say! Not only Sikhs, but Parsees, Christians. All the minorities are to be neglected.' Mr Samudra seemed to have made a resolution to seize anything spoken by Mr Richardson as if it constituted British policy and to attack it. 'That's precisely it!' he shouted. 'Divide and rule, that's your game. We want to call ourselves Indians and you insist that we continue to call ourselves Hindus, Muslims and Sikhs.' Mr Richardson held up a hand and with the index finger of his other hand began to tick off each of the fingers, 'And Parsees and Christians, not forgetting the aspirations of the Maharashtrans, the Tamils, the Gujaratis!' He held up the two hands and brought them together with a sharp clap, adding, 'Oh the problem is not just religious, but within each religion one of language and caste.' Pointing an accusing finger at Mr Samudra, he said, 'Do you blame the Crown if a Brahmin won't shake hands with an untouchable?'

Nabibullah Khan entered carrying a large brass tray, holding it up at shoulder height. Steam rose from the tray, beginning to permeate the room with the aromas that made one's senses fall into a dream of luxury as if one had become a resident of the Moghul court. The crowd parted to give Nabibullah Khan passage to the dining table. He was followed by two young men, sons of the Chutney Lady, also carrying trays. The three laid out the food, went back to the kitchen with their trays and returned with more dishes, repeating the journey several times until the table was heaped with basmati rice cooked in saffron with slivered almonds, lamb korma, kofta curry, fish steaks coated with a garlic and red-pepper paste and fried, brinjal and aloo sabzi, cauliflower with ginger and black mustard seeds, chana dal, chopped onions, tomatoes and coriander leaves in vinegar, peeled and thinly sliced cucumber in yoghurt with burnt cumin seeds, coconut chutney, dhania chutney, mango pickle, gajjar halwa, kheer with pistacchio nuts, and a large shining brass jug containing iced water.

For a quarter of an hour while people served themselves and began to eat with the ravenous rapidity of those who, before they have begun, have resolved on the combination of dishes that are to be their second and third helpings, the room filled with the noise of serving spoons knocking against dishes and voices rising in eager expressions of compliments. Seeing Mr Richardson helping himself from a plate on which he had heaped rice, lamb and meatballs, Anwar-bhai said to him, 'You must miss your Sunday roast.' No knives and forks being available since the common custom was to eat with one's hand, Mr Richardson was eating with a spoon. 'You have to admit,' he said, 'a well-done roast is beyond compare. With boiled new potatoes, of course, and cabbage. A most healthy diet.' Mr Samudra, quickly eating rice and lentils and keeping an eye on the fish steaks which he planned to devour next, commented, 'Healthy, did you say, Mr Richardson? I suppose that's why it's as tasteless as hospital food.' The turmeric in the korma sauce had produced yellow stains on Tilak Singh's beard below his mouth and he looked as though he had put on make-up for some clownish act. 'I'll eat English cheese and drink Scotch whisky any time,' he announced. 'While they drink our tea,' Mr Samudra added.

Any statement about the British was for Mr Samudra a signal for confrontation with the imperial power. Yet he saw no irony in the fact that his own physical appearance in a white suit together with a cheroot stuck in his mouth presented a caricature of an Englishman in the tropics as seen in American films. What is more, he spoke English to everyone, including his servants who did not understand it and to whom he therefore repeated everything, barking a command in English and then shouting it immediately in Hindi. 'Taste is only a passing show,' Mr Richardson said, working with difficulty on a fish steak with a spoon. 'It gratifies the moment, but at what cost to the digestion! Whereas a well-done roast . . .!' Mr Samudra swallowed his last mouthful of rice and lentils, glared at the fish steak Mr Richardson had picked up and, seeing that it was the very one he himself had had his eye on, therefore compensated himself for his loss by picking up two pieces. 'Ah, your roast-post is all very well in your foggy London,' Anwar-bhai remarked, 'it is the food of Christians in cold climates. Leave us to our sun and spices.' Mr Samudra nodded his head, a partially chewed fish steak in one hand, and said, 'Please . . . just leave us.'

Tilak Singh's beard had acquired more yellow patches and since his lips, too, were stained by the gravy it was difficult to tell at once where his mouth was when he spoke. 'I have nothing against roast beef, if I may say so in the presence of Hindus,' he declared. 'And I have nothing against roast pork either, if I may venture the remark in a Muslim household. I am also an impartial admirer of wine, whisky and beer. Therefore, my friends, it follows that Sikhs are the most unifying force in India.' He raised his glass, regretting to himself that it contained only water. His declaration had sounded like a speech and therefore Mr Menon said, 'Hear, hear,' although he himself had not actually listened to Tilak Singh's words. He happened to be next to the old Sikh's young wife and his response to her husband's speech was calculated to please her. Mr Menon looked at her with a smile to see what effect his endorsement of her husband's words had had, and she, nearly blushing, said in a very soft voice, 'He loves to eat bacon.' Mr Menon found this incomprehensible piece of information somehow encouraging, and, hoping to establish a secret bond with Manika, confided to her, 'I'm going to become a vegetarian the day India becomes independent.'

'I see,' Manika said, shaking her head in a manner signifying satisfaction, thus convincing Mr Menon that he had made a considerable advance in her affections. He could not imagine her making love with her white-bearded husband. What, he wondered, had persuaded her family to arrange such an odd marriage? Tilak Singh was at least 60, and possessed neither wealth nor fame. Manika looked 22; certainly, she was not yet 25. It must have been a shock to the poor girl on her wedding night to have the ghostly figure of Tilak Singh come to her bed. Where did his beard go when he kissed her? If Manika lay below him while Tilak Singh kissed his bride, the beard must have gone right over her beautiful small breasts all the way to her navel. It was a preposterous image. Revolting, Mr Menon considered. Perhaps there was no sexual love between them. Ah-ha. Mr Menon pondered the implications, thinking of Manika entertaining a young lover. Mr Menon could not admit such a possibility. Old though he was, Tilak Singh was a vigorous man. Sikhs were famous for being virile. The British called them the martial race, keeping them happy with flattery, and they had certainly established a reputation for being merciless in battle and sexually extraordinarily potent. He found it unbearable to think of it, but old Tilak Singh must be going at it ferociously. Poor Manika! Feeling sorry for her led him to believe that she must long for tenderness, a thought that naturally made Mr Menon conclude that she must already be entertaining a desire for him, and would be receptive to his advances should the opportunity arise. So that, warmed by her soft voice saying, 'I see,' he declared, 'Just let the war end, India will be free!'

Mr Menon could not have explained what the war or India's independence had to do with his fantasy about loving Manika. While he imagined her private life and tried to hold her attention, the conversation around him was getting louder. It was all about the freedom movement. He heard it without listening to it and therefore his declaration to Manika was only an unconscious response to something Mr Samudra had said. Tilak Singh, who kept his ear attuned to what was being spoken to his wife, said loudly, 'Yes, the war will end, and the Japanese flag will be flying in Delhi! You call that independence?' Mr Richardson was outraged that anyone could even think that the British would not win the war. 'Your Mr Gandhi,' said Mr Richardson severely, 'will become a Muslim before the Japs win any war.' Tilak Singh was engraged. '*My* Mr Gandhi, Mr Richardson?' he shouted. 'My Tara Singh, if you like. My Guru Gobind Singh, if you like. But never *my* Mr Gandhi! The man is a Gujarati.' Anwar-bhai said in a conciliatory voice, 'What is this Gandhi-shandi nonsense? The man doesn't like eating, so he fasts, having discovered that the British are terrified of weak people.' Mr Samudra threw his mouth open in the manner of a hippopotamus, guffawed and then glared at Anwar-bhai. 'Yes, make fun of India's living saint,' he said, 'fall right into the British plan to make Indians ridicule their own leaders. Oh yes, that will certainly expedite our independence!'

'Independence is only Hindi-pendence,' Anwar-bhai mocked, expressing a common Muslim fear. 'Your Mr Jinnah,' Tilak Singh said, 'wants to cut the Punjab in half. Why, the man does not even *speak* Punjabi!' Mr Samudra smiled at this little thrust against the Muslim idea of dividing India. Seeing that Mr Samudra was about to light up one of his smelly cheroots, Anwar-bhai remarked, 'At least he smokes good cigars.' To that Mr Richardson thought fit to add, 'And eats pork, I hear, which is tactless, to say the least, for a man pretending to lead the Muslims.' Anwar-bhai said to him, 'Pork-shork has nothing to do with it, Mr Jinnah is talking about a state for the preservation of Muslims, not a state for the preservation of Islam.' Mr Richardson reminded Anwar-bhai of the significance of symbols, saying, 'And I suppose dumdum bullets had nothing to do with the Mutiny.'

Roshan's father judged that all sides of the question concerning independence had been discussed and decided the moment had come to offer entertainment to the company. The mention of the name of the famous Kashmiri singer Malika Pukhraj of Jammu was enough to change instantly the tone of the gathering. Vocally or by clapping hands, everyone, including the several women who had remained quiet all this time, expressed delight that their host had acquired a complete collection of the great singer's records. Receiving a signal from his father, Roshan went to the Cossor radiogram. In the room suddenly become silent, he ceremoniously changed the needle on the arm of the player, taking a shiny new one from the small tin. Having fixed it, he carefully placed the needle on the revolving record and, turning away from the player, saw the look of intense pleasure on everyone's face as Malika Pukhraj's voice came on, singing about the return of spring, as if the music that each heard came from the soul of India or from that undefined, misty area that the inner self saw in vivid clarity and recognized as the soil of its origins.

4 M.K.G.

There was a fifth room in the flat that was kept shut on Sundays. Roshan's father opened it at seven o'clock on Monday mornings to let in the Chutney Lady to sweep the floor before, an hour later when he had breakfasted and taken his bath, he entered the room to sit at the desk in front of the Remington typewriter to assume the duties of M.K. Ghulab Import & Export Ltd, of which, during the first year, he was both the managing director and the clerk.

Mohammed Karim, Roshan's father, had given careful thought to his company's name. Before moving to Bombay, he had been known as Karim Sahib in the largely Muslim community in the Punjabi city where he had worked as the manager in charge of exports for a manufacturer of sports goods. When the war broke out, he was travelling in Europe, sending back orders for cheap badminton rackets and soccer balls; returning hastily to India, he was gripped by two ideas: the war required Britain to use its resources, especially its men, in Europe, thus relaxing its administrative vice on the Empire and making it easier for an Indian entrepreneur to establish himself; and secondly, the war created a demand for goods which Britain itself no longer had the manpower to produce. Between the ship docking in Bombay and the Punjab Mail taking him back to Lahore, he had conceived the idea of opening his own business. He had been gripped, too, by a feverish longing to live in Bombay, for the city throbbed with the excitement of commerce which filled a young businessman's mind with dreams of financial success. As the train rolled out of the lush island into the dusty interior of India, Mohammed Karim fantasized about the business he could create in Bombay. His tongue sounded out the idea. Mohammed Karim Ltd. The idea thrilled him. He thought of his son and was seized by a greater thrill. Mohammed Karim & Son Ltd. He imagined he was the founder of the great commercial empire which was handed down from father to son for generations. The British would leave

226

India after the war. It had to happen sooner or later. Mohammed Karim & Son Ltd would open offices all over India. Mohammed Karim would be one of the country's great business magnates. Like Tata and Birla.

He was travelling in a second-class compartment in which there were three other men. They had inevitably talked about the war and the independence movement; the news about Mr Gandhi's condition in jail where he had begun a hunger fast was the subject of their longest discussion. The Indian leader's action made each of the four men feel a peculiar nationalist pride. One of the men was a Maharashtran, and he suddenly said, 'Now if Mr Gandhi would stop calling Muslims and the untouchables his brothers and showed he was a true Hindu, then we would have a real leader.' The other two men agreed emphatically. There had been no necessity for Mohammed Karim to give his name as yet, and when they exchanged names he gave his as 'M.K.'. The Maharashtran stared at him. 'M.K.?' Mohammed Karim laughed and said, 'That's right, just like Mr Gandhi. Mohandas Karamchand. M.K. Badmintonwala. Traveller in sports goods.'

When Mohammed Karim returned to Bombay with his family and set up his business, he remembered the Maharashtran's contempt for Muslims and, realizing that the man's prejudice must be shared by the majority of people in spite of Bombay's cosmopolitan pretensions, decided not to use his conspicuously Muslim name for his company and not to call himself anything but M.K. Having hit upon the coincidence of sharing Gandhi's first two initials, he therefore invented a third, Ghulab, the common Indian word for rose, and called the company M.K. Ghulab Import & Export Ltd, which began to be known as M.K.G. 'Just like Mohandas Karamchand Gandhi,' he liked to remind people.

5   A Changed Man

The Christian boys assembled in the chapel at the start of the school day. Roshan watched them go into the long room and kneel in front of the statue of the woman with a baby in her arms. They called her the Virgin. It was a mystery to Roshan why she was called the Virgin and he was somehow terrified by the idea; he imagined that the state of being a virgin had to be succeeded by its opposite and therefore some cataclysmic violence had to be the doom of the woman in her lovely painted gown of bright blue with golden stars on it. There were other statues in the chapel and many paintings on the walls. During Lent the statues were covered with purple cloth. Always, there were lit candles in the chapel illuminating the large picture of Christ on the cross.

Roshan envied the Christians the visual evidence of their deity. When they told the story of their religion, they had pictures and statues for every event. They had music, too. Brother Batista played the organ and a choir of boys sang beautiful hymns. Brother Batista was a young Portuguese from Goa who was dark-skinned and had wiry black hair; he taught General Knowledge and said Bach was the greatest composer. INRI it said on the picture of Christ. Roshan did not know what INRI stood for and he did not ask. Indian National Religious Institutions. No. Of course not. It must be some code knowable only to Christians. God looked out of a blue sky with huge white clouds around Him. It was that part of the sky through which you went if you went to heaven. Christians had a picture for everything. A boy named Gomez had shown Roshan a book of religious pictures. There was Eve with an apple in her hand. Pure white skin she had and golden hair, slim body and small breasts that you wanted to eat with the apple. Susanna with the wonderful breasts and massive thighs bathed in voluptuousness watched by the lustful elders. Everything was clear. King Solomon with black curly hair and red sensuous lips. And you could see films of Christian stories.

King of Kings. Gomez said that no actor needed to play the part of Christ. Every time they made a picture about Christ a miracle happened. Christ himself played Christ.

Hindus had a lot of statues as well. Their temples were full of them. Hindus rang bells and chanted in the temples. Ram–Ram all day long. Complete pandemonium on the harmonium. Om Om Om Om. They had funny-looking gods. Elephant-headed Ganesh. Monkey-headed Hanuman. Krishna had blue skin.

Parsees worshipped fire and offered their dead to the vultures. Sikhs had pictures of saints.

Only Muslims had nothing at all, just words. Religion for the brain only. Except during Ramadan, when you starved the body.

INRI. In the Name of Roshan, Inshallah!

While the Christian boys were in the chapel, the others had a lesson called Moral Catechism. Questions and answers about Sin. Hindus, Sikhs and Parsees, and Roshan the only Muslim in the class, all of them with one idea in their mind at the age of 13 – girls – reciting by heart some Englishman's version of a common faith with which to make Indian boys upright. Morally erect. 'Sir,' Roshan's friend Bhatia asked the teacher, 'will I go to heaven if I am morally erect?' Bhatia was a clown. When he had a mischievous thought in his mind his eyes looked Chinese behind the thick lenses of his spectacles. 'Sir, what is a supine attitude?' Through the open windows the Christian choir could be heard. Brother Batista at the organ, the boys singing a robust hymn, conducted by the English priest, Father Brooks, whose favourite hymn it was. Onward Christian soldiers.

'Funny idea these Christians have of religion,' Bhatia said. 'They make it a bloody war they've got to go and win.' With Hindus everything was love, Bhatia said. 'Kama bloody Sutra, man, the gods are the biggest bloody fuckers.' Bhatia was precocious in his study of sex. He had worked out religious differences in a graphic sexual symbolism. Muslim mosques were full of beautiful curves with the dominant domes the shape of full breasts, and, naturally enough, it was the men who went inside the mosques, not women; Christian churches had spires, which Bhatia said were representations of thorns and reminders of pain because Christians thought ceaselessly of punishment; Hindus, however, shamelessly displayed lingams in their temples, had statues of lascivious naked women being ogled by their gods, and the rising mound of the temple was shaped like a cock, everything was plain and beautiful sex, and that, said Bhatia, explained why India had such a large population. Hindus would never go on a crusade, never idealize women as some ethereal and unobtainable creatures, but would seize every opportunity, and position, to fuck.

Brother Batista said that religion was the rock of society. In his General Knowledge class, Brother Batista talked about everything. India was lucky to have so many religions, it was like having so many layers of rock. The country was solid. Bhatia said that Brother Batista took a broad-minded view because it showed Christians were tolerant. It was their way of saying they were superior. 'False modesty and sublime hypocrisy, that's Christianity for you,' Bhatia said. 'What's sublime?' Roshan asked, thinking that it was something that lurked underneath something else. 'Rita Hayworth is sublime,' the Parsee boy, Adi Jamshed, said, rolling his eyes. Roshan realized that he had understood aright and said, 'Oh.'

'We can build unity out of diversity,' Brother Batista said. One thing led to another with Brother Batista. He was like an amoeba. Splitting off endlessly. He would start the General Knowledge class with a quick quiz on the ten highest mountains in the world, and before the boys could answer he would be talking about the peaks of knowledge, and that for some obscure reason reminded him about a famous game between two great chess masters, which in turn led him to talk about politics as a game of chess, so that he ended by rambling on about the nationalist movement in India. The boys loved him because he enjoyed talking so much they did not need to listen to him and could use the time to copy their algebra homework for a later class. Roshan and Bhatia, however, sat at the front, for they found Brother Batista's unpredictability a source of excitement. They felt that what he said about the nationalist movement was serious.

Much of his talk about imperialist oppression, with its references to Gibbon, was above the heads of the boys, but Roshan and Bhatia caught an excited sense that Brother Batista was for the freedom of India. This made him an exception among the priest teachers. Most of the others came from England or Italy, with the principal, Father Marconi, known among the boys as Father Short Wave because he was a small man, a native of Milan; and they talked as if the street outside the window was in some town in Yorkshire or Lombardy. Roshan had noticed that Christians did not like to look at India and were always trying to superimpose European features on indigenous scenes; one Christmas holiday he had visited the flat of a Christian friend and had been astonished to see that little balls of cottonwool had been stuck to the ceiling of the sitting room, with some of the balls hanging from threads, to create a pathetic imitation of snow. Brother Batista was the only Christian he knew who actually spoke the names of Mr Gandhi and Mr Jinnah and even went so far as to say that Mr Churchill was wrong.

Although only Roshan and Bhatia paid any real attention to Brother Batista, somehow Father Marconi always knew what he was saying in class. Bhatia said that Father Marconi received radio waves inside his head. He was tuned to the whole school. That is why Bhatia never jerked off in the school bathroom. 'You might as well go to his office and do it in front of his desk,' Bhatia said. 'Plop-plop on his blotting paper.' Adi said it was Father Brooks, the Englishman from Yorkshire who was a left-arm bowler and made himself friendly to the boys, who spied on Brother Batista and the two other Indian-born priest teachers. Adi said his father had explained to him how the school was a perfect example of perfidious Albion. 'What's perfidious?' Roshan asked, wondering if it was something shockingly sexual that someone did to someone else. 'What Delilah did to Samson,' Bhatia said, but Adi went on with his father's explanation. 'The school is run by Italian missionaries, right? Okay, so the British can claim not to be responsible for what is taught. But they make sure the Italians employ two or three Englishmen disguised as priests, so that they can spy on the whole operation.' 'What did Delilah do to Samson?' Roshan asked. 'Shit, Roshan,' Adi said, annoyed that he had not heard his father's neat theory, 'don't you know, she cut off his balls!'

Father Marconi was seen to take Brother Batista on a slow walk down the long corridor beyond which was the soccer field where the boys were making a racket during break, and have a long chat with him. Brother Batista went away on a retreat for ten days. Miss Miranda from the lower school, where women teachers taught the younger boys, came to substitute for Brother Batista. She was young and fair-skinned, with black wavy hair. The boys looked gleefully at one another, amazed at their luck. Before school began each morning, they would stand in groups outside the building and watch the lady teachers arrive. Miss Miranda in her high heels and swinging skirt and tightly fitting blouse was always a sensation. It was like being in a dream, seeing her enter the class in place of Brother Batista. Like a magical moment in a film when the girl of your dreams is standing right in front of you and you don't know what to say. The boys gaped at her and stared at her tight blouse. Adi wanted to be excused. He needed to go to the bathroom. Miss Miranda's gorgeous voice filled the room. What did the class know about the Lake District? Nothing. The class was in no condition to know anything. It just stared at the beautiful vision. Well, there was a poet called William Wordsworth. He loved the beauty of nature. Poet? Beauty? What did he know about beauty? Had he seen Miss Miranda in her tight blouse? Miss Miranda imparted general knowledge about the poet and his district. The class heard a strange and seductive music and dreamed of slowly releasing her trapped breasts out of that tight blouse. Adi returned from the bathroom. He was stooped and looked pale. Miss Miranda said the class had to listen to a poem. I wandered lonely as a cloud, she began. They could see her floating in the blue sky, her skirt billowing up. What did the class know about the Mother of Parliaments? Nothing. What did the class know about the Boat Race? Nothing. Did the class know why British postage stamps had no name of country printed on them? No. Could the class say if Holland Park was in Amsterdam or in London? No. The class had lost its voice. The class's tongue had been cut. The class had become paralysed by visions of lust. But when the bell rang and Miss Miranda walked out, her skirt swinging and her high heels going tippety-tip, the class burst into a wild roar and two of the boys slipped out and rushed to the bathroom.

Father Brooks arrived for the algebra class. Several of the boys who habitually used the General Knowledge period to copy the algebra homework realized that they had not done so. The brightest boys who answered the questions Father Brooks put to the class found that all knowledge of algebra had vanished from their heads. The forty-minute period was a disaster. Worse was to follow in English grammar and in physics. By the end of the day twenty-three of the boys from the class of forty had received punishment ranging from writing lines to receiving six strokes of the cane on the palm of each hand. The whole class was given extra homework by each of the three teachers. Brother Batista's absence of ten days was therefore a time of great tribulation for the class. It was a time of torturingly wonderful illusions and of painful reality. Miss Miranda began their day filling their minds with dreams of sexual glory and Father Brooks ended it by caning them.

Brother Batista returned a changed man. He had shaved off his hair. Instead of looking smaller, his head seemed to have become enlarged. His skin had got darker. Bhatia said it must be that he had been trying to acquire a halo. You did that by shaving your head and sitting in the sun all afternoon. The sun burned down and made your skull glow. Brother Batista had failed to acquire a halo but the retreat had changed him profoundly. He had prayed and fasted for ten days. At first the change in him seemed to be only one of external habits. He spoke slowly and with deliberation and did not continually break off into a succession of associations. His speech had become measured and ponderous. He walked with his hands folded across his stomach as though he wished to appear middle-aged when he was not yet 30. His lessons became boring. Now if he mentioned the ten highest mountains in the world, it was to talk about geology and the fallacious evidence of the fossils. When Father Marconi passed Brother Batista in the corridor, the boys saw Father Marconi nod and beam with satisfaction. 'Old Short Wave's got his head-phones on all the time,' Bhatia commented.

But exactly two weeks after his return, Brother Batista began a General Knowledge class by showing pictures of the flags of several European countries and asking the boys to identify the country which each represented. When this exercise had been completed, Brother Batista asked, 'Who can come up to the board and draw the flag of India?' Adi volunteered. He went up and made a clumsy drawing of the Union Jack. 'What flag is *that*?' asked Brother Batista, his voice slightly sarcastic. 'Is that the flag of *India*? Are red, blue and white the colours of *India*?' The class grew suddenly tense. Four or five boys at the back who had been copying the algebra homework put down their pens. 'No, sir, that is the Union Jack, sir,' one boy said. 'Yes, sir, that is indeed the Union Jack, sir,' said Brother Batista with undisguised and bitter sarcasm. 'And where may I ask is the flag of India to be seen? India is a country, is it not? You and I are Indians, are we not?' The boys were stunned. Had Brother Batista gone mad? He had begun to talk like Mr Gandhi. His meditations during his retreat had made Brother Batista a fanatical nationalist. He had kept his views to himself for a fortnight. And then, as Bhatia said, 'The dam burst, man, the whole bloody Ganges came pouring out of his mouth.'

The Short Wave picked up every word of the extraordinary oration. He happened to be walking from the chapel to his office at the beginning of the period and, hearing some words through the window that opened on the corridor, decided to stand near there and listen to what followed. Brother Batista declared that it was the duty of every Indian to join the independence movement and proclaim the cry of Quit India from the rooftops. He had seen Christ in a dream and Christ looked like Mr Gandhi and therefore it was his duty as a Christian to support Mr Gandhi.

Father Marconi returned to his office and sent for Father Brooks. Adi, who had gone to the bathroom at the end of the period, which he habitually did several times a day in order to take a quick walk past the lower school to look at the lady teachers, saw Father Brooks go hurriedly to the principal's office. 'The lid's going to blow off,' Adi reported. 'Brother Batista is bound to be considered seditious,' Bhatia remarked. 'What's seditious?' Roshan asked. 'Greta Garbo is seditious as Mata Hari,' Adi said. Roshan remembered Greta Garbo's voice. Foreign women had such wonderful voices, they only had to say 'Hello' and you were mad with lust. Father Brooks did not turn up for algebra class until the period was all but over. No teacher had come to replace him. The boys discussed Brother Batista. Roshan, Bhatia and Adi practised their parents' signatures as they talked.

During the lunch break the three boys went to the restaurant where they could buy a cup of tea for 1 anna and share it by pouring it into three saucers. They pooled the rest of their pocket money to buy cigarettes. Finding that they had enough money to purchase three front-row 4-anna tickets at the cinema as well as three cigarettes each, they wrote notes to their teachers from their parents that required them to go to the dentist, the doctor, the ophthalmologist, and went off to see Errol Flynn.

Brother Batista was seen to be playing the organ the next morning while the Christian boys sang their martial hymns, but he did not go to the classroom to teach General Knowledge. Instead, a man turned up who was so small he was shorter and thinner than the undernourished vegetarian South Indians in the class. Even the most easily intimidated boys who sat stiffly silent all day long felt released from the necessity of obedience. The little man was an irrelevance and therefore he became invisible to the boys while he, content not to be ridiculed, spent the period talking to himself and left the boys to copy homework, chat among themselves or go to the bathroom without being excused.

The following week, Father Brooks was at the organ and Brother Batista was nowhere to be seen. No one could tell what had become of him. Then one day Adi returned from an excursion to the lower school with an excited look on his face. He had information from Miss Miranda! She had set a test to her class and was standing by the door looking at the clock in the corridor. Adi had the daring notion of speaking to her. 'Please, miss,' he said to her, 'remember when you came to my class instead of Brother Batista, you asked a question about British postage stamps. I never did find the answer.' She looked back at her class of little boys working dreamily at their test and listened to Adi pleading to be given the answer. She told him, and then said, 'Poor Brother Batista! Funny how people suddenly lose their minds.' Adi was a quick thinker and he immediately seized the opportunity to ask, 'Where did they send him?' Miss Miranda assumed from the way Adi put the question that Brother Batista's fate was common knowledge. She casually answered, 'Some asylum in Poona.' Adi's impulse was to run at once to the class and tell his friends, but he was clever enough to stop a moment longer and say, 'Believe me, miss, all the boys wish you had taken his place. You are number one in General Knowledge.' The young woman was touched by the flattery.

Roshan and Bhatia envied Adi. He had talked face to face, one to one, with Miss Miranda, and got her in his confidence. They were naturally obliged to concede him a leadership role. Adi was quick to see his advantageous position and seized the opportunity to advance a private goal. In his own community where he played in the evenings and during the holidays with other Parsee boys he had been engaged in much the same activities as Roshan was with Chandru and Mona. Adi had developed a passion for kissing boys on the mouth while pretending he kissed some Hollywood actress. One day when talking to Roshan he saw in his features the lips of Olivia de Havilland. He had become desperate to enjoy the illusion. So, when he found himself the leader of the group, he called Roshan and Bhatia and three other boys to a meeting on the roof of the school building. Of the three other boys, one was a Christian, the second a Jew and the third a Sikh, so that with the Muslim Roshan, the Hindu Bhatia and the Parsee Adi, the principal religions of India were all accounted for. Adi announced that they were the founding members of the Brother Batista Secret Society. Each of them was to be known as a BA – Batista Agitator.

Adi pointed to the mountains on the eastern horizon and said, 'Somewhere there is Poona where our sacred leader is confined to endure his glorious martyrdom.' The boys looked towards the mountains and Roshan asked, 'What's martyrdom?' The Sikh boy said, 'Matadom is the wife of papadom.' Adi gave him a severe look and continued. 'Our Society will serve his noble quest for the freedom of India.' The boys suddenly felt themselves become taller. 'Therefore, our number one resolution is that we believe in the Quit India movement,' Adi said. 'Quit India!' all the boys said loudly together. 'Our number two resolution is that we are first and foremost Indians regardless of religion, caste or creed.' The boys looked doubtfully at one another before a surge of blood in their heads made them feel magnanimous in reducing religion to a secondary matter, and cried aloud, 'Indians first!' 'And our number three resolution is to convert everyone else in the school to a BA.' The boys murmured assent and felt privileged to be chosen as leaders. 'And now,' said Adi, 'we have to swear allegiance to the Society.' Everyone immediately said, 'I swear!'

'No,' said Adi, 'just to say it is not enough. We have to seal our agreement.'

'Varesdavax,' said the Sikh boy.

'Not on paper and not with wax,' said Adi, 'but as brothers, as men of honour.' He paused a moment and then came up with something he had made up with which to win his end. 'Like the knights of old whose chivalry brought beauty and harmony to the world and who believed that an oath taken by one's lips was sealed with the lips of one's comrade, we shall seal our loyalty to our cause with a kiss.' And looking at Roshan, on whose face he saw the beautiful lips of Olivia de Havilland, he concluded, 'Each one of us must kiss everyone else.'

'*Kiss?*' said Bhatia, disgusted.

'That's revolting!' exclaimed the Christian boy.

'The kiss of loyalty,' declared Adi, raising his hands to the shoulders of the Sikh boy, having decided to keep the pleasure of the Olivia de Havilland substitute to the last.

'You sister-fucker Parsee crow-eater sodomist, keep off!' said the Sikh boy, flinging up his arms to repel Adi.

The Sikh boy's mouthful was echoed by the others. 'You chaps know nothing about chivalry,' Adi said sulkily, knowing that he was defeated, and made for the door to the staircase.

Going down, Bhatia said confidentially to Roshan, 'I've an idea. Why don't we write a sympathy letter to Brother Batista and take it to

Miss Miranda. She will know where to send it.' Roshan understood
Bhatia's strategy: it was a way of getting even with Adi, for he was
not to be allowed to remain the only one to have enjoyed the distinction of having received a personal interview with Miss Miranda.
Roshan agreed, and wrote the letter during a break while Bhatia
watched approvingly. Roshan got the top marks in English composition and could also write verses. He was beginning to acquire a
reputation in the school for his imitations of the poets in Palgrave's
Golden Treasury.

Miss Miranda received them with a smile, said she would see
what she could do with their letter, and told them to hurry back
to class. Just as they turned round to leave, another teacher, Miss
Bhosle, came in to see Miss Miranda and the boys almost ran into
her. 'Sorry, miss, beg your pardon, miss,' they said, getting out of
her way, but Roshan still collided with her. She held him back and
stared at him a moment with her hands gripping his arms. Roshan's
eyes were at the level of the red dot in the middle of her forehead, and
he saw the coarseness of her dark brown skin and the oily black hair
which was parted at the middle and wound in a thick, long plait. She
released his arms, staring at him curiously with her large black eyes,
then raised a hand as if to strike him but passed it almost caressingly
across his cheek and let him go. It was the way his mother touched
him. As he finally got out of her path, the stern look on her face
was transformed to a smile that showed slightly protuberant teeth
behind her somewhat thick lips.

The boys scampered down the corridor, and Miss Bhosle said to
Miss Miranda, 'Receiving visits from your admirers?' Miss Miranda
smiled and cast a glance at her class of 7-year-olds who were making
a murmurous sound while they attempted the drawing task they had
been set. 'No, they brought this for poor Brother Batista,' she said,
showing Miss Bhosle the letter. 'Nice handwriting,' Miss Bhosle
said and read the letter. 'How charmingly written,' she declared.
'Since your departure the school is like a garden in winter,' she
quoted from the letter, 'the flower beds are bare and the birds sing
no more.' She returned the letter to Miss Miranda, adding, 'Very
poetical, I must say.'

'It's that Roshan,' Miss Miranda said. Miss Bhosle remarked that
she had heard of him. 'His writing is as beautiful as his looks,' she
said. 'I noticed,' Miss Miranda said, 'you couldn't resist stroking
his cheek.' Miss Bhosle sighed, and said, 'That's why I came, to

take a closer look. A garden in winter. Oh, my!' Miss Miranda's little boys had begun to be noisy, reminding Miss Bhosle that she had neglected her own class for too long, and she returned to it.

Miss Bhosle was 27 years old and lived with her widowed mother and two married brothers, whose wives and children brought the number of the family to eleven, in a three-room flat in Matunga. A marriage had been arranged for her when she was 14, but the father of the prospective bridegroom had cancelled the arrangement one day before the wedding, accusing Miss Bhosle's parents of having misrepresented their caste and given an exaggeratedly inflated impression of the dowry by disguising the negligible amount in a column of figures which constituted a hypothetical inventory of the family's possessions and not a simple statement of the proffered dowry. The two fathers had nearly come to blows, so violent was their dispute. Scandal was heaped on the family, and the young Miss Bhosle's fate was to become a widow without becoming a wife. When her father died of a heart attack two years later, her mother said that he had never recovered from the blow of the daughter's broken marriage contract, thus blaming the young girl for her father's death. Her mother's unwillingness to find a husband for her was a form of punishment for the presumed crime of having killed her father, and Miss Bhosle, who had done nothing at all but remain meticulously dutiful to her parents, was cast in the role of the eternal victim. Sometimes she wished she had been a real widow so that she could have ended her worldly torments by leaping on her husband's funeral pyre. Her only consolation was that she had received an education and could teach at the primary level, and so lose herself in her work. But the boys from the upper school, full-grown men some of them, or so they seemed to her, passing by the open door of her classroom, were a continuous source of palpitations in her heart. Like a garden in winter. And the birds sing no more. What a poetical young man! She felt like crying.

6   Miss Bhosle in Love

Roshan's words echoed in her mind for several days. She saw a wintry desolation in the crowded flat where her nephews and nieces raised a riot all day long. It was hot and suffocatingly humid in the streets when she took the circuitous path to the school, going by way of a small park which was aflame with flamboyant red-flowering trees. She thought of the park as an English garden, its trees stripped bare by icy winds. 'And the birds sing no more,' she repeated, although a noisy argument was going on among the restless crows in the trees. In her more placid moods, Miss Bhosle fancied herself a Jane Austen heroine, one whose sufferings must end with a wholly satisfying marriage; but when embittered with her fate, as increasingly of late, she imagined herself an impetuous heroine who went riding over the moors through a fierce winter storm to be with a forbidden lover. Since life denied her the ordinary and customary expectations of her class, her mind therefore unconsciously sought, in a world composed so far entirely of fantasy, the extraordinary and the exotic. In the mundane reality of her background the most unthinkable horror would be to be touched by a Muslim male, and so she was most marvellously shocked by her own inclination which longed to take young Roshan to her bosom and crush him with so much ardour that he became sucked into her bloodstream.

A small boy came and stood in front of Roshan during break one day and said, 'Miss Bhosle wants to see you.' It was some weeks since the incident when he had run into her. During that interval he had turned 14 and believed himself a full-grown adult, an illusion sustained by his being taller than the majority of the boys, even the most senior. He had made a mark in the school cricket team, which fact alone bestowed upon him an enviously heroic stature among the young boys; among the seniors and even the teachers, he was admired for his English accent, which, unknown to them, he had acquired at the cinema by listening attentively to Robert Donat,

239

Charles Laughton and Laurence Olivier, so that his recitations of poems had attracted a school-wide reputation. It was difficult for Roshan not to have a considerably conceited opinion of himself and believe that he could perpetrate no wrong. What, then, could he have done that Miss Bhosle wanted to see him?

She sat at her desk during a free period, marking exercise books containing the attempts of her little boys to write the English alphabet. Roshan knocked on the frame of the open door, walked in and stood in front of her. She remained absorbed in her work for a moment and then looked up. 'You sent for me, miss?' he said.

'Your name is Roshan Karim, is it not?' she asked, tapping a red pencil against the open page of an exercise book.

'Yes, miss.'

'I see.' She placed the pencil down, folded her arms and leaned against the desk. When she closed her lips, Roshan could see the tip of her two front teeth protrude between them. 'Mr Carvalho was telling me you are very gifted in English.' He stared at her, pleased. 'That you recite poetry very well,' she went on. 'And that you can even write poems.'

'I like Mr Carvalho's class very much, miss,' Roshan said, trying to be modest.

'So, you like English literature?' She leaned her neck forward which, from his point of view, had the effect of raising her chin, so that when she closed her mouth the protruding teeth seemed to be pointed at him.

'Yes, miss, very much, miss.'

'I do, too,' she said, smiling suddenly. Roshan thought this a strange confession from a teacher. 'I have many books,' she continued, 'and I think you might enjoy reading some of them. I've brought three and will be happy to lend them to you.' She paused, and added, smiling again, 'Later we can discuss them.'

Roshan looked obviously flattered. The books were beside her, on the desk, and she picked up the first one. '*Tales from Shakespeare*,' she read the title, but before she could say anything else, Roshan quickly said, 'By Charles and Mary Lamb – I've read that, miss.' She glanced at him, surprised, and was astonished to hear him say, 'They're not as good as the plays.'

'What, you've read Shakespeare?'

Roshan incongruously remembered the pleasing fountains and

felt slightly embarrassed. 'Well, some of the plays, miss, and the poems.'

'The poems? You mean the sonnets?'

'The sonnets, too, miss.'

Miss Bhosle realized that there was more to Shakespeare than she herself knew, and to prevent a revelation of her ignorance picked up a second book and said, 'This is a book they use in grammar schools in England, a selection from Byron's *Childe Harold's Pilgrimage*.'

Roshan took it from her, flipped through its pages, and handed it back, saying, 'That's a good poem, miss. I like the part about the Battle of Waterloo.'

'What, you know it, then?'

'Yes, miss. Byron is a favourite with me.' Seeing an opportunity to show off, he said, 'I know a lot of him by heart. You want to test me, miss?'

'Recite me some, then.'

Roshan thrust his chest out and began, 'Once more upon the waters! yet once more!' Miss Bhosle stared at him in wonder and admiration as his beautiful recitation filled the empty classroom. Her third book was a schoolboy story which she realized would be beneath the youthful prodigy's contempt, and so she quietly covered it with the other two.

Later, she was shocked by the proposal she made to him, knowing that she would never have done so had she premeditated it, but, applauding his recitation, and regretting she had left her best books at home, she asked if he could not meet her in the park – her little English garden – in the evening where she could give him some books and also have the opportunity to talk with him about their favourite poems. Hearing this proposal, the image that came to Roshan's mind was of himself meeting his friend Chandru in the evening as was their custom: Chandru would make some usual suggestion, such as walking to Dadar to see the girls out on their evening stroll, and he would surprise Chandru by saying casually, 'Very sorry, old chap, but I've got to go and meet a girl.' The actuality of Miss Bhosle before him did not attract him in the least; but the opportunity of making an impression on Chandru with the romantic idea that he had a rendezvous with a woman was too good to lose, and so he agreed to Miss Bhosle's proposal.

Chandru was indeed amazed. He first thought that Roshan was being fanciful, inventing a story just to make him envious. But when Roshan said that Chandru could follow him to the park and see for himself, Chandru was obliged to believe. He congratulated his friend, but a surge of envy made him think to himself the affair was nothing more than an enthusiastic teacher wanting to help a gifted student. Tall and fair-skinned, Roshan was good-looking, but Chandru could not believe a Hindu woman with a Maharashtran name would want to be touched by a Muslim, and a Punjabi one at that. So he affectionately slapped his friend on the shoulder, said how lucky he was to be on the verge of making it to a woman's bed, but kept to himself the thought that the truth had to be less romantic than Roshan had represented it. When he saw Roshan go off, however, he felt bitter that he himself had been born with such a dark skin. 'Black bloody pygmy,' he said in that wallowing in self-hatred which is an expression of an extreme love of the self.

Roshan had seen only the amazement and the envy, and went off pleased with the effective little drama he had contrived without realizing that having persuaded Chandru that he was on the threshold of a romance necessitated that he himself believe his own fantasy. Miss Bhosle was not yet at the corner entrance to the park when he reached there. It was just past sunset. Only one distant street-light had come on. Groups of young men were loitering on the pavement, but the crowd was quickly diminishing as people made for the restaurants and the more brightly lit areas of the district. Miss Bhosle, who had already twice walked past the corner before Roshan got there, suddenly came up to him and said, 'Oh, there you are! Sorry I'm late. My little niece would not let me go without hearing a story.'

They entered the park. Roshan suppressed the disappointment he experienced when she came up to him and he saw her thin, somewhat stooping figure while she spoke as if she lived as a dependant among rich relatives. The smell of oil from her hair, somewhat repulsively sweet, had reached him before she did. But as soon as they began to walk across the grass towards the empty bench against the far wall where the park ended his imagination was flattered that a woman walked with him. She was risking her reputation to be with him, for theirs had to be an illicit attachment. He was thrilled to think that some mysterious punishment was to be their fate; imagining himself a famous tragic lover, one who was immured with his beloved and spent what little time was left them in the living tomb singing heartbreaking duets, he needed to see her as some delicate beauty.

When they reached the bench, she said, 'You'll think me wholly forgetful, but as you can see I haven't brought any of the books.'

'It's too dark to read,' he said, sitting down next to her and looking down at the space, which he reckoned to be six to nine inches, between them.

She laughed, thinking his remark very witty. 'It was my little niece, you see,' she explained. 'If I'd picked up a book, she would have asked me to read from it, and as it was she'd already delayed me.'

Roshan said it was nothing, he knew a lot of poetry by heart, and glanced at her, expecting to be asked to recite some. But, 'She's so naughty,' Miss Bhosle said, putting a hand in front of her mouth and laughing, and proceeded to narrate a series of episodes exemplifying the niece's naughtiness. The narration generated associations of the deeds of the niece's siblings and cousins. Miss Bhosle chatted on, laughing frequently, always raising a hand to the front of her mouth when she laughed and letting her head wobble as she did so; then, dropping the hand and closing her lips to swallow before she continued to chat, her protuberant teeth pressed down on her lower lip a second – at which moment Roshan looked away from her each time and thought of the lips of Rita Hayworth. It had grown quite dark. Two distant street-lights cast a dim glow in the park. There were three other couples on the neighbouring benches along the wall. Roshan had seen two men lurking under the trees by the entrance, obviously seeking some voyeuristic opportunity, but could see them no more.

He had also ceased to hear Miss Bhosle's chatter, but sat convincing himself that he was in the garden of the Capulets, having just scaled the wall to be below Juliet's balcony. It suddenly occurred to him that he had to hold her hand. He would need to give an account of his tryst to Chandru, and honour required that there be no false representation of the affair. He wondered how he should reach for her hand. Should he let his own hand creep up towards her when she dropped it to her side or on her thigh? Or should he snatch it boldly? He looked at his own right hand which was on his knee and found that he could not command it to move. It seemed to have gone cold. And then he thought that it had become separated from the arm. It was just there, fixed to the knee. He pinched it with his left hand, and felt nothing. He remained perplexed for a few minutes, and then, a mosquito suddenly buzzing in his ear, the hand flew up instinctively to flick it away. At the same moment, another mosquito buzzed in Miss Bhosle's ear and she flicked at it too, and the coincidence resulted in the two hands grazing each other. Roshan was relieved. He could now truthfully say to Chandru, 'Well, touching hands is as far as we went, it was our first night together, what do you expect?'

At last Miss Bhosle stopped her chatter and said, 'My, it must be getting late.' The banality of her remark was about to make Roshan lose his illusion of a grand passion when she said, 'Well, Lord Byron?' – words that kept him confirmed in his fantasy and provoked from him the spontaneous quotation,

> 'She walks in beauty, like the night
>   Of cloudless climes and starry skies . . .'

He paused dramatically, and would have recited the rest of the poem, but Miss Bhosle rose from the bench, saying, 'And time flies!' He was briefly disappointed not to have been allowed to show off his knowledge but then thought that he might have forgotten a line or stumbled over a phrase, and therefore her interruption was providential in keeping only the sound of his mellifluous rendition in her memory and not what might have been a faulty longer performance. As they walked across the grass, she tripped on the root of a tree, and could only prevent herself from falling by quickly grasping his arm. He was thrilled, and heard himself saying later to Chandru, 'And of course it was natural that she should hold my arm as we walked.' When they reached the gate, she said, 'I'll go out first. You stay about two minutes before leaving. And I promise you. Tomorrow at the same time. I *will* manage to bring the books!' She walked out, and another thrill pulsed through his veins, and he framed another remark for Chandru: 'Parting really is a sweet sorrow, but we shall meet tomorrow.' He rehearsed variations on famous literary utterances as he walked home.

But he did not see Chandru that evening. While walking from the park, he was struck by an idea. He would write a poem that would remind Miss Bhosle, when he gave it to her next morning, of their evening together. He would write a poem that sounded just like Byron! The opening phrase came to him, and when he reached home and Zakia said to him, 'You missed an all-Saigal programme on the radio, where were you?' he answered, 'Don't bother me now, I'm feverishly possessed by an idea right now.' Zakia stared at him and said, 'My oh my, we are all hot and bothered with ideas now, are we?'

Roshan waved a dismissive hand at his sister and went straight to the corner where he kept his exercise books, and quickly wrote down, 'She stalks her duty like the light' and stared at the words for half an hour in utter amazement at the brilliance of his own mind and also in the misery of not having the rest of the poem pour out of his brain in two seconds. He wrote the Byron poem out from memory, then wrote his version of the first line next to it, and spent another half an hour staring at the page. Finally, the second line emerged on the page and he rewrote the two opening lines as:

> She stalks her duty, like the light
>   Of doubtless times and scary sighs

and began to feel a terrific exhilaration in his mind. The excitement alternated with anxiety and misery because each succeeding line refused to come spontaneously and easily but had to be struggled over, making him think for long periods that he would never be able to find it and then being struck with wonder and self-admiration when he succeeded.

The next morning, Roshan slipped out of the General Knowledge class, walked to Miss Bhosle's classroom, found her repeatedly shouting 'Quiet!' to the little boys making a din, held out a folded piece of paper to her, saying, 'A message for you, miss,' and proceeded from there to the bathroom where he found Adi washing his hands.

Miss Bhosle read the poem, and read it again. She could hear her heart beating. It was a love poem, she was certain. Although she could not understand a word of it and failed to make the connection with Roshan's aborted recitation in the park, she thought it a beautiful poem. How wonderful to have someone write a poem to her! She fell into dreaming. Her classes were a succession of infantile riots. Miss Miranda came across the corridor, tippety-tip in her high heels, to see what was happening. Paper aeroplanes were flying above the yelling heads of the boys. Miss Bhosle gazed at the far wall and smiled. Oh, said Miss Miranda to herself, she's in love, and returned to her own classroom. Miss Bhosle was dreaming of becoming a poet herself and living in an arcadian fantasy where on the cool, green bank of a limpid river she and Roshan spoke poems to each other all day long. She thought of herself as Sarojni Naidu, 'the Nightingale of India', and Roshan – well, of course, he could only be Rabindra Nath Tagore. It pleased her to think of him as having a long white beard. That would make him look older; saintly and wise. She would become his eternal disciple. But she was soon filled with regret. Her beautiful poet was a Muslim. He would prefer to be called Ghalib or Iqbal, never Tagore. Her teeth pressed down on her lower lip.

When she was leaving the flat in the evening to go to meet Roshan in the park, she ran into her younger brother Shankar. He was soaked in his coarse cotton shirt, sweat was pouring down from under his orange-coloured Gandhi cap on his head, falling in streams down his cheeks. He was carrying a bamboo stick like a rifle on his shoulder. 'Where have you been,' she asked, 'to the battle of Waterloo?' He looked scornfully at her for the offensive reference to a British victory, and she quickly added, 'Ah yes, it's Quit India, twit India with you all the time! You think you're going to send them packing with bamboo sticks?' He glared at her, and said, 'Yes, and the Muslims, too!' She regretted having taunted him for his attachment to the band of young Maharashtrans who met every day for martial training and had their heads filled with talk of India for the Hindus. *Hindu-Hindu Hindustan!* they chanted constantly. In her instincts she sympathized with their fanaticism, but her own condition of having been condemned by religious zeal to a chaste widowhood made her want to reject her brother's militancy, and her regret was the deeper since the outburst she had just provoked from Shankar served to emphasize the treachery she was committing by loving a Muslim. She left him, telling him that she was going for a walk with a girlfriend, and hurried through the crowded street, her mind filled with the exciting possibility that the future held for her some extraordinarily heroic suffering. She was in love with drama and longed for situations of emotional intensity that involved brutal confrontations, so that she could escape from the grinding boredom in which she was compelled to live, and it was this longing for passionate variety that she saw in her mind as a love for a Muslim boy.

Roshan had arrived early and was waiting by the gate of the park. He did not notice that she carried no books and she did not give an excuse for why she had again failed to bring any. Since her brother was on her mind, she began to talk about him as they walked into the park. He was 25 years old, she told Roshan, who listened politely though the only words he wanted to hear from her were whether or not she liked his poem and how she thought it compared with Byron's. The bench they had sat on the previous evening was occupied by an old man in a crumpled suit with a pair of narrow spectacles balanced on the tip of his nose, trying to read an English newspaper in the failing light, but the bench at the far end of the wall, behind which a street-lamp had come on, was empty and they made for it. Shankar had been working in a textile mill for six years, she was saying. He should have gone to college, but he had married young and needed a job to keep his family. What did Roshan think of people marrying young, she asked as they sat down.

Roshan had no opinion on the subject, and sighed, hoping she would remember his poem. 'It's fate,' he said, because he could think of nothing else to say. 'Look at Gandhi-ji,' she said enthusiastically. 'He married when he was thirteen, and look at him now. He's a saint.' Roshan nodded his head and repeated, 'That's fate.' She laughed slightly with her palm held in front of her mouth, with the middle finger covering the length of her nose, and said, 'Everything's written, it's all there on the lines of your hand. Don't you think?'

Roshan had never thought about this question either, but he saw a possibility and held up his hand and asked, 'I wonder what mine say.'

She seized his hand and peered closely at it, clicking her tongue in her mouth and saying, 'My oh my, what a complicated destiny!' She passed her thumb along the lines as if she followed a prescribed procedure for deciphering them. 'What a long life, and what a life of action!' Her hand was almost squeezing his. 'But such a settled love life,' she went on, 'a long and happy marriage. And look here' – she ticked off several grooves on the side of Roshan's palm – 'my oh my, so many children!'

'What about my talent line?' Roshan asked, hoping she would talk about his poem and wanting also to prolong her holding his hand so that he could tell Chandru that they had become inseparable. She examined his palm again, passing her thumb over each of the principal lines, rubbing the palm with her own and then feeling it with her fingertips. 'Oh, talent! Why, look here, see the crossing of these three lines that make the shape of a six-pointed star? One man in ten million is born with this. A great surgeon at least. Or a famous engineer. Or a very, very famous actor.'

'I wonder if Byron had a similar star on his palm,' Roshan hinted, but she let go of his hand and held up her own in front of her face for a moment, and, before dropping it to her lap, remarked, 'Mine is just a mess.'

'Let me see,' Roshan said, and she, pretending that he could have no interest in reading her future, answered, 'No, no, please.' Her tone suggested that he persist and so he said, 'Come, it's only fair.' She gave the impression of surrendering under duress and timidly brought up her hand for his inspection, saying, 'Please be kind, mister palmist.'

Roshan held the hand in both of his and stared at the crazy lines on the palm. He studied them for a long time, playing with his thumb as she had with hers. It was getting dark. Finally he said, 'You will receive gifts.' She waited to hear more. 'Things wonderfully made,' he said when she said nothing. 'As if they came from Byron.' She took the statement as a form of flattery, sighed, and exclaimed, 'Such happiness!' He realized that in order to continue to hold her hand he needed to furnish her with more information about her future, and so he studied the lines for a while longer and then declared, 'A most complicated and difficult love life.' She sighed again and said, 'I was afraid so!' He ended his reading by saying, 'Your life will be like a poem, full of perfect rhythm and beauty.'

When they parted to meet again on the following evening, for she suddenly remembered she had not brought the promised books, his satisfaction at having held her hand for much of the time they had sat on the bench was somewhat soured by his not having been able to elicit from her one comment on his poem. At first he thought her silence must mean that the poem was bad and she did not want to hurt his feelings by telling him so. Then he consoled himself with the thought that, of course, she was being polite. It was bad manners to express the sort of praise he had expected. Besides, a girl could not say some things. Why, he was a fool not to realize the truth! All the attention she had given his hand was her way of thanking him for having written what he had!

He thought of various ambiguous images with which to impress Chandru with the rapid progress his affair with Miss Bhosle had made when a line came to him: 'You held my hand under the starlit sky', and was again seized with the inspiration to write a poem. Miss Miranda saw him deliver it the next morning when she stepped out of her classroom to see why there was such a noise coming from Miss Bhosle's; the look on Miss Bhosle's face when she received the piece of folded paper from Roshan struck Miss Miranda as revelatory. 'Ah-hah,' she said to herself, observing the handsome young man walk dreamily away. The science teacher gave a zoology lesson that afternoon, and some remark about tigers suggested to Roshan's mind the line, 'A tiger springs out of my heated blood'. He wrote it down, deciding to use it later in his next poem, but found that he could think of nothing but the line that must follow and so felt compelled to write the poem while the class learned facts about animals. When the lesson ended, he slipped out and walked quickly to Miss Bhosle's class to deliver the new poem.

During the next week, Miss Miranda saw him pass by her door several times each day on his way to Miss Bhosle's classroom, and each time she said, 'Ah-hah.' Miss Bhosle had become the idea of the loved one in Roshan's mind; she was an object of his poetical devotions, more a ghostly glow of a female being than a real woman. To her, he was the forbidden male whom she so longed to possess in secret that she shivered with ecstasy at the thought of her implied transgression. They continued to meet in the evenings in the park, reading each other's palm or seeing a mosquito on the other's cheek in order to have an excuse to touch. One evening, darkness having fallen, Roshan drew her hand to his lips and kissed it. She responded by holding his and placing it against her cheek. He thought of Merle Oberon, and sighed. A tear fell from her eye to the back of his hand, and she cried softly, 'God, why do we have to suffer such a fate!' The moment called for a dramatic gesture and he turned and held her firmly by the arms. She dropped her face on his shoulder and sobbed and then placed her cheek against his, saying, 'How can this be, how can this be?' He slowly turned his face and touched her cheek with his lips. It was wet. 'It must be God's will,' she whispered, 'marrying Hindus and Muslims to make India one.' He paused, taking his lips away from her cheek, where he had felt no sensation although he had been thinking of the evocative language in which he was going to describe his first kiss to Chandru, and reflected on her portentous statement. Before he could come to any conclusion, her lips fell against his. It was a brief, close-lipped impression, and she quickly withdrew and assumed a stiffened, remorseful pose, but for him it was a moment that made him one with all the lovers of literature and films. He was too thrilled with himself to say anything and her pose seemed to forbid a renewed embrace; and she, expecting a romantic declaration, found her prolific poet had gone dumb. The two sat in silence till it was time to go.

A man stood leaning close against the wide trunk of a tree and, unseen by the lovers, watched them walk across the grass towards the gate where the woman left first. He hastened out of the park after Roshan and contrived to take a good look at his features under a street-light, deducing from them and from the fair skin and the boy's height that he must be a Parsee or conceivably a Punjabi Muslim. The first possibility filled him with revulsion, the second with disgust and murderous hatred. He ran after the woman.

Miss Bhosle was walking serenely along the crowded pavement. At last she had a lover! A young boy who kissed her tears. Whose lips were like rose petals. At last she could dream of passion. But suddenly a hand grabbed hers and began to pull her violently through the loitering strollers, and she screamed aloud but immediately suppressed her scream seeing that the person who did so was her brother Shankar. 'Come, come,' he was saying, 'you're going to see something.' She was nearly running in order to keep up with him. His rough hand gripped hers tightly as he dragged her along, and she cried at him, 'Stop, you're hurting me, let me go I tell you!' He threw a fierce glance back at her and hissed, 'I'll show you what hurting is!' And quickened his pace, obliging her to run, her body stooped, her hair falling in front of her over her shoulder. 'Shankar, let me go, I tell you,' she shouted at him, realizing what had happened, 'I'm your elder sister, let me go!' He did not relax his grip and dragged her all the way to the family flat, pulling her up the stairs, through the front door, straight to the sitting room where his brother and his wife had already placed their bedding on the floor and were squatted on it listening to the radio news, held her now by the wrist and forced her to turn her face to his, and slapped it sharply, demanding, 'Tell me who it is, tell me his name!'

She saw her elder brother Laxman reach to turn off the radio, his eyes, which were on her, taking on a severe look and revealing he understood the cause of Shankar's anger. 'I will only tell you this,' she said in heroic defiance. 'He's a Muslim.'

Shankar stared at her incredulously and then slapped her hard three or four times. 'He's a Muslim,' she cried back at him viciously, an exhilaration surging within her above the pain, and thrilled by the scandal she was raising within the family, she cried out more loudly, 'He's a Muslim!'

Laxman stood up and pulled her away from Shankar. 'Is this true?' he shouted at her, and hit her harder than had Shankar. She cried aloud in her pain, some blood trickled from the corners of her mouth; and she could not even repeat the pathetic defiant phrase, so quickly had the one moment of heroism in her life come and vanished. 'With a Muslim?' Laxman thundered at her and, receiving no reply, beat her mercilessly, shouting again and again in a voice full of contempt and hatred, 'With a Muslim?'

Laxman's wife watched grimly from the floor. Their mother had appeared at the door from the kitchen and stood stonily, feeling a sudden pain in her breast on hearing that her daughter had been consorting with a Muslim. The children stood in the door from their bedroom, five round faces with large terrified eyes, and watched their aunt being punished for some awful crime that they could not understand.

7   Adi's Dilemma

After his failure to get his friends to seal the oath of allegiance to the Quit India movement by kissing one another, Adi entered a phase of demonstrative meditation. Although he went with the others to the restaurant during lunch and shared his cup of tea with them, he spoke very little but merely sat there smoking his favourite Black & White cigarettes. In class, too, he had become quieter. He continued to escape to the bathroom as often as he could manage but whenever someone saw him there all he was observed to be doing was washing his hands obsessively.

With Roshan and Bhatia in the restaurant one day, he was staring at the door to the kitchen from where the tall dark-haired waiter Ibrahim with greying crinkly hair was emerging in his usual style of carrying three or four cups of tea in their saucers piled one upon another on one palm while with his other hand he carried an equal number of full glasses of water by inserting his thumb and fingers into the glasses so that one saw the digits distorted through the water. Ibrahim served the customers at a nearby table and Adi kept staring at the door which continued to swing. Ibrahim went back, gave the door a kick and disappeared into the kitchen.

'Poor Ibrahim, we've put him in a bad mood,' Roshan said.

When he had brought them their single cup of tea a few minutes earlier, he had shown them a picture postcard that portrayed two naked men simultaneously performing fellatio, each receiving what he gave by lying in the opposite direction to the other. 'Got this from Cairo,' Ibrahim said, grinning. 'That's filthy,' Bhatia said. 'Disgusting,' commented Roshan. Adi merely looked at the card and returned it mechanically to Ibrahim, who said, 'You boys don't know what's good for you.' Bhatia said to him, 'Piss off, sodomist.'

'He'll cheer up soon enough,' Roshan said.

'He's always looking for someone to bugger,' Bhatia said. 'Filthy fucker, trying to pick up boys by showing them dirty postcards.'

Suddenly Adi surprised them by breaking his silence. 'It's not worth it,' he said.

'What's not worth it?' Bhatia said.

'I mean nothing's worth it. What's the use when I can't even have the illusion that I'm the only one?'

'He's talking to himself,' Roshan said.

'Listen,' Adi said, becoming animated, 'can you imagine the billions of women who have enjoyed sex before you were ever born? And can you imagine that there will be billions after you're dead who will find their greatest joy in someone else's cock?'

'So, what are you saying, you'll settle for men?' Bhatia joked.

'You want to go and cheer up Ibrahim?' Roshan said flippantly.

But Adi, paying them no attention, went on. 'And even in your lifetime, while you're still young and vigorous and think what you see in the mirror is terrific, even right now, at this very minute, in England or France, or right behind that door of the private dining room, there's a woman loving it from a man who's not you!'

'Suppose you could have every woman in Bombay,' Bhatia said. 'No, every woman just in Matunga. No, not even that many. Every woman in this block of buildings. You'd be devastated, man! You'd die of fucking.'

'You could become a Muslim and marry four,' Roshan suggested.

'It's not what you could do or what you're allowed to do,' Adi said. 'It's when you know you have a self, you then have a craving to be omnipresent.'

'What's omnipresent?' Roshan asked.

'Jane Russell's omnipresent,' Bhatia said.

'I was talking to a young woman who came to a tea party my mother gave,' Adi said. 'She was pretty and looked very interestingly at me when I talked. And then, do you know what she said? "Oh, that's so amusing I must tell my Mody," she said. "Who's this Mody?" I asked. "My fiancé," she answered. She'd given the impression of looking only at me, listening only to me, the whole world was excluded from her attention but me, but, dammit, all the time she was thinking of her fucking Mody.'

'You should read about the Greek gods,' Bhatia said.

'What about them?' Roshan asked.

'They were exclusive fuckers,' Bhatia answered. 'Just like Adi wants to be.'

'Only one god can be exclusive,' Roshan argued.

'And he's yours,' Bhatia said sarcastically. 'Muslims are such monomaniacs.'

'False,' Roshan said. 'We can have four wives.'

'The Greeks preferred buggering boys,' Adi said. 'Greek love, it's called.'

'Your Krishna was a pretty active fucker,' Roshan said to Bhatia.

'A model for all of us to emulate,' Bhatia responded.

'Try imitating him and see where it'll get you,' Adi said.

'Straight to the bathroom,' Roshan said, and added, ''Tis better to have buggered and tossed than not to have buggered at all. Alfred Lord Tennyson.'

'Celibacy is the answer,' Adi said. 'If I can't have it all then I refuse to take any. Why put myself in a situation where I will always be punished? I'll be celibate. Like Christian priests.'

'Oh, balls, man, they fuck all the time,' Bhatia said. 'Even the Pope has nephews and nieces.'

'What, he sleeps with his sister?' Roshan asked.

'Do you know why Catholics are forbidden to use contraceptives?' Bhatia asked.

'Why?'

'Because their priests can't very well go to the chemist's and ask for rubbers. It protects the myth of celibacy. Everyone has to breed like mad so that the priests can do it on the sly.'

'Celibacy is the answer,' Adi repeated to himself. 'If I can't do it all the time then I won't do it ever.'

8 Miss Miranda's Commission

Roshan had a poem to deliver to Miss Bhosle the morning after she had kissed him in the park but she was not in her classroom. When he had walked away from the park the previous evening it was in so high a state of self-esteem that he alone seemed to have the privilege of existence. The crowd in the street, and the buses and the hand-drawn carts were no more than ghostly phenomena on the outer edge of his consciousness which was absorbed in an exquisite egotism. He had received a kiss from a woman! That one event in the history of the universe had effected a marvellous transformation in the young man, stimulating within him an exultant ecstasy. He had done it! Received the gift of the female's adoration of his self. His vanity flattered, he perceived self-love as an intimation of love, suppressed the plain, unattractive figure of Miss Bhosle, substituting for it an archetypal female form, and was suffused with a mystical glow as if his soul, having discovered the eternal other with whom it must consort, had commenced to dance. But in this awakening within him of an abstract idea of love he preserved an element of mundane drama with which to relish an earthly poignancy: he reminded himself that Miss Bhosle was a Hindu, a fact that would inevitably be a source of trouble and pain and therefore a fact likely to bestow distinction upon their love.

But Miss Bhosle remained absent for the rest of the week. Roshan went to the park in the evenings and sat alone on the bench where he had received the kiss, and enjoyed being melancholy. He assumed she must be ill to be absent from work. He sat on the bench imagining her beside him, kissing him again, and shedding tears at the sadness of their love. He was impressed by the fact that fate was being cruel to him, separating him from his beloved. When darkness fell, he tried to force tears out of his eyes so that he might know the full force of his suffering.

When another week had passed without Miss Bhosle returning to

255

school, his solitary drama became tedious and he ceased going to the park. There were other events to engage his interest – cricket games at Pavilion Hill, weekend excursions to Juhu beach with the family, long walks with Chandru during which he could pretend not to be interested in the pretty girls they passed because he had told Chandru of his love for Miss Bhosle. By the end of the month, he was quite bored with having to look sad and to seek pleasure in suffering. Then he found himself stopped by a small boy in the corridor during a break and summoned to the presence of Miss Miranda.

She was alone in her classroom, marking exercise books at her desk, and called him in when she saw him come and stand in her door. Her black, recently permed hair was not just wavy, as in the past, but fell in profuse ringlets about her light-skinned face, and he noticed, as she leaned on the desk, her breasts in her tight blouse were drawn close together and uplifted so that a bulging fullness was revealed below the neck. 'I've some important information to give you,' she said, 'but I can't do so here.'

'What's it about, miss?'

'You'll have to be patient. It's nothing to do with school. That's why I don't want to talk about it here. Can you meet me after school?'

'Yes, miss. Where?'

She thought for a moment and said, 'Wait for me outside. When I come out, follow me at a short distance as far as the cinema.'

'All right, miss,' he said, smiling, excited both by the assignation and by the mystery surrounding it, and at the same time beginning to formulate a remark for Chandru – 'Oh, by the way, Miss Miranda, the one with the luscious tits, asked me to go out with her.'

'Remember to wait,' she said. 'I'll be out ten or fifteen minutes after the bell.'

'Yes, miss. I'll be there, miss.'

Miss Miranda watched him go and thought Miss Bhosle had been unlucky to have had her liaison discovered so soon, the boy was so handsome. The poor woman had suffered the consequences of a forbidden passion without enjoying its pleasurable benefits. But she must have been deluded to believe she could have any sort of affair with so young a boy, she was old enough to be his mother, and, on the top of that, was nothing but a dry stick. These thoughts, affecting to be objective and expressive first only of a concern for the afflicted Miss Bhosle and then of a criticism of her presumption that she could be loved by a handsome youth, were in fact rooted in subjectivity, for seeing the absurdity of Miss Bhosle's desire she unconsciously advanced the normalcy of her own, her vanity being stimulated by the opportunism of the self which is always on the lookout for gratification. If she felt pity for Miss Bhosle's age her real feeling was a delight in her own comparative youth, and if she thought of her as the poor woman who was unattractive it was to think of herself as the fortunate one who was beautiful.

But she had not come to a conscious realization of her motives when, leaving the school that afternoon, she walked past Roshan and heard him begin to follow her. Most of the boys had already disappeared and the street as far as the cinema was nearly empty. There was a crowd of people on the pavement by the cinema, especially by the showcase windows full of stills, and she stopped and waited for Roshan. 'Let's go in there,' she said, indicating the restaurant on the side of the cinema. It was crowded with young men who buttoned their eyes on Miss Miranda's tight blouse as she marched right through the long room to one of the small private rooms where women went to be served to avoid precisely the sort of male attention that Miss Miranda had just received. Roshan walked proudly behind her, thrilled with the glances of envy the men threw at him.

From past patronage of the restaurant, Roshan knew the waiter who came to take her order. He was Moosa, the brother of Ibrahim at the other restaurant, and also given to suddenly producing pornographic postcards. Moosa now gave Roshan a knowing look which at once suggested congratulations, discretion and, as the private rooms had cunningly placed mirrors in them, the hope to be allowed voyeuristic gratification. Miss Miranda asked him to bring two cups of tea. He brought them quickly, also carrying to the table two glasses of water in the style of his brother, with his fingers dipped into them, the digits looked paler than the rest of his hand, and as he turned round to leave he gave Roshan a sly wink.

'I went to see Miss Bhosle,' Miss Miranda had just been saying. 'She was able to send me a message, a postcard, requesting me to go and see her. It was difficult to find the right time. One of her brothers works the night shift at the textile mill and there are also her two sisters-in-law and her mother. Anyway, I managed to see her alone. Well, there was a niece present.'

Miss Miranda sipped her tea and waited for Moosa to go before telling her story. Miss Bhosle had had an accident that had made her . . . 'Well, an invalid almost,' Miss Miranda said, pausing to find some generality in order not to have to say that Miss Bhosle's face was scarred and that she had lost two teeth. Roshan stared at her, hardly hearing what she had to say though she continued to give him a version of Miss Bhosle's condition that the latter herself had approved. There was no mention of the ferocious beating for her audacity in going out with a Muslim boy, nor of the fact that her brothers had forced her to resign from her job, confining her to the flat in the situation of a widow who is obliged to fast, thus compensating themselves for the loss of her income by spending the minimum money for her keep. Roshan vaguely heard again something about her being incapacitated and unable to work and listened to none of the fabricated details, for he was in an ecstasy of self-admiration. In a private room with the beautiful Miss Miranda! Chandru was going to be amazed, Adi was going to die of envy. Kissing a Hindu girl one day and going into a private room with a Christian beauty the next, what a Don Juan! So that he was suddenly shocked to hear Miss Miranda say, 'Only you can save her. That's what she asked me to say to you. Give her your word and she will have something to live for.'

'My word? To do what?'

'Why, to marry her. I can take the message to her.'

At that moment, for the first time, Roshan saw the pitiable figure of the woman whom his mind had lately entertained as a lover. He felt again the sensation of the kiss that he had boasted about to Chandru as 'deep and lingering' and knew it for what it was: a lifeless, dry pressure against his lips, with her protruding front teeth touching his upper lip and inducing within him now a feeling of revulsion. He looked at Miss Miranda's lips. Full and slightly parted, the upper one like Cupid's bow, a slight gleam where the light caught the tips of her teeth: there, it seemed to him, resided the mystery of passion that he so longed to enter. Her black eyes, shining brilliantly, awaited his answer. 'My father will kill me, miss,' he said.

She smiled, drank her tea, and said, 'How about this? I'll tell her your father has found out and has you watched. There's nothing you can do.'

'Yes, miss. That's correct, there's nothing I can do.'

'Or wish to, if you could.' She jerked her chin very slightly as she spoke and a shiver went through her glossy black ringlets, provoking a shiver of intense delight within him.

She changed the subject, asking him questions about his work at school. She had heard about his poetical talent, she remarked. He was flattered. 'Oh, yes, miss, I know a lot by heart.' Inspiration hit him and he sat up straight and recited,

'She walks in beauty, like the night
Of cloudless climes and starry skies . . .'

As he recited, he observed that unlike Miss Bhosle, Miss Miranda watched him with admiration and seemed to be receiving the words as a personal tribute. She praised his elocution when he had concluded.

She took a 2-anna piece from her purse and stood up, saying while she pressed the coin into his palm, 'Will you be kind enough to pay the man as we go out?'

That night Roshan was convinced that he had to write a poem. But the sound of *Miranda* would not go out of his brain and he could only think of *veranda* which sounded ridiculous. He remembered with what deep feeling she had looked at him when he had recited Byron to her, and found himself looking at the imitation he had written:

She stalks her duty, like the light
Of doubtless times and scary sighs . . .

Miss Bhosle had never really acknowledged that poem. It was almost as if he had never given it to her. Therefore, why not present it to Miss Miranda?

The next morning he calmly walked to Miss Miranda's classroom, saw her look first in surprise and perhaps a little alarm when she saw him standing in her door and then smile and jerk her head to indicate he could enter. 'Please accept this, miss,' he said, handing her the poem on a folded piece of paper, and quickly retreated, his heart beating and his penis throbbing, for that gesture of hers, the sudden sharp tilting of the chin and the resultant shaking of her mass of glossy ringlets of hair, accompanied by an aggressive smile, was like an invitation to her arms.

The morning break brought a little boy to him, bearing her message. 'Same time, same place.' It was a small piece of paper, torn from the corner of a page in an exercise book, but Roshan, holding it concealed in his palm and pretending to be wiping his mouth, furtively kissed the blank area below the words where surely her hand must have rested as she wrote.

They went again to the restaurant after school. Moosa raised his eyebrows and cleared his throat in a meaningful manner in Roshan's hearing. But after he had brought the tea and gone, Miss Miranda said to Roshan who sat timidly opposite her, hoping his internal palpitations were not extremely visible, 'I knew you were poetical but not that you were such a marvellous poet!'

He relaxed spontaneously, smiling, and she, struck by the beauty of his smile, went on, 'You have a lot of talent, a *lot* of talent. This is a very *sweet* poem,' she said, bringing out the poem from her purse. Her emphasis suggested to him that she believed the poem to be addressed particularly to her, and he said, 'I hope you like what I think of you, miss.'

Indeed she did so, though she did not immediately confess it. She understood the theme of duty as meaning the duty they had to their own religion, to be true to it, while the imagery of time offered the consolation of hope, and she was convinced the two ideas were a perceptive statement of her own deepest feelings. 'Roshan,' she said in a lowered voice that struck him as hauntingly erotic, 'please do me the kindness of not calling me miss. My name is Alicia.'

'Alicia,' he said softly as if in a dream.

'That's nice,' she said, leaning forward and quickly patting his cheek. He closed his eyes a moment to make the sensation last longer. What luck, he thought, to be with a Christian girl. Christian girls did not think of themselves as Indians and were like American film stars, whom they loved to imitate, and touched men openly, not like Indian girls who were taught to remain in horror of physical contact.

'So, you don't miss your Miss Bhosle?' she asked, almost as if she were teasing him.

'I haven't thought about her for twenty-four hours,' he answered, astonished, as he did so, at the facility with which one acquired the language of a flattering lover.

She deliberately stared at him with wide open eyes while holding a smile upon her lips indicating that she dared him to proceed. He plunged straight into that provocative gesture. 'I've thought only of you,' he said.

He could not have chosen a thought that appealed to her more had he known her secret mind. The nubile young woman who tormented the fantasies of the schoolboys was the eldest of seven children for whom she and a young brother named Fernando were the only consistent providers, one paying the rent of the overcrowded flat in Bandra and the other buying the provisions for the large family that promised to increase yet more. The father, Manuel Miranda, was of obscure Goanese origin; though nature had neglected to provide his skin with the appropriate pigmentation, he considered himself a European because he was born a Christian and spoke only English. He resented his black skin that obliged him to seek work with Hindu entrepreneurs to whom he considered himself superior; they, in turn, despised his European affectation, and if they employed him at all it was out of a sense of irony, to show who possessed power and, with that, a real superiority. Mr Miranda consequently sought consolation in gin, which somehow guaranteed his kinship with the English, and when he was not doing his unencumbered Catholic duty to Mrs Miranda, he took his pleasure in the infamous Foras Road where his choice fell exclusively on Maharashtran women from whom he relished a whipping because they were the same race as his employers and he craved to experience physically from the women what the men inflicted upon him morally, enjoying furthermore the privilege of buying with the money earned from the men the right, when the whipping had drawn his blood, to crush the women under the weight of his enormous belly. Consequently, when he was employed, Mr Miranda was seldom home, but the less he was at home the more he was in a condition to lose his latest job. The rest of the family, including the mother, who apart from the seven living children had seen three others go to an early grave, longed for the day when she could bear no more children, had become accustomed to Alicia being the principal provider and saw her as newly hatched birds perceive the larger bird who returns to the nest, one from whose mouth to pluck out what sustenance they can. Of attention and consideration, let alone love or gratitude, Alicia received nothing from her family. Her siblings choked her with their pestering for money, and she hated her mother for expressing the fear that her 22-year-old daughter might marry and abandon the nest, convincing Alicia that the few occasions that presented themselves when she could be with other families among whom there were suitable young men of her age were deliberately sabotaged by her

261

mother in order to prevent an economic catastrophe in the Miranda household. So that when she heard Roshan say, 'I've thought only of you,' it was as if she were like one who had long been trapped under the rubble of a collapsed house and had suddenly heard a beam being lifted and saw the renewing light come pouring into her life.

Leaving the restaurant, they lingered by the showcase of stills outside the cinema. Tyrone Power, who appeared sword in hand in several of the pictures, was a favourite with her, she said. She liked men with black hair. Roshan took that as a compliment to himself. 'I heard it's a terrific picture,' he said, hoping she would look away from him and not notice he was blushing. But his suddenly darkened cheek emboldened her to become more familiar. 'Is it really that good?' she asked, slightly decreasing the distance between them. 'I haven't seen it, but I heard it's very good,' he answered.

'Tomorrow's Wednesday,' she said, her lips quite close to his ear. He understood what she meant. School ended early. And even before she could make the suggestion that she had already implied he was formulating a statement for Chandru: 'Sorry, old chap, no pleasant fountains this Wednesday, I'm off to the pictures with Alicia.' He saw her black eyes gleaming at him in the bright light, and said, 'Yes, I'll see you in the lobby for the three-thirty show.'

She had in fact said nothing at all after stating that the next day was Wednesday, but was pleased that she had not needed to, and went away delighted to have the image of her young poet in her mind to distract her from the misery of her family.

The poet lived up to his name the next day when during each of the four morning periods he appeared at her door and delivered a poem. The poems dated from the night and the days immediately succeeding the solitary kiss he had received from Miss Bhosle and had been intended for her eyes. Returning home with the excited knowledge that he was to go to the pictures with Miss Miranda, he had been overcome by the idea of the female's generosity to the male, that she should come to him as a gift more priceless than any he had desired. He wanted to give her some rare gift in return and could only think of writing her the greatest love poem ever written. But try as he might, nothing would come. His brain was too excited. He was stuck for rhymes. If *Miranda* suggested only *veranda*, *Alicia* was even more difficult; after two hours of whispering the word, and being distracted much of the time by erotic dreams, he had realized that words like *creasier* and *greasier*, which might just pass for rhymes, were too ridiculously inappropriate, and could think of no others until he hit upon *lease here*. But the discovery of a rhyme did not lead to the discovery of the image and the poem would not come. Looking at his earlier poems, he was surprised how everything in them had fallen perfectly into place, and despaired of his talent, wondering whether he would ever be able to create again with such facility. Then he remembered that no one had seen several of the earlier poems. He copied them out, inscribing beneath each that day's date, and enjoyed the pleasure of delivering them to Miss Miranda in the morning.

Although he had, on the pretext of having to pay an additional fee for the use of the chemistry laboratory, obtained money from his father, Miss Miranda insisted on buying the tickets, which, he was glad to observe, were for the rear of the balcony, the most expensive seats in the cinema, generously cushioned and covered in red velvet. From there, before the lights went out, he could see down below, on the wooden seats of the front two rows, some of the boys from the school, and believed himself to have been singled out for a life enviably superior both in the height it could maintain and the luxury it could enjoy. Three other couples entered the balcony before the film began. Each, immediately on entering, glanced round, saw where the others sat, and took the remotest available seats, and thus, when the lights went out, the four pairs occupied the four corners of the twenty or so rows of the seats in the balcony, Roshan and Alicia on the rear right.

The problem was on what excuse should he hold her hand. An exercise in palmistry was out of the question. He became sharply conscious of a perfume she wore that had the effect of exciting his senses. He had not been aware of it before and wondered if she had not furtively brought out a little bottle from her purse when the lights went out and quickly applied some before the screen lit up and British Movietone News began to show pictures of the valiant efforts of the air-raid wardens in London. The picture disappeared from his mind and he found himself sinking physically, but weightlessly, in a forest of heavily perfumed flowers. The smell changed to the sickly sweet aroma, both awfully attractive and slightly repulsive, of a jackfruit that has split open, and he found himself, aged 8 or 9, up on the hill with Mangal and Rusi, hidden behind a boulder, watching the enraged lovers in their violent embrace. The association that followed was of Miss Nogueira's green skirt swinging past him in the aisle in the classroom and his curious sense that there was a potent, and a terribly desirable, smell behind the smell of the talcum powder.

He came out of his dream when he began to feel a pressure against his right arm. Alicia had rested an elbow upon the arm rest between their two seats and was leaning a little towards him so that the point of her left shoulder fell against his arm. He remained still, not knowing whether he should acknowledge the signal, if it was one, and exert some reciprocal pressure and see where that led; but, fearing that her position might not be a calculated move at all but only an unconscious one and that a move on his part would only serve to remind her of her lapse and so make her maintain a deliberate distance from him, he remained still, preferring to keep what he had than to lose all by wanting more.

But Alicia was saying something. In fact, she had been talking in a low voice while he had been sunk in his reverie. The images of blitzed London evoked many sympathetic sounds from her, a considerable shaking of the head, and several statements about what the poor Londoners were suffering. He could scarcely discern her words over the loud British commentator, but found a distinct pleasure in the murmurous sound at his ear and, leaning his head a little closer to hers as if his motives were only the innocent one of wanting to hear her speech, he accidentally increased the pressure against her shoulder and was thrilled to see that she did not withdraw. At one point, clicking her tongue against the roof of her mouth and shaking her head at the sadness of people made homeless by the bombing, her curls brushed against his ears and almost touched his cheek. He was grateful to the dark, for a tent had risen in his lap.

Several trailers of forthcoming attractions succeeded each other. Roshan loved the MGM lion; he had a passion for the white-robed woman who seemed to be throwing Columbia's bolt of charged electricity straight at him; and Paramount's circle of stars around the mountain peak filled him with a desire for some purer, higher air where beautiful female forms floated. Sometimes what excited him was not the film itself but the fact that *he* was watching the film, that it was a private engagement of the disengaged self that contemplated mysterious alien images and found them somehow comfortingly its own. But now, with the pressure at his arm, the soft murmur of Alicia's voice in his ear, and her perfume swirling in his brain, he found himself at still another remove from any immediate present. Reality had disappeared altogether.

The main feature began. Alicia became quiet. Roshan shook himself back into reality, but the titles had no sooner begun than he fell into his dreams again. Alicia renewed her commentary. The sound of her voice soothed him, seeming to take him over some ocean. Tyrone Power appeared on the screen in close-up. Alicia turned her head slightly towards Roshan and said something. He did not catch the words and, stretching his neck a little, whispered, 'What?' She turned her head a bit more and with her lips almost touching his ear, said, 'You look just like him.' He glanced quickly at the screen. Tyrone Power was still framed in close-up. Alicia's hot breath tingling in his ear, Roshan looked back at her and saw that she had been watching him since making her declaration. 'It's the black hair and dark eyes, and the nose too,' she said, moving her head closer to his so that her words were almost spoken into his mouth. Her breath seemed perfumed as its warmth reached his lips. The flickering light from the screen gleamed in her eyes.

What should he do? He needed to say something complimentary in return but his mind had gone blank; even the name of the actress playing opposite Tyrone Power would not come to his mind – besides, she was a blonde. Alicia's mouth was so close to his that he had only to raise his chin an inch and he would be kissing her. But supposing she took that as an affront? He could not presume to kiss her when he had not even held her hand to see whether she would let him retain it. In his scheme of sexuality, a love scene was initiated by the holding of hands, and proceeded from there, one step at a time, according to a strict order, each new step increasing the tension and excitement, offering a little release to the anxiety of desire and increasing its force by successive delayings until the body was overwhelmed by rapture. The idea that he could begin directly with a kiss seemed contrary to his private superstitions. She looked away while he debated his situation. Shifting her position, she leaned a little more to her right, so that he lost the advantage he had earlier enjoyed of being able to press against her shoulder.

She became absorbed in the film. He stared at the moving picture but saw nothing, being caught up entirely in the problem of holding her hand and of the second theoretical step, of raising it to his lips. There was nothing he could do as long as she remained leaning to her right. He shifted in his own seat, hoping the action would encourage her to rearrange herself, but she remained perfectly still and had even stopped murmuring her commentary upon the events on the screen. Should he have attempted to kiss her after all, he asked himself, reflecting back on the moment that now seemed to have been a beautiful heaven-sent opportunity. Should he regret his loss or should he be glad he had not done anything foolish to offend her? He eyed her left hand. It lay in her lap, partially concealed in a fold of her skirt. If he were to attempt to seize it he would touch her thigh. The image of doing so was erotically exciting but also too brazen, and therefore forbidden, an act.

She gasped suddenly, threw forward her head, bending it towards her lap, and raised her right hand to put it down her blouse below the back of her neck. 'What happened?' he whispered, lowering his head towards hers. She raised herself and, bending her head in his direction, said, 'Please help! Something fell there, a spider perhaps, I can't reach it.' He was confused for a moment. 'Oooh!' she added as one in pain. He put his hand through the neck of her blouse and felt the top of her back. 'Lower,' she said, unfastening the top button of her blouse to loosen the opening, 'and to the right.' He plunged deeper and moved his hand over her smooth skin. 'No, lower still. Oooh!' He had the thrilling sensation of touching the strap of her bra, and then began to feel the area below it, to her right. 'Oooh,' she moaned, 'it's gone to the left!' He shifted his hand to that side. 'No, back to the right,' she said, her head now against his chest while he was turned towards her. He found himself stroking her back, massaging it gently, and was astonished to encounter no objection from her but instead a contented soft moaning as she pressed her head to his chest.

She raised her head to his shoulder, her curls falling against his cheek. His stroking of her back had become an undisguised caress. She said softly, 'That feels nice.' He raised his other hand to the back of her neck and stroked it gently. The approving little sound – half sigh, half moan – that came from her struck him both as an endorsement of what he did and an invitation to proceed further. His hand moved from her neck and found her cheek and touched the delicate flesh there. She raised her head from his shoulder and placed her cheek next to his, moving it in a slowly rubbing action. A little turn of the face and his lips were against her cheek. She held herself still against the pressure of his lips, and then leaned back a moment to gaze at him. 'My handsome Tyrone Power,' she said to his lips before joining them with hers.

9 The Theology of Love

When he returned home, Zakia walked in a circle around him, sniffing with her head thrown back and nose held conspicuously in the air, and said, 'My oh my, we have been taking a bath in rose water, have we, or' – she clicked her tongue in her mouth and shook her head disapprovingly – 'seeing some naughty lady.'

Roshan felt a sudden bump in his chest and realized he smelled of Alicia's perfume. 'I was at Bhatia's after school,' he quickly invented, 'with some boys, and two of us decided to dress up as girls in his sister's clothes. Bhatia brought out his mother's lipstick and rouge and a big bottle of perfume. You should have seen me. I looked just like you, a real beauty.'

'Pitter patter, it doesn't matter if you'll but flatter,' Zakia said in a mocking voice and ran off. Roshan hastened to the bathroom and soaped himself furiously under the shower, not wanting to be detected by his parents the way he had been by his sister. But he was so saturated, in his mind, with Alicia's perfume that he could not appreciate his own true condition, and only hoped that three thorough latherings with the sandalwood soap would cleanse him sufficiently of the evidence.

After the shower, he decided his best course was to remain secluded as long as possible, and so he went to his little desk in the corner and, until it was time to emerge from there for the dinner which the family took together under the ceiling fan in the sitting room, he presented, to his parents and to the servants as they passed by the open door from time to time while pursuing their own concerns, a most pleasing picture of a clean, well-behaved and studious boy. As he sat attempting to complete some homework, his mind, however, was receiving again Alicia's kisses and he kept passing his tongue over his lips to feel again the moist fullness of hers. 'Kissing with inner lip', the phrase from Shakespeare, in recent months a theoretical prelude in the imagination before visiting the pleasant fountains

267

with Chandru, was his own immediate reality, and the sensation was the greater for the poetical association.

But he became unexpectedly oppressed in his mind when a certain question assailed him. Had Alicia eaten any pork that day? Christians commonly ate bacon for breakfast. If she had, he wondered if she had washed her mouth afterwards. How vigorously would she need to brush her teeth, how thoroughly rinse it before the least trace of the impurity could be removed? The question troubled him deeply. Could it be that in kissing her he had kissed bacon grease? His perception of the situation worsened when it next occurred to him that she could also have had a ham sandwich for lunch. Ham and cheese sandwiches, with a little pickle, were a favourite with Christians. His memory of the thrilling taste of the interior of her mouth became hideously polluted. His tongue had touched her teeth and that had been unexpectedly exciting, but what if, doing so, his tongue had caressed a minute morsel of ham stuck between the teeth? The whole idea was decidedly revolting. His misery intensified when he thought that a lifetime of eating pork must surely have created a sort of lining around her mouth, thus becoming a permanent presence in her saliva. Theologically speaking, he was done for. It's hell for you, old buddy!

After dinner he went out. It was the hour when Chandru stood leaning over the balcony of his flat, watching the traffic go by, on the lookout for his favourite actress who was sometimes seen to drive by in her Studebaker, with its beacon-like lights on chromium rods, on her way to her residence in the newly fashionable district of Chembur. Roshan waved for him to come down, and presently the two strolled together, as they usually did if they met at this hour, to the back of the building which housed the British soldiers, and in a secluded nook there shared what cigarettes they had between them.

Roshan was eager to tell his friend of his afternoon at the cinema and had been rehearsing alternative preambles to see which would be the most tantalizing and potentially the most sensational. But Chandru looked extremely solemn and seemed distracted by some crucial introspection which filled him with a great passion or despair. When Roshan had called on him the previous Wednesday, he had, on opening the door, presented a shining, chalk-white face that had first startled and then amused Roshan. Chandru had become so depressed by the dark pigmentation of his skin, which he saw as the cause of his failure to attract any girl, that he had undertaken an experiment of his own invention. He had bought a jar of Pond's cleansing cream and another of Pond's vanishing cream, seeing pictures in magazine advertisements of fair-skinned women claiming to use the two creams; he was convinced that the principal reason for the practice was to lighten the colour of their skin. Why else should one of the creams be called *vanishing* if it did not make blackness vanish? To enhance the efficacy of the remedy, he devised the procedure of covering his face with the shining cleansing cream and then dabbing on that a liberal quantity of talcum powder. His face was supposed to absorb the beneficial effects of such a chemistry for two hours, after which it was to be washed with warm water, thoroughly dried, and finally rubbed with vanishing cream. After the first experiment he was convinced that there had been a visible lightening of his pigmentation, and when Roshan found him looking like a clown who has made a mess of putting on his make-up it was the occasion of his seventh application of the remedy to cure him of his desperate problem. But when the time came to wash his face and to rub on the vanishing cream, Roshan, on seeing him present his new face with the expectation of receiving objective confirmation of his progress, laughed and ironically said, 'Princess Elizabeth is bound to mistake you for a handsome fair Englishman.' Chandru turned away embittered, hating the friend he loved for being fairer and taller.

Chandru had abandoned the experiment with Pond's and begun instead, although he was not 15 and was smooth-skinned, to shave, superstitiously never expressing in words, even to himself, the idea that he hoped thus to scrape away the offending layer of blackness. Each time he met his Punjabi friend, Roshan had some titillating gossip to narrate, and it struck him that to remain an auditory voyeur was the worst fate of all. Each day brought enviable new success to Roshan, advancing him in sexual experience which would remain out of his own reach until his mother arranged a marriage for him, and because he was, as he with exhilarating bitterness called himself, loudly shouting the words when he was alone and stood in front of a mirror, a 'black bloody pygmy', the arranged marriage would inevitably be to, he also shouted, 'some black bloody Brahmin'. And, turning away from the mirror, adding in his bitterness, 'What a race of fucking untouchables!' The Christians and the Parsees were doing it as teenagers, and his Muslim friend had joined their ranks while he remained an untouchable, though born a Brahmin.

Although Roshan was eager to give him the news of his latest success, there was something about Chandru's mood that prevented him and the two sat smoking silently, hearing, without paying attention to it, the noise coming from the windows of the British soldiers in the building. Chandru threw away the stub of his cigarette and broke the silence with the dramatic words, 'I came to a very important decision last night.' Roshan, caught in the self-congratulatory egotism of a young man who is ardently embraced by a beautiful woman, did not believe that anything could be more important than his own experience of the afternoon, but was magnanimously prepared to let his friend have his say first. It would be a little, warming-up trailer to his own sensational feature. So, giving Chandru the benefit of a concerned look, he asked, 'What about?'

'God,' Chandru answered, and remained portentously silent for a minute. Then, regretfully shaking his head, he solemnly and sadly declared, 'I cannot accept his existence.'

'What,' Roshan cried, 'you don't believe in God?'

Chandru mournfully shook his head and expressed an emphatic, 'No.'

'But you Hindus are polytheists anyway,' Roshan remarked. 'You're not going to be sent to hell for eating pork.'

'No, only be reborn, probably as a pig whose fate is to be slaughtered and eaten by Christians.'

Roshan laughed at the thought, but Chandru threw a castigating glance at him and said, 'Better to go to hell a man than be reborn a pig.'

Roshan pondered which was the superior alternative and Chandru began to give his deeper reasons for his atheism, listing, and expatiating upon, the problem of evil, the horrible vindictiveness of an eternal punishment, the opium of the masses, and several other of the labels attached to the subject that he had come across in his reading. It was more than Roshan had, and he, impressed by Chandru's range of thought, was prepared to concede his thinking was intellectually impressive, but was unwilling, for himself, to risk the certainty of hell by first offending the deity with his distant flirtation with pig meat and then rejecting him altogether. Just when he thought the subject was exhausted and he could begin to talk about his own affair, he heard Chandru say, 'All religions are nothing but entrenched bureaucracies.'

Roshan looked at him incredulously. Chandru was really asking for trouble. 'They exact taxes, levy fines, inflict punishments,' Chandru went on. 'They make and define their own laws. Everything is calculated to keep the bureaucracy running smoothly and unthreatened by any dissident voice. It is a licence to print money. Look at the Pope. Look at the Agha Khan.'

'The Agha Khan is fat,' Roshan said.

But Chandru was not going to be distracted by facetiousness, and, ignoring Roshan's comment, warmed up to his diatribe against religions. Roshan realized that it was going to be impossible to tell him about Alicia's kisses, the man was in no mood to listen. When it was time to go home, Chandru parted with the mysterious declaration, 'How can you know what is in my heart?'

During the next several days, while Chandru seemed perfectly normal when they were with others on the cricket field, he maintained a gloomy silence when alone with Roshan, and when the latter described what he had been up to with Alicia in the darkness of the cinema, instead of expressing interested admiration, or making some ironical comment dictated by envy, Chandru remained as though he had heard nothing, looking sadly with a fixed trance-like gaze at some distant object. Exasperated, Roshan finally asked what troubled him. Slowly, as if it pained him exceedingly, Chandru turned his sad head and stared into his eyes with a look of infinite melancholy. 'How can you know what is in my heart?' he repeated from the earlier time.

'Well, tell me, then, for God's sake!' Roshan said in his exasperation.

His mournful friend made to walk away, halted, stared up at the sky, turned, and slowly walked back to where Roshan sat. 'So, you love a Christian girl?' he said. 'You had a brief affair with a Hindu girl, and now you're deep in it with a Christian.' He paused, nodding his head significantly, and continued. 'And what if I am in love with a Muslim girl? Wouldn't it be better if the bogus bureaucrats of religion did not tell us we could not love one another?'

'What, in God's name, are you talking about?'

'In no god's name, I hope, only in mine. Have you not understood what I have just confessed?'

'Confessed? What?'

'If I say I am in love with a Muslim girl who can I mean?'

271

Roshan thought for a moment, and his first feeling was that of panic that the chastity of his sister should be threatened by a Hindu boy. But that was succeeded by the knowledge that the idea was farcical. Chandru had only to utter a word and Zakia would lash him viciously with her quick tongue until he sought escape in reincarnation. He hated Chandru for entertaining such a notion, and realized in that moment that all his talk about rejecting religions had been an attempt to eliminate the one great obstacle between men and women in India. By declaring himself an atheist and a despiser of religions, Chandru had effectively asked not to be seen as a Hindu; but like the cosmetic creams that had been of no help to his skin, all his talk could be of no help in changing an ideology. Roshan decided not to reveal to him the foolishness of his desire and the irrelevance to it of his theological ideas, and, convinced that the melodrama would exhaust its futile action within the tormented man's mind, he said to Chandru in a sympathetic voice, 'She's only thirteen, my dear chap. You're going to have a long wait.'

10 The Blinded Vision

Since Roshan still had the money he had obtained from his father on a false pretext, he invited Alicia to a film in the city's premier cinema, the Metro, famous for its air-conditioning. It was a thrill, whenever he was in town, just to walk past the lobby of the Metro and to be touched by a tiny tongue of the cool air emanating from there, exciting just to stand there and look at the stills in the window of the latest MGM release. He had gone and reserved two seats, for a Saturday afternoon performance, in the very last row of the upper circle. Alicia was most flattered. No man could have done anything more special.

The event, however, did not live up to his fantasy of just the two of them in the throbbing cool darkness fondling each other, for the majority of the seats were taken. There was nothing to do but hold hands and lean shoulder against shoulder, and remain silently absorbed in the film. Alicia was not even able to make her comments on the picture because when she tried to do so several heads in the three rows in front of them turned round and someone went, 'Shooo!' Although frustrated, she looked extremely pleased when the film ended and they walked out into the hot sunlight, delighted by the privilege she had enjoyed of having spent Saturday afternoon in the Metro.

They walked along the Maidan where several cricket games were in progress. The air was filled with the cracking sound of a ball being hit, people clapping softly, and some of the food-vending hawkers calling out. A huge dust-laden banyan tree scarcely moved in the slight breeze coming from the ocean. A crowd stood in a circle near the pavement, and when Roshan and Alicia reached it they saw what the crowd was gaping at: a man had buried his whole body except for his head in the sandy ground, just his head – long locks of grey hair, ash-smeared dark brown face, the eyes open but not looking, nor blinking, with the chin resting on the ground – appearing like a pumpkin that had been left there. His tongue stuck out of his mouth, a long pin pierced through it, so that he could neither withdraw his tongue nor take into his body anything but the hot, humid air that entered his nose. Drawn in front of him, a continuous line chiselled with the point of a knife in the bare earth, was the map of India: the head, therefore, apparently stuck on a peak in the Hindu Kush, looked down towards the Deccan plateau that tapered away from his face, and in the middle of that crude representation of the country was inscribed the Sanskrit figure for *Om*.

Roshan and Alicia quickly walked past the crowd after observing what fixed its awed attention. It was pleasanter to look at the nearest cricket game. But further down, towards the end of the Maidan, taking up the space of an unused cricket pitch, a group of men in orange-coloured Gandhi caps and white shirts of coarse, homespun cotton, were brandishing bamboo sticks in an unmistakably martial drill, accompanied by loudly threatening words in Marathi. A line of policemen in their blue uniforms and yellow flat-topped caps watched them from a distance. Roshan and Alicia instinctively hastened their steps in order to suppress the associations that the militant Hindus brought to mind, calling for an India which was purely Hindu.

The couple turned towards Churchgate, becoming briefly caught in the crowd coming out of the station, and walked past the monumental edifice of the Eros cinema. After stopping for an ice-cream near the Brabourne Stadium, from where sudden bursts of applause and roars of the crowd at a cricket match could be heard, Roshan and Alicia came to Marine Drive and sat there enjoying the refreshing sight of the blue-green Arabian Sea and the cool breeze coming over its surface and cleansing from their minds the spidery webs that had sprung there from seeing the buried man, the Hindu militants and the crowds pouring out of Churchgate station. Here at last they could take pleasure in looking at each other without the troubling knowledge that the world around them meant to exclude them from its future.

They resumed their walk, talking about the film they had seen, and, without having chosen that as a destination, came to Chowpatty beach. A crowd of people milled there among the food vendors. Roshan suggested eating some vegetable fritters with hot tamarind chutney. When she did so, Alicia quickly sucked her lips and then blew them out, and said, 'Whew!' He was astonished to discover that she had never tasted that native combination and talked of hot food as if it were something so utterly exotic that it was a brave adventure to taste it – as though she had been born in England and had only just stepped on Indian soil. He offered to buy her a glass of sugarcane juice, for there was a vendor nearby crushing long lengths of sugarcane through his press, in which he was also placing little pieces of ginger root to cut the cloying sweetness of the cane. But Alicia preferred a lemonade, and kept making a whistling sound, complaining that the hot tamarind had set her mouth on fire, until she had begun to sip from a cold bottle. Her reaction to the Bombay street food reminded Roshan of his worry that she must eat pork, and the thought oppressed him. He did not want to talk about it. There could be no doubt that she did. But he did not want any confirmation. Fearing that, surrounded as they were by the food stalls and the spicy smells and a crowd of ordinary Indians enjoying indigenous tastes, she might suddenly, in an unconscious flaunting of a sort of racial superiority, allude to the forbidden meat as a delightful delicacy, he directed her away from the beach and towards the bus stop, suggesting they go up to Malabar Hill and visit the Hanging Gardens.

The single-decker bus climbed up Malabar Hill, going past houses set in large gardens with uniformed Gurkhas or Pathans guarding the gates. Roshan noticed that the Gurkhas were forever knitting something of khaki wool while they stood as watchmen, whereas the Pathans squatted on the ground or sat on stools and were invariably absorbed in cleaning, or merely stroking, a rifle. His observation that the men performed obsessively out of native habit something that was irrelevant in their new environment was lost on Alicia, however, who commented, 'Poor chaps, they have to stand there all day long.' A Riley drove out of one of the gates and briefly showed a glimpse of an Englishwoman. 'I wonder where she can be going?' Alicia mused, imagining the woman enter some dazzling ballroom.

Roshan plucked at Alicia's arm, suddenly deciding to alight from the bus sooner than they needed to for the Hanging Gardens. He wanted to show her the spot where he had gone several times by himself. It was a small deserted area on which nothing had been built. The land seemed to tumble down the hill in a succession of straggly bushes. There was a boulder there among some high trees where he had come and sat on previous occasions, and he took Alicia to it. She made a little sound of intense delight when they arrived there, and said, 'My, how spectacular!' Down below them was Chowpatty beach, the people whom they had left some twenty minutes ago milling about like ants; then the sweep of Marine Drive and the green-blue ocean, and the tip of the reclaimed land where Bombay ended. 'How beautifully silent it all is,' she remarked. 'The city glittering there, all the way to the Gateway of India, how terribly, terribly beautiful.'

He held her hand, looking around to see if they were observed, and they sat down on the boulder. 'What are you thinking of?' she asked when he had remained staring at the view. He glanced at her a moment and looked back at the view again. She gasped without knowing whether her instinctive response was to the suddenly heightened brightness that radiated from his eyes, revealing in that moment a beauty of unspeakable brilliance, or whether it was the sharp realization of happiness that, whatever disintegration or fragmentation was the self's imminent destiny, there was, during this passing moment, a solidity, a wholeness, a knowledge, perhaps, of love. And looking at the view, she felt a flutter within her breast, perceiving in that vision of Bombay a passage opening towards some vastly illuminated, and therefore physically unrecognizable, embodiment of the sacred. She leaned her head to his face and kissed him softly on the cheek.

He gave no response but remained absorbed in staring at the city, perceiving clearly in his mind those landmarks that were too distant to be visible. All the city's throbbing activity had become frozen, and he saw the inhabitants of Bombay as a joyful body of celebrants stopped at some charming moment in its processional gaiety, like the figures in Keats's urn, and he saw himself as the privileged witness of that eternal truth and that immortal beauty. So that when he at last sensed the warmth of Alicia's lips on his cheek it was as if he had been stung there, and drew back in a sudden shudder. He recovered quickly from the surprise of her presence, and, throwing a glance around him and remembering where he was, held her shoulder and pressed his cheeks to hers. She attempted to move, wanting to kiss him, but he held her still, for there was a burning sensation in his eyes, the first intimation, inexplicable in this moment of complete happiness when his spirit was possessed by an exceptional calm, that the brightness there had dimmed and he did not want her to see that what replaced it was the glistening moisture of tears. 'I will like to be yours,' she spoke in a whisper near his ear. 'I will like to give you everything.' The ocean could be glimpsed beyond her shoulder, but he was unable to see it, and her softly spoken words seemed to pierce his ear. He drew back sharply, turning aside his face. She flung her head against his chest, throwing her arms around him, and cried, 'Oh Roshan, Roshan, what are we going to do?' And it was she who was sobbing while he, his hand gently stroking her neck, stared at the city, blindly, through the moisture that remained frozen like gum on the bark of a tree.

11 · Under the Virgin's Gaze

There was a half-holiday at the school early in the following week because of some obscure event in the Christian calendar that necessitated priestly homage to a saint. Roshan had agreed with Bhatia and Adi not to let their parents know about it so that, pretending to remain at school, they could spend a conscience-free afternoon at the cinema admiring the charms of Ruth Roman. But Roshan received a message from Alicia just before the morning classes ended, and instead of going with his friends he found himself, after he had quickly swallowed the lunch he had brought from home, accompanying her on the suburban train to Bandra.

High over King's Circle went the train, thuka-thuk, thuka-thuk, the moist wind blowing through its open doors and windows. Then it sped over Mahim Creek, tick-tick-ticka-tick, tuck, tuck, ticka-tick, the wind, dense with humidity, bursting through the carriage. Alicia's curls were flying about her face. The crowd of men in the carriage eyed her. She smiled at Roshan, not caring who observed her, and he smiled back at her and looked out at the rushing light and the blue blur of the marshy creek, pleased, and yet embarrassed, to be noticed by others. In his uniform of blue shorts and a white shirt covered with dark patches of sweat, he felt he must look younger than he was while Alicia, with her high bosom in her usual tight blouse, was a mature woman. But the exterior light dazzled him and, together with the noise of the train and the wind rushing through the carriage, gave him the peculiar sensation of his own being becoming unfamiliar until, the train slowing down as it approached Bandra, his seeing a distant church on some high ground suppressed the threat he felt of some inexplicable loss.

From the station at Bandra, they had a fifteen-minute walk to the building where she lived. A lot of girls in their blue-and-white uniforms from St Andrew's School stood at the bus stops or walked on the pavement towards the train station, going home for their half-holiday. In their blue skirts prescribed by the Catholic school, it was difficult to distinguish who were not Christians, which almost all of them were not since the Christians would already be home, Bandra being their special district.

Alicia led him down a narrow street and then out into a wider avenue. Scores of children were playing outside a row of buildings, in the second of which she lived with her family on the third floor. Two little boys accosted her just by the entrance to the building. 'My darling brothers, Tony and Frank,' she said to Roshan, and then spoke sternly to them before giving them an anna each with the instruction to keep away from the flat for the rest of the afternoon. 'That's the male side of the family,' she said as they climbed up the dark staircase. 'Except for Fernando, who will be at work, and Dad, who can be anywhere between here and heaven. Or hell,' she added, after surmounting the final steps and arriving at the door of the flat. A shrieking noise was coming from within and Alicia, opening the door, glanced at Roshan and said, 'Sounds like a mad house, but come on in.'

They entered a narrow hall at the end of which two girls of about 13 and 14 stood in possession of each other's hair, each bent in the posture of being about to pull the other right out of the flat. 'Miriam! Claudia!' Alicia shouted at them. 'Stop that this instant!' Without removing her hands from the other's head, each turned to look and, seeing the boy with Alicia, instantly let go and stood erect. 'Go at once to the kitchen and stay there till I come to see you,' Alicia commanded. The younger of the two marched off with her head theatrically inclined in the air while the elder stood passing her hands over her hair and thrusting out her bosom in her ragged and grease-spotted cotton frock, staring at Roshan with the tip of her tongue showing in the corner of her lips. 'Did you hear me, Claudia?' Alicia shouted at her. 'Uh-huh,' she answered, pushing forward her right arm with the hand still at the hair so that the elbow gave a little jerk which had the effect of producing an undulating movement across her bosom. 'Why, you little hussie!' Alicia, quickly giving her purse and some exercise books she was carrying to Roshan, sprang upon her and dragged her away.

She was gone only a moment, but another girl appeared, taller, but no more cleanly dressed than Claudia, stood sideways in front of Roshan, put her hands upon her hips, turned her torso so that her waist seemed incredibly narrow and her bosom remarkably developed, and raising her head slightly, said, 'Hell–oh,' letting her voice sound even after the word could no longer be extended. The returning Alicia leaped at her, attempting to push her back to the room she had come from and saying loudly to her, '*Maggie!* You go right back to your little kennel!'

'Margarita is the name, my dear Alice,' she said, resisting the elder sister's force. 'Margarita Miranda,' she addressed Roshan over Alicia's shoulder. 'Alice's beautiful and irresistible *younger* sister. How do you do?'

'*Bitch!*' shouted Alicia.

'Jealous Alice!' she shouted back! 'Alice, Alice, full of malice.' In a softer, seductive voice, winking at him, she said to Roshan, 'None sweeter than Margarita.'

Alicia twisted her hard at the shoulder and forced her to turn around and face the direction she had come from, saying, 'Better stay away if you want money for the Saturday matinée.' The sister allowed herself to be thrust back through the doorway, while singing aloud, 'Come and greet her, the sweet Margarita.'

They had to go through the same room and Roshan saw that Maggie had collapsed on a bare mattress on the floor. As he walked past, Maggie pulled the skirt of her frock up to her thigh, raising her bare leg, put a hand inside the skirt, clicked her tongue in her mouth, and said, 'Parading a man through a young woman's bedroom, what next, I ask you!' 'Slut,' Alicia hissed at her. Three other mattresses were piled against a wall on which hung a faded calendar with a picture of the Virgin Mary. Some clothes were heaped in a corner. 'Sweet sixteen, oh what luck, luck, luck,' Maggie sang. 'Oh if I had a man I could . . .' '*Stop that!*' Alicia screamed at her before she could utter the rhyme, and dragged Roshan out of the room.

They came to a narrow corridor which had a wash basin bolted to a wall on one side and a small room on the other, which was obviously a lavatory. Alicia, walking a step ahead of Roshan, pushed closed its door that had been left open, but could not seal off the smell which had already flowed out of there and stiflingly permeated the corridor. Passing the wash basin, Roshan saw its enamel had long begun to flake and that its inside was covered with rust. A damp rag hung from a nail next to it. An open door at the end of the corridor led to a room. Roshan followed Alicia into it and was relieved to find that a wide window on its far wall let in a flowing stream of fresh air. The potent smell in the corridor had begun to fill him with nausea.

Before Roshan could take in the particular images of the room, he heard Alicia say, 'What are *you* doing in here?' Roshan saw that there was a bed under the open window and a stout woman with grey hair lay asleep in it. Alicia grabbed the woman's arm and pulled it sharply, saying, 'Mother, get up, please, this is ridiculous.'

The woman sat up, shaking her head in the confusion of one suddenly woken from a deep sleep. 'Oh, it's you,' she said and yawned.

'I told you I was coming home early,' Alicia said to her. 'And I told you to put some order in the house. Instead it's like coming to some animal shelter – full of bitches on heat.'

Roshan was shocked at Alicia's words to her mother, but observed that the mother had remained inattentive until Alicia's final phrase, and that it was only the pause followed by a louder, angered harshness of voice that seemed to penetrate her brain. 'Oh the girls, the girls!' she said helplessly. 'Do you know what Claudia has been boasting of?'

'Mother, I don't want to know right now,' Alicia answered, restraining her exasperation.

'She offered to kiss Father Stanislaus during confession just to get out of doing penance for the sin of touching herself.'

'Mother, we can talk later?'

'She claims Father Stanislaus took her up on her offer.'

'Mother!'

'In the confessional,' the mother went on. 'How could she? I said, not believing her. Oh, she says, I just got out and went into Father Stanislaus's side of the booth and sat in his lap. It was like sitting on three fat thighs, she says.'

'Mother, will you please open your ears and hear what I say' – Alicia spoke loudly at her – 'and will you please open your eyes as well and see that I have a visitor.' She held her mother's shoulders and began to direct her out of the room, saying to her, 'You have no business to be messing in my room. It's the only thing I ask for myself, I give you everything else.'

The mother had at last noticed Roshan and turned her head to see him as she was led away. 'He's nice,' she said while Alicia pushed her through the door. 'Are you going to marry him?'

Alicia closed the door when she had thrust her mother out. 'God,' she said, turning to face Roshan who was just then putting down her purse and the exercise books on a chest of drawers opposite the bed, 'what a mad house!'

Roshan smiled and took her hand, not wanting her to be embarrassed. They sat on the edge of the bed. Apart from the chest of drawers with a mirror above it, there was a small cupboard on the top of which was placed a wooden statuette of the Virgin Mary, her face shining pink, her dress a bright blue covered with golden stars.

'Let me go and change,' Alicia said, 'this blouse is suffocating me.'

She removed her shoes and put on a pair of slippers and, taking a garment from one of the drawers, went out of the room. Roshan glanced out of the window from where the pleasant breeze was flowing, thinking it must face the ocean. It opened out on to a wide balcony, though there was no door to it from the room. He leaned over the bed and looked through the window. A door from the next room gave passage to the balcony, and a rusted old metal folding chair with a string attached to one of its legs was left abandoned on its side near the door. He was right about the ocean: one tiny triangle of blue some five streets away could be glimpsed past several intervening buildings. Withdrawing back to his earlier position on the bed, he stared at the Virgin Mary, and was struck by the flattering thought that he was sitting alone in the bedroom of a woman who had just gone to prepare herself for him. More than his expectations were raised. The room became transformed in his mind to one of splendid proportions, with high gilt-framed mirrors and a canopied bed with cool white satin sheets, and he imagined a woman as lovely as Ginger Rogers enter there in a flowing white gown and immediately begin to dance with him across the shining parquet floor.

Alicia returned in a blue frock of coarse cotton, carrying in her hands the clothes she had earlier worn. She placed them on the chest of drawers and Roshan saw among them the strap of a bra – just a few inches of it sticking out in a loop from between neatly folded skirt and blouse, but it was sexually the most provoking thing he had ever seen. In his fantasies, he had always relished the moment when his hands were at the bra, gently caressing the straps and the cups, probing knowingly, prolonging the captivity of the breasts so that their release would be the more dramatic and thrilling. Female underwear was a topic of considerable debate when he was with Chandru and Mona, with speculations on whether there were, on a bra, hooks to be unclasped or elastic bands to be tugged at or some secret female trick that would never be known to males.

Mona had excitedly revealed one day that he had had the good fortune of discovering a bra of his mother's carelessly left behind in the bathroom and had examined it closely. The thing was *far* more complicated than they had imagined. Chandru and Roshan gaped at him incredulously when he proceeded to describe a network of bones and wires and said how if one did not remove two of the bones and loosen a certain joint in the wires the bra would never come off. *Never.* But there was the little loop sticking out from between the skirt and the blouse! His expectations had risen higher.

She stood before him. The glare from the window lit up her light-coloured face and brought out the lively gloss in her hair. The brightness gleamed back from her eyes, too, but the mood reflected there seemed ambiguous, as though some profound hesitation held her in check. She raised a hand and touched his hair. Her fingertips slid down his cheek. He held her hand and drew it to his lips. 'The Virgin watches over me in this room,' she said. He kept his eyes on her hand and kissed the tip of the middle finger, drawing it slightly into his mouth, not knowing how to understand her words. 'But she can't see you,' Alicia added, falling upon him, pushing him back across the width of the bed, 'my beautiful heathen!'

His head fell to just below the window while his legs remained dangling over the edge of the bed. Alicia, holding her arms in front of her bosom and resting her legs away from him, had her hands pressed to his shoulders and her mouth on his. Her arms dug into his chest uncomfortably and he tried to push them away. She shook her head in disagreement. Her closed lips moved over his. He tried to press his tongue against them to unseal them but she would not permit that either. He thought it odd that in their other meetings she had lamented the lack of privacy but now that they were alone she had assumed the stiffness of an unexpected modesty. Hoping that it was only an initial shyness, he decided to remain patient, becoming a passive recipient of her close-mouthed kisses, which, surprisingly, soon become boring, oppressively so. Finally he was obliged to shift his head so that she lifted her face from his and rearranged herself to lie on her side. He too turned on his side, so that they faced each other, curled across the width of the bed with their feet sticking out over the edge.

He raised a hand to her cheek and stroked it. She touched her nose to his and then pressed her forehead to his lips, shaking her head like one troubled by her own desire. He moved his hand to her shoulder and then to the bare upper arm, meanwhile moving his face to kiss her lips. Stroking her arm, he debated whether he should quietly drop it to her bosom, but just then, almost as if she anticipated his thought, she drew up her arms and crossed them across her chest. He leaned his head away from hers and sighed. She grasped his face in both her hands and they stared at each other. 'Isn't it enough just to be together?' she asked. 'We don't have to sin,' she felt it pertinent to add. 'There's no sin where there's love,' he said, inspired. She let go of his face and thrust her head down against his chest. He held it there, his fingers in her hair. She seemed to have gone into an internal dialogue, for when she suddenly raised herself it was with a changed resolution, the argument of desire having defeated every scruple, and she turned him on his back and came to his lips with her mouth open, her teeth and tongue gleaming with saliva.

Roshan was in an ecstasy of delight, finding her pressed the length of his body, and in that flow of passion he embraced her hard and was maddened to discover that his hand encountered no resistance when it held itself against one of her breasts. The coarse material of her frock made it seem as though he held a dry sponge and his fingers probed the little gaps between the buttons. And then, of all the wonderful miracles to take place so quickly one after the other, he found that she herself was rapidly undoing the buttons, the opening was already sufficiently wide, her hand held his and was in the act of pushing it through the opening and his fingers were touching the swelling flesh.

Something crashed outside the window, a boy's voice said, 'You bloody fool!' and there was the sound of steps scampering away. Alicia sprang up and shouted, 'Tony! Frank! You little shits, come back here this minute!' She jumped out of the bed and went running out of the room in her bare feet. Roshan sat up, breathing hard, not knowing whether what suffocated him was receiving so generous a quantity of Alicia's passion in so short a time or the frustration that it should be terminated so abruptly, leaving him with a throbbing and an oozing erection. He looked out of the window. The metal chair lay fallen below it. He wondered for how long the two boys had been watching them. Seeing a shadow move slightly, he leaned further out of the window. Claudia stood at the far end, her elbows on the metal railing, in an aspect innocently meditative, though not a convincing one, being quite obviously hurriedly composed. She slowly turned her head and gazed at him. The sun was behind her and she appeared to him in silhouette, somehow a troubling darkness of outline. But the pressure inside his shorts troubled him more and, hearing Alicia's screaming voice now coming from the street below, he decided to go to the lavatory.

The lavatory door was slightly ajar and he quickly pulled at it. And halted with a sudden revulsion. The powerful smell seemed to have built a brick wall there that would require a stubborn, or a foolish, sort of courage to scale. But in that instant his eyes penetrated the thick layers of the smell and he saw the terrifying and hideous sight of Alicia's mother squatting over the hole in the floor, her eyes closed, and straining hard, her mouth open and wrinkles on her forehead. He pushed back the door immediately, hearing just then the explosion that relieved her, and, panting, returned to Alicia's room, his own trouble by now shrunken and reduced merely to an unpleasant wetness. He was making blindly for the bed but stopped just a foot away from it.

Claudia reclined in it on her side, an elbow on the mattress and propping up her head against the palm of her hand, the skirt of her grease-spotted frock pulled up to her waist, a leg raised and her other arm stretched out with the wrist on the knee and the hand dangling loose. Roshan stared at her speechless. She looked bemusedly at him, the tip of her tongue moving delicately in the corner of her lips. 'What is your pleasure, sir?' asked she demurely. Seeing that he merely gaped at her dumbfounded, she raised the hand that rested on her leg, drew it along the thigh and over her waist up to her right breast, against which she pressed it while simultaneously letting her tongue slide across her lower lip and then, closing her eyes, sighed, 'Aaaah!'

Roshan turned round and made to dash from the room. Claudia laughed and he paused a moment by the door. Even her laughter had a strong sexual pull – as if it were a sound that had the power to suck into the cavity whence it emanated the whole being of the bewildered male. He ran from it, but only to collide with the mother just then emerging from the lavatory. 'Oh, I beg your pardon,' he said, trying to go round her. But with the wash basin causing an additional obstruction the passage was too narrow and the mother's confused movement blocked his escape, so that it seemed for a moment that he was engaged in a strange sort of dance with the stout grey-haired lady. 'Promise me,' the mother said, 'you won't marry Alice.' He was amazed not so much by the demand as by the singular circumstance in which it was expressed. 'I promise, I promise!' he cried at her, and she, as if they were discussing the question over tea, said calmly, 'Why don't you put it in writing before you go?' He shouted back, 'I will, I will!' Satisfied, she scurried away through the room where Maggie lolled on the bare mattress.

That being the only way out, Roshan followed. By the time he reached there Maggie had jumped from the bed to the further door and leaned on her shoulder against its frame while blocking the passage with an arm stretched across it. 'Where you to off to, sailor boy?' she winsomely asked. 'Wasn't that a neat trick, Claudia getting Alice to run out of the house leaving her bed empty for her to hop into? She's a witch, is Claudia.'

'What do you mean a trick?' Roshan's curiosity arrested his flight and he waited for an explanation.

'Oh, she set up Tony and Frank to watch the show and then pulled the chair to send them flying and Alice running after them. Works every time. Beats me why Alice don't close the window.'

'She's done that before?' Roshan asked, his male sense of exclusive possessiveness outraged.

Maggie tilted up her chin, heaved her bosom and gave him a haughty smile that implied a superior knowledge, suggesting to him that he knew nothing. 'You got a girl in every port, sailor boy, but you're dumb ignorant about your girl back home,' she said, reciting, he was certain, something she had heard in a film. 'But you're right to run from Claudia,' she continued. 'She's such a witch, she's made a sinner even out of Father Stanislaus. *This*,' Maggie added with a dramatic flourish, throwing up her arms and hugging herself, 'is where *you* belong.' The suddenness of the gesture and the ringing tone in her voice as she raised it for emphasis sent a current of lust crackling through Roshan's veins and he stood stunned by the shock, wanting thoroughly to be crushed by the girl. But he clenched his teeth, closed his eyes, breathed in deeply and took a determined step towards the door while Maggie still hugged herself, leaving a narrow gap through which he could escape. It was completely filled, however, the moment he reached it.

The mother had taken that space and he nearly crashed into her. 'Here it is,' she said, waving a piece of paper in one hand and a pencil in the other.

'Oh Jesus!' exclaimed Maggie, and her shoulders drooping resignedly she went and sat on the edge of the mattress.

The mother thrust the paper into Roshan's hand and held the pencil up for him to take. He was too confused to be able to read the slanting scrawl, which would have proved almost illegible were he calmly in possession of his rational faculties. 'Mother,' he heard Maggie say, 'why don't you get it in your head that you can't get rid of Claudia by making a boy sign that he'll have her.'

Roshan remembered that that was not what he had undertaken to sign. He looked hard at the words on the paper and was able to decipher a statement agreeing to marry Claudia. 'I've nothing to do with Claudia,' he said, holding out the paper to return it to the mother.

'You promised to sign,' the mother said sharply.

'Yes, that I would not marry Alicia.'

'That's correct,' the mother said, holding up the pencil for him to take. 'If you marry Claudia then you won't be able to marry Alicia, right?'

'But I don't want to marry Claudia!'

'Why, what's wrong with her?' demanded the mother.

'She's got big tits for a girl of fourteen,' Maggie said.

'You be quiet,' the mother commanded her.

'Ask Father Stanislaus,' Maggie said, laughing. 'He'll even tell you how much they weigh.'

'Maggie!' the mother cried at her, but when the girl responded with a louder burst of malevolent laughter the mother screamed, '*Margarita!*' and darted towards her. Seeing his opportunity to escape, Roshan ran out of the flat, dropping the piece of paper behind him.

Once out of the building, he stopped and looked around him to find his bearings and saw Alicia, holding Tony and Frank, each by the ear, on either side of her, walking in his direction. He pretended he had not seen her and began to walk away towards a crowd of people on the opposite corner, but she had seen him and shouted his name down the street. He was obliged to wait. When she was some twenty feet from him, she stopped and spoke sternly to her little brothers, shaking her hand in front of their faces as if about to slap them, and then let them go.

'What happened?' she asked, coming up to Roshan.

'What do you mean what happened? Claudia just jumped into

your bed, and when I ran from her I got ambushed by Maggie.'

'Those two bitches! I'd told Mother to send them out for the afternoon.'

'And your mother wanted me to sign a paper agreeing to marry Claudia.'

'Jesus!' Alicia jerked up her head, rolling her eyes and clicking her tongue.

'How many men have you had there in that room?' he asked, looking deeply pained.

'Why, who said anything about my having men? I don't know any!'

'But Maggie said . . '

'Maggie said. Listen, Maggie and Claudia are a couple of lying, conniving bitches.'

'I don't know what to believe.'

Without either making the suggestion, they began to walk away from the building as though each needed to meditate silently but without leaving the other. They walked side by side for some ten minutes, aimlessly cutting across several streets. He noticed that her feet were bare but that she appeared perfectly oblivious of the fact. In her loose frock, her hair quite dishevelled and her face covered with sweat, she was unrecognizable from the tight-bloused beauty who arrived tippety-tip at the school. Wilder and earthier now, the odour flowing from her animalistic, she seemed a creature driven by a raw passion. Suddenly she stopped and, looking up at the building outside which they stood, held his hand and said, 'Will you come in here for a minute?'

They were outside a church. 'Why?' he asked, finding himself mysteriously threatened by another person's religion.

'Because I want you to believe me,' she said, leading him into the church. It was dark inside, with a smell of mildew coming from the plaster walls. Candles lit up a few of the statues beside the high windows through which the sun would have penetrated but for a thick layer of grime. A few old women knelt in the pews, flicking the beads of a rosary, their eyes shut, their mouths praying in a low murmurous whisper. Roshan followed Alicia, feeling a little scared that one of the watching saints might spot him for an infidel and fearing, too, that he himself might make some discovery that might challenge a truth held by his own religion. Alicia stopped under a statue of the Virgin. She took his right hand and placed it upon her heart and, raising her own right hand to touch the feet of the Virgin whose painted eyes seemed to look down upon them with personal concern, she said, 'I swear to you in the sight of the Holy Virgin that I have told you the truth.'

Roshan was greatly impressed by her little ceremony once they were out of the church and safe from some divinely retributive influence that might instantly exact a penalty for a passing impious thought, such as his delight that in giving him her heart Alicia had in fact given him her munificent left breast to hold. They walked now hand in hand, thoughtlessly wandering through the streets, as if the silence that they preserved had acquired a holy sanctity from the Virgin. After some time they were surprised to come to the point known as Land's End and realized that had they deliberately plotted a journey from the flat to Land's End they could not have chosen a more direct route, so that it seemed that some destiny had guided their footsteps.

They climbed down among some rocks and sat on one, looking upon the sea crashing against the barrier, some of the spray coming to their faces in cool prickly needles through the air. She was going to express to him her despair and bewilderment with her family, but the words remained unspoken. He was experiencing a confused and a contradictory pulsing within his blood, not knowing what to make of the little explosions that made the heart believe itself now divinely gifted and now satanically cursed. His mouth and his hand had received and touched the sources of love but the sudden flash floods surging in his mind had been of lust. But words were failing him, too, sitting there under the clear blue sky, looking at the swelling sea that, reaching the land, exploded in great floral bursts. The immensity of blue under the intense light of the high afternoon sun was brilliant, blinding.

12   Incident on the Grand Trunk Road

Bhatia passed a piece of paper to Roshan. Roshan read on it the line, 'All things that rise must fall,' saw the invitation to be smutty but avoided it and wrote, 'As will the Tower of Pisa.' He passed the paper to Adi, who, after a moment's thought, added a third line, 'In parts three divided is Gaul,' and returned it to Roshan. Roshan wrote a fourth line, 'And so is Julius Caesar.' The completed verse was returned to Bhatia, who chuckled over it, but, glancing at Roshan and Adi, shook his head disapprovingly to complain against their failure to be indecent. He gave them a fresh opportunity by writing on a new sheet of paper, 'In the evening brightly rises Venus.' Roshan threw a smile at Bhatia before making up a second line.

The history teacher, Father Mendoza of the short legs and round torso and round dark brown face and no neck, consequently known as the Giraffe, was, as usual, going on and on, this time about the Congress of Vienna. Some of the boys in the class who listened to him were struck by the word Congress, which had the association in their minds with Mr Nehru in his white cloth cap, and imagined the Congress of Vienna to be something like the Indian National Congress with frock-coated European men in white cloth caps, and were considerably confused. The others played silent games among themselves, for Father Mendoza's history class was longer than the reign of Queen Victoria and made everyone feel they were getting old without doing anything. Father Mendoza kept exercise books piled at the front of his desk. All the boys knew that the exercise books were there to hide a textbook from which he read non-stop for forty minutes, looking at it in a funny way – sometimes askance, sometimes with his chin raised, sometimes by appearing to be looking down on something fallen to the ground – pretending not to be reading but naturally to be pouring out knowledge stored in his head.

Clocks went dead at the sound of Father Mendoza's voice. Minutes collapsed into the dust, the hours evaporated. He read about the Thirty Years War and the forty-minute period took a hundred years to pass. And the Hundred Years War went on for an eternity. Europe was forever at war. Like now, for the second time in the twentieth century, and the century only in its fourth decade. For homework, the boys had to learn the dates of the wars and the dates of the English kings and queens and the dates of Marlborough and Napoleon and Wellington and the dates of the Habsburgs and the Bourbons and the House of Hanover and the House of Windsor and the dates of the Bloodless Revolution and the Industrial Revolution and the French Revolution. Cannons to the right of them, cannons to the left of them, what a bloody massacre, nothing but one long torture, history.

Adi had devised a system by which to comprehend all those dates and European names. He had renamed the European countries as cricket clubs and made their wars Test matches with the dates representing the winning score. The kings and queens and the eminent warriors and politicians were given the names of contemporary cricketers so that their dates could be learned as career statistics. Thus Wellington became Vijay Merchant, Nelson the dashing batsman Mushtaq Ali, and the favourite Napoleon the famous Parsee batsman Rusi Mody. Adi shared the system with Roshan and Bhatia, who introduced their own variations into it in order to perceive the interminable European conflict in images from their own background.

But the Congress of Vienna was like the famous timeless Test match, which, intended to guarantee a result, instead guaranteed universal boredom. The verse-writing had degenerated into filthy doggerel, and even the most shocking rhymes were no longer amusing. The wretched forty minutes would not pass. What a mountain of piled-up boredom it was, the world's history. And then suddenly the latest European war burst upon the school in a series of tremendous explosions that sent the instantly fragmented glass from the windows flying through the classroom, slicing across the arms and cheeks of several of the boys.

There were shouts and screams. Some of the boys went dashing out, others threw back their desks and ducked to the floor. Roshan, running out, saw that Father Mendoza's mouth was still open but instead of words a low scream came from it, for there was a bleeding gash across his cheek, from where his blood was dripping down upon the open book below his chin. 'The Japs, the Japs!' the boys were shouting down the corridor, running out of the school. The last of the explosions was the loudest of all, striking like a thunderclap on the roof of the building which seemed to shake as in an earthquake. More windows sent their glass flying through the air, the splinters shooting through the rooms and the corridors like paper planes aimed at the ears of the unwary. Boys fell to the ground, bleeding and screaming. 'The Japs, the Japs!' the others yelled.

Roshan stopped running as soon as he was outside the building and found his friends standing on the pavement looking at the school. An alarm had gone off and could be heard outside, tinkling weakly while the boys poured out of the school. A gloomy silence fell. The boys who had been screaming and yelling looked back on their school in quiet fear. No one asked the question but everyone wondered what had happened and looked around for evidence. No bombs had fallen from the sky, which was cloudless and dully blue. There was no fire, no earthquake. Then a distant rumble could be heard, like the charging of horses over the horizon in westerns. 'It's the Japs!' someone shouted. Others took up the cry, and hordes of yelling boys went running down the street.

Bhatia asked Roshan if he had any money on him. Four annas. Adi had 4 annas, too. The three pooled the money, deciding that if the Japanese had at last invaded India then the three friends should go and share a last cup of tea and smoke as many cigarettes as they could before the end came.

Ibrahim walked past the tables where he had been serving, choosing to go round a table where two small boys sat drinking lemonade so that he could stroke their heads, and threw up his arms in welcome when Roshan entered with his friends. 'All my beautiful angels are safe,' said he. 'Get us one cup of tea and three saucers,' Adi said to him while Bhatia went to the counter where the proprietor, a moody and uncommunicative Parsee, sat sorting out some coins, and bought six Capstans. While the proprietor opened a new packet and counted out the cigarettes, Bhatia asked, 'What happened, do you know?' The proprietor raised his heavy eyelids, stared at Bhatia, turned his head wearily and looked out of the doorway on his right, stared again at Bhatia and shrugged his shoulders. Bhatia picked up the cigarettes and his change and was turning to go when he heard the proprietor say, 'Nazi submarines.'

Ibrahim was coming up with the cup of tea when Bhatia got to the table where Roshan and Adi sat. 'Did you hear that?' Bhatia asked. 'It was Nazi submarines.'

'Where?' asked Adi.

'In the harbour I imagine.'

'No, it wasn't Nazi submarines,' Ibrahim said, placing three saucers in front of the boys and the cup of tea in the middle of the table.

'Your boss just said it was,' Bhatia informed him.

'The boss always thinks there's something hidden that makes things happen,' Ibrahim responded. 'What you just heard, my little angels, was the arse of the world being split.'

'Oh, get lost!' Roshan said to him, while Adi asked, 'Don't you ever think of anything else?' and Bhatia added, 'Go bugger a goat!'

A thin bald-headed man with a beaked nose and round-rimmed spectacles, immediately recognized by the boys as the Bengali Nationalist, entered and said aloud, 'Subhas Chandra Bose be praised!'

His presence woke the moody proprietor out of his lethargy and he called out, 'Hey, you're going to buy a cup of tea or simply coming in here to make a speech?'

'Speech, can speech be necessary,' demanded the Bengali Nationalist, 'when the sky has spoken?'

'In that case get out of here,' the proprietor commanded.

'The Indian National Army has struck,' the Bengali Nationalist declared, making a small tour past the tables while aiming for the exit. 'Subhas Chandra Bose be praised! The great Bengali leader has given us our freedom!'

The proprietor, who was rarely given to extravagant speech, shocked the boys by shouting at the Bengali Nationalist, 'Go piss in the Hooghly!'

'Bengal for ever!' the Bengali Nationalist shouted from the door as he left.

Two Sikhs who had come in while the Bengali Nationalist was shouting his slogans laughed at his departing figure, and one of them said, 'Pathetic fool, two drops of rain fall in the desert and he will tell you the clouds come from Bengal.'

'It's a mutiny, that's what happened,' the second Sikh said as the two went and sat at a table and called for cups of tea.

'Mutiny?' Bhatia asked from two tables away.

'That's correct,' the Sikh answered. 'Indian sailors took over a ship in which they were setting out for the European war and turned the guns on the British.'

'That's what you heard,' the other Sikh said, 'twenty-one pounders smashing a British ship. It sank in the harbour.'

'The tricolour is flying from the Gateway of India,' his friend said.

Several of the other boys and some men in the restaurant shouted nationalist slogans in Hindi and there were two minutes of unrestrained jubilation. The proprietor came out from behind his counter, looked dreamily across the room, walked to the door and went out. He could be seen strolling on the pavement and gazing in. When the noise subsided, he wandered back in and resumed his position behind the counter where he picked up a newspaper and began to read it.

Roshan and his friends sucked the last of the tea from their saucers and lit their second cigarettes. Waves of a distant murmur had been reaching the restaurant and now a distinct commotion could be heard. The boys paid for their tea and went out. The main road that ran as a central artery in the island and became, when connected to the mainland, the Grand Trunk Road, on which one could travel all the way to the Khyber Pass, was three streets down and the boys, hearing the noise coming from there, hurried in that direction.

A long procession of humanity filled the main road. Poor people pushing hand-carts piled with their belongings, families crowded in bullock carts, their eyes staring out in mortal fear, and thousands others on foot seemed to be making a hurried exit from Bombay. They chattered loudly as they walked, some waited or cried aloud and some merely mimed the gestures of lamentation. A cloud of dust had risen in the air which was heavy also with an increasingly disagreeable smell. People stood in doorways of shops and were crowded in the balconies and windows of the buildings that lined the main road which, though its name changed with each district it traversed, was also known as the Delhi Road.

But the procession was not a response to the nationalist cry, 'Let's march together to Delhi!' They were people in flight. The island had exploded in their face. One instant of terror, and they were fleeing to the security of a larger land.

'What's happened, what's going on?' voices called from the doorways. But mostly the watchers of the exodus were silent, being too amazed by what they saw.

'Communal violence?' Roshan heard a voice ask, echoing his own apprehension. Some small misunderstanding sometimes led to Hindus and Muslims killing each other by the hundred followed by one group fleeing to a safer district. But the humanity that was fleeing from Bombay was clearly of mixed religious composition, for he could recognize Sikhs and Hindus and Muslims in the procession. For once, they were all together pursuing a common aim. What were they all running from, what had happened? Nazi submarines, mutiny, who knew the truth? How quickly the Indian had learned to run from the place he had made his home! A rumour in the air, and he was on the road.

Then another apprehension seized Roshan. What if his family also needed to flee? His parents must be waiting anxiously for him, he ought to run home. Whatever catastrophe had struck Bombay remained a mystery, but he must hurry home and be with his family. Bhatia said there could be nothing to worry about. 'Look,' he said, pointing to the human procession, 'these are all poor, illiterate people.' Adi concurred, and said, 'People like us don't take to the road just like that. We don't even know yet what's happened.'

So they waited on the pavement where the crowd had swelled from more curious people coming from the side streets to see the remarkable sight of thousands of people in flight. Roshan noticed that a group of six or seven young men wearing orange-coloured Gandhi caps pressed near them. A new rumour had sprung up concerning the explosions. The British were leaving India. The Viceroy had come down from Delhi secretly in a carriage attached to the Frontier Mail. Overnight, ships of the Royal Navy had filled up with high-ranking English officials and their families. And then, sailing out, they had fired their guns to smash the Gateway of India.

Adi thought it a naïve explanation and dismissed it. 'Just you wait,' said the man in an orange cap who had conveyed the rumour, 'Gandhi-ji will be proclaiming the Hindu Republic of India on All-India Radio any minute now.'

'What rubbish,' Bhatia said. 'Gandhi-ji never talked of a Hindu Republic.'

The other orange-capped men took offence at this assertion, and one remarked aggressively, 'Let's not even say India, let's use the proper native name, Bharat, Bharatmata, Hindustan, land of the Hindus.'

Bhatia looked askance at Roshan to see how his Muslim friend

295

was reacting to this flow of exclusively Hindu nationalism, and instinctively wanting to show his allegiance to him, answered back to the Hindu claim, 'India is for all Indians, whoever they are.' Seeing that the men in the orange caps stared angrily at him only emboldened him, and he went on, 'Look at the National Congress. It has Pandit Nehru-ji and Maulana Abul Kalam Azad, Hindu and Muslim, sitting side by side, leaders of free India for all Indians. No one ever talked of a Hindu India. Least of all Gandhi-ji.'

'Hey, this man's a Muslim!' one of the angered men exclaimed aloud.

'No, damn it, my name's Premchand Bhatia,' Bhatia shouted to declare his Hindu identity.

'He's lying!' charged the other. 'Pull his pants down, and see if it isn't a cut-off one.'

Bhatia, sensing that the group of orange-capped men was on the verge of becoming a violent little mob, attempted to dart out of the crowd. But two of the men sprang on him and threw him to the ground, and in a moment a third had torn off his pants and a circle of orange-capped men stood gazing down upon his uncircumcized penis. Bhatia yelled obscenities in Hindi. Roshan had become terrified. He imagined himself in Bhatia's situation and a wave of cold fear ran down his body. Seeing the men momentarily absorbed in confirming that Bhatia was a Hindu gave Roshan his chance to slip away, but he did not want to abandon his friend. Adi was making a sign to him to leave but he shook his head in refusal.

The men pulled up Bhatia from the ground and pushed him aside. And now they noticed Adi and Roshan. Frustrated by being proven wrong, they had become more enraged. They stood frozen for a moment, surveying the two boys with eyes that looked murderous. 'We're Parsees,' Adi shouted at them. 'I'm Adi and he's Jamshed.' Roshan was unable to utter a word. The men seemed about to accept Adi's word. The two boys were fairer skinned and taller than Bhatia and looked Parsee. But suddenly one of the men cried aloud, 'He's lying!'

The group made to move towards Adi and Roshan. Adi quickly tore at the buttons on his trousers and pulled out his penis and shouted, 'Parsee, Parsee! Can't you see?' The men stopped. One said almost resignedly, 'Go shove it into your sister's cunt,' and turned away. The others began to follow.

But one of them remained standing, staring with great curiosity at Roshan. The boy seemed vaguely familiar, as if he had seen him before in some shadowy light. Parsee or Muslim. The man moved closer to Roshan. 'Parsee, didn't you hear!' Roshan attempted to shout but the words were stuck in his throat. Adi had rearranged his trousers and now saw the man menacingly step towards Roshan. Bhatia had also composed himself, managing somehow to tie his torn pants across the waist. The man looked grimly at Roshan and suddenly recalled the image he had been seeking. His sister in the little park with a youth while he stood hidden against the trunk of a tree. And then when they left the park, he had hastened out and taken a good look at Roshan's features under a street-light. The very youth! And not a Parsee, but a Muslim, as his sister had declared.

Bhatia and Adi now stood on either side of Roshan. The man looked back to call to his friends but noticed that the gathering crowd had increased the distance between them while they went searching for some other victim. Obliged to act alone, he suddenly struck out at Roshan, his two fists rapidly pounding Roshan's abdomen and, as he staggered forward, the man struck his rib-cage and then his jaw, sending the boy staggering back. The beating was fast and of vicious ferocity. Before Adi and Bhatia could move to their friend's defence, the man was gone, pushing aside people in his way and shouting to his companions in the distance, 'There's a Muslim here, there's a Muslim here!'

Bhatia began to go after him but Adi held his arm and checked him. 'They'll all be back in a minute and finish him off,' Adi said to Bhatia. Stopping, Bhatia looked back at Roshan and saw him helplessly doubled over, his arms across his stomach, blood dribbling down his chin. 'We should take him to safety first,' Adi said, dodging past a man in his way and going to hold Roshan up. 'Maybe we should take him to Ibrahim,' Bhatia said over the head of the man Adi had just side-stepped past and going to join in the rescue. But Adi had another idea. In the huge and noisy procession of humanity that still continued on the Delhi Road a string of bullock carts was at that moment being driven past. 'Let's get him among those women,' Adi said, pointing to a cart on which stood five or six women in bright pink or purple saris over apple green or aquamarine blue blouses of the type that left the midriff exposed.

The two carried Roshan through the crowd on the pavement,

shouting, 'Fainted, fainted, please step aside, fainted, fainted!' Reaching the front of the bullock cart, Adi held on to Roshan while Bhatia jumped up into the cart, shouting at the women, 'Quick, quick, there's an injured boy, come on, help, quickly!' The man sitting at the front with his legs sticking out and his bare feet rhythmically beating with his big toes the rear sides of the bullocks to drive them on shouted at Bhatia, 'Hey, donkey, go bray in your sister's cunt!' One of the woman who had seen the injured boy said loudly, in a scolding voice, 'Hey, Desani, what a way to talk!' But another woman, also touched by the boy's plight, spoke to the driver in his own language, 'Listen you, Desani-Pissani, when you go to hell you'll beg the devil for a donkey to lick the sores on your arse, why don't you do a good deed for a change?' But it was a third woman who achieved the desired result. She simply walked up to the front, threw a stinging slap to the back of Desani's head and, bending towards his ear, shouted, 'Stop right now, goddam sodomist!'

Roshan was put aboard the cart, the women making room for him amidst the heaped luggage that consisted of two rolled-up mattresses, large boxes made of tin, several earthen jars and one empty bird cage.

'What happened?' the women asked, and Bhatia quickly answered, 'Got crushed in the crowd.' The women gazed sadly at Roshan and clicked their tongues. 'Poor thing,' one said, and another, 'Hai, what a pretty boy!'

His throbbing head propped against a mattress that leaned vertically against the side of the cart, Roshan saw as if in some hallucination a large woman with yards of purple about her bend over him and stroke his cheek. He longed for the tenderness to be real. A bump on the road made his head sway. His eyes rolled and his breath came in short gasps as a pain swelled from his stomach. If only the woman would grasp him in her arms, enfold him within the embrace of her munificent body, draw him inside her flesh into the fluid world of her being – but a sudden sharp pang from his stomach made him cry out and throw up his hands to hold the woman's arms. She was not there. In that momentary extremity of his pain, before it became a dull ache within his body, his vision was clear and sharp, and he saw the woman standing with her friends and talking while gesturing towards him, and he noticed that a numberless crowd of people followed the cart. Men with sunburnt wrinkled faces, a loosely wound turban on their heads, nearly hunchbacked women in dirty cotton saris, concave-chested and with what wrinkled flesh still clung to their bones covered with sores, and children, thousands of big-bellied, saucer-eyed children on rickety legs, naked in the swirling dust.

'He's shivering,' Adi said, his hand on Roshan's forehead. 'He's hot and cold. Probably delirious.'

'There's a dispensary down the road,' Bhatia said. 'Half a mile from here. Maybe there'll be a doctor there.'

Then they remembered that Roshan in fact lived in a side street off the Delhi Road just past where they hoped to find a doctor.

Adi squatted down beside Roshan and held him by the shoulder. Bhatia looked down at his friend and wondered how seriously he had been hurt. The man was a brute. Fast and furious. Bang-bang, phut-phut, smash, and phew! He was gone, the fucking fanatic. Poor Roshan. Must feel he has broken glass inside his rib-cage. Something damaged for sure.

Bhatia glanced at the buildings to see how far they had travelled. The pavements were still crowded with onlookers. 'Where are you all going?' he asked the woman nearest him.

'Wherever God will take us,' she replied.

Receiving such an answer, Bhatia realized that it was futile to expect a rational explanation of the events. 'What began this great procession out of Bombay?' he nevertheless asked.

'It's the government wanting to get rid of the poor,' she answered, and Bhatia abandoned his enquiry, knowing that the only discourse that could be expected from the woman would be a mixture of superstition and untruth. ———

'And other undesirables,' the driver morosely added to the woman's statement.

'Listen to the jackass!' the woman mocked.

'Queen of the night,' the driver muttered. 'Madam number one in the parade of beauties.'

The procession suddenly halted. Just ahead was a large roundabout bisected by a tram line. Four other roads normally made the roundabout a busy junction but now they were blocked by lines of policemen. Seven British soldiers stood on the tram line where they had parked three jeeps to block off that passage, six of them in a group beside the jeeps and the seventh, an officer, closer to the Indian crowd. The British soldiers watched two Indian police officers talking to some men in the crowd.

Bhatia jumped off the cart and made his way to where the Indian officers stood gesticulating and speaking loudly in Hindi. What was the panic about, one of the officers was scolding a group of men. Why this great exodus? There had been an accident in the harbour, two or three ships loaded with ammunition destined for the eastern front had blown up, that was all, who was spreading all the stupid rumours and causing panic? Go back, disperse, return to normal.

Worried about Roshan's condition, Bhatia had a bold idea. He walked up to the British officer who stood just behind the Indian policeman and said, 'Please, sir, excuse me, sir, but there's a boy here has been wounded.'

'Go talk to a policeman,' the officer said and looked away from Bhatia.

'Please, sir, it is serious, sir, not much time to talk, sir.'

The officer cast a cold gaze at Bhatia. 'You heard me.'

Bhatia clenched his teeth to still the sudden surge of rage. He said in a choking voice, 'The boy's a Muslim, sir.'

The officer did not even look at him but, throwing his chin up, made to walk towards where the other six British men stood in a group. Bhatia spoke after him in a rush of words, 'He was beaten by a Hindu, sir, a Hindu in an orange cap, he's a Muslim boy, sir, believe me, sir, I am a Hindu myself and I am telling you the truth, he's a Muslim boy and was beaten by a Hindu and you've got to save him or there could be a riot here, sir.'

The officer finally stopped and turned round. 'Where is he?' he asked.

'There, sir, in that cart, sir.' Bhatia pointed.

'Harrington! O'Keefe!' the officer called to his men. Two of them stepped forward, saying, 'Sir!'

'There's a wounded boy in that cart. Go check on him, will you? And if he looks serious take him to a hospital at once. On the double!'

His body being moved touched off a pain within Roshan and he came vaguely into consciousness. Though the blurred image of the staring faces of the crowd created a strange sensation of being lifted above the surging humanity, the feeling that overpowered him was that of sinking within its great mass, like a bird fallen in a pack of excited hounds.

13 Time's Outcast

'Look at the sea, how still! Like a sheet of glass,' Nurse Nabuco said, glancing back from the window at Roshan's mother who sat in a rattan chair next to his bed. 'Just like our sweet, quiet patient. So silent and so beautiful!'

His mother's eyes were closed while she obsessively flicked the beads of a rosary and quietly repeated some prayer, moving her lips urgently as if she feared the time for its completion was insufficient. Hearing the nurse's amiable chatter, she shook her head, like one awakening suddenly, opened her eyes and, leaning forward, blew her breath, which was charged with prayer, at the face of her son, and kept blowing while she turned her head so that the length of his body would be touched by her pious plea.

Nurse Nabuco came to the side of the bed and leaned over his face. 'When you're stronger, we'll place a chair next to the window so you can look at the sea. Would you like that?'

Roshan's still eyes saw her face a foot away from his. Dark brown and almost triangular, the chin was so pointed, with curly black hair, and dark brown eyes that gleamed so generously bright he almost felt a warmth from them on his cheeks. 'So calm he is!' she said, turning her face to the mother.

The mother's fingers worked at the rosary. The whisper that escaped her lips was a fragment of Arabic.

Nurse Nabuco touched Roshan's cheekbone with her fingertips and softly drew them down his face. She traced the outline of his lips with her index finger and then tapped his nose gently. 'Hello, handsome,' she said, smiling. 'Ain't I your favourite girlfriend?' She stroked his cheek, her face very close to his. 'Won't you speak, my beautiful darling?'

The mother spoke aloud the conclusion of the Arabic prayer and blew her breath again at her son. Nurse Nabuco stepped back from the bed, and said to the mother, 'The doctor must be right. He hears everything. You can tell it from the rhythm of his breath. He knows everything.'

'How can we be sure? He won't say anything.' There was despair in the mother's voice.

Nurse Nabuco walked to the window and drew the curtain halfway across to cut the glare. 'Like a mirror, the sea,' she said as she did so. 'The doctor's quite certain though he's waiting for the tests to be completed,' she said to the mother. 'He will be all right, you'll see. Before you know it, there'll be delegations of mothers coming to ask you for his hand, he's so, so handsome. Such a catch! Do you know what, if you didn't sit there watching him I think I'd steal him myself!'

The mother would have been scandalized by such an assertion from a Christian girl did she not believe Nurse Nabuco was only trying to cheer her up.

'But I'm an old woman,' Nurse Nabuco said, mockingly self-deprecating.

The mother could not help laughing, knowing the nurse had only the previous week turned 21. She had brought a piece of her birthday cake to share with her favourite patient.

'Hai-ay,' the nurse clicked her tongue and sighed dramatically. 'Here is my prince charming, but what can I do, his mother watches him like a dragon!'

The mother laughed aloud now. Nurse Nabuco was too comical. 'Go on with you,' she said.

Nurse Nabuco glanced at the patient to see if her talk had had any effect on him. He remained as before. Eyes open, breathing quietly, silent.

She looked out at the wide curve of Marine Drive. The usual crowd thronged Chowpatty beach. Beyond Malabar Point the ocean had begun to swell and white points of gleaming light seemed to pierce the vast blue. She drew the curtain across the entire window. How sad it was, the handsome boy just lying there as if the world about him were water and no sound reached him.

Roshan heard each of her words. The warm, amiable quality of her voice sounded clearly in his ears. Her Goanese-Bandra accent was just like Miss Miranda's, though Nurse Nabuco's speech had a ring to it which Miss Miranda's did not. There was a distinct music in her voice. He wanted to tell her that her voice was lovely. Her Christian name was Carolina, she had said, and he wanted to tell her it was a charming name. Each time she leaned over him and talked to him with her face so close to his he wanted to tell her she was beautiful. It was not the presence in the room of his mother that prevented him. There were times when his mother went to the bathroom and Nurse Nabuco was alone with him. He was unable to talk. His voice would not come. He could speak no words.

His senses were sharper than before, and his capacity for knowing the world he inhabited had intensified. His memory was so vivid, he sometimes felt himself present again in some past event and was astonished, when he realized he had only been remembering, at the reappearance of forgotten tastes and smells. Sometimes it seemed the remembered event was not one from the past but from the future, but that, he was convinced, was merely a confusion in his brain. But he could not work out how long he had lain in this room. He knew it was a room in a clinic on Marine Drive in the city of Bombay. He did not need to be placed by the window to see the ocean. He could see it with his eyes closed. He knew, too, that it was an expensive clinic, and that his father had gone into debt to save his son. But he could not tell how long he had been there. Weeks, months. He had no system of reckoning time. It was almost as if he had been cast outside the dimension of time and could only float among random appearances of images of events that claimed to be his reality.

The British soldiers had taken him to the nearest hospital after Bhatia had pleaded with them. The blows he had received made him look mortally wounded and the British officer, not wanting a communal riot in the streets when his government had enough problems with the war and had just suffered a setback with ammunition-loaded ships blowing up in the Bombay docks, had seen the immediate necessity of trying to save the boy. But the hospital had found nothing to be alarmed about. Bruised ribs, a slight cut inside the upper lip. No more. He was kept overnight for observation and discharged the next morning. The parents' relief at his recovery was brief, however. Roshan would not leave his bed. He would not explain what, if anything, pained him: he uttered no sound; and no one could tell if he was awake or asleep, his eyes were always open. Specialist doctors were consulted. He was moved to the clinic on Marine Drive.

A doctor would come, carry on a silent manipulation of his body. Tapping his chest, holding the tongue down with a wooden stick and peering into his throat, looking through a glass into his ears. Some days a second doctor came with him, and probed and fingered as Roshan had often seen his mother do at the market when buying chicken. The two men stood aside and looked gravely at the floor as they whispered to each other. Nurse Nabuco fluttered about the room. His mother sat there, fixed like an idol in a Hindu temple, her breath coming from her as if it were incense that floated continuously about her head. His father and Zakia visited every evening. Zakia had become quiet and watched him with round, worried eyes, staying by the window and sometimes pulling the curtain in front of her. His father talked with a bold cheerfulness that masked his anxiety. Without turning his head to look, Roshan could see his father have a whispered talk with his mother while Zakia observed them, though she pretended to be looking out at the crowd on Chowpatty beach. Roshan did not need to direct his eyes at an object in order to see it. And though the parental whispering was distant and muffled the words reached him as clearly as if they had been spoken in his ear. Money problems, the father was talking about. 'Ninety per cent of my head is thinking of the boy all the time, how can I do any business? What if . . . ?' The mother stopped him quickly with, 'Don't say that!' *Allah . . . Allah*, came from her lips.

He never needed to look or to listen. Yet all experience reached him with great clarity. When he attempted to focus on the present it dissolved instantly into the past and he fell into the habit of re-enacting events in his memory with such an obsession for minutiae that the particular event seemed to be happening for the first time and it was a surprise to discover at its conclusion that he had been lying in a bed and only dreaming about the past. Sometimes the discovery of his condition seemed merely an imagined event, as if his healthy body were running about chasing a soccer ball on Juhu beach and only imagined an unpleasant fate, thereby superstitiously preventing its happening. One day when his father and Zakia came, he saw them leave and return again the next day, and then he saw them returning a month later, having done so on each of the intervening days, and all their successive comings and goings happened in that one instant of their latest arrival. He thought that years had passed while he lay there. His eyes always open, he was certain that he never dreamed any more. He would see a mountain, its series of jagged, snow-covered peaks sharply defined against a deep blue sky, and he was certain he stood there in the cold atmosphere. Their Pathan servant Nabibullah Khan was there, in a valley at springtime with the snowy mountain in the distance. Whether it was a past or a future moment, or merely the eternally self-deleting present, seemed vastly irrelevant. He was in a train, which was like the Frontier Mail, and perhaps it was because it was so far north and mountains could be seen from the window, but beyond its terminus he travelled on horseback and then on a canoe. Even the canoe had to be abandoned and he was obliged to proceed on foot. 'We shall arrive at the icy waters yet,' a voice behind him said, but when he looked back there was no one there, only roots hanging from trees with vast trunks, forming a curtain so thick he was surprised it had not prevented his passage.

'Drink it all up,' said Nurse Nabuco, holding his hand that held a glass and gently tipping the cold water into his mouth. 'You need a lot of water in this heat. Oh the glare!' When he had drunk the water, she went and drew the curtain across the window. His mother's breath blew over his body.

A vast crowd had gathered on Chowpatty beach. People had come from the suburbs on lorries that flew the orange, white and green flag with the blue wheel at the white centre. They were shouting slogans in Hindi. The city was in a turmoil of independence. Thousands of people were massed upon the cricket pitches on the Maidan. The flag flew from buildings. Loudspeakers rang aloud with patriotic songs and with speeches. The voice of the people pierced the sky. The sky flowered with fireworks and burst with echoes of cheering humanity.

A group of orange-capped youths roamed the narrow streets behind Mohammed Ali Road. Very little light fell upon the deserted streets from the buildings, which had most of their doors and windows closed. Inside the closed flats, people sat grimly silent. The festivities of independence seemed a distant rumour, as if the celebrating country were just past the horizon across a border which excluded them.

Then someone saw the youths in the streets and could tell in the darkness that their caps were coloured orange. It was a provocation. They had got their India and were flaunting it. Coming to their doors and yelling in Hindi and Marathi. Abusing the name of God. Telling them to eat pig. Two men, armed with knives, ran out of an alley, shouting the name of God. There were screams in the night. Puddles of blood. Vengeful crowds flowed into the narrow streets. Roshan was running before them. A line of policemen, bamboo sticks in hand, charged from a side street and held the crowd. Shots were fired in the air. Roshan slipped into a doorway. A man stood there holding a dagger in the air, looking with horribly gloating eyes at the blood dripping from the blade. Roshan ran past him and came to a courtyard. A crowd sat there on the ground, wailing and crying in the direction of the open door of a room. There was a bed in the room. Mahatma Gandhi lay on it. He had just died.

The radio was on in the room. Nehru was talking. Bells were ringing. The night air boomed with fireworks. The hour of destiny. Soft as a lover's, Nehru's voice. A train had stopped in a vast plain green with sugarcane and wheat. It carried the dead lying in their blood that still flowed from their flesh. No sound, no motion, just the slow oozing out of the blood from the carriages of the stopped train in the middle of that vast green land. Gandhi's head was propped against pillows, he stared sadly at the people gathered round his bed beseeching him to take a sip of water. But several fires had started in the village and women were running down the dusty streets calling to their men to come back from the dead. Lorries, decorated with garlands of marigold flowers and flying the tricolour, rushed through the streets, the men in them shouting in jubilation. Roshan was in one of the lorries, squeezed among the men. He, too, was wearing an orange cap on his head and shouting with the men. Hindustan, Hindustan.

Squeezing the warm water out of the sponge, Nurse Nabuco scrubbed it across Roshan's chest. 'Here is the heart that beats only for me,' she said in her ringing, cheerful voice, rubbing the chest with a white towel when she had sponged it. 'You're going to be nice and clean, as for a wedding party.' She inhaled deeply, bowing her head quickly so that her nose nearly touched his left nipple and her lips seemed to graze his skin, and said, 'And you smell so fresh you could be getting ready for your own wedding! Ain't I your lucky bride!' And she smacked her lips just above his left nipple while at the same time putting the sponge into its enamel bowl and slapping away the towel so that Roshan's mother, sitting nearby with her rosary, heard nothing untoward and kept her eyes closed, concentrating on her prayer. The sudden kiss sent a shivering sensation through Roshan but his body seemed to remain immobile and his eyes did not blink.

Nurse Nabuco combed his hair and rearranged the pillows behind his head. She caressed his cheek. 'There,' she said, 'his imperial majesty is ready to receive the ambassadors.' She leaned back and asked the mother, 'Doesn't he look just royal? Hai-ay, I shall go to an early grave, I know, with a broken heart.'

The mother completed her prayer and opened her eyes. She stood up, saying, 'Help me with this chair. They'll be here soon.'

The two women carried the rattan chair with its faded pale green cushions and placed it near the window. Nurse Nabuco came back to the area that had been cleared and did a quick pirouette. Her skirt fanned out and swirled around her knees. Footsteps could be heard in the corridor and she stopped, smoothing her skirt down her thighs.

'There you are, Carolina!' a bright voice said from the door. Roshan recognized the voice a second before he saw Miss Miranda come into the room. A thrill passed through his body although its surface remained still.

'Alicia!' Nurse Nabuco greeted Miss Miranda. She stepped back, stood erect, threw an arm in the direction of Roshan, and said, 'His imperial majesty the emperor of Bombay and his dominions of Elephanta, Ajanta and Ellora welcomes you to his court!'

The two girls laughed as if what had been spoken was some private joke that they had long shared between them. But Roshan's mother, a little alarmed by the outburst of gaiety, whispered loudly, 'Nurse!'

Without turning his head, Roshan saw that more people were entering the room behind Miss Miranda. There was little Miss Mimi Engineer, the art teacher from the lower school, who was always seen in a stooping posture, with her face shaking continuously as if her life were dedicated exclusively to making the gesture of refusal. Even when she expressed agreement or accepted a gift the movement of her face suggested disapproval and rejection. But she had beautiful grey eyes and a sensuous mouth, making her a puzzling contradiction to men attracted to her, for when they gazed at those features the eyes would never stay still for any prolonged contemplation and the mouth would appear to quiver nervously, so that the men inevitably turned away from her in frustration. Behind her walked Father Marconi, his hands clasped across his protruding stomach. He had undone the top two buttons of his white cassock and sweat could be seen to have collected at the base of his neck. He kept his head lowered as though he wished to regard only the ground below his feet, so that as he looked up his eyebrows remained raised and gave him the appearance of someone for whom experience is a succession of surprises. He was followed by Bhatia and Adi, both

307

looking like model senior students, with their hair perfectly in place and their mouths shut.

Not seeing Roshan at the school for several weeks, Miss Miranda had set her little boys questioning the senior ones and had been able to piece together a loose and somewhat wrinkled fabrication of what had transpired. Then a chance meeting with Nurse Nabuco, a family acquaintance, had given her precise information that she wore about her like mourning, desperately wanting to go and see Roshan but not knowing how to do so in the face of the obstructive social conventions. She set her little spying boys at work again and had confirmed what she already vaguely knew, that Roshan's closest friends were Bhatia and Adi. The plan she hit upon was to take a delegation from the school to visit the sick boy. She chose Miss Mimi Engineer from among her colleagues because the art teacher never talked in the staff common room, and then persuaded Father Marconi that it was the duty of the spiritual leader of the school to visit one of his brightest pupils who had been hospitalized. Father Marconi's going with them would serve two purposes: he would make the visit look official, and since he would go in the school car, an old black Morris with curtains at the windows, it would save her the expense and the discomfort of travelling by bus.

She allowed Father Marconi to step forward and stand beside the bed, his head bent low. Roshan's mother saw him from the window and felt alarmed. Father Marconi seemed to be saying a prayer. She quickly turned her head away and looked out of the window. She was terrified that the Christian priest might make the sign of the cross over her son and thus nullify every prayer that she had uttered. His hands still clasped upon his stomach. Father Marconi made a quick little gesture with his right index finger which could be seen as the sign of the cross and which need not be generally noticed. Having done his duty, he stepped back and turned his lowered head to glance round the room. He decided that his next duty was to say a few words of consolation to the mother. She heard his steps approaching and began vigorously to flick the beads on her rosary.

Miss Miranda took his place by the bed and stared sadly down at Roshan's unblinking eyes. Nurse Nabuco came and stood next to her and said with her customary extravagance, 'Look at him, Sindbad the Sailor, Mr Number One Pirate of the blue oceans, plunderer of treasures and stealer of girls' hearts, Oh I could die!'

While Nurse Nabuco's voice rang in the room, Miss Miranda

leaned closer to Roshan, and said in a whisper, 'Oh, Roshan my dar-ling!' She withdrew quickly, closing her mouth tight and swallowing hard to suppress a choking sensation. Miss Mimi Engineer had come up to her other side and glanced down at Roshan, her head saying no, no, no. Bhatia and Adi remained behind by the door and saw glimpses of their recumbent friend, much of whose body was blocked by the women standing near the bed.

The mother flicked the beads of the rosary furiously and opened her eyes. Father Marconi stood right in front of her and her eyes fell upon the cross on his chest. 'Allah, Allah,' she whispered to herself, terrified that the communication she had established with heaven was being sabotaged. It was bad enough the Hindus on Chowpatty beach making their idolatrous offerings to the ocean, obliging her to close the window to prevent their prayers entering the room and polluting her pure devotion, but this priest had to come right in with his cross. She had stealthily observed his feet since he had entered, even when pretending to keep her eyes closed. He had walked into the room in a straight line, turned sharp left to the bed, then retreated and completed the interesecting line before following along the straight line to where she sat by the window, thus making a sign of the cross on the floor. She knew the tricks of these Christians. 'Allah, Allah,' she whispered. Father Marconi looked down upon her and said, 'So sorry.'

Bhatia and Adi were able to stand by the bed when the women stepped back and went to talk to the mother. 'Watch it, Roshan,' Bhatia whispered into his friend's ear, 'I wouldn't have a single thought in my mind, if I were you. The Short Wave's right here in this room. I didn't even say what I just said!' He added in a very low voice, 'You should have seen us in his old hearse. The Short Wave was squeezed against Miss Mimi and her head seemed charged with electricity, shaking faster than ever.'

Adi, who heard Bhatia's attempt to be funny, was not amused and looked sadly down at his friend. He had not known till the last minute that Miss Mimi Engineer was to be one of the party. She depressed him. As soon as he saw her come to the car with her eternally shaking head he went quiet and had scarcely spoken a word since. Miss Mimi Engineer paraded the curse of the Parsees, to be fair and beautiful and pathetically deformed at the same time, to appear from one perspective gifted by nature and from another to be conspicuously mocked. He lamented his fate, seeing in Miss

Mimi Engineer a model for the wife that would be chosen for him, with whom he would have children who would perpetuate the curse. It was another of the dilemmas that made him want to remain celibate, but he knew that would be impossible, for already, at 16, he felt that if he could not find soon some way of experiencing real sex he would have to take up a shocking suggestion made to him by a male cousin.

Roshan saw himself arrive at the school, late as usual in order to miss the first period of compulsory moral instruction that he loathed. Being a senior boy and having been appointed to the team of monitoring prefects, he had worked out with the other prefects a mutually beneficial system of ignoring among themselves the very precepts they obliged others to observe. It was Holy Week again, and passing the long room where Brother Batista used to play the organ while the Christian boys lustily sang the hymns, he heard the little bells ringing. Always Ram-Ram in there, Shiva, Krishna, tinkle, tinkle, and great puffs of incense. He hurried past and pretended he was patrolling the corridors, looking for miscreants and shirkers. From the open windows of the classrooms he could hear the moral instruction going on in top gear. In front of each class stood a fat little man with an orange cap on his head shouting away in Hindi so pure it sounded like Sanskrit. He walked into the lower school to escape from the harshness of the alien language. Miss Miranda had gone and Miss Bhosle was back. Luckily she did not see him pass her door. But the next classroom had a teacher who too looked exactly like Miss Bhosle. The lady teacher in each of the succeeding classes wore a sari and had a large round dot in the middle of her forehead. Going back to the senior school, Roshan had to pass the principal's room. Father Marconi had gone. A new principal sat there, a man named Mr Bhagwan. He was talking loudly in Hindi to Mr Ramdas and Mr Krishan. Roshan remembered that his first lesson, after the moral instruction period, was with Mr Krishan who taught Hindi grammar and that later in the day Mr Ramdas expected the class to recite by heart sixty lines from a Sanskrit epic. As he walked through the corridor, the bells from the temple became louder and louder. The boys in all the classrooms had stood up and had donned orange caps on their heads. They were all chanting loudly in Sanskrit. Then they were shouting at the top of their voices. Hindustan, Hindustan.

Allah, Allah, he heard vaguely and felt his mother's warm breath blow across his face. Then he thought the air that touched him came off the side of a white mountain peak, imbuing him with the cool grace of heaven. He opened his eyes. His mother was just then retreating from his bed and going out of the room. Nurse Nabuco had come in with her little white enamel basin and a towel folded over her arm. 'Time for a bathy-bath,' she said cheerfully, 'the hour for a scrubby-scrub, *and* . . .' she paused, putting down the basin and the towel and lifting Roshan's head away from the pillow to begin removing his pyjama top, before adding triumphantly, 'the minute to take off his clothy-clothes!'

She sponged his forehead and cheeks, his neck, shoulders and chest. She rubbed the fluffy white towel over his face and then the chest, moving her hand vigorously and letting the towel slip and continuing to stroke him with her moist little hand. 'Here we go round Roshan's heart, Roshan's heart, giving him a warning,' she sang as she stroked, 'and here we go kissy-kiss early in the morning!' And she quickly threw her face at his chest and kissed him smack-smack on each nipple. He gasped at the sudden pleasure that ran through his body. A low, distant sound had escaped his lips. Nurse Nabuco looked up at his face. His lips were slightly open in their attempted expression of delight. Nurse Nabuco glanced around and listened. The mother had not returned yet and nor could her footsteps be heard outside. Nurse Nabuco regarded Roshan with eyes that beamed with a new brightness. 'Ah-hah!' she exclaimed, and then dropped her face against his and kissed him long and hard on the mouth, driving her tongue into it.

'Ooooh!' came from Roshan's mouth when she withdrew from it, hearing the mother's footsteps down the corridor. Nurse Nabuco looked amazedly at him. First, her surprise was with herself, at the sudden snatching of pleasure from the captive boy, but then the greater surprise that she had in the process released his voice that had remained silent for so many months. She gave him a quick little smack on the mouth again, saying, 'And what do you say to that' – giving him another kiss – 'and that' – one more – 'and that?' – one more. 'Oh Carolina!' he responded. 'That's my wonderful Roshan,' she said, kissing him once more, and then beginning to busy herself with the towel and the basin for the mother had just reached the door.

14   Recovery and Loss

Roshan quietly opened the door of the long room on the left of the school's entrance hall and looked in apprehensively. A young European priest was playing at the organ. The Christian statues and pictures were still in place. A boy was polishing some brass object by the altar and another arranging some flowers there. The priest was absorbed in his playing, a meditative and melancholic piece evocative more of some patriotically nostalgic, rather than spiritual, feeling. Retreating into the hall and going towards the corridors that led to the classrooms, Roshan found the old divisions between the Catholic boarders and the secular day students still prevailed: the former were assembling for their morning service while the others went to their classes of Moral Catechism. Nothing had changed.

And yet as the days passed in the old routines Roshan felt the order to be illusory. In the history lesson, Father Mendoza, his face now scarred, had advanced in his interminable reading from his concealed textbook from the Congress of Vienna to the Revolution of 1848, but he seemed a waxen figure placed at the head of the class to pass the boys' time in a pretence of learning. When Bhatia slipped to him a piece of paper with the line on it that read, 'He met a boy in the Khyber Pass,' Roshan glanced at it and conveyed it to Adi without exploiting the suggestive rhyme. He had a disagreeable sense of being forced to perform previously rehearsed actions, as if his friends had entered some conspiracy to maintain around him an elaborate fiction that, repeating carefully chosen actions from his past, protected him from the threat of change. Adi returned the paper to him, having added a second line, 'Pretty as a girl in a summer frock,' thus giving him a choice of two suggestive rhymes. He stared at the paper and was conscious that Bhatia and Adi were looking sideways at him, and more out of a desire not to let them down than with any conviction that he had not become trapped in some hoax calculated to conceal from him some harsh new reality, he wrote down a third line, 'With

312

lovely cheeks and lovelier arse,' and conveyed the paper to Bhatia. Bhatia laughed aloud, and this response seemed to Roshan to be an exaggerated reward for his having gone along with the game. Father Mendoza looked up in the direction of the three friends, saw no untoward disturbance in the making, and continued reading, surprised – since the moment's inattention made him attentive to what he read – that where he thought he had been describing the events in France the words now coming from his mouth related some drama in Hungary.

Roshan excused himself and wandered to the lower school. Miss Mimi Engineer's little boys seemed engaged in acting out a vivid drama illustrative of the scenes of 1848. Bits of coloured chalk and paper missiles flew about the room between two groups while Miss Mimi Engineer stood beside her desk, her hands clasped in front of her thighs, her body stooped forward and her head going no, no, no. Order prevailed in Miss Miranda's class where the children were concentrating on copying out the alphabet. Miss Miranda walked up and down the aisles, stopping beside a boy here and there and bending above him to guide his hand along the ruled paper. Roshan stood by her door a moment until she noticed his presence there. She smiled but quickly turned her attention back to her students.

Her behaviour was the only real change at the school when he returned to it after five months away. She seemed pleased by his recovery but had made no attempt to see him. He found it strange that she should have taken the trouble of devising a clever strategy to visit him at the clinic but now that he was again available for the intimacy they had formerly enjoyed kept scrupulously away. After waiting vainly for some boy to come to him with a message from her, Roshan had walked into her class one day and handed her a message. He had received no answer. One afternoon, he waited for her to come out of the school after it was over. She refused to stop, saying she could not miss her train and added that one of her brothers was ill. He started to walk with her, but she said they ought not to be seen together so near the school. Roshan believed her at first that she had family problems that claimed her time. He longed to renew their embraces, and began to write a poem about a woman divided between her duty to her family and her passion for her lover, hoping to demonstrate to her that passion should take precedence over duty; but the poem that he wrote came out as an altogether different idea: it was about a woman who takes a new man when her first lover falls ill. And it was through writing the poem that Roshan discovered the truth. Later, when he happened to see her with her new boyfriend, who bore a very close resemblance to Nurse Nabuco, the evidence seemed dully redundant; it was only a visual projection of a truth already perceived by his imagination.

He enjoyed the luxury of talking with his friend Chandru about the Betrayal. Chandru, who had used the excuse of wanting news about Roshan when he was at the clinic to see Zakia every day, had convinced himself of being similarly betrayed by a woman. His meetings had amounted to standing below the balcony of her flat in the evenings when she had returned from her daily visit to the clinic and receiving from her from above, for no more than five minutes, general answers to his questions about Roshan's condition. But in his own private world of unbearable anguish, in which he was always the suffering lover fatally doomed to separation from the beloved, Zakia's commonplace answers became translated into an eloquent language of love; and, of course, he nightly rejoiced at the coincidence of the beloved appearing on a balcony so that he could believe himself a Romeo, and when he wished Zakia good night it was in a poetical voice which he was certain communicated more than it expressed. So that when Roshan returned home and Zakia had no more reason to appear before Chandru, the thwarted Romeo sought solace in poems that lamented the fickleness of women and their propensity to betray the hearts of sensitive men. Secretly, Chandru was delighted with Miss Miranda's going off with another man. It made Roshan Chandru's equal again, and he was no longer obliged to listen to the details of Roshan's love-making which filled him with painful envy.

The two crossed the bridge over the suburban railway line and walked towards Pavilion Hill to join the others in a cricket game. Roshan noticed that a woman with three naked children near her sat next to the foot of the bridge trying to light a fire on a small brazier. An old ragged sheet of coarse cloth was attached at two corners to the criss-crossing rusted iron of the bridge and to two pieces of bamboo stuck in the ground at the opposite ends, and in its shade were placed a bundle of clothes and some rolled-up bedding. One of the two rail-way tracks was no more than ten feet away, and the mother, blowing at the tiny heap of tinder and coals from where a wisp of black smoke curled up into the air, called to the children to mind the train that was screeching down the track towards the station just past the bridge.

Mona came running after Chandru and Roshan when they had just crossed the bridge. He carried a new cricket bat which had Walter Hammond's autograph printed on it. Roshan touched the engraved letters of the flowing signature and felt the presence of the great man in the wood just below where it said 'English Willow'. Mona withdrew the bat and tucked it under his arm, possessively. Roshan saw willow trees growing under a grey sky, the trees sucking the moisture in the air as if each drop were a run to be stored up inside the tree-trunks to be released on sunny summer's days on lovely green squares, from the cricket bats to which the trees would eventually be transformed. But Mona had brought out his autograph book and was showing them his latest prize. C. K. Naidu. The tall, lean C.K., famous for hitting sixes. But as if that were not enough to fill the other two with envy, Mona brought their progess to a complete halt by announcing that he had written a letter to Lord Wavell asking for his autograph. After overcoming their secret regret that they had not themselves thought of doing so, Roshan said, 'The Viceroy will never answer,' and Chandru added, 'The Viceroy write to an Indian boy? Never!' Mona was certain he would. 'And that's only going to be the beginning,' Mona declared. The other two looked at him suspiciously. When he had Lord Wavell's autograph, he was going to write to Winston Churchill. To Number Ten, Downing Street. It sounded like a magical formula. But Chandru dismissed Mona's ambitious plan by saying, 'Your letter will never reach him, there's a war on.' Mona was emboldened to reveal his larger, hierarchical plan. After Churchill he was going to write to King George VI for his autograph. And when he had that, he would write to the Princesses Elizabeth and Margaret requesting them to follow their father's example.

Roshan understood the entire purpose behind Mona's strategy of beginning by trying to obtain the autograph of the Viceroy. It was to hold in his hand a piece of paper touched by the fingers of Princess Elizabeth. Roshan knew exactly what Mona would do once he held that piece of paper, and slapped him on the back and congratulated him by calling him a son of a pig in Punjabi.

They joined the other boys on the field and began the game, which was now played with proper equipment and not, as in their younger years, with a home-made bat and a used tennis ball. Mona's new bat seemed to give him extra power and twice he slammed the ball into the hillside. Roshan had to go chasing after it one of the times

315

and going where he had seen the ball land among some bushes he suddenly stopped. There was a potent smell of human faeces. He saw that the area behind the bushes was covered with excrement, and noticed in the distance, at the foot of the hill, something he had not observed before. Several little huts had sprung up there. He retrieved the ball and went running back into the open air away from the smell. The huts must have come up when he was in the clinic, he thought, throwing the ball at the wicket and watching its perfect trajectory through the air as it curved across the space and landed with a thud in the wicket-keeper's gloves.

As at the school, so at his games with his local friends there seemed to be a continuation of established routines, and yet he could not entirely be rid of the idea that his world had become insecure. It was as when he went one weekend with his parents to Juhu beach and, filled with the exuberance of newly restored health, ran the length of the beach and found himself alone at its southern end. There were some rocks there that he could climb up and jump from one to another; leaping from one of them, he failed to make the rock he had aimed to land upon and fell in the intervening area of sand. It was a pleasurable fall, crashing into the wet sand upon his heels with his legs bent; but the pleasure was of very brief duration, less than a second perhaps, and was succeeded by terror, for he had landed in a notorious area of sinking sand. Had the rock he had aimed for not been immediately at hand to be quickly grasped, held on to and used to pull himself up from where his legs had begun to sink, he shuddered to think what might not have happened. He could no longer trust the seeming solidity of the world. He remembered the parade of hallucinations to which he had not been able to close his eyes as he lay in the clinic unable to produce a sound from his throat. Certainly, it was a relief to observe that reality had not become so degraded as in the involuntary projections of his imagination, but walking slowly up the beach, his body still shivering from its sudden terror, he could not trust the firmer sand over which he had only a few minutes earlier run with such energetic freedom, and the ocean at whose waves he had lately flung himself with perfect composure, diving at the base of the great lifting mass of water as if he were leaping into his bed at home, the ocean, too, now seemed to possess a malignant murmur underneath its boisterous roar and to have prowling, out in the deep, a clawing current beneath its mirror-like surface.

Mona smashed the ball again over the heads of the other boys. His new Walter Hammond bat seemed to be working like magic. It was impossible to get him out. Roshan had seen a Don Bradman bat at the sports goods shop. He had touched the Don's signature on it and wished he could buy the bat. But he could not ask his father for the money. His father had gone into debt to pay for the clinic. Crack! Mona sent the ball whizzing through the fielders. Wally Hammond. Would he play like the Don if he had the Don Bradman bat? English willow. There was magic in that wood. What a bold idea, writing to the Viceroy. Funny about Lord Wavell. Roshan remembered dreaming about him. No, it was not Lord Wavell. That was the funny part. He was the man who was not Lord Wavell. A younger man, from England. In a white navy suit, like an officer of the Royal Navy. Rear-Admiral Viscount. But he was coming out of an aeroplane. No, it was not a dream. Roshan had seen him with his eyes open, lying in the clinic bed. He was not Lord Wavell, who was not a navy officer, he was the Viceroy of India. Crack! God, if I had that Don Bradman bat I'd hit the ball over the hill all the way to Poona! He knew the most potent figures in his imagination had been the orange-capped men but he suppressed thoughts about them, forcing himself to replace that image as soon as it surfaced in his mind with some scene from a film with his favourite actress in it. Hedy Lamarr with eyes like diamonds. Once when Bhatia had mentioned a procession in which they had found themselves among a crowd of people senselessly fleeing from Bombay, Roshan had not known what he had been talking about. It was impossible he should have been in a crowd of humanity and not remember it.

They played until it was nearly dark. Although the ball remained visible minute by minute after the sun had set, when Mona cracked the ball past the boundary again and it took five minutes to find it, the interruption of their continuous perception dramatically altered their vision and they realized that they could no longer see the ball.

Crossing the railway, Roshan saw in the light falling from the small lamps on the bridge the family that had made its house below it. Two of the children had gone to sleep under the cover of the sheet attached to the bridge. The mother sat beside them, near the brazier, watching the husband eating with his fingers a small mess of rice and lentils on an earthen plate. A train was clattering down, tucka-tuck, tucka-tuck. The beam of its headlight briefly fell upon and vividly illuminated the third child who sat between the two tracks, defecating. The train rattled past the child, its lit-up carriages filled with people.

His mother and Zakia were watching out for him from the balcony of their flat. But neither complained how late it was when he entered. He knew that he was being observed for any variation of behaviour. His mother spent more time praying than in the past. Sometimes when he sat reading and happened to look up he could tell from Zakia's hasty movement of her eyes that she had quietly been staring at him. The two women lived in terror of his suffering a relapse. No one talked of what had afflicted him, as if to talk would be a superstitious error, like unwittingly looking at oneself in a broken mirror, an action bound to crack the protecting shell in which the self was encased and show its composition to be fragmentary.

But this evening the father was in an elated, triumphant mood. He had outbid his business competitors and won an order to supply the British armed forces in India with football clothes. Within days, the flat became a small factory with the beds being pushed up to lean standing against the bedroom walls during the day and being replaced by twelve sewing machines that were stacked at night in the balcony and the entrance hall. Twelve small dark men chattered away in Tamil as they rocked on the pedals of the Singer machines and deftly moved pieces of cloth with their stubby little fingers to sew together the multi-coloured shirts to supply the hundreds of distinguishing colour combinations of the many clubs into which the British had grouped themselves in their endless pursuit of order, discipline, and class rules. Sometimes Roshan would pick up a newly completed shirt and put it on and shuffle about the balcony like a centre-forward dodging the full-backs in the penalty area. Then he would stop, overcome by the strangest sensation, his own body seeming to become in that moment the body of the Englishman who would soon be wearing that shirt.

The father's success with this one order led to other successes, and within a year of Roshan's recovery the family had regained more than its former middle-class prosperity. There were dinner parties every other Sunday when again the ageing Tilak Singh, with his snow-white beard longer than ever, and his young wife Manika, grown slightly plumper and more voluptuous, were invariably the first to arrive. The dark-skinned Mr Samudra still drove up in his stately style in the old black convertible Morris but he had abandoned his Churchillian cheroot and demeanour and instead smoked home-made Indian *bidis* and wore Indian clothes of Gandhian home-spun purity. Mr Richardson, who until lately had claimed to be an Anglo-Indian, now kept a white cloth cap on his head in the style of Mr Nehru, declaring it was the best protection he had discovered for his bald patch. Only Anwar-bhai had remained unchanged and continued to be a cynically bemused commentator on the conveniently altered attitudes and convictions of his friends. He narrated the fable of the goat that imagined it wore a tiger's skin, but his obvious moral was lost upon the party.

But the talk was, as before, about the politics of independence. 'Believe me, there will be a Japanni surrender any day now,' Anwar-bhai declared. 'With America stronger and stronger, there can be only one outcome of the war.'

'The writing is on the wall,' Mr Richardson stated.

'And that can only mean the end of British rule,' Mr Samudra said. And that led to the usual web of opinions. Partition was inevitable. A grave mistake, cutting the country in two. What minority guarantees can you have? Why, it would be freedom for all! Ha, a fool's freedom. You and your Pakistan. Then what do you want, a parliamentary democracy? Very nice, very pious to want democracy when it perpetuates Hindu rule. India is Hindustan. Then give us Pakistan.

'Divide and rule, that is precisely the British idea!' Mr Samudra protested. 'You're only giving them an excuse to prolong the Raj.'

'No,' Anwar-bhai responded coolly, 'you know the Raj will end and you're simply bent on snatching complete power. You don't want to share it with Muslims, with Sikhs, with Christians, with no one. Democracy is your alibi.'

'But a secular state . . .' Tilak Singh began, but Anwar-bhai cut him short with, '"Look at me, I'm only a sheep," said the wolf peeping out of sheep's clothing.'

Mr Richardson advanced the idea of dominion status. Under the impartial and benevolent supervision of the Crown. You and your Crown! Another fool's paradise. But the best spirit of compromise. Baa-baa. And your princely states, the Jaipurs and the Barodas, what about them, then, just dying to go back to feudal times! I repeat, parliamentary democracy is the only solution. Don't make me laugh, let me see you shake hands with your own untouchables first. God, what a prospect, the independence of India!

Anwar-bhai spoke of the principle of contraries. Don't you

remember, he raised a rhetorical finger, Jinnah wanted nothing but unity. Everything constitutionally correct. But Gandhi reduces it to an issue of slaughtering cows. So Jinnah's forced to seek a state of his own although he never wanted one. Just to escape the treachery of popular symbols. Civil disobedience says Gandhi, cunningly striking the imperial power where it's weakest. But that creates an atmosphere of lawlessness and gives a licence to extremists to kill innocent people. Gandhi wants Hindu–Muslim brotherhood but he is himself proclaimed a Mahatma, emphatically a Hindu saint. Muslims will never follow a Mahatma and if he doesn't live up to Hindu expectations of Hindu exclusiveness the Hindus will kill him. Jinnah wants a state where people are equal and free but instead he will lay the foundations for religious fanaticism and create a country in which he himself would be better dead than alive. 'Contraries, my friends,' Anwar-bhai concluded, 'everything happens by opposites. Gandhi's love of peace will create a civil war, Jinnah's love of law will fuel that civil war, and each man's high principles will spawn a race of barbarians.'

As always, the arrival of the food put an end to the talk. Nabibullah Khan no longer headed the servants who carried in the many dishes. He had believed the family's troubles threw a malevolent shadow over his own destiny. Roshan's illness, which he understood showed no visible physical symptoms, had to be a curse. Nabibullah Khan did not want to eat the food of the cursed. Not being able to rationalize his thoughts, he became generally resentful and performed his duties as if under protest, in a surly and sluggish manner. One day he was sent to town on an errand – some things Roshan's mother needed at the clinic – and he took the opportunity to loiter among the distractions of one of the main streets. An extraordinary coincidence occurred. A Pathan had just held up a bank and driven away from it in a jeep. As he drove he laughed and threw bundles of notes into the air. He seemed to be highly entertained by the action of throwing money at the crowded pavement and it was not long before he had thrown all the money away and been stopped and arrested, as broke as he was before he had robbed the bank, and became a unique example of the man who laughed all the way from the bank straight to jail. However, during the few moments when he enjoyed his lunatic fantasy of bringing wealth to mankind, one of the bundles he flung out landed bang against Nabibullah Khan's chest and fell to his feet. Thus one Pathan enriched another without knowing it, and while his generosity sent him to jail it freed the other from exile. Nabibullah Khan pocketed the money and quickly slipped through the crowd, making for the Bombay Central station. There he bought a third-class ticket to Peshawar and spent the rest of the day asleep under a bench, waiting for that night's departure of the Frontier Mail.

Roshan had not been surprised to discover that Nabibullah Khan had left their household. It was one more fact among many that had transcended the linear flow of time, and when, finally arriving at the historical moment, as with the replacement of Lord Wavell by Lord Mountbatten, the naval man stepping out of an aeroplane, the event took place that had already been recorded in his imagination, it occasioned in Roshan neither surprise nor curiosity. During the first months of his recovery he had been puzzled by an ambiguous phenomenon in reality: some of it seemed stable and constant, as it had been before his illness, and some of it had become elusive and unfamiliar, as if walking in the sunlight he was being overwhelmed by shadows; and when some of the most hideous images experienced during his illness, which he had explained away as hallucinations, began to manifest themselves as national events, he believed that to be proof not of his mind's capacity to predict the future but of his self being cast out of the dimension of time. It was, he realized, the eternal condition of the poet, to appear to be a prophet when in fact nature had taken away from him the common conception of mundane hours and minutes.

The great events occurred. The war ended. The British soldiers vacated the building next door and it was soon filled with a dozen Indian families. The parade ground and the vast depot around it where tanks, jeeps and anti-aircraft guns had been stored were transformed into building lots. With blocks of flats going up, Roshan could no longer see the railway tracks where daily he used to come running out to the balcony to watch the Punjab Mail gliding into Bombay. Where the British soldiers had paraded were now streets overrun with the thousands recently arrived from Sind and the United Provinces and Gujarat and Bengal.

The clamour for independence filled the air. From the balcony Roshan watched what he had already seen when he had lain in the clinic bed, his eyes wide open all night. Lorries flying the tricolour went past packed with men shouting slogans. Men tore at one another with knives. Gandhi fasted. Roshan stood beside Gandhi's bed in the Bengali village. Gandhi's face was smeared with ash. Hindu and Muslim men stood shamefaced at the foot of his bed but would not speak to one other. Two men glared at each other across the bed. Each had murdered the other's family. Gandhi's round spectacles had slipped down his nose. Gandhi's eyes were fixed in a stare. A woman knelt on one side of the bed, a glass in her hand offered to Gandhi. The glass was filled with warm blood. Opposite her, on the other side of the bed, knelt another woman, a brass tray in her hand offered to Gandhi. On it was the heart of a man murdered a minute ago. The hour struck. Nehru's voice came on over the radio. Long years ago we made a tryst with destiny . . . Soft as a lover's, Nehru's voice. Long years ago my father took me on a journey to the Hindu Kush and said if you could climb the highest peak and looking south spread out your arms you would embrace all of India. Long years ago when the living heart was plucked out of my body and I watched the women kneeling beside Gandhi's bed and saw the hour had come when he must break his fast for the woman who held the glass in her hand had begun to raise it to his lips. Drink, father, my blood.

15 The Station of the Dead

Bells were ringing in the new temple near the suburban railway station. Roshan and Mona walked hurriedly past it towards the old iron bridge. The priest's voice in the temple seemed to pursue them down the street. Ram, Ram. Mona was swinging his Walter Hammond bat and talking about a recent visit to Amritsar. The Frontier Mail up, the Punjab Mail down. Mona was comparing the two trains. Chandru and some of the other boys were trailing behind them. They had stopped to go into the temple and were now coming out with a line of ash smeared across their foreheads. Mona said that each train had its unique points. He wished he could travel on both simultaneously. There was one station in the Punjab that both the trains used to go shooting through at top speed, Mona said. But now they slowed down and crawled through the empty station. Everyone held his breath when the train crawled through making no noise. The blood on the platforms still looked fresh. Five months after independence there was still fear. Anything could happen. There were still murderers about. A drop of cold moisture fell in Roshan's stomach. It is the station of the dead, Mona was saying. No train stops there but no one dare speed through there either. A train going to the new country of Pakistan had been forced to stop there. Everyone on it had been killed. I wanted to put my head out of the window, Mona was saying. But all the windows had been pulled up. To keep out the smell of death. Mona swung his Walter Hammond bat in his right hand as he walked. He had flung his left hand over Roshan's shoulder. Roshan remembered the time three or four years earlier when he had been alone with Mona in Chandru's flat and they had desecrated the Hindu kitchen. They had kissed each other on the lips. No trains go through the station of the dead at night, Mona was saying. No one wants to run over ghosts.

Chandru and the others had caught up with them. They came to the bridge and scampered up the steps to get away from the potent smell of human excrement. A dozen families now made their home under the bridge, having put up some kind of lean-to on the side away from the station and used the station side as their lavatory. Coming to the bridge, the thing to do was to hold your breath and run. But when the boys reached the top of the bridge and were hastily crossing it a man standing halfway across it stopped them. His eyes were swollen and red. He looked distraught. He raised his arms with the palms of his hands to the boys and said, 'Where are you all going?'

Mona held up his Walter Hammond bat and answered, 'To play cricket.'

'Ah, to play cricket.' The man nodded his head, and repeated with an exaggerated suggestion of irony in his voice, 'To play, of course, to play.' He paused, looked down at his feet, which were bare, and suddenly stared up at the boys with tears flowing down his cheeks, 'And it is nothing to you that Gandhi-ji is dead. Oh no, it is nothing to you that the Mahatma has been assassinated! Hay Ram, Gandhi-ji gives his life for your freedom and all you can do is to play!' He fell to weeping uncontrollably for a few moments. The boys stood petrified, not knowing what to say. They had heard the news the previous day. It had not occurred to anyone that it was somehow wrong to carry on living. Several had talked about the assassination late into the night and listened to the speeches and reports on the radio. But by morning the shock had passed. Gandhi wasn't going to come back if they didn't play cricket.

A train had arrived at the station and many people who had disembarked were coming up the bridge. The weeping man turned aside. The boys stood back to let the crowd pass. Roshan held on to an iron post as he looked down the tracks. Another train was approaching from the opposite direction. Immediately below him a swarm of naked children were playing between the tracks. His hand on the iron post slid down and encountered some embossed letters. He looked closely, for the letters had become the same colour as the weathered old iron, and read:

HOSKEN & BULLER
LIVERPOOL

and then clasped his hand over the words as though he needed to conceal them from the eyes of others.

'Let's go home,' Chandru said, turning around. All the boys, released from the tension by Chandru's decision, quickly followed him and the group became swallowed by the crowd flowing over the bridge.

Roshan and Mona walked past the temple where some of the Hindu boys again disappeared. Bells were ringing. The priest's voice echoed from within the temple. Ram, Ram. 'Hé Ram,' had been Gandhi's last words. And Nehru's voice had come on over the radio. *The light has gone out of our lives and there is darkness everywhere.* Nehru's voice like a betrayed lover's. The light has gone out, Roshan repeated walking past the temple.

Chandru caught up with Roshan and Mona some distance from the temple. The three walked silently towards the block of buildings down the road, where they lived. From a side street there suddenly burst upon their hearing the sound of drums being beaten. It was an erratic pounding sound. Soon some bugles joined in. The combination was not musical so much as noise intended to catch people's attention. A band of some forty or fifty youths marched down the street led by the bugles and the drums. They wore orange-coloured cloth caps and chanted slogans in Hindi. They were marching in the direction of the temple and grew louder as they approached it.

A bus was coming down the street. The procession came out of the side street and obliged the bus to halt. 'How much money you got?' Mona asked. Neither Roshan nor Chandru needed to count the coins in their pockets. 'And I have two rupees,' Mona added when they had said they possessed 8 annas each. 'Let's go to town!' They ran to the bus stop and waited for the procession of the orange-capped men to pass. The drummers were beating furiously as they approached the temple. The bugles had become shrill. Roshan remembered the new Hindu students at the school. They were not like his friend Bhatia. They carried orange-coloured caps in their pockets and wore them during the lunch break when they paraded by themselves on the edge of the cricket ground. The new Hindi teacher Mr Shelvankar led them on their martial exercises. Mr Shelvankar was short and fat, with a round, bald head that seemed to rest on his shoulders without the need of a neck. He did not wear a suit and a tie like some of the other male teachers who were not priests, but dressed like a Maharashtran in a white shirt of coarse cotton over a *dhoti*. When he came to a class he spoke only in Hindi. He spoke loudly and his voice boomed out of the window and the door into the corridor and down the length of the school. You could hear him when he was in another class. He spoke a Hindi which even Bhatia could not understand. Suddenly he would roll his eyes and chant in his booming voice from some Sanskrit epic. 'The man's crazy,' Bhatia said. 'Complete number one lunatic.' But everyone had to say 'Yes, sir' to him in Hindi. 'I wish the Short Wave would tell him to pipe down,' Bhatia said, 'his yelling gets on my nerves.' Adi laughed cynically and said, 'That's just what he'd like, just what he's trying to provoke. If the Short Wave says anything that can remotely be interpreted as criticism of Hindus, that's the end of the Catholic mission. Goodbye Father Brooks, Father Mendoza, go to sleep for ever, here come the orange caps!' Roshan found it impossible to learn the Hindi alphabet and had come to an arrangement with Bhatia. He wrote Bhatia's English essays and Bhatia wrote his Hindi exercises. The strategy in class was to remain dumb except to say 'Yes, sir,' in Hindi. They had yet to work out a plan to cope with the coming exams.

The procession finally cleared out of the street and disappeared into the temple where the bells began to ring louder than before. The three friends boarded the double-decker bus, climbed up the steps and found seats at the front, above the driver. The bus crossed the middle of the island, from Sion in the north to Fort in the business district. The conductor came up. 'Where are we going?' Roshan asked. 'Let's make it to VT,' Chandru said. 'No, no, let's make it the end of the line,' Mona said, who sat by himself with the Walter Hammond bat held between his knees.

The bus went off the main road before approaching Dadar to serve an area inhabited principally by Parsees. Roshan looked down on a park where seven old Parsee men sat in a line, their heads tilted up. One of them was talking but the others also had their mouths open. Their eyes seemed made of glass. There was one who could not control the nervous movement of his face. Just like Miss Mimi Engineer with her beautiful grey eyes. Always saying no-no-no-no with her face. Mona saw the Parsee men on the bench and said, 'Hey, Roshan, what's worse, to kiss a pork eater or to kiss a crow eater?' Roshan answered, 'It depends on how carefully the moustache has been trimmed.' Chandru laughed and said, 'You Punjabis!'

The bus filled up at Dadar. A man boarded it a few stops later. He carried a basket in his left hand and in the other he held up three or four black arm-bands of which the basket was full. 'In remembrance of Gandhi-ji, four annas, in mourning for the father of the nation, four annas,' he chanted in Hindustani though his voice betrayed the intonation of an Urdu speaker. No one paid him any attention. The conductor ignored him at first but when the man became louder to see if he could get a customer and at the same time cut his price by 50 per cent, the conductur shouted at him, 'Go stick them on your grandmother's nose, this isn't the bazaar.' The man left, saying, 'What a way to talk, hai-Ram.' Roshan felt sorry for the man whose features and accent clearly marked him as a Muslim but who was pretending to be a Hindu.

Some of the shops were closed. Black sheets were draped over their padlocked doors. Groups of men stood talking on the pavement by the textile mills. The conductor kept ringing the bell all the way to Byculla to inform the driver not to stop, the bus being full. There, several people left the bus and as many got on it. The crowds on the pavement now became immense and spilled on to the road, slowing the already congested traffic. A general noise of vociferous humanity filled the air, but no words, or slogans, could be distinguished in the waves of a muffled sort of roar that swept across the road. The slow progress came to a halt when the bus reached a junction on Mohammed Ali Road. There vast crowds thronged the streets in every direction. The noise was louder, shriller. The traffic crawled forward a few yards at a time. The crowd in one street was running towards some distant destination. Then a bell was heard. A fire engine trying to get through. When the bus had moved a little further and another side street came into view, smoke could be seen rising from a building.

Roshan observed, without seeing, the recurrence of history that he had already witnessed during the months he had been sunk into silence. Someone behind him in the bus was saying, 'But it was a Hindu who killed Gandhi-ji.' Someone else answered him, saying, 'No, no, the Muslims had to be behind it, why should a Hindu want to kill the Mahatma?' Roshan did not need to raise his hands to his ears to stop the words from entering. His body had evolved spontaneous procedures with which to block out unpleasant sensations. His Hindu and Sikh friends were silent. Chandru looked out sadly at the crowd which seemed to be driven by some agitators in its midst, for now Hindi slogans could be heard. Mona stroked his Walter Hammond bat and wondered whether he should not let his hair grow, like other Sikhs.

More bells could be heard. They seemed to be ringing with a desperate urgency as if someone wanted to clear away some vast obstruction with one loud gesture. Car horns added to the din. Some siren had also gone off. Then the bus began to move uninterruptedly, though slowly. An unfamiliar smell came through the windows. A smarting, searing sensation hit the eyes. Someone shouted, 'It's tear gas!' People without handkerchiefs pulled up their shirt ends to protect their eyes. Roshan bent his head towards his lap and held a handkerchief against his eyes. Tears had sprung from them.

The bus accelerating, the air in it, which had possessed only a momentary hint of tear gas, cleared. Roshan wiped his face and put away his handkerchief. His eyes were red. Most of the passengers left the bus at Victoria Terminus. 'Hey, Roshan,' Mona asked when the nearly empty bus moved on, 'if VT is Victoria Terminus, what's VD?' Roshan answered, 'Victoria Dermatitis.' Mona asked, 'What's dermatitis?' Roshan answered, 'Inflammation of the skin.' Mona said, 'I thought yours was cut off!' Roshan answered, 'That's correct, which is why I can't get VD.'

They left the bus at Flora Fountain and stood laughing in front of the bare-breasted maiden in one corner of the monument erected some decades before by the British, who could not have guessed that Indian boys would rename it Lowra Fountain, the substitute being a common native word for the organ just referred to by Mona. Exchanging coarse jokes, they walked away towards Colaba, Mona with his Walter Hammond bat on his shoulder as if he carried a rifle.

The emptier streets, with their cleaner buildings, and the sense of camaraderie between the three boys that sprang from the sharing of vulgar jokes restored the easy gaiety that characterized their friendship. They were released from the tension that had closed them from one another in a strange mood of resentment and regret when the bus had stopped on Mohammed Ali Road.

But here too, near the shipping warehouses, a crowd had gathered, though a thin one. Some office clerks stood in a group and shouted at the sparse traffic going to the docks to stop work as a sign of mourning. The people in the few taxis and cars and a number of luggage-laden lorries that went past looked curiously at the demonstrators as if their shouts were aimed at someone else and proceeded with their business. The clerks seemed content merely to be gazed at, for theirs was the sort of demonstration calculated not to achieve any real end but only to make the demonstrators feel good. Mona, walking with a military air with the Walter Hammond bat on his shoulder, led the boys away from the futile spectacle of the clerks and headed towards the Gateway of India.

They stopped at a café for a cup of tea. The radio was on and played a selection of sad songs from Indian films. Men sat at the tables, drinking tea and smoking cigarettes, and talked animatedly. One behind Roshan was saying, 'Believe me, Pandit Nehru can cry all he wants to to impress the public but secretly he must be glad. Now he won't have Gandhi-ji to stop him sending troops into Kashmir.' His companion clicked his tongue in disapproval of an expression that was nearly sacrilegious. 'Believe me,' the other said, 'time will prove it, Pandit Nehru will be glad not to have Gandhi-ji to nag at his conscience any more.' 'Hay-ay.' His companion seemed saddened by the prognosis.

Mona ordered a boiled egg and toast. Chandru went to the counter and bought cigarettes for himself and Roshan to smoke with their tea. Roshan moved to another chair so that he could be closer to the radio and not have to listen to the man analysing Gandhi's death as the Prime Minister's opportunity. But the whole room seemed to be talking about the same subject, and though Roshan listened to the playback singer Mohammed Rafi's Urdu words that flowed lugubriously from the radio the words he heard again and again were Nehru–Gandhi, Gandhi–Nehru being uttered by the men around him.

A cool breeze blew through the arch of the Gateway of India. The usual crowd strolled about the precincts of the monument. Evening was falling. Mona leaned upon his Walter Hammond cricket bat as if he stood at the crease. Roshan bowled an invisible ball at him. Mona drove the invisible ball into the crowd. Chandru leaped up and caught the invisible ball and threw it jubilantly into the sky. The three friends walked through the arch of the Gateway of India. A small vessel was sailing back from Elephanta Caves. But from their left came the urgent noises of an ocean liner. A bell rang out several times. A steam whistle blew startlingly loudly. Just at that moment the crowd strolling about the precincts of the Gateway of India began to run in the direction of the café. 'It's Gandhi-ji, it's Gandhi-ji!' someone shouted.

The three friends ran after the crowd. People had packed into the café and stood in a mass between the tables. Most of the crowd was obliged to stand outside on the pavement. Everyone was dead silent. The Hindi words on the radio could be heard in the street. Everyone's head was bowed. It was evening on the banks of the Jumna river in the nation's capital. Gandhi-ji's pyre had just been lit.

It is a beautiful fire, the flames evenly distributed. In the middle of the pyre there is a round orange glow brightening each moment like a glorious sun. And now the Mahatma's body is framed in a dance of flames.

A small heap of ash, Roshan saw . . . and already observed the ceremony twelve days hence on the banks of the Ganges, at the confluence of the sacred rivers, the Ganga and the Yamuna, over a million people crowding the banks, of the immersion of the ashes, and Nehru speaking in the language of India *The last journey has ended. The final pilgrimage has been made* and a tide of garlands rises around the ashes in the voyage of the self without being towards . . . but now Roshan again heard the commentary on the present and shrank from it, withdrawing from the crowd, and began to hasten towards the Gateway of India, hearing a ship's bell strike.

The white P & O ocean liner had just begun its journey to England. Roshan stood under the arch of the Gateway of India and watched the brilliant white ship slowly sailing past, its decks crowded with people who still waved in the direction of the dock. *SS Stratheden*, he read. He had climbed to the topmost deck and stood away from the crowd and watched the Gateway of India receding as the steaming ship left the murky waters of the harbour and entered the blue ocean. The monument looked like a small box of matches on the edge of a table. Tiny people moved around it like ants. Roshan went to the opposite side of the deck. The ship was sailing past some small islands, each with a hilltop temple. He walked to the bow and, finding the crow's-nest unmanned, settled in it, making for himself a position from where he could not see the land. The stiff breeze that had been blowing exhilaratingly over the deck was nearly a gale here in the crow's-nest. The ship was racing through an immensity of blue. A cold, benumbing spray blew at his face, hitting his eyes like sharp needles.

16 But You

But you are not 7 years old when in the still pitch-black night long before dawn you are awoken and for some minutes you wander sleepy-eyed among the rooms where familiar voices are ordering do-this-do-that preparations for some undreamed-of journey. There are sacks and bundles beside doorways and your father's voice is broadcasting instructions to the whole house while he himself rearranges the items in an old leather suitcase. 'Do we need blankets?' your mother's voice asks loudly from one room. 'Do we need more towels?' As if in answer, your sister Zakia starts singing. 'Yes, we do, oh yes we do!' and your father shouts back from another room, 'Just two hand towels, the hosts will provide the rest.' But your grandfather says, 'Better take a blanket or two, just in case.' Your grandmother, who is helping Zakia tie up a bundle of her clothes, picks up her nonsense song and sings, 'A blanket or two, oh yes we do!' There is your aunt Faridah in the kitchen, her eyes in tears from the sharp smoke rising from the brazier, who shouts, 'How many boiled eggs you want to take?' From two rooms away your mother shouts back, 'All of them, there are two dozen in the basket.' From another room your grandfather jokes, 'It's your wedding, Faridah, you take all the eggs!' Your father, whose two fists are pulling at the ends of a cord that he is tying around the old leather suitcase, shouts, 'Don't forget the salt and black pepper.' Your Uncle Mansur is chasing a hen round the courtyard where you go to escape the inexplicable confusion in the rooms. A rooster is crowing aloud vigorously while the hen goes cluck-cluck-cluck as she dashes just out of Uncle Mansur's reach. Uncle Mansur is 15 years old and whenever he sees a dog or a cat or a hen he has to chase it. Completing a second circle round the courtyard, the hen dashes into the house where people, seeing its wild dash around the rooms dodging in and out of the chaos of luggage, clap hands or stamp on the ground or yell at her to chase her away so that she comes dashing back just when Uncle Mansur has reached the door and, confronting him, flaps her wings violently, is momentarily airborne, flies over Uncle Mansur's shoulder, lands in the courtyard, hops and dashes for a few yards and takes off again into the air and alights upon a branch of the guava tree. Cluck–cluck–cluck she goes in her irritation and the rooster, looking confused and panic-stricken but continuing to pretend he is in charge, crows vehemently as if welcoming the dawn. But it must be the middle of the night, for the sky is full of brilliant stars. You hear your father calling Uncle Mansur to help with the luggage. A glow from the house is casting a dim light on the pomegranate bush and the round little globes of the ripening pomegranates look like small lanterns hanging in the air. You put your fingers around a pomegranate, first just to touch its shiny leathery skin like a cricket ball's, but then find yourself clasping the fruit. A little saliva spurts from below your tongue and you feel a sharp edge on your lower front teeth. Your hand has tightened over the pomegranate. A trickle has formed at the corner of your mouth and your hand pulls the fruit free from the branch. You run to a further corner of the courtyard and crouch there in the darkness, tearing at the pomegranate's leathery skin with your teeth. A sharp, sour taste of the unripe fruit pierces your gums and sets your teeth on edge, but you bite deeper and harder and rapidly chew the dry seeds in the scarcely moist flesh. Just then you are being called. Your father and your grandfather and Uncle Mansur are all shouting your name. The rooster stops crowing. You chew, swallow and spit double fast. The fruit is so sour it's pinching your gums. Now your mother's voice is calling too. You stuff the remaining pomegranate into your mouth and chew and spit treble fast and run to the house. It is still far from dawn when the family is parading out of the house and walking to the railway station under the eerie light of the street-lamps. Your mother has made you wear a new pair of navy shorts in which you have neatly tucked a clean white shirt. You are thrilled to be wearing new black boots and cannot take your eyes off your feet as you march along with Uncle Mansur, helping him to carry a large sack that contains several small bundles. You regret it is not daytime and your friends are not in the street to see you in your new boots. Left-right left-right, you march. Your father and grandfather are carrying the large suitcase between them, changing sides from time to time. Inside the suitcase is your new dark blue sweater that your mother knitted a month ago. It has a pattern like two snakes wound together. Already long before sunrise it is hot and you are beginning to sweat. The dust is catching in your throat. But you are going where you will be able to wear your new sweater. Your grandmother and Zakia are walking together. The two are always carrying on some nonsense duet. You hurry along with Uncle Mansur, trying to get out of hearing range from Zakia's nonsense that drives you crazy. Your mother and Aunt Faridah are carrying a basket of food between them. Aunt Faridah is big and slow and reminds you of a cow. You always like sitting in her lap and putting your arms round her neck. She sighs as she walks. She has a sad face. But she cannot be really sad. She is wearing new clothes of red satin so bright and shiny you think it is her blood you are seeing in the dimly lit street. She is going to get married and so she sighs and has a sad face. You will be eating sweet rice on her wedding day. The sour, bitter taste of the unripe pomegranate stays in your mouth but because it is your secret it is therefore a sweeter taste than sweet rice with pistachios and cardamom seeds in it. Next thing you are at the railway station, on the platform under the open sky which is still black and full of stars. You look at the arm of the signal with its red eye. The station master walks up the platform. A lantern with a red light in it swings from his hand. It looks like a red pendulum is swinging from the end of his arm. There is a smell from the fields of wheat growing. There must be goats sleeping nearby, you can smell them too. Then you see the big white eye of the engine coming out of the black distance and becoming a piercing light. Clanking and screeching the engine comes to a halt and lets out a long hiss. It is only pulling three carriages and is coming to stop at a small country station but the noise it makes, you think it is pretending to be at the head of the Frontier Mail coming into Peshawar. Your father and grandfather are hurrying to the door of a carriage. Uncle Mansur has already jumped on to the train before it comes to a stop and has claimed a long bench in the third-class compartment, an act that proves unnecessary since the carriage is nearly empty. There are only two men in it. They wear beards and look pious and it is decided that your mother, grandmother, aunt and sister need not travel separately in the women's compartment. You run to a window seat. You plan to put your head out if Zakia and your grandmother start their nonsense duets. You are going to listen to the rushing air instead. Then off you move with a sudden jolt and clank with the engine going chuff-chuff shoo-shoo-shooo. Warm air rushes in. You look out of the window but can see nothing in the darkness. Chukha-chukha chukha-chukha, the engine settles down to a slow rhythm and ticka-tick ticka-tick go the wheels of the carriage. You doze off. The train stops and starts several times. Your father decides to eat a boiled egg although your mother says it is not yet time for breakfast. Everyone wants to eat a boiled egg. The train stops at a station where there is nobody. Then after a long run when the wheels go cutta-cut cutta-cut the train slows down to a crawl while another train goes thundering past. 'That's the Mail, that's the Mail,' Uncle Mansur shouts. It has many carriages. They are brightly lit up. You see hundreds of faces rush past. You think you are looking at the cinema screen in the darkness. The thunder suddenly stops, the train has disappeared and it is blacker dark outside than it was before. Your little train resumes its earlier slower rhythm, chukha-chukha chukha-chukha, and then begins to screech and puff and put on a big show. You arrive at a large station and your father is shouting from the window at a porter and the porter jumps into the carriage before the train stops. Soon everything is being transferred to the longer train on the opposite platform. The train seems full, overflowing with people. It is so long you cannot see its beginning or end. It has one carriage that is painted silver. Uncle Mansur tells you that it is air-conditioned. Always cold inside even when the train is going through the desert in the middle of the day. It is reserved for the English. The Governor of the Punjab travels in it when he goes to Bombay to catch the ship to England. You look at the mysterious silver carriage with its closed windows. Suddenly there is a commotion on the platform. Two English soldiers are marching across the platform. Behind them walks an Englishwoman, followed by four porters carrying brown leather suitcases. Tall and straight she is with a green pill-box hat on her wavy blonde hair and a beautiful white neck like ivory. She wears a light lime-coloured coat over a frock of printed cotton. You can see red and green flowers and leaves as the skirt of her frock swings out and about. Her calves and ankles stand out below the coat. Her green high-heeled shoes match her hat and the green on her frock. She walks quickly, decisively. Her hair bounces up from her shoulders with each step, her chin rises and falls. But her eyes, blue and unblinking, are seeing nothing. Another English soldier marches behind the porters. For a minute or so every eye is upon the Englishwoman. One of the soldiers opens the door of the silver carriage. The Englishwoman enters the compartment. The platform is again busy with Indian families arriving and departing. The Englishwoman's luggage has gone in, her door has been locked, the English soldiers stand outside the next door of the silver carriage where the porters are taking some of the luggage. You are told to go with the women to the women's compartment in which there is more room. You refuse, stamping your foot on the ground. You see dust rise from your new boots, and so stamp both feet hard on the ground. No, you won't travel in the women's compartment. You squeeze in with the men. Some people are still trying to get off while many more are pushing in with their luggage. And some who are staying on the train are calling out to the tea vendors on the platform. The men are tall and lean. Many have beards and turbans and are wearing clothes of coarse cotton. Four of them are sharing a hookah which is filling the compartment with smoke which smells almost sweet but which irritates your eyes. Everyone is talking about the Englishwoman. What is she doing in the middle of the Punjab? She must be the governor's daughter. No, no, an actress. What actress, what are you talking about, where is the studio for the shooting? Your shooting-looting can be done outside too, on location it's called. No, she is the Pindi district commissioner's wife. What, and has an escort of three soldiers? Exactly why she has to be higher up, royalty perhaps. There is not enough room in the carriage for everyone and so you make a deal with Uncle Mansur to take turns to sit down. He wants to stand first so that he can be by the door when the train starts to move. You are staring out at the crowd on the platform when you see the people are slowly passing out of your sight and you realize that the train has begun to move. There is none of the laboured chuff-chuff of the smaller train. This one is imperceptibly easing out and then gliding quite smoothly and just when the platform is about to disappear there is a burst of powerful acceleration. The smoke from the hookah that had been hanging in the compartment and drifting about the ceiling rushes out. You look out in wonder at the dark grey land, amazed to be sitting in the most famous train in all India with an Englishwoman with a neck like ivory three carriages ahead of you. You have never experienced such speed. A thin line of light appears on the eastern horizon. There is a change of sound from the wheels of the carriages before yours and you lean towards the window, trying to get a glimpse out past the crowd of men. *The Chenab, the Chenab*, people are saying even before the wheels of your carriage go ctunk-ctunk over the bridge and you manage to see a gleam on the water's surface of the broad, dark river. But soon the sky is lit up and you are racing across the cultivated land, green with cotton and wheat and rice, you are crossing another beautiful river, the Jhelum, and the land is beginning to undulate and tilt, for there far to the east and the north, beyond the horizon, are the great snowy mountains, the Karakoram Range and the Hindu Kush. It is your turn to stand and you find a spot between two large men standing by the window of the door, and you squeeze yourself between them. There is a green infinity to the land saturated by the melting snow from the great mountains. The fastest train you've ever been on seems suddenly slow as hurtling through endless space the speed seems reduced to a crawl. One of the two men between whom you stand shifts a leg and you are able to get your head close to the window. You put your hand out a little and see it invisibly slapped back by the rush of the wind, you are going so fast, though when you look at the green land you are not moving at all. There is the huge engine! The track curves to the east and you can see the engine and the first five or six carriages following the curve. And there is the silver carriage, closed and mysterious though you know its secret. You wonder if she is looking out at the land and dreaming about the mountains beyond the horizon. White as the snow on the mountains her neck. A gleam catches your eye and you look away from the silver carriage. There is a little quivering brightness in the vast green. Some river perhaps, or a pool of water left by a recent rain. You stare because it is getting bigger, like the headlight of the engine coming into the country station at night, coming closer and closer towards you and blinding you with its brightness. You put your hands over your eyes. When you look again, for a moment you cannot see anything. There is only the white glare. Then you see a sugarcane field and the wide bend of a river, the green of the land and the silver of water under the blue sky. You go hurtling across the land and yet you're crawling. Then you're slowing down to come into the station. In the commotion of alighting from the train at Rawalpindi, you look at the silver carriage. The Englishwoman's compartment door is closed but two of the soldiers from the next compartment are walking towards it. One of them knocks on the glass in front of the shuttered window. A louvred section is raised and then the glass. You see part of a hand. Small white fingers. A brief dialogue takes place. The window is sealed closed again and the soldiers return to their own compartment. Uncle Mansur had run off to the women's carriage as soon as the train entered the station and is now escorting your grandmother and the others to where you are with your father and grandfather and the luggage. Even above the noise of the crowd on the platform, you can hear Zakia going, 'Pindi, Pindi, I feel so windy,' and your grandmother responding with, 'I'm a Punjabi, you're a Sindhi.' You hope your grandfather's cousins with whom you are going to stay have a large house where you can find a place to hide from your sister and grandmother who drive you crazy with their nonsense. In her red satin clothes, Aunt Faridah walks with her veiled head lowered. She is going to be married in three days. She has to look as though she is full of sorrow. After the wedding, she can look happy. After the wedding, your father has promised to take everyone to Murree. Up in the hills, in the cool air, hooray, you will be able to wear your new dark blue sweater with its pattern of two snakes wound together, a pair of woollen socks up to your knees and your new black boots, hooray, hooray, hooray! Your grandfather's cousins live in a flat on the second floor of a building in a street full of shops and pavement vendors. Boys and girls your age and older are running about the flat. Zakia stares at them with contempt. There are many adults. While everyone is talking you take a quick walk round the flat. There are four rooms in it. You try to count all the people. There are twenty-three. There could be twenty-five, you are not sure, because the children are running around wildly and showing off to you that this is their playground. You go and stand on the balcony. A crowd of people is loitering in front of the shops. Some go in, some come out. The pavement vendors are shouting out their distinctive cries. A bullock cart is moving slowly down the street, blocking the passage. Four cars behind it are honking their horns even though it is clear the street is not wide enough for them to overtake the bullock cart. You remain on the balcony. The crowd below is interesting to watch and you don't have to pretend to like the children in the flat. Looking into a room you can see that Zakia has caught the attention of four of the children. From the way she is talking and moving her eyes you know she is reciting some of her nonsense to them. Everyone is always impressed the first time, especially adults who are bigger fools than children. Your father is restless and goes out. He is always looking for a better job. His dream is to start his own business. The bridegroom's people arrive.

His parents and grandparents and a youth who is the bridegroom's younger brother. The bridegroom himself does not come. Large trays loaded with sweetmeats are brought out. The children go wild. On Zakia's prompting, some of them yell, 'I eat a sweet, I run on my feet.' You don't know if you should stay for the sake of the sweets and go crazy or steal out and wander down the street to escape from Zakia's nonsense. What really makes you mad is that the adults think the chidren are being so clever. You decide to do both, stay for a while and stuff yourself with sweets and then slip out. But when the tea is being passed in the thick white cups without saucers the adults go shoo-shush at the children. They have had enough of the children going wild. They want to talk and get to know one another. There are presents to exchange. Plans to discuss for the wedding. There is talk of money. Your grandfather says there is property. Land in eastern Punjab, just across from Jammu. You have never heard about this land. You imagine green grassy slopes with almond trees on the banks of rivers that flow through your grandfather's land. The bridegroom's father nods his head in satisfaction. They have talked about some of this before and are going through the formalities once again. But that there is to be land too for his son's dowry is a surprise to him that has made him very happy. You just like *you*, he says complimenting your grandfather, and is lost for words to express his praise. It's a rich land, your grandfather says, giving the bridegroom's father a copy of a deed to the land. The bridegroom's father admires the calligraphy. It looks Persian, he says. From Moghul times, your grandfather hints. A gift from the emperor Akbar. The bridegroom's mother is talking to your grandmother and mother. She is talking about her youngest son, the youth who has come with the bridegroom's party. He knows his mother is praising him and sits with his head lowered but is hearing everything and you can see he is pleased. He can speak high-class Urdu. His vocabulary is so advanced he can speak like a Moghul prince. And you should see the poems he writes! Just like Ghalib. What a gift from God, his Urdu! Like honey in one's mouth. 'Come, Usman,' she calls to the youth, 'why so shy? Here are good people begging you to recite a verse.' Usman gives a performance of being reluctant but soon recites a dozen verses. Sitting cross-legged, a hand raised to his head with the thumb stuck into his ear and his eyes closed, he declaims the verses in such pure Urdu you stop breathing. You are living 200 years ago when the language flowed from your mouth like honey. Usman recites verses about moths and flames and breezes that touch the petals of a perfect rose. Everyone applauds when he finishes. Your father comes back from his tour of the city. Usman recites two or three verses again so that your father can applaud, too. When the bridegroom's party goes, people continue to praise the young man's pure Urdu. Uncle Mansur starts to talk in an affected Urdu but even Zakia laughs at him. The conversation goes back to Punjabi and is again about the wedding. But something terrible happens the day before the wedding. The bridegroom's father arrives when he is not expected. His voice is abusive even as he is climbing up the stairs. His voice booms into the flat and sends the children into the corners. The coarsest Punjabi flows from his mouth, words that are vile and smelly as though the man had drunk cheap country liquor and now vomited uncontrollably. Your grandfather shouts back with a thicker flow of filth and the next thing a sewer is running from the bridegroom's father's mouth. He is accusing your grandfather of lying. Somehow he has found out. Your grandfather has no land to give to his children. He was only pretending. Like it was a joke. Everyone knew he never had any land. His daughter's dowry is a fraud. The bridegroom's father has not thought it funny. He spits on the dowry that is not there. He does worse in his anger for having lost the land that came as a gift from the emperor Akbar. He says he shits on your family. Your grandfather does worse than that, he says the bridegroom's father is the shit inside a pig's intestines. The foul smell hangs in the air for two days. The wedding day comes and goes. Aunt Faridah sits crying. Your father has gone into a deep silence. Grim-faced, he walks out of the flat and paces the street below for hours. You can see him from the balcony. Back and forth, back and forth. His eyes on the ground. There is a crowd in the street but he walks back and forth as if he paced an empty corridor. He is the only man in the family with a good job, manager at a factory making sports goods. Your grandfather works as a construction supervisor but there is no construction sometimes for months. Uncle Mansur is a carpenter's apprentice. Only your father makes steady money. It was his money paying for his sister's wedding but the grandfather, with nothing to give his daughter, had a fancy deed drawn up to a land that did not exist. Your father knew nothing about it until the deception was exposed. And now he is walking back and forth in the long prison corridor of the street where men move out of his way because they can see that he is like one who is punished so badly no pity can comfort him. Then, grim-faced, he walks up to the flat and in a quiet voice says everyone is to go back home on the next day's train. There is to be no family treat to Murree. You think of your dark blue sweater and your woollen socks. He leaves the family to chew on misery and goes away for the rest of the day, returning late at night when you have gone to sleep. The next morning he tells you he is going to take you to the mountains. You and I are going on a trip, he says. Only you and I, everyone else is going home. You don't say anything because he has been so angry for two days and you cannot be sure what he means. What mountains, you wonder. Only yesterday he said no one was going to go to Murree. But everyone is sent away and you and your father remain standing on the platform, watching the train take the sad family back towards home. Then you cross to another platform which is deserted and wait for the train going north, to Peshawar. You sit on a bench and watch your father walk up and down on the platform. He is talking to himself, muttering words which you can hear. You are shocked. He is cursing his own father. Imagining he has land, he is saying. Ha! Land flowing with milk and honey. Near Jammu, if you please! He doesn't have 2 annas to call his own from one month to the next. Thinks he is Mister Big Shot direct descendant of the emperor Akbar's tax collector. Not 2 annas, not 2 annas at any one time in his pocket. Only a counterfeit deed to a land that doesn't exist. Just a paper dream. Your father is agitated, much troubled in his mind, and he walks up and down, up and down, cursing his father. Land, who has land, he suddenly asks aloud, looking at no one. You feel uneasy. A train is expected and people are beginning to crowd on the platform. Some people watch your father talking to himself. What can they think of him but that he is a madman? Who has land, he asks again. A couple of men who happen to be walking past quicken their pace. One of them looks back and your father says, Where is this so-called inherited land? Tell me that! But the train arrives and you are relieved that your father has not gone crazy. In the crowded compartment he is himself again talking about business opportunities. You realize he has undertaken this journey in order to get away from his own father who has let him down. Obscurely, you sense his heroism. Seeing his father's error, he has said nothing, only sent him back home with the rest of the family and taken you, his son, and found an excuse to go off somewhere so that tempers can cool down. He said nothing when the family was still in Rawalpindi, he remained quiet when everyone was getting into the train to go back home, and only then, with you as the solitary witness, talked like a madman walking up and down on the platform. And now, among the men travelling to Peshawar, he is his old self, his real self, the man who admires commercial travellers, who loves the language of business and uses a phrase such as 'letter of credit' as if it was from his religion. He accepts the hookah offered him by a Pathan, puffs coolly on it and asks what is the profit margin on untanned animal skins in the Northwest Frontier. A group of Punjabi merchants forms around the Pathan's hookah. A lovely delight in imagined profits from a variety of businesses joins the men together in a warm comradeship. Your father sighs, getting to the truth of the matter. You can sell a goat, he says, or a camel, why, you can even import textiles, but . . . he clicks his tongue on the roof of his mouth and his companions stare at him sadly, knowing what he says is true . . . where are the real profits, he asks, where? They all know. In London, Manchester and Leeds. And one merchant adds, 'And with the unholy middlemen of the British, the Hindus of Bombay.' Another agrees and says, 'The very men who are financing their Mister Gandhi.' The conversation turns to politics, and each man falls into a dream of an unreal India, a land full of conspiratorial men with treacherous motives. *Ctunk-ctunk, ctunk-ctunk.* The conversation ceases. Everyone looks out of the windows. The train is trundling over the Indus river. Everyone's eyes are filled with admiration and wonder. There are rivers and rivers, but this is the great Indus whose banks were the destination of the dreamers and invaders who wished to find India and make her their own in a choking embrace of jealous possession. Your father is calling to you to look. But you are already seeing and in your mind you are looking at more than you can see because what you are seeing you will re-vision many years later when you come to stand on the banks of the Thames, the Mississippi and the Amazon. But for now you are in the heart of the mystery of primeval water with its source in the Himalayas, and there is a throbbing within you because your father has said he is taking you to the mountains, it is as if the blood that pulsed within you were a mirror image of the swift current of melting ice within the heaving surface of primeval water and you are certain that the Indus is within you. Now you are completely lost. You do not hear the train, you do not see Peshawar when you arrive there. You do not think to admire yourself in your new dark blue sweater or the sheepskin coat your father buys for you. You are lost, lost. Even the fact that the Frontier Mail is standing on the opposite platform and is preparing for its departure for Bombay makes only an incidental impression upon your brain. Your mind registers, but you do not immediately hear, your father saying, 'Ah, Bombay!' But later you will remember hearing him and seeing a look of longing on his face as if the train had brought to his consciousness his buried dream of becoming a businessman in the great city. You see as a dull gleam on the edge of your vision that two silver carriages are attached to the middle of the train and vaguely you recall the Englishwoman with the green pill-box hat and blue unblinking eyes and have an obscure thought about English soldiers in their khaki uniform and governors with plumed hats and the Viceroy giving a speech on All-India Radio, but everything is dimmed and distant, the whole world has become foreign and strange, you are so utterly lost. Afterwards, you try and work out the chronology of real time and the geography of real roads beyond where the railway did not go. What possessed your father to go beyond where railways and roads ended, where trails through mountain passes were scarcely perceptible? He was mad with his own father for having claimed a land that his family had possessed only as a dream. And he was madder still to discover that his father's wild claim had aroused a hunger within himself for possession. All he could do was to punish himself as if suffering were a form of consolation, a soothing version of self-pity, by entering the region in which an unattainable land rose before one's eyes in an unimagined white, abstract beauty, the earth lifting up vertically to heights no human had yet conquered, a land that literally could not be possessed and even the successive empires could own it only on maps. But you, lost in your mind when your eyes fell upon the Indus, have awoken in a cold northern town where the high mountain air is making you pant. You find your father is still mad and his journey is not done yet, that he is doubly punishing himself by keeping on going north, away from his father's imaginary land, and after seeing the Frontier Mail, rushing away from his own dream, which could prove equally false, of a successful business in Bombay, and so he bitterly pursues a punishing opposite course. You go higher yet and higher, in a lorry, then on horses, on a canoe across a broad, fast-running stream, then on foot, and by now the air makes you light-headed and sometimes you laugh for no reason at all. Icy streams go tumbling down. Flowers grow on their banks. You gaze down on a valley, which looks like a silvery grey oval of ice but its bed where many streams flow down to form a lake is emerald green with grass around the royal blue lake. But you do not linger there, though the sight of the valley fills you with a futile envy, it is so perfectly lovely and so completely inaccessible. But you are gasping for breath now, having risen higher. Precipitous walls of mountains rise before you. They are miles away, but you are in a land of unusual perspectives where measurement of space and time is an absurdity. There! your father says. The Hindu Kush. The great crown of mountain peaks lit up golden in the morning sun on the head of India that no human hand can reach. And the invaders, so pompous in their conceit of conquest, when they come here all they can ever conquer is illusion. But you looking at the Hindu Kush or at your father's dream of it aware of the unbearable beauty of white snow on white ice reinventing your father among glittering peaks so as not to suffer alone in your afterlife the curse of your beginning no longer not yet 7 but all the ages you must be before your body becomes a drop of moisture frozen in one of the tiny cracks in the ice alone in this land of origins this crunched up vertically thrusting land of suggestive distortions in exile even in your first moment from which there is never an emancipation could you come to an inch of the wall of ice and crack its surface like a geologist certain there must be an important fossil in the rock-face that crucial missing link deposited in the ice smashing wildly and shouting in the unechoing ice-bound valleys But you But you But you

AUTHOR NOTE

Zulfikar Ghose was born in Sialkot, Pakistan, in 1935, lived in England from 1952 to 1969, and now resides in Texas where he works as a professor at the University of Texas. He is married to the Brazilian artist Helena de la Fontaine.